NORA'S MASK

Hi Willie,

Enjoy the adventure!

ROLIENA SLINGERLAND

Evil is unspectacular and always human and shares our
bed and eats at our own table

W.H. AUDEN, *Herman Melville*

PROLOGUE

Nora

TWIN COULEES, ALBERTA, 2013

Life is good. Not perfect. But good. Even the late afternoon sun agrees, winking at her through the gaps in the blinds. White, lacy curtains frame the little picture window that stares out at a small yard.

Nora's little sliver of paradise.

Well, almost.

Her heart pulsed. *Darling Henry.*

She blinks quickly and pauses, but only for a moment. She slips into her mental armor –the squaring of shoulders, centering herself with a deep breath, and the humming of a familiar Pakistani melody. Most days, this seems to work. Henry is playing at the periphery of her mind – there, but not really.

She gropes for the next dish soaking under a tower of bubbles. With a flick, she sends her long braid tumbling over her shoulder for the umpteenth time where it sways in gentle rhythm with her body. Soon, it will creep over her shoulder again like a persistent child.

Her fingers search again. Three more plates. A quick glance at the plain silver watch mounted on the edge of the sink tells her it's 4 pm. No rush here. Three red roses on her windowsill catch her eye. Tomorrow, she will paint their likeness on canvas, immortalize their perfection before the satiny petals bruise and wilt. She reaches out to stroke one, leaving a trio of mating bubbles clinging to the petal. Admiring the fragile spheres for a moment, she pops them with her breath, almost feeling bad for marring something so perfect.

It is a good thing love is not like that, she thinks.

She turns off the tap, and the pipes groan in protest.

There is a scratch at the door. She shakes her head. Silly cat. Always trying to get in. One warm afternoon, he had come in through the open door and had found a penchant for her kitchen and its fragrant smells ever since.

Hanging her dishtowel on the oven door handle, she stops for a moment, then shrugs. Houses have their own heartbeat, her grandfather once told her. If you listen quietly, they speak to you in the shifting of beams and the creaking of floorboards.

As if on cue, a train roars in the distance. She can imagine it, long and sleek and faraway, hugging the track, still a dot on the horizon. Usually, there is something comforting about it. Three times a day on the hour, the beast comes to life.

She reaches for the cupboard above the sink. Two candles and one wine glass. Reg wouldn't be home until tomorrow. Glass for later, candles for the tub. A night of relaxation and pampering is in order. Merlot, a soft Afghan, and a fire.

Thunder-like rumbling sounds in the distance. The cupboard door shakes lightly as she closes it.

She sets the wine glass and candles down on the counter, and the goblet trembles for a moment as it is released from her fingers.

Then, she feels it. Like a whisper at her neck. Rubbing the back of her neck, her fingertips feel the staccato of the pulse in her jugular.

The ground is beginning to shudder as the beast grows louder.

She whips around, and her hand flies to her mouth.

A black hood, a mask. Gliding closer.

She grips the counter behind her on either side. "Who are you?"

Silence stretches between them.

She presses her body against the counter as if hoping it will absorb her.

"I – " The walls of the house are now trembling. A hollow roar swallows her voice.

He moves closer. She presses further back, the edge of the counter now cutting into her skin.

Without looking, she feels behind her. There it is. Cheap leather. Her fingers dig in deep as she casts all hope upon it. Her arm jerks, and the wallet tumbles by his feet.

He walks past it.

"Please!"

Suddenly, he flings out his arm. A blur.

Something cold and wet slaps her face. Her head snaps back. Hundreds of fiery needles dig into her flesh. She claws at her eyes, her nose, her mouth.

Then, she is on the floor, writhing, and rocking back and forth.

Water – she needs water. She tries to get up. Darkness crowds in. Somewhere in the distance, there are screams piercing the air.

Raw, desperate, animal-like.

With one final roar, the monster rushes past. Windows rattle and bang in their frames as the house gives one last shudder.

DAY 1

Marc

AUGUST 28, 2014

He turned off the motor and rolled down his window. This was it. The end of his journey. As he ran his eyes over the decay in front of him, his heart sank.

Was this rundown house with its blistering paint and cock-eyed shutters the resting place of the gems? Reluctantly, he opened his car door and allowed a quickening wind to jostle him. He couldn't turn back now. Not when he'd come so far. Not when so much was riding on his success.

He got out, pushed a lock of hair from his eyes, and climbed the porch, stepping over its rotting planks. A gust of wind shoved him towards the door. In the distance, he heard the soft drone of a motor. He touched the wall and ran his hand over the rotting boards as if he were exploring a wound. He had no doubt that once restored, the house would be a breathtaking sight.

But the gems. Already he could see it: *Local Reporter Saves Twin Coulees.* Okay, he could do without the melodrama; he'd had enough of that. He didn't need the spotlight either. He'd found his niche at the Twin Coulees Gazette. And now, he'd found his chance to help his hometown – to give back after a lifetime of miserable regret. Then there was Arizona, his precious wife, the woman who met him at the crossroads of his life. She had given him the hope and courage to pursue his journalistic dreams. Even more, she had supported his desire to return to God, even willingly going to church with him for the first time ever.

His hand reached for the rusty doorknob. Had this place been condemned? Nothing was boarded up. The knob protested as he slowly turned it. Faintly, he registered the crunch of gravel behind him.

He sensed it before he felt it, a blow to the back of his neck.

Then all was black.

• • •

Dark shapes swam in front of him and then slowly settled. He blinked once. Twice. But the layer of darkness remained. He scrunched his nose and felt the tightness of something around his head. A blindfold. He moved his arms, but they would not budge. His wrists were tightly bound to something on either side of him. He must be sitting on a chair; it was hard and uncomfortable, the nerves in his buttocks partially numb. He moved his legs but found his feet were bound together.

His heart raced as he strained against the ropes. Where was he? Why was he tied up? He probed the fabric of his mind, like fingers working through cloth. Then he remembered. Gravel drive. Large house. Door opening. Then nothing.

The cool air held a pungent odor, like that of a science lab. But it was the quiet that made him stop and listen hard. There was nothing, not even the ticking of a clock.

"Anyone? Please help," he said softly, testing the waters.

He tried again, louder.

He was alone. Seconds slid into minutes. His head hurt. His heart galloped. Was he in the house of the gems? In the middle of nowhere? When were they coming back?

His legs began to shake. They? Who was *they*?

He sucked in a deep breath. *Please, God, help!*

Then he heard it. Softly at first. The faraway whispering of the Chinook wind as she climbed over and through the trees, swirling around the edges of the roof, scrambling over the shingles, pressing, nudging, feeling for him.

She laughed knowingly, and the little hairs on his arms stood up.

How long would he be sitting here? Had he been left here to die? He envisioned his blood gathering in stagnant pools in his lower limbs, his muscles shrinking until only a dusty skeleton bound with rope remained.

Had someone else been after the gems before him? Had he walked into a trap?

"Help!" He suddenly yelled. "Someone – *anyone* – help!" His throat felt raw.

The wind grew louder. She infiltrated the crevices and spread through the attic. Like an insane woman, she laughed at him, frolicking on the beams.

He pulled forward, muscles straining. But his wrists were too tightly bound. He banged his feet on the ground and yelled again, "Help!" But she sucked in the words and muffled them, all the while hissing around him. Her claws slid under the door, between the jamb, probing, reaching for him.

It was growing inside of him, that nebulous lump. He wanted to carve it out, to still the vibrations in his legs, the shivers racing up and down his spine.

She began shrieking and wailing, banging the walls and clawing the windows. He strained against the ropes, like a desperate man wanting to crawl out of his body and mind, until they bit into his flesh.

She lashed at the walls until they shuddered under her breath. He rocked himself back and forth. Nausea crept to his throat, his nostrils. His breathing became swift and ragged.

She was coming. For him.

DAY 16

Basil

CALGARY, ALBERTA, SEPTEMBER 2014

There was a shiver in the autumnal air. Hoarfrost clung to the pine needles. A few spruce trees stood in line like tightly drilled soldiers while the sinewy limbs of birch and poplars clawed the air. Basil Andreas edged his sky-blue Cutlass down Southland Drive. Constable Andreas. Okay, Constable Andrews. One could only offer polite pronunciations of one's own name so many times before it becomes annoying.

A new town. A new life.

Steam escaped from the hood of his car. Radiator. Again. He patted the dash in the long-suffering way a parent ruffles the hair of a mischievous child. Myra had taken the Honda Pilot. He gripped the steering wheel tightly. Today, he would try to put Calgary behind him. Never mind that he had not picked this transfer from a silver platter; rather, he had been strongly encouraged.

The steam grew; billows clouded his vision, forcing him to pull over. He punched the steering wheel. Time to call a cab. This one was for the junkyard. Tranny almost gone; brakes not too dependable. Besides, his lanky frame was meant to pivot and jump on a volleyball court, not apply horsepower to the rear of a car.

• • •

Twenty minutes later, he was folded up in the backseat of a white cab. He settled back into the ripped leather seat and reminded himself this was just a bump. His entire life was in two suitcases crammed in the trunk. That and the searing memories he carried with him.

He glanced out the window. The Albertan sky was the perfect stage for nature's unparalleled drama to unfold. Lightning flashed over the prairie, illuminating the gray thunderheads primed and ready to unleash an arsenal of baseball-sized hail – hail that would shred the vast carpeted fields of bright yellow canola blooms to ribbons. Nature was one force to reckon with. It could inspire the most unimaginative of hearts, and instill great awe and wonder, but boy, could it destroy.

"Reg Clarkson," the man smiled into the rear-view mirror. His eyes were pewter gray. "You from Twin Coulees?" The collar of his plaid shirt looked freshly starched and pressed, and Basil could imagine gentle fingers carefully ironing out the wrinkles. Some previous injury had left a small cleft in his chin. Calloused fingers on the steering wheel drummed to some inner beat.

"No. Calgary." Basil stretched his limbs out diagonally, his toes feeling desperately for space underneath the front passenger seat. The car was pristine. The air held a pungent blend of Lysol and pine air freshener.

"Getting outta the rat race, huh? Sometimes, I hate the busyness of city life, particularly in Calgary. He clamped his hands tightly on the steering wheel. "I'm from Twin Coulees myself." He reached for his cup holder that held a lone candy wrapper. He dumped that into his garbage can. "Best view of Calgary is from my rear-view mirror," he chuckled. He felt around his console, coming up empty-handed. "Ah crap," he muttered, then shrugged.

"Yup," murmured Basil. He breathed in deeply and looked out of the window. "It's a rat race." He hoped his short answers would effectively shut down the conversation. He ran his hands down his thighs and began playing with the buttons on his coat, popping them open and pressing them closed repeatedly. His tongue felt like a wad of sand-paper. Running a hand through his reddish hair, he tugged on one of the fleshy protuberances from the side of his head that some called ears and others wings.

"Planning on staying for a bit?"

"RCMP. Transfer."

The man suddenly sat straighter, and his application of the brakes was no feather-like touch either. "Sorry, speedin' just a bit." He grinned sheepishly, running his fingers through neatly combed hair.

Basil shrugged. "Off-duty. It's all good." He closed his eyes, fatigue pressing down on him.

"A police officer, huh?" The cabbie said. "Good for you. Not the easiest of professions, I imagine."

"It's good, it's bad, it's ugly."

"Yeah, no doubt, hey?" He chuckled. "Any tales of valor?"

"It's never what the public imagines. Lotsa paperwork. Lotsa heartache. Lotsa ho-hum, too." He opened his eyes and saw a small, weather-beaten sign, Wine and Spirits. He shifted uncomfortably in his seat.

"Yeah, I understand." the cabbie's voice dipped. "There's always the ugly underbelly folks don't see."

Basil looked at him expectantly, but the man did not parcel out more. He cleared his throat. "Well, Twin Coulees is a nice town. A bit off the beaten path, but it has all the amenities. Plus, a new mayor finally introducing some reforms. The last mayor did that town in; strung everyone along while knocking back one wobbly pop after the other."

Basil nodded. "You know what they say: social reform is like a late-blooming teenager."

The cabbie nodded. "Yup, that it is." They're cleanin' up downtown too. Real problem with street girls." He shook his head.

"Age-old issue at that."

The man nodded again. He scanned the console beside him, his brows furrowed. "Well, uh," he suddenly slurred, "new mayor is the one forgin' change down there."

Basil glanced at the cabbie's face in the rear-view mirror. There was an odd, puckered look about his neck, a loss of color.

"Gotta hand it to the man." The cabbie's fingers lost their purposeful rhythm. "Has…has his work cut out for him, but he's a real bulldog…he's a…he's a real go-getter." He blinked wildly for a second. "Don't take no for an answer. Politics in his blood." He slowed down the car and sped up again, and Basil felt an uncomfortable lurch in his gut. "Tongue is slicker than a sword. Sometimes," he cleared his throat and rubbed his eyes, "big problems, uh, need big solutions."

The sky began to rumble. Basil pulled his face away from the mirror, but not before noticing the man close his eyes and then widen them in exaggeration. The car swerved slightly. Basil's right foot pressed hard to the floor. Traffic was merging in fits and starts like an obstinate zipper. "We're not gonna beat thish one," the cabbie slurred, looking at the darkening sky. They were nearing High River. The radio forecasted a strong hailstorm.

"Perhaps we should pull over," Basil suggested, clutching the door handle.

The cabbie merely grunted, fingers fumbling inside his shirt pocket. The car swerved again, this time enough to make Basil pitch in the backseat. "Visibility is gonna be –"

"Careful!" Basil cried, his hands shooting out to grab the headrest in front of him. He stiffened as the man's head suddenly dropped. His hand slid off the wheel. Horns blared, and cars swerved around them.

There was no radio to call this in, but instincts kicked in. Get the car to safety and then deal with the cabbie. Basil slid snake-like over the passenger seat. Take control of the brake and steering wheel. Basil kicked the cabbie's legs to the left. He thrust his left foot onto the brake pedal. He flicked on the four-way emergency flashers. Pressing his lanky body against the cabbie, he merged the car onto the shoulder as traffic whizzed past. He yanked up the emergency brake. With uncharacteristic strength, he pulled the cabbie's body flat onto the two seats. He began alternating chest thrusts and breathing air into his mouth. "Push hard, push fast," he coached himself, all the while thinking, *He's gonna die, he's gonna die!* The awful sound of cracking ribs made him freeze momentarily, but then he remembered his training from Depot days: *You'll hear ribs cracking; good, it means you're doing it with the force you need. Now, remember: do not stop; keep pushing.*

For a second, the cabbie's eyes fluttered open and then closed again. A buzzing suddenly enveloped Basil. His breath came hard and fast.

Not again! It was her eyes, green with the odd brown fleck in one of them, pleading. Heat slammed into him.

He gritted his teeth. *Focus. Focus.* He pumped the cabbie's chest again.

It was the sudden rap on the passenger window that jolted him back to reality again. He looked up into the squinting eyes of an RCMP officer.

Not exactly how he envisioned the next chapter of his life would begin.

• • •

With the ambulance en route, Basil leaned back against the passenger seat of the cop car. He thanked Constable Wally Kennedy again for giving him a ride.

"No worries. Good save back there! Hey, can I bring you home, or...?"

Basil smiled dryly. "Twin Coulees RCMP Detachment, please."

Kennedy looked puzzled. "No need to fill anything out."

"Just transferred here."

"You gotta be kiddin'!" Kennedy's wide face was wreathed in smiles. "One of the Force! Welcome to our neck of the woods, Basil! *Basil*," he repeated the name. "Now, whadya do to get stuck with something like that?"

Basil chuckled lightly. "She didn't like the name Bill."

Kennedy said, "Good name in man and woman, dear my lord, is the immediate jewel of their souls."

Basil stared at him.

"The good ole' Bard."

"What?"

Kennedy looked at him and smiled. "Shakespeare!"

"Oh, right."

Wally shifted his large frame. "How long you a part of the Force?"

"Nearly three years."

"You're still new – "

"New?"

Wally lifted a hand in defense. "I was going to say 'new and fresh.' Now, don't take it the wrong way. Years on the Force can make you cynical and jaded. If you're not careful, it gets harder to dodge that bullet as time goes on." He smiled ruefully. "Sometimes, I must learn to give my thoughts no tongue."

"Let me guess: The Bard again."

Wally chuckled deeply, his rich and merry laugh shaking his gut like a bowl full of Jello, and Basil felt himself, oddly, relaxing. *This is a man*, he thought with a twinge of envy, *at ease with himself and the world*. He wondered if this was even possible.

"Shakespeare has plenty to teach us. His plays are a window into the human condition. I dunno." He looked thoughtful. "I've always loved literature, particularly Shakespeare. That man had a keen perception of people and their motivations." He looked at his watch then. "Say, you up for grabbin' a bite to eat?"

"Sure." A small part of him wondered how the cabbie was getting on. Had they pronounced him at all? They had gotten a pulse back, but things could still easily go south. He felt a twinge of regret that he had been short with the man.

• • •

Arizona

TWIN COULEES, ALBERTA

His recliner sat untouched in the corner of the living room, the black leather covered in fingertips and the first hint of dust. A worn guitar rested wearily against its frame, its voice now silenced. Sometimes, when she walked too close to the chair, she could smell the hint of Holt Renfrew Cologne

– a whimsical splurge last Christmas – and her heart would suddenly lurch.

August 28. Sixteen days. Soon, it would be a month, then…

Her throat tightened. One day slipping into another like butter through her fingers, and she was powerless to stop it, to turn back time.

Pulling her worn robe around her, she walked to the living room window and thrust a raw, nubby finger between the slats. She jerked back as sunlight stabbed her eyes. Out there, the world was moving on in a rhythm of its own. Stately maple and poplar trees stood in various stages of undress, their fiery garments floating to the ground.

The doorbell jangled. Her pulse raced. She ran to the door and yanked it open. Her heart dropped to her toes.

Mother.

While so many slavishly earn the title, others have it thrust upon them undeservedly. Okay, maybe that was a bit unfair. But here she was, Master Puppeteer. Ready to control the strings for her adult daughter once again.

"Arizona?"

"Mom. What are you doing here?"

"Good morning, dear. How very nice to see you. How am I? Why, fine, dear."

"Mother – " She let the words die on her lips. No protestation could possibly thwart a hurricane dressed in Chanel and wearing the subtlest floral notes money could buy. The best recourse was to be prepared.

And she was as unprepared as ever.

"I *am* your mother, Arizona. I simply wanted to check up on you. See how you are doing."

"You didn't have to drive all this way, Mother. You could have phoned." *It'd be much easier – on both of us!*

"The phone! Impersonal invention if there ever was one." She swept into the room and glanced around, brows furrowed. "Oh, the mustiness! What a dreadful smell! Dear me, does this room ever get aired out?" Her long fingers gracefully trailed deliberate swirls on any dusty surface she could find, and the pickings weren't slim. She moved towards the recliner and made to wipe the leather.

"Mom – no!" She thrust herself between Estelle and the chair.

Estelle frowned. "It's covered in dust and prints."

"I know. Just...leave it."

"Are you allergic to the sun since I last saw you?" And with a pronounced flourish, she stood on tiptoes to draw the blinds. Sunlight burst through the slats, momentarily blinding Arizona and highlighting every dust mote that lingered in the air. Every nerve in her body felt taut like the strings on a violin.

She turned and scanned her daughter's face. "Well?"

"Well, what?"

"Oh, stop beating around the bush! Did you hear anything else from the officer?"

Tears rising, Arizona hugged the robe closer around her. "No." *Tell her!* Her mind screamed. *Just tell her the truth. Then all her theories about Marc will be true – or at least in her mind.*

"There was no evidence of foul play, Arizona. Grown men don't just disappear unless they want to." Her voice softened. "The truth hurts, my dear, but as your mother, I have to say it. Unstable past, addiction," she barrelled on, the overconfident soldier treading a minefield. "It's time to grow up and take stock of your future; purge yourself of this farcical existence you have been clinging to. The relationship was a whirlwind. Too quick and ill-fitted. You are worth more."

Arizona recoiled in anger. It was just like Estelle to take a rich and varied experience and devalue it to an afternoon picnic in the park. But this was low, even for her, like rubbing salt in raw wounds. "You don't know him, Mom! You *never* tried!" She couldn't bear to use the word *didn't*, and all that it implied.

It *had* been a whirlwind courtship followed by a simple court-house affair – everything quick and understated – but assuredly rooted in that deeply growing love between the two. After a flop of a dinner at her parents' resplendent home in Calgary, they'd married without their blessing. She would not soon forget how her mother had looked down her artfully complexioned nose at the man she immediately summed up as sub-par for her daughter. Marc's excitement to meet her had come to naught. Low social standing aside, he had made the mistake of over-sharing his past. Unaware of the portent they presented, he had given her all the ingredients she needed to launch a full-scale attack on him: his previous drug addiction, homelessness, the list had gone on. She had pointedly ignored him at the family dinner, speaking to him through Arizona. Her father, preoccupied as usual, was as polite as a man on a leash could be.

Estelle picked up the simple wedding frame of the couple and sighed. "That's the problem, dear. With money, you just never know if they are in it for love, or..." She let her words trail for effect and put the frame down carefully, then abruptly faced her daughter. "I've always dreamt of a lavish wedding for you, Arizona. My *only* daughter. To a man of your standing, a prosperous life – "

"I *never wanted* that! Besides, Marc left his past behind him. He *tried* to tell you! He has a good job as a reporter. You should see the articles he has written!"

Estelle raised an eyebrow. "A *different* man. They all say that. Usually empty promises, Arizona – "

"You don't *get it*, Mom. Do you really know what's most important to him? God. He started going back to church just like when he was little. She tilted her chin then. "*We* go together."

"Church?" Estelle grimaced. "What has God got to do with this all? Now you are starting to sound like Nana. Let me tell you, God did *nothing* for me. Absolutely nothing. He –" She took in a deep breath and squared her shoulders. "If you truly want to believe in God," she waved her hand dismissively, "then believe He is giving *you* this second chance." Before Arizona could retaliate, she seemed to draw herself together once more. "Oh, darling," she soothed, effortlessly changing tactics and gently lifting her daughter's chin. "Have I not always stood by you, through the good, the bad, the ugly? You deserve better, you know that? This has all been merely several months of, well…painful lessons."

Arizona sucked in her breath.

"C'mon, let's pack your things and go back to Calgary. We can put this little box up for sale and get rid of it quickly."

"Forget –"

"If you want, the police can stay in touch with you from there."

If she wanted? She pressed her lips tight.

Estelle pulled out her rhinestone-studded day planner.

"Mom, that is not –"

"Hmm, I think Justin Sharpe would be the best agent; he is quick and efficient."

"Mother!"

A car horn blasted through the open kitchen window.

Estelle blinked and then suddenly wilted. She lowered herself onto the couch. The scarlet knot of a mouth relaxed.

Shoulders dropped, and busy hands lost their energy. She cleared her throat. "Arizona –"

"They found a note."

"A note?" Estelle sat up straight.

Arizona sank onto the couch and ran her hand over the rough fabric. "Suicide. They, um, they found a note on his desk. It said he couldn't," she took a deep breath, "couldn't do it anymore."

"Oh, Arizona," Estelle shook her head and stood up. "Here is all the proof you need. He left you. Suicide or just walking out…" she paused, her lips pressed tight. "…he still left you."

"No!" Arizona burst out.

Estelle placed her hands on her hips. "Darling, what other explanation is there?"

"He would never just up and leave me," her voice broke. She thought again of his new devotion to God, his desire to live as a true Christian should. A man with such hope does not end it all, does he?

"Look, Arizona, I know it's painful." Estelle moved towards her daughter. "But he isn't the first man to do this."

Arizona's throat burned.

"Look, darling, we need to face forward. Let me help you through this, bring you back to where you belong."

"No, Mom," she pushed against the embrace. "I can manage. Just, go. Please, just leave me be."

"Arizona, you need me." But Estelle was backpedaling to the door.

"No, I don't, not now. Go. Please, Mom!" She opened the door, her hands trembling.

"I will give you time, Arizona, but I will be back. You need me, even if you don't think so." Then, with a pivot of the heels, the mother and master puppeteer were gone.

Arizona closed the door and pressed her body against it. She tried to swallow the large lump in her throat. "Don't cry!" she scolded herself. "*Don't* cry!"

• • •

The Avenger

The narrow road that snaked out of sight was heralded by a rusty piece of signage that clattered in the wind. The dirt-splattered car barely slowed down before it careened down the road, angry bits of gravel spitting up from its tires. It plunged onward, swerving down an even narrower driveway that meandered up and down until it widened in front of a large, austere house.

The thing with Twin Coulees, Alberta, was its deceiving façade. Blink, and you would miss it. Highway 2 zipped on by as if it didn't exist. It was tucked away between two coulees not visible from the freeway, but it was no hick town. The exit was dusty Milner's Road, masquerading as a dead-end country track that disappeared behind some large coulees towards the east. In the afterglow of dusk, it was the brilliance of tiny, jeweled lights that hinted at a little town tucked behind an uneven prairie landscape.

Many esteemed Twin Coulees as that fine collection of properties near enough to access the big city while maintaining a rich community atmosphere. Dude ranches attracted tourists, while cattle ranches supplied a flourishing beef industry. Twin Coulees Meat Solutions was a fully integrated beef processing facility employing upwards of 2,000 people. The availability of prime real estate was attractive with its ideal location, panoramic views of the undulating coulees and foothills, and a price still lower than less attractive lots in Calgary.

It was a capillary off Milner's Road that the car barrelled down out of sight, and then another, before it arrived at a rambling building. In its earlier days of glory and elegance, the building had been a large and stunning white Victorian bed and breakfast, replete with turrets, gables, and an ornate blue trim. Run by friendly and motherly Emma Watson, people flocked from as far north as Dawson Creek and High Level just for a short, relaxing getaway and, of course, her famous crepes. Its Victorian charm had been captured superbly in a well-written piece in *Oh Canada!* Majestic poplars boxing in the large acreage, a sea of green grass, and colorful perennials and shrubs, not to mention her prize roses and tulips, were all tucked away in the serene, quiet countryside infinitely worthy of a double-page magazine spread.

When Emma died, business and home lost their spirit as if a flame had been snuffed out. Her son arrived to claim his inheritance and half-heartedly attempted to continue the venture. Unfortunately, his love of booze led to his ruin. When he did work, his recipe for success lacked Emma's magnetism. Discovering that his mother's name and fame alone did not run a business, he gave up quickly and sold out, only to return east. The home, which had already fallen into disrepair under new ownership, became a sorrowful sight.

For a while, it was a long-term care home. Glossy pamphlets prematurely advertised a state-of-the-art facility complete with elevator and wheelchair access in a rustic Victorian setting. Renovations were well underway when reports of elder abuse, together with a lack of funds to complete the overhaul, ended another venture. For a decade since, the rambling home had stood empty, out of sight and out of mind.

To the outsider, the home stood cold and uninviting, decrepit and forgotten. All romance was gone, as if its life force had been sucked dry. The scars of vandalism and neglect, of peeling blue-and-white paint and sunken steps, would have destroyed poor Emma. Once a panorama of natural beauty and timeless architecture, a celebrated success, Twin Coulees' hidden pearl sat in anticlimactic ruin.

The car came to a halt in front of the house. Slowly and deliberately, he climbed out from the vehicle and gave the house a slow and meticulous once-over. His fingers pushing up the cuff of his windbreaker, he looked at the time. His gaze slowly traveled the expanse of gravel and landed on a spotted reptile of the irritating "ribbit-ribbit" variety. He leapt forward and jumped on it. He continued to pulverize the creature long after the croaking stopped.

He stood for a moment at the edge of the porch. Responsibility weighed heavy on his shoulders. But this forgotten and neglected place was proving to be the perfect spot for his plan. He walked up the creaking porch that skirted the house, allowing himself to be swallowed by the large front door.

Nothing and no one would impede him; justice must be served.

• • •

Basil

Sitting in Gemma's, a little hole-in-the-wall down Main Street, Basil looked furtively at his new colleague. The spicy aroma of hot wings wafted through the air, and he felt his body try to relax for the first time that day, strong coffee revitalizing his cells. His near-death experience had shaken him up, and he suddenly wanted nothing more than to be in his new place with the door closed.

The café was nearly empty with the lunch rush having come and gone. Constable Kennedy intrigued him with his graying hair that licked his collar, and his gut that spilled from his belt. His mouth and calloused hands never seemed to stop moving. His friendly conversation was liberally peppered with Shakespearean phrases, but Basil didn't feel as if the guy was trying to show off. There was something fatherly about this middle-aged cop, something that reminded Basil of his own late father. When he spoke, it wasn't condescending in the least. His slate gray eyes were often wet, as if his soul carried a pain so large that it welled up in his eyes.

"So, who do we have here?" Basil looked up to see a tall gazelle with blonde hair moving fluidly to the table, her hand on her hip, sizing him up slowly. "Since when do you bring company for lunch, Wal?"

Wally laughed. "Easy there, cougar." He winked at Basil. "Gemma likes to give the first degree to any newcomer. Best be prepared. But she makes the best food this side of the foothills."

Gemma scoffed and punched Wally lightly on the shoulder. "You're biased. Doesn't count."

"Basil here is transferrin' over from Calgary."

"Jay's replacement?" Suddenly, her voice had a noticeable edge, and she stood up straighter. Wally nodded as he took a gulp of his coffee. "New and shiny, huh?" But the sarcasm wavered as her voice broke.

"Now, Gemma," Wally warned her, gently taking her arm.

She shook it off and stared at Basil. "Ya think you can fill his shoes, huh? Mighty big, they were."

"Look, Gemma, just git us some of your best grub. How about your famous Colossal Coulee sandwich? Man, I can taste that melted Monterey Jack already. And that steak – "

Gemma refused to be railroaded. "How do you want your steak, huh?"

"Um, medium rare," Basil floundered.

"Medium rare? He liked it well done. But he had taste, y'know?"

"Gemma," Wally interjected.

Basil groaned inwardly. New town, and he was already messing up. "Sorry about Jay. About whatever happened," he spoke softly.

"It's Constable Stevens to you!" She walked away. It was quiet, except for the swishing of the half doors to the kitchen.

"She took it hard. Jay's death," said Wally.

"What actually happened? Basil probed, aware he might be on shaky ground.

Wally's eyes dimmed ever so slightly. His voice was hushed. "I think we'd better leave that for another time."

Gemma returned quite soon with their hot plates, her face impassive, her voice courteous enough. "Enjoy," she said briskly and disappeared.

Basil bit into the sandwich and then realized how hungry he really was.

"So, whaddya gonna do from here?" Wally asked, attacking his food like a starving wolf.

"Do?"

"No car. Gonna call a cab?"

"Nah. I'll give cabs a break for now. Actually, was thinking of walking. Everything's nice and close here."

"Walk?"

"You know, put one foot in front of the other."

Wally waved his hand in dismissal. "No need. Gotta bike you can use. Bit o' rust on it, but thing will do nicely till you've got somethin' more reliable."

"No need to be put out on my account. At any rate," he shrugged his shoulders, "fresh air and all."

Wally ripped a chunk out of his sandwich and shoved the wad in one cheek. "You know what they say about our good ol' weather. Besides, walking with two suitcases?"

Basil laughed. "It's been done before."

"Nope. Not in this town." He jabbed his chest with his thumb and continued, tongue-in-cheek: "Can't have you lookin' like Orphan Annie. We got a reputation to uphold."

Basil lifted his hands in defense. He *was* low on cash. "Duly noted. For the sake of getting off on the right foot and all, I think I will take you up on your offer."

Wally lifted his cup. "Well, as they say, welcome to Twin Coulees!" He swirled what was left and threw it back. Moments later, he tilted his body to retrieve a wallet from his back pocket.

Basil lifted one hand and used the other to grab his own wallet. "My turn. Keep things nice and even, you know?"

Wally grinned. "Keep this up, and I think you'll fit in quite nicely."

• • •

The Boy

TWIN COULEES, 1974

He moved inches from the cage, bent over, and stared solemnly at the brightly speckled snake curled up in the corner. Its forked tongue darted in and out with lightning speed.

"Hungry, aren't you, Hercules?" The boy asked quietly. The snake's eyes glinted, and the tongue continued to thrust in and out as it slowly uncoiled its body.

The mouse's tail was warm between the boy's fingers. It pumped its limbs in desperation and squeaked as it hung there suspended. The boy sniffed, glaring at the dangling creature. His shaking fingers grasped the vermin's body, and he squeezed, his eyes closing. Long after the squeaking had died, his whitish fingers relaxed, and blood flowed freely once more. Opening the cage door, he thrust the broken body into it and slammed the door shut. Swiping angrily at the dampness on his cheek, he stood rigid. His bedroom door opened.

"Son?"

"I fed her to Hercules."

"Her?"

"Peggy."

The large man turned to look at the faded portrait hanging askew on the wall beside the cage, his features hardening.

"One may smile and smile and be a villain."

"Good." His large, calloused hand squeezed the boy's thin shoulder before he turned to walk out of the room.

• • •

Nora

TWIN COULEES, 2014

Paintbrush in hand, Nora Clarkson sighed deeply. She stared at the half-finished ocean scene before her. Or at least what was supposed to be an ocean scene.

She'd lost her touch. That was all.

She tossed her brush into the soapy basin next to her. Despair crouched deep within her gut, like a monster ready to wrangle itself from within. It was like she'd taken her blood and guts and smeared them across a white canvas. The dabs of despair – ugly strokes of black – seemed both malevolent and painful.

She moved to the small kitchen to scrub the last marks of oil paint from her small hands and stared at the miserable sky outside her studio window. Gray clouds joining forces, ready to send whatever their Maker intended. "At least you are free," she murmured to the clouds. Nora was a prisoner in her own home. Oh, not forced, mind you. She could leave whenever she wanted to. But one can only bear the stares and whispers for so long. She could hide behind her traditional Muslim niqab, but its reception depended on the status of Muslims in the media. If she had not known this status a month ago, she was in no doubt when she raced home one day wearing spit on the front of her niqab, the insults still ringing in her ears. Most people in Twin Coulees were not racist, but she had an uncanny knack of bumping into those who were.

Hanging the kitchen towel on the stove handle, she pondered the irony of it all. She'd left a prison of sorts in Pakistan, only to enter another here. At least here it was bearable, thanks to Reg.

Reg. Her rock in the storm that had become her life, her thread to the outside world. Where would she be without him? Leaving her studio, she stopped short of the hall mirror. *Don't be an idiot,* a voice inside whispered. *Don't look!*

Trembling fingers pulled her niqab close around her face. At one point, she'd hated the traditional Muslim dress. She'd detested the way it erased her individuality, the way it reminded her of her low station in life. But now it made her feel safe.

She moved away from the mirror and walked to the fireplace mantle, Reg's eyes drawing her in, and she could not help but smile – at least as far as her skin allowed. Her dependable, loving Reg. Quiet and intense, her rock. He looked so very smart in his soldier's uniform. He was proud of holding a part-time position in the Canadian Army Reserves. He wasn't one of the super attractive types, but then she didn't mind; she'd never trusted the good-looking ones.

She closed her eyes and savored the memory of when she met him for the first time.

Nora had breathed in the warm October air, surprised she could still go outside in sandals. She'd rushed from her last house-cleaning gig to the nearest Sobeys to pick up groceries so she could cook a late supper in her apartment. Her stomach grumbled noisily as visions of curried rice and naan bread danced in her mind. Humming softly, she scanned the busy street for a cab. *Look at me!* she thought proudly. *A strong, independent woman in my own right.*

The two large bags of groceries strained her thin arms, but she didn't mind. A sense of satisfaction filled her. Her dream of coming to Canada had been realized. She shifted the bag to her hands and, for a moment, allowed the tightening plastic handles to dig into her fingers. Trying desperately not to spill them into the street, she attempted to flag down a cab.

Relieved as one finally pulled up to the curb, she limped to the car. The shopping bags banged awkwardly against her knees. The lower one tore open and spilled its contents all over the sidewalk. She scrambled to collect her items, her cheeks flaming. Tears scalded her eyes as she debated how she was going to collect her things, no one stopping to help her. Cans of food…personal items – horrors! – rolling every which way, a few stopping just short of the edge of the sidewalk, tottering precariously on its edge.

"Here, let me help!" came a low voice at her elbow. She looked up into kind, smiling eyes – such unique gray – and realized he was her cabbie. At that moment, the city fell away, drained of all color and all activity but him, sunlight glinting off his dark brown hair.

Without waiting for her response, he collected her groceries together and grabbed a small cardboard box from the trunk of the cab to put the wayward items in.

What a gentleman! she thought. Arms aching with relief, she allowed him to take her groceries and place them onto the backseat.

"This plastic stuff can't hold anything," he said. "They stuff 'em so full and send you on your way."

"Thank you so much," she responded softly, her cheeks finally cooling. What a spectacle she must have made. The thought made her cringe once more.

He dismissed her apology with a wave. "Enough food to feed an army," he chuckled.

"Actually, it is hopefully going to last me for the next two weeks."

"Wow, just for you?"

Red spots quickly stained her cheeks once again. *He must think I'm a pig,* she thought.

"Oh, sorry, no, that's not what I meant," he quickly added. "I just figured an attractive woman like you must, you know, be married or something. Please, I'm sorry!"

"It's okay," Nora responded, although not at all put off by the effusive apology. In fact, she found it kind of endearing.

"Really, I shouldn't have pried like that. I'm not usually so forward. Here, let me begin again. My name is Reginald Phillip Clarkson, and I am pleased to be your cabbie." His eyes twinkled with humor.

She trembled a little as he looked deep into her eyes. So intense. So direct. "That's a mouthful. Nice name, though."

"Thanks," he grinned. "I think so."

This time, Nora laughed and relaxed her small frame against the seat cushion. There was something about him that intrigued her; not that she could explain any of it. "My name is Nora. Actually, it's Aynoor." Now, why did she tell him that?

"Beautiful; so exotic." His voice was low and deep. For a moment, she just savored it quietly, her heart thumping in her chest.

"It's not, you know, familiar around these parts. I'm Pakistani. Some people have difficulty pronouncing it. I read the name 'Nora' in a book and thought it was close enough."

"Pakistan. Wow. Are you trying to Canadianize yourself?" He smiled in a friendly manner.

"Sort of, yeah. I guess so. I don't like standing out."

"I don't think you were meant to fit in."

If she had been blushing before, her cheeks were now flaming. She was used to one-liners back in Pakistan, but somehow, this time, it felt special.

"You know," he said, turning to her slightly. "This is very unorthodox of me, and something quite unprecedented, but would you like to go for a coffee with me? Maybe you can tell me all about Pakistan. You are my last fare for the evening. Unless, of course – never mind. How very presumptuous of me." He lightly punched the steering wheel. "Of course, you have other plans. Look – "

"Sure." She blinked. Had she just said that? Although every voice of reason in her head, particularly those of her parents, told her he was just a stranger and it was not proper to just go off with a man like that, her heart silenced the voices instantly. For some reason, it felt so right.

He pumped his fist in the air. "Yes!" Nora blushed once more at his emphatic response. "You can call me Reg," he added.

That evening, she'd fallen hook, line, and sinker. Reg, as she would come to call him, was like an open book: what you saw was what you got. Not like some of the men her parents had paraded in front of her – men whose lives were too much like a complex puzzle. She was surprised at how quickly he won her over. He was a good ten years older than her, but when you find the right one, the pieces fall into place just like that.

Of course, she married him.

• • •

Nora put down the gold-toned frame and picked up the white, heart-shaped frame standing next to it. The photo suddenly blurred. Darling Henry Phillip Clarkson, their little boy. How she missed him!

She set the frame down and walked to the bathroom to run a hot bath. She tried to ignore the only mirror in the house – one that taunted her daily. Only one time did she allow herself a hurried glance and the hideousness that stared back at her and nearly drove her over the edge.

She slipped off the veil and then her other clothes and slipped into a terry robe.

Soon, steaming water filled the tub. She cranked the tap and then quickly glimpsed in the mirror. The hazy image peering back at her was, as usual, safely hidden by a shroud of mist, the clearly delineated scars so blurred they lacked a sense of realness.

But then a tear of heavy condensation rolled down the mirror's surface, and a gasp caught in her throat. The apparition that stared back at her was more grotesque than she remembered. Frozen, she stared as tears like liquid pain trailed down the unfamiliar face before her.

The phone rang then, jerking her back to reality. It was Twin Coulees General. Reg had been in an accident.

• • •

Nora gripped the cold receiver to her ear.

"He will be alright," the nurse quickly reassured her. She explained what happened. "He is ready to be discharged. Are you able to come pick him up?"

Nora sat down. He could have died! "Um, yes, uh, no, I can't! Look, I'll send someone." She began picking her lower lip. How could she go to the hospital? She had barely been in public since the incident. Her fingers lightly ran the crevices and scars of her face. She was a monster. Of course she could not go to the hospital. They would all stare. The whispering would start. Children pointing. The looks of pity. She squeezed her eyes closed.

An unsteady hand hung up the receiver, and the accusation began: He was there for you every time you needed him. She glimpsed his tool belt lying on the floor. He worked so hard for their little family. Cabbing and part-time maintenance for a few businesses around town. And never complaining.

And here she was, not even able to bring herself to get him when he needed her most.

Trying to make sense of everything, she poured herself some coffee. The pot shook, and hot coffee splashed onto her arm. She shoved the pot back onto the hot plate, her arm smarting.

It was then she suddenly realized she was in the exact same place where the intruder had found and attacked her. The ground started shifting under her feet. The tables and chairs began moving. She reached for one of the closest chairs, but it would not stop spinning as darkness descended upon her.

• • •

"Nora? Nora?"

Nora opened her eyes. A very blurry Reg looked down at her. She blinked and widened her eyes as his form slowly cleared. She was lying between the kitchen table and the counter. A stinging sensation drew her attention to her arm. Realization washed over her. "Reg? Are you okay? Who brought you home?"

"Gladys from work. I'm fine, at least I am now."

"I am so relieved, Reg! I was worried. You had to call a cab. Sorry." She *was* sorry. She had not been there for him when he needed her.

"It's fine. I felt it coming. I thought I had more pills left. It just happened so fast." He sighed. "What are you doing on the floor?"

She shook her head. "I must have passed out. Burned my arm. Just a little."

"You burned yourself?" Immediately, he dropped to her side. "Where? How?"

"The coffee. I was just being clumsy. I'm fine. Look, it's just a small patch."

He carefully took hold of her arm. "Did you run it under cold water?" He glanced at the cupboard above her. "We have aloe vera gel. Here," he moved to the cupboard, "let's put some on."

She obliged, clambering to her feet. "I'm sorry, Reg, I just lost it." Such a pathetic mess, she was.

"Lost it? Why?"

"Because – "

"Why, Nora?" He persisted, his face wreathed in concern.

"I just couldn't anymore, Reg. It all hit me suddenly. My face – the fact that I am a prisoner in my own home. Everything!"

He reached for her hand. "Oh, darling. One day at a time."

"I came here to be free of them – of *everything*." She tried to swallow. There had only been a tinge of remorse as she watched Pakistan grow smaller from her plane window until it was a mere figment in her mind. Freedom beckoned. A future blooming with possibilities and potential as the plane touched down in Calgary, Alberta. She could become her own person. "Now, I'm just a prisoner."

"Oh, Nora." He drew her towards him.

She searched his face. "It was all my fault, Reg. I refused Amir. I *had* to have my own way – to be different."

"No," he grasped her shoulders. "You wanted to make your own choices."

"I *left*."

"Nora, wanting freedom – independence – is not a crime."

Her heart ached. Aman's sweet, brotherly face. Her mother's soft hazel eyes. How was it possible that the people you've lived with for your entire life would want you dead? "To them, it is." She drew in a deep breath. "Sometimes – sometimes, I feel like I'm living a nightmare."

"I know, I know," he soothed. With much tenderness, he took her jaw in his large hand and stroked her scarred chin with his thumb. "My beautiful Aynoor."

She pulled back, a surge of resentment suddenly ballooning in her stomach. She reached for the veil that wasn't there.

"Nora, it's okay. I've seen it all before. You were and will always be beautiful to me."

She pulled against his embrace for a moment longer and then gave in. She lay her head against his chest, her face downwards, drawing comfort from the familiar mix of sweat and cologne.

"We have each other, Nora," Reg murmured. "They loved you so long as you played to their song and dance. Your wants – your dreams – didn't matter to them. But they do to me."

She nodded and tried to rub away the hammering beginning in her temples. Her father's accusing voice sounded in her ears; her mother's lips pinched tight in disapproval.

Reg stroked her back, and she felt the comforting beat of his heart. "Some day, you will face the world again."

She pulled herself back once again and looked into his eyes. "I can't. Please don't make me go out there. I'm not ready!" How could she convey the desperation she felt? Reg was a fixer, a man of action. But she didn't want to be fixed yet; she didn't dare embark on that journey.

"Shhh, Nora. I didn't mean right now."

Dropping her head into her hands, she whispered: "I'm so sorry I didn't come get you, Reg."

Reg took her shoulders. "I'm fine, aren't I?"

She nodded.

"Here," he suddenly offered. "Let's see what we can do about your arm."

• • •

Basil

The row of duplexes stood tall and narrow on an even narrower street. Colorless and drab, they huddled together in solidarity like tattered orphans. Wilson Street was a dead end, its serpentine pavement different shades of gray stitched together like a quilt with old and new patches creating an uneven surface. Smoke spiraled from each chimney, thin serpents slowly uncoiling against a backdrop of gray and blue. Though the homes might be uninspiring, they were neat and functional. And quiet. He liked that. He needed quiet. His mind was chaotic at the best of times. The street's occupants were no doubt eking out a living somewhere in the small town. No bikes littered the front yards, no balls rolled aimlessly down the street. No laughing children ran carefree, playing a game of tag or showing off their latest techno gadgets.

He ran a hand through his reddish hair, rolled back his aching shoulders, and coolly appraised his new home: Number 14. The duplex was small but appeared well cared for. He stood on the threshold, remembering the last one he'd crossed over. But that time, he had Myra in his arms. Stop it! He shoved the thought to the back of his mind. Never in a million years would he have guessed he'd end up in this situation. Alone. But he'd made up his mind to push forward, to begin anew. No one promised change would be easy.

One suitcase in each hand, he took a deep breath and entered the room. The strong smell of stale cigarette smoke and bleach assaulted his nostrils. The landlord promised clean, but he obviously was not referring to air quality.

Basil dumped the suitcases on top of each other and turned to bring in the bike – a simple green mountain bike with plenty of life in it. He shook his head and chuckled. Wally. A man who did not take no for an answer.

He turned to his suitcases. The black one, that was it. His hands fumbled as they undid the clasp. He threw back the flap and carefully lifted out the square bottle with the black label. Jack Daniels. It shook in his hands. He unscrewed the lid and placed the opening at his lips. Cold wetness and then exploding heat filled his throat, then belly.

Jack had been with him when he was at rock bottom. The amber liquid had warmed his soul when the frigid gusts of memory left him shivering; it had pried the tight hold of his nightmares and chased the memories away, albeit temporarily. It promised so sweetly to never leave him, to anesthetize his tortured soul. It always delivered. He could not say the same for God. Where was He when Jules died?

Centred again, he glanced around him. The furnishings were sparse but clean. The couches were a faded plaid, with Ikea-style coffee tables. Mottled beige carpet ran through the living area. Brown kitchen cupboards and off-white walls slightly dated the home, making it tired and lackluster. Small windows peered sorrowfully from behind drab tan muslin as if trying to hide their sun-streaked nakedness. What feet had walked over these floors? What conversations had these walls been privy to? A cheap Walmart reproduction of a Mona Lisa hung slightly askew on the living room wall. He straightened it without thought. Her benign smile was the only warmth cast over the room. He found himself, oddly, smiling back at her.

Slowly, he opened each cupboard and drawer. If he was going to live here, he wanted to know the place inside and out. With ease, he ran his fingers over the top of the door frames. Thick dust, like greasy fuzz that did not come off easily, spoke volumes. Mentally, he cataloged the pen-stained drawers, the chipped faucets, and even the crumbs packed tightly into those hard-to-reach places. Each person may have left his mark in some way, but the house was an empty shell, a soulless and bloodless corpse. He paused in the windowless bathroom to splash cold water on his tired face. The pipes clanged and shuddered with effort. A cold draft snaked its fingers around him.

Suddenly, there was a prick of something at the back of his throat and an odd feeling deep in his belly. He cleared his throat and kept looking out the window. What was he doing here?

The tiny master bedroom's double window peered into a small yard. The upraised claw-like arms of the aspen tree swayed stiffly in a suddenly cold breeze. It stood like a lonely sentinel, garb-less and weary. The small space of grass was patchy and discolored, and weeds of questionable origin had wrestled their way through, stalwart and feisty as only weeds can be. The glass of the window was cold to the touch. His breath turned the streaked glass into patches of fog into which he trailed his finger in snakelike movements.

Fall was fading fast, and so was he.

Peering upwards at the sky, he noticed thickening stratus clouds. Snow was coming early this year. Soon, winter would seize this little village in a searing grip of cold. Winter. There would be no Christmas this year. What was there to celebrate?

Myra. He said her name aloud. It merely echoed off the empty walls. Inside, a spark still glowed feebly; some days, it was a very weak spark, almost like a dying ember. It kept him afloat. Barely. Enough energy to endure this transfer, to live this new life. But memories, like quicksand, threatened to suck him in.

He opened the window to allow in fresh air, and the drab curtain stirred to life. Satisfied, he returned to the living area. He was no interior designer, but he knew he desperately needed to infuse the space with some color, whether through flowers or art.

Dropping himself onto the couch, he placed his large feet on a diagonally placed coffee table, the landlord's simple gesture, perhaps, at introducing some style to the otherwise rigid room. Shifting his feet left striations on the dusty surface. Okay, maybe the rooms weren't super clean after all. He sat up and sighed. For a few minutes, he drank in the silence, the hum of the refrigerator the only noise in the background. He closed his eyes briefly, but even silence can become loud and oppressive.

He scooted his butt closer to the suitcases and undid the clasp of the gray one. T-shirts. Jeans. Only two pairs. Wrinkled. When was the last time he'd bought any clothes?

He sighed, then opened his wallet and took out a photo. Even as he did this, he wondered why he was going down this road. It was a form of emotional masochism. A smiling face looked deep into his eyes, light brown eyes radiating affection and joy. But that was a lifetime ago; another world; another universe. He shoved the picture back into his wallet and turned on the radio.

Distraction was good.

"...Heroic rescue today on Highway 3. A cab driver was saved from an almost definite fate as his quick-thinking passenger brought him and his car to safety on one of our busiest highways. The man suffered from hypoglycemia due to a pre-existing condition and lost control of his vehicle. Thanks to the bravery of his passenger, he is now on the mend..."

Today was about moving forward, about embracing a new chapter in his life. But was it even possible? On the one hand, he felt like he was dying, but he had saved a man's life – a man he didn't even know. There was a whole lot of irony in that.

DAY 18

Arizona

A sharp ring wrangled Arizona from a deep sleep.

Her hand shot out from under the covers, and she slammed the alarm clock.

It sounded again.

She pried open her eyes and stared at the luminous digits: 5:00 am. She groaned.

Suddenly, she sat up, eyes wide. In one fell swoop, she threw back the covers as cold air rushed in. She struggled into her robe, rushing to the door.

She pulled the door open. Her heart dove. It was not him. And definitely not Mother. Unless she had developed a penchant for band-aid skirts and allowed someone to take artistic liberty to the canvas of her face. Hair gathered in a limp pony, a tight, sequined shirt on a skeletal frame, railroad tracks up both arms...

"You done?"

Arizona blushed. "Sorry."

She shrugged. "I know it's early. Can I?" She gestured at the warm kitchen.

Arizona rubbed her eyes and moved aside. "Um, I guess."

The woman fumbled for a Virginia Slims from behind her shirt and tried lighting it with shaking hands, her chipped red thumbnail repeatedly slipping on the lighter's edge.

"Here, let me." Arizona lit her cigarette and returned the lighter.

"Thanks." The hard edge to her voice softened somewhat. Fatigue, drugs, and drink had written their narratives on her body in the rounded stoop of her shoulders and the glaze in her eyes. "Flippin' feet." Arizona watched in surprise as she kicked off her high heels and liberated her red and swollen feet. "Look, can I bug you for a quick coffee? I don't wanna drag this out. I can't do that."

"Coffee?" The wall clock shouted 5:06.

"Please."

"It's really only five," she hesitated. "Do I know you from somewhere?"

"Shoot, sorry! Seraphina LeCaure." She thrust out her hand. Arizona enclosed the spindly fingers in her own. They were cold and clammy and leathery. "Yeah, it's early, but please, let's get this over and done with. It's stupid hard as it is."

Arizona blinked and stepped back. "Okay. It'll just take me a minute."

"Arizona Stuart. Finally." She ran her long fingers through bleached straw and scanned the tiny kitchen.

"Finally?"

"Marc's spoken of you."

"Marc?" Her fingers clenched the coffee pot handle, and cold coffee sloshed against the inside of the glass.

"Oh, all good stuff," she waved her hand. Arizona watched as she tapped her cigarette against the plant pot centered on the kitchen table that held her prize ivy, allowing the ashes to fall onto the soil. Smoke trailed from her cigarette and cast hazy swirls above her head.

Arizona jerked the tap, and water rushed into the pot. She sucked in a few deep breaths, and with a flick of her wrist slowed the flow of water. She watched it rise to line four...then six...and finally, eight. She dumped five heaping spoons of fresh grounds into the filter. Today, it would be strong. Ghastly, but strong.

A hacking cough tore through Seraphina, and she sank onto a kitchen chair.

"You don't sound too good," Arizona managed, punching the auto button.

"It's just a matter of time." She drew her legs underneath her, and they stuck out like sharp blades. Purplish lines threaded out from the crook of her knee, and Arizona was surprised her flesh was able to dimple.

"Oh." Arizona grabbed a dishtowel from the stove and clutched it tight.

Seraphina stretched her arms out on the table and rested her head on them, eyes closed. For a moment, the only sound was the hiss and sputter of the percolator.

"Can I call someone?" Arizona tried again, running a hand through her knotted hair.

The woman just shook her head and coughed again. Each time, the spasm took whatever breath she had. Arizona worried the little mole at her elbow and stared at the pathetic vision before her. Seraphina smelled of the night streets, of deep-fried oil mixed with dust and sweat. Her eyebrows had been shaved off and replaced with exaggerated inky arches.

Little lines spider-webbed from her closed eyes, and her cheeks were sucked in. No makeup, no matter how richly layered, could hide the lurid paleness of her skin.

And Marc had known her?

"Can't put it off any longer," the woman suddenly wheezed, lifting her head. "It's killin' me, but now is best, before, you know." Her voice sounded strained as she used her energy to dig in her leopard-print handbag."

"No, I *don't* know," Arizona jumped in.

But Seraphina did not seem to hear. "I kinda expected Marc to be here. Oh, got it!" She paused for a moment and drew in deeply once more. "Such a load of junk in this bag." She dropped a legal-size envelope onto the table.

Arizona edged toward the table and stared at the stained and battered envelope. "What is this?"

"Legal documents." She slumped against the chair, a veiny hand massaging her collarbone.

Arizona's scalp squeezed tight. "I feel like I am supposed to know something."

A smile slowly untwisted the woman's grimace. "You do have a sense of humor." She drew in another deep breath and then sat up business-like. "But I don't have the energy. Here." She pushed the envelope towards Arizona. "Malcolm's papers."

Arizona stared at her. "Who is Malcolm? What papers?"

Seraphina began to chuckle, but it died on her lips. Her eyes probed Arizona's face, the smile wavering.

Suddenly, it slid off. "You're not –"

Arizona shook her head.

Seraphina struggled to rise before standing there, holding onto the table. "Where *is* Marc?" She demanded.

A muscle jumped in Arizona's jaw. "Gone."

"Gone?" She cocked her head. "To work?"

"No." Arizona's throat suddenly ached. She bit her lip and dropped the towel onto the table. First her mother. Now this. "I don't understand."

"They say he is, uh, that he committed suicide."

"Suicide," Seraphina whispered, sinking back into her chair. Arizona could see the woman searching her face in vain for a sign she was joking while fumbling for a cigarette. She shook her head then and thrust a fresh cigarette between her lips. "I never saw that one coming."

Arizona stared at the table. The indentations of Marc's pen stared at her from the soft wood surface. He always wrote hard and furious when caught up in his work.

Seraphina's lighter shook and finally spit out a fiery plume on the third try. She sucked in hard. "I'm sorry. I really am." Exhaling a cloud of smoke and stifling the start of a cough, she covered her face with her hands, the cigarette clamped between her fingers.

Suddenly, she lifted her head. "Wait a minute." She stabbed the unfinished cigarette into the ivy's soil. "You mean, he never...?"

"No," Arizona bit off, glaring at her ivy plant.

Seraphina pulled her arms tight to her, panic bubbling beneath the surface. "He was s'posed to take Malcolm! It was all arranged."

"What is arranged? Who is Malcolm? Please! I am in the dark here." She dug her hands into the pockets of her robe and pinched her flesh. Hard. She knew Marc had been with another woman before he'd come into her life, and he'd struggled with the guilt since, but that it had led to a child?

"He's my son!" Another coughing fit. "My little boy," she gasped, stabbing her finger in the direction of the front door, "who's sleeping out there. In my *car*."

Arizona turned her head in the direction of the driveway. A small car sat in the drive, its back end dipped lower than the rest of its frame. Moonlight spilling over one side revealed part of its blue, rust-tinged body. A back window was partially lowered. If she thought she might have been hovering in some state of sleep, she was no longer.

The woman he'd known before she met him. "How old is your boy?"

"Three. It's a long story. He never knew Malcolm existed. Until recently. He was going to take him," she struggled for breath. "Now what?" She looked around frantically as if an answer was somehow lodged in the wall.

Arizona dug her nails into the flesh of her arm this time and winced. Then it hit her like a bucket of ice water. "You killed him."

Seraphina looked stunned, as if she'd been slapped.

"You blackmailed him, didn't you?" Tears burned at the back of her eyes.

"How dare you!" Seraphina bit back. "What do you think I am?" She struggled to her feet once more. "He was so happy he had a kid." Another cough sapped the energy from her thin frame. "It takes two, you know?" Her voice broke.

Arizona sank wordlessly into a chair. *Marc's* chair. Her mind spun with half-formed thoughts. *What have you done to me, Marc?* Seeing the glimmer of pain in Seraphina's eyes, she impulsively reached out to touch her arm. "Why are you trying to give me your child? Don't you have family to help?"

Seraphina fumbled for Arizona's hand and clutched it tight. "*You* are all the family he has."

Arizona simply stared at her.

"I'm very ill."

Arizona blinked. The walls around her seemed to close in. She moved to the edge of her seat, turning her head to the kitchen window – to the distance beyond. A child? She couldn't take care of a child! Her life was a mess now. It was all she could do to stay afloat herself.

But it's *Marc's* child too. Her heart squeezed. But she was no mother. And toys. She had none, nor children's books. There was a spare bed. What did he like to eat? Was he potty trained? The vise around her hand clamped tighter.

"You're his only hope." Seraphina blinked in frustration, but tears have this stubborn way of escaping, and they led a wet path down her sunken cheeks.

In her mind, Arizona could see Estelle's look of shock. Her cherry red lips forming that perfect 'O' of exaggerated horror. In desperation, she would remind Arizona of who she was and where she'd come from, and demand to know why she dared to even *contemplate* doing something. But then, Mother never did approve of anything she did.

"I'll take him." She blinked. Had she just said that?

Seraphina stared at her for a moment. "For real?"

Arizona nodded. "For real." A lump wedged itself in her throat.

A smile cleared her face. But then it disappeared as she began to rub her sternum.

"Are you okay?" Arizona said.

She squeezed her eyes. "It's getting worse."

Arizona reached to support her, but she sank from the chair to the floor. Arizona dropped beside her and rubbed her back, looking around her frantically. "I'll get help!"

Seraphina tried to speak, one hand suddenly clutching Arizona's arm.

Arizona shook it loose. "Hang on. Please hang on!" She grabbed her cellphone off the table.

She fumbled. It slipped, and she grasped it before it hit the floor.

"Send an ambulance!" She barked at the calm lady who answered. "I need help. This lady – I think she's having a heart attack!"

Seraphina slid further until she was lying on the floor. Arizona froze. "Hurry!" she yelled at the dispatcher. She watched in horror as the woman's arm stopped its frenzied movement and fell limp onto her abdomen before sliding to her side.

She dropped the phone on the table. "Seraphina!" She crouched beside the woman and patted the pale face. With shaking fingers, Arizona picked up the wrist and felt for her pulse – it was there. But faint, thread-like.

• • •

The ambulance ferried away the frail woman. She had barely known Seraphina, but for a moment, there had been a connection, albeit stretched thin and taut.

"Ma'am?"

Arizona blinked. The police officer shifted from one foot to the other, his eyes searching her face with concern. "Where's the child?"

Malcolm! "He must be in the car. She said he was sleeping in there." The two hurried to the battered Cutlass. It had seemed like hours since Seraphina had arrived, but probably only an hour had elapsed. What had the child seen?

When the officer yanked the door open, they were both stunned to see a brown-haired boy still buckled in a crumb-infested car seat, fast asleep, the little fingers of one hand clutching an earlobe. Arizona felt so relieved. His road ahead was sure to be difficult enough. The sudden flood of light from the officer's flashlight made the child's head jerk. He started blinking. The little boy opened his eyes wide. Immediately, he shrunk back as if hoping to be absorbed by the ripped vinyl seat.

For Arizona, the effect was like being doused in ice-cold water. She was looking right into the face of Marc.

"Do you want me to call Child Protective Services?" The officer gently prodded.

Arizona paused, her lips tingling. She played with the flap of the envelope and then shifted the package from one hand to the other, the crisp paper wilting in her sweaty palms. She turned to her small home, peering at her with its sorrowful eyes, and then the boy's trembling lip. She noted the stain drool had left on his chin and took in the dirty, mussed clothes. She felt the officer's searching eyes on her once again. She cleared her throat. "No. I have these. We'll be fine."

• • •

That night, she slid into a terrifying nightmare. A whimpering sound finally pulled her out of its grasp.

She woke, trembling and perspiring, her heart galloping in her chest. The whimpering was still ongoing, coming from the direction of the guest room. She pulled the blankets up to her chin and tried to place the sound.

Malcolm.

There it was again. A frantic plea this time. "Mommy!"

She clambered out of bed, noting that even her dresser, the pictures on the wall, the curtains, everything felt strange.

She tiptoed softly into the spare room. The tiny form lay dwarfed in a twin-sized bed. Sheets were twisted around his body.

Her shoulders tightened. She crept closer to the bed. Was he awake?

The floorboards groaned.

She froze.

His eyes were still closed, though dewy at the corners. He gave a small sigh and popped his thumb into his mouth, his other thumb and forefinger working the lobe of his ear. How terrified he must feel, she thought, having been torn from his mother and placed in a strange house.

For a long moment, she watched him sleep. The familiar markings were all there. The sloping of dark hair, the down-turned mouth...

Salt in a raw wound.

His hand fell from his face, and his breathing evened.

She exhaled, feeling her muscles finally uncoil. Like a thief, she slunk back to her room.

She inspected her once-again raw fingers, bitten to the quick, in the narrow slat of moonlight. The silence and darkness of the night draped over her with the weight of a lead blanket. Tears pricked her eyelids, but she refused to give in to them. Their impending power frightened her terribly. It would not stop with tears. They were merely a distressing harbinger of what was to come. It did not take a psychologist to explain to her that the effect would be like a snowball gaining ground and size. It would crush her.

She nudged the curtain aside and peered into the starry sky as if searching for answers. *Marc, where are you?* They merely twinkled as they had done for centuries, unaware of the trials and tribulations of mere mortals below. *Please, God, don't leave us! Let Marc be out there somewhere. Alive.*

She touched the blanket on her bed and then stopped. Tea. Maybe something herbal would beckon sleep once more.

In the kitchen, she measured a teaspoon of loose-leaf chamomile tea and added it to an infuser, watching the boiling water take on a golden-brown hue. "I did the right thing," she argued to the steaming brew.

Suddenly, an image of Melody popped up in her mind. What would *she* say? Her legs began to tremble. The feeling wormed its way up through her limbs, her bones, her tummy. Was she getting ill? Was this how the crying would start? She half sat down as the tremors increased, and, with horror, she discovered an ocean of laughter bubbling from within, unstoppable, pushing its way out until she was carried away on violent waves.

Spent, she laid her head on her forearms, her sides aching, breath coming out in short gasps. Lifting her cup of tea to her mouth, she winced as the scalding liquid touched her tongue.

She thought of Seraphina in the hospital.

I'm very ill. What did she mean? Cancer, some degenerative condition?

She pushed away her tea and stood up. Seraphina would come back for Malcolm. It was amazing what hospitals could do, epicenters of the latest in medical technology.

This was just a stepping stone. She could do that.

She dumped the last dregs of her tea in the sink. Imagine placing a child smack dab in the wreckage of your life.

DAY 19

Nora

The sky over Twin Coulees was a dazzling interplay of pinks and purples that cast crowns of burnished gold on the tops of the trees, painting each leaf. Peaceful and idyllic, infinitely worthy of being captured by the strokes of a paintbrush and rendered eternal on canvas. Using her bare toes to slowly push the swing on the narrow porch, Nora tried to find solace in its repetitive creak and groan. She noted with delight that the sunflowers she'd planted were blooming nicely. The street, lined with duplexes and tiny bungalows, was quiet. A cool wind fingered her scarf and played with the dark tendrils of hair that escaped. Soon, it would be too cold to go outside. She would be sealed up like a prisoner unless she could scrape together courage. The large sunflowers seemed to bob their heads in agreement.

Sunflowers – the flowers Reg had brought with him to the hospital when he came to visit her – the sun captured and handed to her. Instinctively, she held them away from her face.

That was Reg. Meticulous, organized. She'd only mentioned once before that sunflowers were her favorite, but he'd remembered. It was the first smile she had cracked – a painful smile – behind the bandages, but this simple act had touched her. Through the haze of memory, she remembered certain events quite clearly: the pain, the fatigue, fighting the infection, visits from police, the surgeon.

"We can give you a new face," Dr. Bekar had stated, steepling his smooth, manicured fingers. The downtown Calgary office was like a room out of a high-end hotel. Luxuriously patterned carpets, soft, sage walls, and oaken paneling. His face was chiseled and smooth – flawless. "There are options available to you, Mrs. Clarkson."

"Technology," Reg breathed, leaning forward in his chair, hope plastered over his face.

Nora simply stared.

"Absolutely." Dr. Bekar turned his attention to the enthusiastic man before him. "Medical science is amazing." He swiveled his chair back to Nora. "One option is grafting."

"Grafting?" Nora repeated.

"Correct. We would take skin from a discreet part of your body, like your thigh, and graft that to your face to reconstruct it."

Her inner thighs burned.

"In your case," he peered at her, "we would do a split-thickness graft. The area is quite large, but the wounds are not terribly deep."

He leaned closer to Nora, and she could smell his expensive cologne and coffee breath.

"May I?" he asked, moving his hand toward her face.

She nodded mutely.

The small, pale hand inched toward her face. She closed her eyes as fingers stripped away the shawl. She sat there naked. Opening her eyes, she saw his eyes travel across her face, the slight flicker in their depths.

The shock was there. So slight, just a whisper, but it was there.

His warm fingers lifted her chin, and he studied her face, one finger daring to slide over its ravaged contours.

Nora dug her hands into the folds of her skirt.

"This type of graft has a greater chance of taking and a quicker healing time."

Dr. Bekar dropped his hand and sat up straight again. Nora's breath rushed out.

"What are the complications?" Reg forged ahead while Nora huddled at the sidelines.

Dr. Bekar straightened up in his chair. "Like any extensive procedure, you're faced with risks. But this does not have to be her case," he quickly stressed. "There is a chance – a *chance*," he emphasized, "that the graft doesn't take. At the very least, skin tightening, and discoloration are difficult to avoid."

A buzz filled the room. Nora picked out the words floating around like fragments. "Bleeding…infection… numbness."

"We have different cards we can play," Dr. Bekar continued as if this was all some cruel game.

Reg's eyes were huge, like a little boy in a toy store, and he nodded enthusiastically.

"A face transplant."

"Face transplant?" Nora squeaked.

Dr. Bekar smiled and gestured at a poster on the wall. "It is a new frontier, but it has been done successfully. We replace your face using tissue from a donor."

A face lay against a dark background like some malleable rubber mask, slightly dented in on one side. Two yawning holes stared at her. Bloodless. Soulless. An actor's dressing prop waiting to come to life.

Something suddenly bubbled deep inside her, incipient laughter. Her body shook.

"Nora. Be serious," Reg tapped her arm.

I could paint this, she whispered. Then stronger, "I would call it: *The Face With No Eyes*. Oil paints," she barrelled forward, "would neatly emphasize the ridges, the – wait a minute." She held up her hand. "I could call it *Scraps of Me Stitched Together*."

"Nora, please," Reg begged again.

She hiccupped.

"It will be – " Dr. Bekar began.

The spasms of laughter deep within grew like an unstoppable force, wrangling upward. She tried to hold them in her throat.

Until she no longer could.

The doctor and Reg looked at each other helplessly.

The laughter died as suddenly as it started. Two pairs of eyes probed hers.

"So, I would be wearing someone else's face." She touched the uneven craters of her face.

"Well, essentially, yes."

Reg turned to the doctor and frowned. "She would look like someone else."

The tall, well-heeled man leaned back in his chair. "That is another way of putting it. But," he enunciated the words carefully, "she will never again look like she did formerly. This will make her face more presentable. Allow her to move about in society without feelings of inadequacy."

Silence mushroomed in the room.

"Look," Dr. Bekar hastened to add. "She would not have the facial expressions of her donor. The brain regulates emotion. She will still be uniquely her own person."

"Under another person's face." Reg rubbed his own face.

Nora tried to envision what she looked like formerly. Her fingers gripped the sides of her chair as she realized right then that she could not remember.

Suddenly, she felt Reg's hand on hers. She looked down. Her fingers were digging into his flesh, and he was trying to disengage them.

"Sorry," she whispered. He squeezed her hand for a moment, and something flickered in his eyes.

"Me too."

The walls of the room moved, and she felt as if she were tipping over. Dr. Bekar floated before her. She squeezed her eyes closed and inhaled deeply.

"Honey?"

"Mrs. Clarkson?" The doctor's voice intruded.

She opened her eyes.

Suddenly, she scrambled to her feet. "No."

Dr. Bekar put down his pen.

Reg half rose. "Darling – "

"I can't."

She ran out of the office, Reg begging her to stop, to reconsider.

She stopped just outside the building, winding the scarf tightly around her face.

Eventually, she chose the skin graft. It was partially successful. After a few infections and much pain, the graft took, although she was left with keloid scarring.

Medically, she was a success.

A blanket term if you could call a lifelike quilt a success.

For many miserable months already, she'd been living the life of a hermit, wrapped in a cocoon of fear, humiliation, and self-imposed guilt. For the first months, she hadn't looked in a mirror. For the first months, she'd wanted to die.

She didn't care anymore. No longer did she resemble Nora Clarkson. She'd lost her son and face. Her smooth cheeks and slight dimple, and even the petite nose her friends back home had always coveted had shriveled under the drops of acid, like paper under intense heat. Hideous and frightening. They apologized profusely. She no longer cared. Part of her had died that day anyway...

The sound of a motor broke her trance, and she quickly looked up. The duplex rental across the street had been unoccupied until the past few days. She tried to push away a gnawing sensation in her gut as a tall, dark-haired man in a black hoody stepped out of a beat-up car. He seemed to look right at her for a long moment, and Nora felt hair standing straight up on her arms. She took in a deep breath, ready to bolt, when she realized he could not see her behind the weathered porch column and the aging maple.

She saw then the cellphone in his hand and expelled the air, feeling slightly dizzy as she did so.

DAY 20

Arizona

She lay like a corpse tucked in the hospital bed, tubes and wires snaking from her arms and chest. An oxygen mask pressed tightly to her face, the skin blanched around its edges.

Machines whirred and hissed and sucked in the few rooms arranged strategically around a central administrative area.

The ICU fishbowl.

Arizona perched on the edge of her seat, twisting and untwisting her hands. She'd gained entry to the ICU by the skin of her teeth.

A stocky nurse breezed into the room with a smile on her freckled face. "Just a couple more minutes of visiting, please."

Arizona nodded. "Is she gonna be okay?"

The nurse rehung the clipboard and inserted her pen in her front pocket. "Overwhelming infection in one so compromised – "

"Because of her – "

"Heart condition. Now her lungs are also severely weak with pneumonia. Time will only tell." She moved toward Arizona and squeezed her shoulder. "I'm sorry, dear. I know it's not easy."

Then she was gone.

Arizona stood and moved to the bed. *Wake up, Seraphina,* she thought. *There is still hope. You just must fight; fight hard. Your little boy is waiting for you.* She looked down at the milk-soaked stain on her shirt. "You have to," she whispered this time.

Seraphina did not blink or move. Only two days ago, she had burst into her world and dumped cigarette ashes into her prize ivy.

And left her a little boy.

Arizona turned to the small window. Darkening clouds hung like a mass of sodden blankets that dripped and dripped.

She swallowed hard. "Please, Seraphina." She laid her hand on the woman's spindly leg and stroked it, willing health into her. Straightening a fold in the blanket, she turned and hurried out the room.

The elevator could not descend fast enough. Moments later, glass sliding doors sealed her from the world of antiseptic smells and sounds of death. She shivered. Lifting her face to the sky, a few drops glanced off her nose.

But she kept her face upturned and sucked in the fresh air.

• • •

"Mrs. Stuart," Constable Kennedy greeted her. He sounded weary almost. Resigned.

She lifted her chin with boldness. "Have there been any developments?" Her hands already felt clammy and jittery.

He shook his head. "I'm afraid not, ma'am. As we've indicated, until other evidence surfaces, our hands are tied."

As we've indicated. Part of her wanted to run, but the stronger part kept her rooted to the floor, to press for answers, to keep searching. She owed that to Marc. To herself. She hugged her arms to her body. A phone rang in the background. "So, you believe it was suicide?"

"We must follow the evidence, ma'am. Right now, there are no signs of foul play. Prints on the suicide note are exclusively his. But then again, with no body – "

No body. "Does this happen often?" she pressed. "A suicide and no body?"

"It is definitely not the norm, I will give you that. But it is not unheard of, either."

"What if he was killed?" Her voice sounded strained to her own ears.

Constable Kennedy shifted. "We are looking at that angle, too. Every possibility is on the table."

She rubbed her face. They *had* interviewed coworkers, acquaintances, and scoured the area. So far, due diligence had been done.

She pulled her purse to her. "There were no signs," she grasped for some thread to hold onto. "Here," she groped in her purse and produced a thin, stapled stack of papers. Her sweaty hand slapped them on the counter between them.

His thick fingers moved the papers toward him. *Suicidal Behaviour.*

She ran her tongue over chapped lips and leaned toward the counter. "It says in here there are signs. Victims exhibit behavior before – but there was none!"

"Mrs. Stuart – "

She stared at the papers as if willing him to look closer, to flip through them.

But he simply moved the stack about, his fingers feeling the edges. His eyes never left her face. "With suicide, the signs are not always there. Please, don't blame yourself." He rubbed his shoulder as if she were a splinter sitting deep beneath its surface. "We are ninety-nine percent certain here there was no foul play."

She gripped the counter's edge until her fingers ached. His face was too smiley, his gut too big. She jutted out her chin. "Ninety-nine percent. There is still one percent. *He* could be the one percent!"

"Until we have evidence to prove otherwise – "

"Are you giving up?" Her fingers strangled the strap of her purse.

He rubbed his face. "Of course not. But manpower, resources are all limited. We will keep looking."

Keep looking. Placed on the back burner. She bit her lip and blinked away her suddenly blurred vision. They were all the same. Her mother, Constable Kennedy, even Mel. Tiptoeing around like she was a house of cards that would topple at any moment if the card of "truth" was pulled out.

• • •

Her steps slowed somewhat once she was outside. Like a predictable pulse, the busyness of Twin Coulees marched on. Cars honked; people chattered. Everyone had destinations – a purpose.

Then she saw it. The darling little café where she and Marc had enjoyed many a date.

"C'mon, Arizona," he had coaxed her one afternoon.

She scrunched back into her seat. "Marc, put that away. I hate my picture taken!"

He pointed the snout of his camera in her direction and laughed. "I report and photograph, my dear. And you're the perfect subject to shoot."

She felt her cheeks blotch. "Why me?"

"Newly renovated café. Happy customer. Front page news." He leaned forward, a swath of dark hair falling above one eye. "And a beautiful one at that."

"Oh, get out of here!" She swatted him. "Front page news. Okay," she conceded, "*one* picture. Hope that fancy gadget of yours doesn't break."

He took the picture then laid his camera down. The smile slid off his face. He examined his fingernails as if there was something there that intrigued him.

She sipped her latte and watched his face. The cleft in his chin, his thin lips. Downturned, of course, unless it morphed into a grin.

He toyed with his coffee cup and then looked at her. "You are hoping for children someday, aren't you?" he asked quietly.

She sat up straight. "You don't?"

"I do. I do. It's just that – "

A long shadow cast over their table. "Stuart!" It was Dawson Williams, news reporter for the Gazette. The two clasped hands, the conversation forgotten.

A horn suddenly bleated, and she realized she was standing in the middle of a crosswalk. Her armpits dripped. A thick layer of moisture sucked the silk to her skin. Even her stockinged feet felt wet and made squishy sounds when she walked. If she took off her shoe, no doubt she would leave a wet imprint on the concrete.

What had Marc been trying to tell her that day? Did it have anything to do with Malcolm? With Seraphina?

Malcolm. She had to get back home. Relieve Melody. Deal with the little boy so unceremoniously dumped into her life.

A stepping stone, she reminded herself, *just a stepping stone.*

• • •

Arizona stabbed her key into the lock.

Then she remembered.

She dumped her purse and scanned the room. A small hurricane had ripped through the kitchen and living area. Toys and books strewn all over. Melody-style. She bit her lip.

"Over here!" Melody waggled her fingers over the edge of the couch.

Arizona took in the wilted bloom. Her legs were tucked underneath her. A bright skirt billowed around her like an Asian fan. She was not a beautiful woman by industry standards, but there was an attraction in the bold angles and planes of her face and lithe body, in the high cheekbones and long fingers. A strong woman who was too strong for many men – too independent, too confident, though not arrogant. In that tall fortress, Arizona saw a human balm that slathered vulnerable people in love, with just the right hint of common sense and wit.

"I might be a teacher of hormone-driven teenagers, but this has me all done in," she sighed with a grin, running her fingers through her long bob.

Arizona could not help but smile. Essays slashed in red lay strewn around. "I don't think," she said, picking one up, "they would dare too much after seeing one of these."

Melody straightened up with a laugh, bracelets jangling. "Oh, they are used to this. But that poor child is a pendulum, I tell you. Goes from not talking to a full-out tantrum. And then crying for his mom. I read to him and played with him, and now," she indicated the closed bedroom door, "he is fast asleep. Started rubbing his eyes and playing with his ear."

"I see he wanted more juice than you were willing to give?" She pointed wryly at the stain on Melody's bright pink shirt.

"Yep," Melody pulled a face. "I am officially bushed."

Arizona plopped on the couch beside her. Students loved Melody. They lapped up her over-the-top, flamboyant style, her acerbic wit.

She got them.

They got her.

But what worked for her students would be lost on a little boy.

"So?" Melody probed. "How did it go?" She wound her fashionable scarf around her neck.

Arizona sank into the couch with a sigh. "She looks awful, Mel. Wrangled my way in. Place has tighter security than a jail. She is so bloated and so pale, like a…" She swallowed. "Just awful." The corpse-like woman swam into view, tubes threading from every orifice, eyes sunken shut.

"What exactly is wrong with her?"

"Some genetic heart condition is all I managed to get out of the nurse, and only because she figured I knew. Complicated by pneumonia, I believe."

"Can they do a transplant?"

"I don't know." Truth was, she had not dared ask. "I left the desk my phone number. Told them I was caring for her son, and if they needed me for anything, they could call. They said they'd keep me updated."

"Wow." She gestured toward the spare bedroom, her face falling. "He asked for her. Nearly broke my heart. Told him she was in the hospital and doctors were taking care of her. But I don't think he understands."

Arizona's heart ached, and she shook her head. "He wakes up with nightmares, crying for his mommy. Soaked from sweat and pee. Having a child, even temporarily, is harder than I thought."

Melody agreed. "Now what?"

Arizona stared at her. "What do you mean?"

"Is she going to make it?" Melody asked carefully as if she was sidestepping a path of hot coals.

Arizona stood up and picked a few books off the floor. "I'm sure she will. A long road, but she is young. Medical science is amazing. Besides, she has a boy to fight for."

"What if she doesn't make it?" Melody persisted, organizing her papers into a neat stack and dumping them in her chic handbag.

"Medical science – "

"You keep saying that." Melody's voice dipped. She began fingering the bright beads around her neck.

Arizona escaped to the kitchen with a few dishes and began filling a sink with hot, soapy water. She needed to tidy the place, to establish order once more.

"Science can only do so much," Melody's voice intruded from the other room.

Goose pimples erupted over arms dipped into scalding water. She didn't answer. Picking up a plate, she scrubbed it over and over until her fingers were red and raw. The tap ran at full blast, drowning Melody's voice. The sky from the kitchen window suddenly darkened. Clouds hung heavy and bloated.

...her swollen face, fingers...

Melody was suddenly at her side. Arizona jumped, and a cup slipped from her fingers into the tower of bubbles. "There are limitations, Ari. You know that."

She nodded and swallowed. "I know." It was time Melody left. She had things to do. Laundry to organize, dusting, waiting bookkeeping clients... "Thanks for watching him, Mel," she managed.

Melody opened her mouth then shut it again. She squeezed Arizona's arm. "Anytime, Ari. I gotta get home. Phone you later, 'kay?"

Arizona simply nodded and leaned over the sink. She heard Melody's retreating footsteps. The click of the door.

"She will make it," she repeated the mantra over and over.

A sudden torrent of rain pelted the window.

DAY 21

Marc

He opened his eyes. The pulse of blood in his ears felt like tiny, relentless hammers. He remembered now. The blow on his head. The welt on his left temple. It was the second blow that had rendered him unconscious.

What day was it? No radio today – static or otherwise. Was it two weeks? Three? Sometimes, his blindfold was taken off for a few moments, though he never saw his captor. When this happened, his eyes hungrily devoured the walls of his prison. He needed some image, some sense of where he was, or he'd go mad. Wallpaper peeled like blistered skin, and jagged cuts spread over the wall where the sinews of the house – its rusting pipes and weathered framework – showed through.

A few medical textbooks sat on a long, worn dining table. Medical student? Doctor? He could not see completely into the kitchen area. A wired cage housed a large, striped snake. When his blindfold was taken off, he glimpsed its thick body as it weaved and undulated through the cage, its forked tongue darting with lightning speed, always ready to strike. The terrified squeaking of its prey always set him on edge.

One night, blindfolded, he'd heard moaning – or was it a scream of terror? It was the first clue that he was not often alone in the house. When he called out, no one answered. The darkness he inhabited merely extended his nightmares. Classical music played almost constantly – Bach, Mozart, Vivaldi. He was thankful for that.

By now, Seraphina would have been by. With his son. She'd hunted him down with their little boy in tow weeks ago. This was his son, too, she'd argued, and would he help with child support? He could not deny it; the resemblance was striking. His son – his precious, innocent boy, albeit a flesh and blood reminder of how far he'd fallen. He'd agreed instantly to her pleas for him to take custody of Malcolm. God had given him the chance to do what was right – to make amends for his past. A sob caught in his throat. Now he might never see Arizona or Malcolm again.

He knew he needed another plan of escape. Day after day, he sat on a hard chair, feet and hands bound, his mouth gagged at the whim of his captor. Most days, he sat alone; hours stretched out into oblivion. He moved each muscle group as often as he could to prevent atrophy, but still they burned, and nerves pricked and felt numb in no order.

His arms ached as the heavy-duty rope burned into his skin. Again and again, he strained against the ropes, often dreaming of escaping, only to awaken to the angry biting of the ropes in his flesh. His legs crawled, and he longed to dig his fingernails into the itchy flesh. How long had it been since his swollen hands, infused with just enough circulation, had touched his face, brought a spoon to his mouth, or caressed his wife's hair?

Arizona. He'd said the name out loud a few times, allowing the sounds to roll off his tongue. But it sounded foreign to him, as if he were mouthing it for the first time.

One time, he worked the ropes on his wrist so they were much looser. But he needn't have bothered. His captor often checked his wrists: "These have come loose, I see," he said nonchalantly and then tightened the ropes a little tighter so that the blood flow was temporarily cut off, and he had to endure endless tingling and burning throughout his hands and wrists.

Another time, only days in, he'd jerked his body upright, despite the weight of the chair, so that he was standing. But he'd lost his balance and fallen over, chair and all. For hours, he'd lain there, twisted and sore, only to listen to the feigned sympathy of his captor when he returned.

Of course, then his feet were bound to the chair as well.

It was with panic he realized his captor did not live here; there were many times when he endured the cold, dark house alone. Oftentimes, he would sing hymns and pray; sometimes, he would talk to himself as if he had a companion nearby.

A sudden scraping sound coming from the snake cage alerted him. He held his body stiff, but a tickle in his throat forced him to cough.

"Ah," a deep voice said.

He jumped.

"Look, Hercules, our friend is in possession of his senses once again."

He imagined the snake lifting its head for a moment and then settling it down again on its content and bloated body.

"Please, I need water."

"Of course." Calmly, the man walked over to him with a bottle of water and carefully poured the liquid into his swollen mouth, wiping any excess water with a paper towel. "Washroom?"

"Yes, please," he said. Then, in a moment of boldness: "Do I know you?"

The man pulled him to his feet and simply ignored him. He allowed Marc to hop to the washroom just off the kitchen. Sciatic pain tore down his right leg, and he winced. Marc closed his eyes as he felt the man tug his pants down and push him onto the toilet seat. He closed his eyes behind the blindfold, out of habit, not modesty. After enduring countless trips to the bathroom, modesty no longer mattered. But he could hear the man turn around, as he always did, allowing a measure of privacy. Amazingly, the other senses picked up the slack when one was severely compromised.

Once seated again in his chair, the man said: "You need to eat, to keep up your strength."

"Strength?" His voice came out strangled. "On three slices of bread a day?" *Strength for what? To die?*

He was silent.

"Fine."

"Fine?"

"Please."

"Much better." He fed him one-inch cubes of bread; that was his ration. Slowly, he forked one piece after the other, and fed Marc as if he were feeding a child. "It's getting cold out there."

"What do I care?" Marc bit off before he could stop himself. "What are you planning to do with me? What do I need strength for?"

"We need to shave you again," the man ran his finger over Marc's stubby jaw. A muscle jumped in Marc's cheek, but he remained still. "I'm recruiting you." His voice was calm and sure.

"Recruiting?"

He lifted another forkful and nudged Marc's lips. "I need a fellow soldier for the next phase of battle. My game plan has changed. I will cast my net wider. I must wake the public. Like fat, lazy flies, they remain sleeping when filth is in front of their eyes."

Battle? Had he heard the man correctly? His speech, Marc realized for the first time, often sounded contrived, almost artificial. When it sounded natural, there was something about it he thought he recognized.

The man was smooth. He played his cards well.

"We will talk of it later. Would you like your blindfold off for a moment?" he asked ceremoniously.

Marc nodded as if he was merely sitting in a barber chair being asked if he wanted a shampoo alongside his cut.

The man deliberately stood behind him as he always did when the blindfold came off. Marc no longer struggled to look behind him. The man anticipated his actions and merely moved in line.

Once again, Marc's gaze landed on the wall portrait. The young woman stared at him – beautiful, almost, with her black hair and green eyes, if not for the look of disdain and the smugness playing at her lips.

This time, she looked different. A red line cut through her face. Her right eye was shredded as if someone had taken a knife to it.

His blood ran cold.

DAY 22

Basil

Basil walked into Twin Coulee's RCMP detachment the next morning, apprehension tugging at his gut.

The detachment was tucked behind some buildings on Main Street as if the place had been an afterthought. It was only accessible from Main via a dark alley, unless one doubled back a block to access it from Queen Street. Perhaps some practical-minded resident had rubbed his bearded chin, gazed thoughtfully at a map of the town, and queried: "Mmm, you know, a police station might come in handy in this town." And then, with a nicotine-stained forefinger, poked the map repeatedly: "Here, there's a small lot. Overgrown with weeds, but we can clear it quickly. And then tuck one in right here! Not on Main Street, but close enough." The simple and functional box managed to stand out from the other architecture like a sore thumb.

He half expected to see Jules bounding up, her hair tied up in a neat little bun, ready to take on the day.

But just a gray alley cat slunk around the corner. Basil

hesitated, then opened the door. A rabbit warren of musty, low-ceilinged rooms met him.

"Hello!" The deep, throaty British threw him for a moment, and even before he turned around, he envisioned a woman with a cigarette limply hanging from her lips.

She wore a stubby, ash-brown ponytail that stuck out like an appendage, and a startling profusion of freckles on a weathered face. When she smiled, her large, white teeth in a slight overbite had Crest written all over them. She was petite but unable to disguise her devotion to the bench press. "Is it raining felines and dogs out there yet?"

"Not even a whisker," he grinned at her mixed-up cliché.

"Good. Welcome to Twin Coulees," she smiled, thrusting out a freckled hand. "Sharon Montgomerey." Did she know about him? He wondered.

"Can I get you a coffee?" She stood up, and much to Basil's surprise immediately engaged in a series of arm and leg stretches.

"Uh, sure."

"Bet you're the sugar and cream combo kinda guy, huh?" She did a series of side-bends, voice straining, eyes never leaving his face.

"You know, black is perfect, actually."

"Low maintenance, huh?" the stubby ponytail disappeared behind the counter, and all he heard was grunting, and then a crash.

Leaning over the counter, Basil saw Sharon twisted into a human pretzel. "Yup, low maintenance," Basil grinned, moving to her side and offering her a hand up.

Sharon cleared her throat, refused his hand, and stood up slowly, shoving her pert nose into the air and smoothing her stubborn hair. "There is nothing wrong with multi-tasking."

"Absolutely not," he agreed.

Leaning over the counter to grab the pot, she knocked off a stack of papers.

Gym enthusiast meets human tornado.

Basil pretended the memos on the office corkboard absorbed him.

"Black it is, then."

He hid a grin behind his coffee.

"Small town, but it's a wonderful place to live. Thanks to our new mayor. He's done wonders for this town. Single-handedly brought down our petty crime rate.

He set his paper cup down. "Sounds like an evolving place."

"We are definitely not a boring place to live."

"Sounds like not." He massaged his temples.

"Basil Andreas!" A rich baritone broke his reverie.

"Better put on your bulletproof vest," Sharon whispered knowingly.

"Mornin'!" The man wasted no time on niceties. "C'mon in my office." There was nothing diminutive about this small pit bull. Round and compact, his very noticeable muscles were coiled up springs trembling with tension, like a fighter aching with anticipation to throw the next punch. And those eyes. Basil swallowed as the man's eyes swiftly and adeptly filleted him, exposing the raw fibers of his soul. It felt like an intrusion, cold and impersonal.

His beefy hand shot out unexpectedly.

"Sergeant Ichabod. Wondered when they were shippin' you here. We've been scratching the bottom of the barrel. Might be small and insignificant on a Calgarian's scale, but we pack a pretty good punch, as you'll find out sooner than later." He lifted his coffee cup to his mouth and swallowed noisily. "Have a seat." He gestured to a cracked leather chair. "They promised you were good. I don't bank on promises.

We'll see." Like a steam engine, he barrelled on. "I don't care if you have an affinity for the ingredients found in certain bottles. We all have our…deficiencies."

No secrets in the Force…

"But you leave them at the door. You can bet your sorry ass I will not rescue you. This is the bottom. *My* bottom. There is no one else to catch you. Be glad that when the big guys flushed you out, you were caught in my sieve."

He nodded. His mouth felt dry, and he ran his tongue over his chapped lips.

"The thing," he said, inspecting his sausage fingers closely, "the thing I hate about small detachments is that we get the leftovers – the refuse. He dragged the word "refuse" out slowly and deliberately, and with more than a dollop of disdain.

Basil stiffened.

"But," he paused deliberately, "refuse can come in handy."

Anson Ichabod. He had been warned about this cutthroat bulldog.

"I run this unit with pride." He sat down behind his desk carefully, wincing slightly, and then suddenly changed his mind. "Knees," he grunted and stood up. He folded his hands behind his back and walked back and forth along the width of his small glass castle: "Just a few things you would do well to remember: half your shift is to be spent on the road, the other half behind the desk doing reports. Be ready to go ten minutes before shift. I detest lateness. Two tickets minimum per shift, and two street checks per shift. Got it?"

"Yes, sir." He ran his hand along his jaw.

"Oh, and a few more things before I forget. "I'll condescend to buy my men meals on the road, but only if you're at least fifty kilometers out of town. And coffee? Take it on the road. We need our members to be visible, as I'm sure you understand. We have a newly formed Police Advisory Committee, and this is one request that has come out of this joint effort. All right, at ease." He waved his hand in the air, and a smile danced at the corner of his mouth. "Basil, huh? I suspect a lot of ribbing must have come your way regarding that label your mother tagged you with."

"It did, sir." He slipped his hand into his pocket and then jerked it out again.

"Good. Then I hope you have a tough shell. You'll need it here." He eased himself into his chair and cleared his throat. "You still having those nightmares the counselor reported?"

"Sometimes. Not often. Look, it won't affect my work, sir." Her green eyes flashed before him, and he gritted his teeth.

Ichabod searched his face. "Alright," he nodded. He took a paper from his desk, crushed it in his large hand, and tossed it in the trash can. "Contrary to what my men think, I tend to give them a long leash. But don't let yourself think for one rosy minute that the leash can't be pulled in, that I can't breathe down your neck if I so please." The phone rang, but he charged onward without missing a beat, as if he ignored phone calls on a regular basis. "I despise volatile situations that members bring onto themselves and the Force. I'm sure I don't have to remind you that we're constantly scrutinized and publicized. We serve and protect *and* keep skeletons out of our collective closet. If you find this impossible, then you'd better be able to bury them beyond reach." Pulling out a hankie, he mopped his generous brow and sighed with satisfaction. In the distance, Basil could hear a lone siren. Ichabod cleared his throat noisily and nodded. "Welcome to our little town, Basil!"

"Thank you, sir." Basil's hand tingled as the life slowly

returned. He was in for an uphill climb.

• • •

The man behind the counter at Twin Coulees Spirits reminded Basil of a walrus. A full sheath of whiskers spread out on either side of his face. The sagging skin shook each time he spoke. He picked up the cheap whiskey blend, turning it in his massive hand like some new object. "Whiskey?"

"Yep." The bottle held his eyes with magnetic power.

"Never had this kind. Stuff taste any good, or just strong horse piss?" He laughed at his own joke.

Basil's eyes bored into the man's fingers, willing them to press the buttons on the cash register. "Depends on the palate."

The man chuckled. "Me?" He stabbed his gut spilling over his belt buckle. "I'm just a beer guy." His gauze-like shirt mated with his lumpy skin, cupping each dip and roll, the sweat stains morphing as he moved.

Basil turned his leather wallet in his sweaty hands. Fingers twitched.

"Mind you," he stroked his whiskers, "that's in the summer. Perhaps this stuff will do when it gets colder, and you need somethin' that burns all the way down.

Basil's tongue felt leathery. He held out his card. "Debit, please."

The man took the card, punched in keys on the register, and waited. He tapped jagged nails on the counter. "Dum de dum," he intoned with a smile. "Thing is a dinosaur. Moves even slower." Suddenly, the card dropped, and he made a big show of bending over. A grunt, and then a florid face popped up again. Moisture beaded his forehead and upper lip as if he'd just stepped off a treadmill.

Basil pressed his body against the counter. He forced a

chuckle, his hand reaching for the bag.

"Enjoy," the man proclaimed with enthusiasm as Basil's fingers snaked around the plastic handles.

On the way out, he noticed a poster plastered neatly to the glass door:

Do you control your drinking, or does your drinking control you?

Perhaps one of these little reminders would be good inside a holding cell for the drunkards they often collected from off the streets.

• • •

Nora

Nora sat cross-legged on the faded floral sectional in the tiny living room, a cardboard box propped on her lap, housing relics of her former life. She fingered the neatly folded letters lying on top of photos and other mementos. Rani's letters – the one connection left to her childhood friend.

Rani.

Was it just stupidity and carelessness, inadvertently letting her family know where she was? Or had she done this out of spite?

It was just her and the box. Reg had a temper whenever and wherever injustice was courted, and any mention of Rani or her family angered him. She remembered his wrath when he put the two and two together.

She'd just come home from the hospital, face bandaged and painful, the world devoid of joy and warmth, the police unable so far to apprehend the man responsible. No unique prints in the home. He must have worn latex gloves, the police suggested. It smacked of careful planning and precision. This was not random. Someone hated her enough to scar her for life.

They considered co-workers, neighbors, people Reg knew from work, people who may have it in for him.

Nothing turned up.

One day, a week or so into the investigation, she got up from a nap to see Reg sitting in front of the bookcase, rearranging his books in agitation. She knew it must affect him terribly to see his wife in such a state. The impotent anger and grief he felt to not be able to change any of it. A loss for him too. A spirit broken, and beauty burned away. He roughly shoved each book into its place. Alphabetically, of course.

She walked to him slowly. He whirled around suddenly as he realized she was there. He grabbed a newspaper lying beside him. "I know exactly who did this to you, Nora!"

"Who, Reg? Did the police catch him already?"

"Catch him?" He laughed, roughly shelving the last book. "Him or them? They'll never catch them. They're long gone."

She searched his face for answers then made out part of the headline in the newspaper: The words she could see on either side of the fold were "Honor" and "Canada."

"Who's long gone? Tell me, Reg! And what is this about honor?"

She peered closer at the paper that unfolded in Reg's hand. It read: "Honour Killings on the Rise in Canada."

"Reg, what are you saying?"

"Your family, or even that guy you were supposed to marry." He poked a finger at the newspaper headline. Nora's head spun. She reached out in time to steady herself against the bookcase. His lips formed words, but it all sounded garbled. A loud rushing filled her ears. "Personal…someone who knew you…"

Her hand flew to her bandaged mouth. "No Reg! That's

not possible! It simply can't be!" She sank onto the couch.

"Why not? You yourself said honor is extremely important to them. Your father was angry when you mentioned leaving. Nora, honor killing is done for far less infractions in your culture. You know this. A vitriol attack – it's so personal!"

Vitriol. Such an angry name for the act that ended her life as she knew it. Father. His black eyes smoldered with barely concealed rage. Venom spewed from his mouth, hateful words cutting her up without mercy as he threatened to disown her. Her mother cried at the disgrace her Aynoor was putting them through. Her eldest daughter. No man good enough for her. Such an ungrateful fool. And then Amir. She'd rejected him. Was this his revenge? "But, Reg, they don't know where I'm staying. How is it possible they've found me?" She clenched and unclenched her hands. Please let it not be true. But Reg was not impulsive. He thought things through carefully.

"You've had contact."

"Not with them!" She fingered a loose thread on the couch and began pulling repetitively at another.

"I don't mean with them! Think, Nora. Think!" His voice filled with desperation.

Please, Reg, you're shouting at me! I've done nothing wrong!" Tears burned in her eyes, and she quickly blinked them away.

Immediately, he looked contrite. "I am so sorry, Nora." He sat carefully down beside her and placed an arm around her tense shoulders. "You've written, no? Your pen pal, that Rana girl."

"Rani," she corrected quietly, dread filling where hope was draining.

"She could have told your family – "

"No, Reg!" She rubbed her collarbone over and over.

He took her gently by the shoulders. "Nora – "

She looked away. Her hand dropped to the couch, and she fumbled nervously with the threads once again.

"Nora," he repeated.

A mewling began. Deep in her throat. Not Rani. "I begged her not to," her voice came out strangled. "She's never broken a pact before." A sob caught in her throat.

"People change."

"Reg," she turned to stare into his eyes, pleading beyond hope that he would agree. "Why would she?"

"Chances are she feels betrayed."

"Betrayed?"

"You left her behind without warning."

The knife twisted slowly with each explanation.

"Don't shoot the messenger, Nora," he responded softly, stroking her hair. "I'm so sorry!" He held her in his arms.

"It's all gone." She drew in a ragged breath.

"What is?"

"My family. Everything. I can't connect with them ever again. Reg," she clutched his large hands, "Reg!" She buried her face into his chest, her small frame shaking with sobs.

"You have me, Nora. I'm your family." He soothed her like a small child. "I will help you face this injustice; I will support you through this all. Remember, my dear, for better or worse. We'll get through this, one day at a time! We'll fight for justice."

She unfolded the letter and stared for a long time at Rani's beautiful cursive before shoving it all back into the box. Memories of happier times.

"Why?" She asked out loud. "Why did you betray me? Why, Rani?" She stood and walked to her living room window and looked out, remembering that the officer had said the use of acid was often personal. He'd asked then if she had any enemies.

Nora laughed out loud as she remembered her shocked response. "I haven't been here long enough to make any."

"Could it have been a racial attack?" Reg had asked. He'd sat on Nora's bed, rubbing her back, his brow furrowed in concern.

"It's very possible," the officer had responded. Everyone grasping at straws. No identifying fingerprints, no trail – nothing.

And all along, it was my family, Nora thought. She remembered a time when a neighbor girl had disgraced her family. Curses had sprung from Father's mouth, and it shook her to glimpse the monster hiding within him.

Mindlessly, she pulled her cardigan sleeve over her hand and wiped a smudge off the window.

Then she saw it. A pale curtain falling back into place. The clear shadow of a figure moving away. Someone was watching her.

Again.

• • •

Arizona

Arizona shook her head when she saw the large wet stain on her front. Malcolm had giggled under the tower of bubbles she'd made for him and splashed his little arms in abandon. "More, more!" he'd shrieked. Shaking her head, she noted that the bubble bath she'd only just bought was merely half-full.

Now, Malcolm was dried and dressed but still frantic with energy. "Song! Song," his voice clamored from the living room.

"Um, okay!" she called out, contemplating whether to

change her clothes. She glimpsed herself in the mirror and did a double take. Who was this stranger before her? Bleary eyes, disheveled hair, and arms straining under laundry. She blinked and looked around. The landscape of her home had even changed. Toys. Books. Everything looked different, as if she'd woken up in a dream world.

For how long now? Three days? Four? She'd called the hospital to check in on Seraphina, but no change.

Carrying the laundry hamper, she walked into the living room and froze. The hamper slid from her fingers and landed sideways, laundry tumbling over the floor. Marc's guitar lay on the floor on its side, Malcolm's chubby fingers violating its sleek finish, running striations in the carefully preserved dust. He slapped the chords, unaware they needed to be strummed to life.

"No! No, Malcolm!" she yelled. Not Marc's guitar – not his precious fingerprints. Without thinking, she grabbed Malcolm by the arm and pulled him away. She knelt next to the guitar, tears forming in her eyes. His prints had disintegrated under the smudging of little hands. She ran a trembling hand over its smooth face and chiseled edge.

Through blurry eyes, she saw Malcolm cowering beside the couch, his head tucked into his dimpled arms. How could she have been so cruel?

"Oh, Malcolm!" She pulled his trembling form into her arms. "I'm so sorry, Sweetie! I didn't mean to yell at you." She stroked his hair and rocked him back and forth. With a shaky voice, she crooned: "Twinkle, twinkle, little star" into his ear.

When she finished, his body relaxed in her arms. With wide eyes, he lifted an index finger to her mouth. "More, more," he demanded.

He fell asleep as she read him one of the board books

she had picked up from the public library. Carefully, she tucked him in and watched him jab his chubby thumb into his mouth and snuggle under the covers. "I know how you feel," she sighed and moved a dark curl from his forehead as her heart clenched once again at the familiar crease between his eyebrows and the slight downturn of the mouth.

• • •

Moving to the laundry room, she found her dusting cloth. It was getting late, but her restless hands needed to be kept busy. And she hadn't dusted in who knew how long. She moved books on the living room bookshelf this time instead of dusting around them. Getting rid of the dust bunnies felt cathartic.

When her cloth bumped into the shoebox holding her childhood photos, she frowned. The box was usually kept in Marc's office. What was it doing here?

But of course! Sometime shortly after Marc disappeared, she'd wanted to look through it, but then the phone had rung, and she'd deposited it on the bookshelf and completely forgotten about it.

She brought it to the dimly lit kitchen and opened the lid. She reached for a photo and stared at the face of a little girl with curly hair and a slightly off-center button nose. Donning a frilly dress, a satin bow in her hair, she was concentrating fervently on blowing out the five candles on her pink-iced cake. Such happy, carefree days. The time slid by as she pulled photo after photo from the box, immersing herself in the days when her father was around more often, and she was too young and innocent to see her mother for who she was.

The kitchen clock coughed, and she placed the photos into the box. Morning would come quickly, and sleeping in was no longer an option.

Then she saw it. A slip of white paper nestled in the corner of the box. Marc's distinctive writing jumped out at her, and her heart began to thump loudly. The only explanation was this paper had fallen from his desk into the box.

Check out the Silver Spoon – all signs point there.

The word 'clue' had been circled, and the word 'there' underlined boldly.

What was this silver spoon? What clues? Marc did not deal with investigative journalism, focusing instead on run-of-the-mill news stories generated in their small town and outwards. Politics, the art scene, hot-button issues, and garden variety happenings – he covered them all, his finger firmly on the pulse of this town. But this had the flavor of something larger, something more "sinister" than what he usually dealt with.

Arizona closed her eyes and tried to remember his last words, the hunger in his eyes that told her he'd found another story he could raise from often skeletal beginnings and tenderly nurture to fruition.

But she could not.

She deposited the note in his drawer for safekeeping. A sudden whiff of cologne stopped her. Her stomach somersaulted.

Far in the distance, she heard a loud truck rumble by. For a moment, she concentrated on the fading sound until she could hear it no more.

DAY 23

Marc

A shadow loomed in front of him. A chair scraped. The shadow lowered.

A fork clanged against a plate. Food! His salivary glands burned. Oh, what he wouldn't give for some juicy meat!

"I thought you might be hungry."

Hungry? Two days with no food or water. Every cell in his body clamored for nourishment, and he moved weakly in response. A piece of bread was placed between his swollen lips like a morsel of sawdust. "Water!" he choked.

Silently, the man poured liberally into Marc's parched mouth.

His muscles uncoiled. "Thank you." His voice sounded muffled against the blindfold.

"You're welcome," the voice responded, calm and even.

He watched the shadow move. "It's been two days. I need to know if I can rely on you to be my fellow soldier." The voice sounded frozen around the edges. His fingers drummed his knee rhythmically.

Marc blinked. "I don't understand."

"Ah!" He could hear the smile in the man's voice as if he'd enthusiastically accepted. "We'll be fighting for justice."

He wheezed. "Justice? For whom?"

"Me. Us. Men everywhere. We'll eradicate a modern-day plague!"

"Plague?" Marc pulled himself up straighter. Knife-like pains shot through his entire body. "Who're we fighting against?"

"Women. *Certain* women."

With a sudden bang, the furnace leapt to life.

• • •

Basil

It was a foul-smelling welcome Basil received at the beginning of his first shift that morning. He'd requested to spend this shift as Constable Kennedy's second member on. Twin Coulees was a small rural town with a lot of gravelly range roads. Policing in a rural area was different than in the bustling metropolis of Calgary. Just barely two years out of Depot, Basil would be the first to admit he was still the new kid on the block, or "new and shiny" – according to Gemma.

The grizzled drunk in the detachment's holding cell had spent the night cooling his heels and sleeping off the alcohol. He sat against the wall, complaining bitterly when Basil walked in. His graying hair had the Einstein effect, and bleary eyes set in a sunken, sallow face followed Basil questioningly.

"You're new. I know all the coppers here." It was a simple statement couched in tired defeat.

"How ya feelin'?" Wally asked with a barely suppressed grin. "Noggin buggin' you at all?"

"Ah, shaddup! How'd I end up in here, huh? You can't hold me like this. Practically illegal. Ain't done nuthin wrong."

"Easy there, Ian. There's no government conspiracy here. They say you were drunker than a skunk last night, tripping over your feet and babbling like a toddler. On top of that, you punched the owner of Tate's Grocery."

"Wait a minute! He was askin' for it! It's my word against his."

"Perhaps. But you were drinking, and he was not; it isn't your first rodeo either."

"Awe, man, you guys have it in for me. Just a bit o' drink ain't ever killed anyone. That guy was eggin' me. Stupid people. Awe man, my head's a bustin'." His scabby hands roughly massaged his head, and he pulled himself up.

"Sign this release, and I'll let you go."

"Yeah, yeah, sign this, sign that."

"You know the drill, Mully. This piece of paper is your ticket outta here today." Mully had to promise to appear at the courthouse on November 23. If he did not show up, there would be up to a five hundred dollar fine. There was one condition as well: to abstain from the consumption of alcohol. In Mully's case, this was sure to prove difficult.

"You got no rights to hold me. I got constitutional rights, ya hear! Ugh!" He groaned and held his head again. He then scratched his name on the signature line, looking defeated as if he was parting with his life savings, and then shoved the paper into the pocket of his ripped Levi's. Muttering under his breath, he stumbled out of the holding cell.

"Get yourself a coffee, Mully; you'll feel better soon."

"Ah, whaddaya care?" He exited the detachment, muttering, "Stupid hangover."

Wally sighed as the door closed. "First order of the

day done. We'll see him soon enough again. One of Twin Coulee's finest upstanding citizens. Not the first time I've caught him walking around aimlessly with plenty of the good stuff swishing around in that keg of his. Not much in the upstairs attic, either."

• • •

"This here is the town's honey hole," Wally noted as they drove his Tahoe down a meandering gravel road on the eastern side of town. They were heading deeper into the countryside dotted with a few homes, ranches, and the occasional small feedlot. The late afternoon was picturesque, with the undulating snowy landscape and an icy sliver of moon peeking from the edge of a cloud like a lemon slice on a margarita glass.

Basil groaned inwardly.

"Just stake out behind that little hill," Wally was saying, "and no one sees you until ka-ching! Money in the municipal pocket. You'll nab many a lead foot going a buck forty out here."

Basil drank deeply from his Timmy's coffee. Lukewarm; it would have to do. "I see Ichabod has a little self-imposed quota going on."

Wally nodded. "It's difficult sometimes, though. Not to hand out tickets but to take the time for it." He tapped his fingers rhythmically on the steering wheel then shifted his frame to a more comfortable position. "We're so understaffed and overstretched; one of the downsides of rural policing." He swept his hand towards the east. "Got a few feed lots and farms stretched all around, and citizens forming their own version of vigilante justice."

"Robberies?" Basil queried. A siren sounded in the distance.

"A rash of them. And the farmers are all proud owners of firearms. Nothin' illegal here. Just a few weeks ago, we had to charge one with opening fire on a perp. The perp got away. I had to lay charges on another one for improper storage of firearms. They need to let us do our job." He opened his door. "For a smallish town, we have our work cut out for us. Streetwalkers and drugs – hard to untangle the two – are the bane of our existence. To support their habit, many druggies are resorting to property theft; farmers are easy targets. The long distances from town and the lack of police presence, and the perps have it easy." He opened his door. "Gotta stretch my legs a sec."

"Can't say I blame them too much," Basil responded, leaning sideways to keep Wally in view. "Don't know much about farming, but I'm sure it takes years to acquire the resources they do have, and with only so many of us to go around, well, puts 'em between a rock and a hard place."

"Point is," Wally stretched his back as far back as possible, and Basil winced at the series of cracking noises coming from his spine, "with Ichabod shoving ticket quotas down our throat, we're left with less time to deal with crime." Stuffing himself back in the Tahoe, he grinned: "Man, that feels much better!"

"Sounds like he's got his blinders on."

"Ichabod? Nah. Guy's a good leader overall. Sometimes, he gets stuck on numbers. He's a perfectionist. But lately he's digging his heels in, even when it might not be the best course of action; sick of the last mayor's song and dance. Anyhow, we all feel the shortage here. Mayor wants us to focus on prostitution and help turn the tide on drugs. The farmers want us to protect their properties. Ichabod feels caught in the middle."

"So, to hit hard on drugs, we deal with the streetwalkers,

which, in turn, will help the farmers, but the farmers want us nearby pronto, and the mayor wants us in town."

"Exactly. And the blame will fall on us no matter who loses."

"They want to have their cake and eat it too, huh?"

"Yup."

A silver sedan rambled on past them. Wally clocked him doing ninety. This one was on the straight and narrow.

"So, this your first rural posting?"

Basil nodded.

"Policing's different here. Tougher to maintain a tactical edge when backup can be many miles and long minutes away. You learn little survival tactics before long, like stirrin' up the gravel with your Tahoe to let the backup guy know you've been there. Wally waved his hand at the scenery around them. There's a certain measure of isolation here. Our resources are finite, and our geographical area is, well, infinite some days. We're stretched thinner than a spider's thread."

"That can be some pretty tough thread, though," Basil chuckled.

"For the spiders, it is. We're hanging on; some days barely. Then, when crime goes up, Miss Muffet and her tuffet are the only winners in the game." Wally smiled. "I run off at the mouth. What about you?"

Basil grinned. "Not usually the talkative type –"

Wally threw back his head and laughed. "No, I mean, *you*."

Basil shifted uncomfortably in his seat.

A Volkswagen Beetle whizzed by, and Wally sat up straight.

Saved by the bell!

Wally noted the Beetle's speed. "Buck thirty! Now, that's

what I'm talkin' about." He hit the lights and sirens, and whipped the Tahoe around, mud spitting up under his tires. Not missing a beat, he continued: "You met any of the other guys in the detachment?"

"Not all of them." The Beetle must have noticed a copper was on his tail, and it wisely decided to slow down and pull over onto the shoulder.

"Hang on. Duty calls." Basil waited patiently while Wally laid down the law. Once on the road again, Wally picked up the conversation: "We've only got three other members: Charlie, Lee, and Bill. Charlie is known as Two-Dads – "

"Two-Dads?"

"Yep, you've got a new car, he has a nicer one – no, better yet, he has *two* nicer ones; if you have one nice house, he must have two. But he's not afraid to get dirty. He's got presence too. Walks casually into a bar, and the rotters know what he's about." He lifted his travel mug from the cupholder, took a long gulp, and shoved it back in the holder again. "Lee is lazier than a hound dog. Likes to drive the lonely roads and show up just a minute too late to take the call, but he is loyal to a fault. Bill likes to strip his duty belt off to sit behind the computer. Gets real cozy and all, and often not even a minute later, puts it all back on. Patient as the day is long. You should see him typing; plunks those keys one at a time methodically and calmly."

Basil laughed. "He and I have something in common."

"Don't think I've ever even seen him riled up. Great with kids, too. Oughta be, though; he's got eight of his own."

"Eight?"

"Eight strapping boys. You know," Wally continued, "off duty, we like to hang out at Shorty's, the local watering hole. It's got a full menu, nice atmosphere; just an all-around great hang-out. Join us sometime."

"Sure."

"Great! Anyhow, speaking of farmers earlier, I need to check on a certain farm."

Bouncing along, Basil drank in the silence stretching around them and closed his eyes. Suddenly, the Tahoe turned wildly and jerked to a halt.

Basil's eyes flew open just as he bounced back against the seat again.

"This shouldn't take but a minute. Hop on out."

Basil obliged immediately. "Guy's definitely not got a feather's touch," he muttered under his breath. The freshly fallen snow crunched under their feet. Wally moved in generous strides, Basil walking close behind in his tracks.

Suddenly, Wally stopped cold, and Basil bumped into him.

"Sorry, walking much too close behind you, but thanks for clearing the path for me," he laughed.

Wally did not respond.

Moving from behind him, Basil searched his suddenly pale face and followed his gaze to where it fell on the ground. The body lay face up and spread-eagled, half submerged in the snow. Two Nike sneakers peeked out from the snow, and half a meter up, the blue fabric of a hoody.

• • •

Arizona

Books were scattered around her on the floor, the voices of psychologists and reignited cold cases. Modern investigative methods updated forensic science. Complex and dense. But it was a handle she could hold on to. She ran her fingers over the cool, worn surfaces. Maybe beneath the covers, there were some answers – some explanation to the questions that spun in her mind.

Her back ached.

Malcolm ran in circles like a toy with a broken connection.

The phone suddenly rang, and she jumped. She raced for it just before it stopped and grabbed the receiver. "Hello?" Her heart slammed against her chest.

Just a telemarketer. Her heart flopped.

"Want bubble juice." Malcolm suddenly appeared at her side.

"No Pepsi, bud." She'd discovered his affinity for carbonated drinks. Water, milk, or diluted juice were not enough.

"Bubble juice! Bubble juice!" His voice increased in pitch and intensity.

She rubbed her eyes. Broken sleep from his nightmares had left its mark. "Okay, just a tiny bit," she said, indicating with her index finger and thumb. He raced for the kitchen, not caring about her rough measurement.

He won in true toddler fashion.

If there was one thing she learned from all this, it was that saying no was almost impossible. Not if you wanted a measure of peace.

He gulped the bubbly liquid and wiped his face with the back of his hand.

Nice one, Arizona. You've just added fuel to the Energizer Bunny.

She walked to the bathroom and shuddered at her complexion. Her eyes were puffy. Her hair was dull. Her cheekbones seemed a tad pronounced. She shrugged and, on a whim, opened the mirrored door of the wall cabinet.

She stopped cold. His things were there. Everywhere. Lining all three shelves. Floss, shaving cream, antacids. Taunting her. His toothbrush bristles seemed hard from non-use. There was a fuzzy layer of dust on his deodorant. She popped off the lid, closed her eyes, and breathed in deep. Spicy and manly.

Her eyes stung.

Sometimes there are no signs.

Constable Kennedy's words played over and over in her mind like a broken record. But what about his new-found trust in God? Was it all just talk? She found that so difficult to reconcile with the image of his shining eyes when he would talk about the Bible.

For days, she had let the police examine evidence: his keys and wallet left neatly side by side on his desk, the typed suicide note with fingerprints on it. His laptop. Orderly and methodical. Just like Marc.

Only grudgingly she admitted they *had* investigated. Interviewing friends, acquaintances, coworkers. They'd canvassed the area, searched for his car.

Nothing. No evidence of any kind.

She pressed her hand against her beating heart. *This is my evidence.* She gritted her teeth. But not enough for them.

It was not black and white, not measurable or examinable.

She slammed the door closed and lifted her chin.

It was up to her now.

• • •

She gripped Malcolm's chubby hand in her own. He didn't want to get dressed and go out. But she had to. Melody was teaching and couldn't watch him.

It was just the two of them.

She would investigate on her own. Ask different questions, approach it all from a different angle. She bit her lip. The "how" part was not exactly clear to her yet.

A stop at the Twin Coulees Gazette was in order. The

place where Marc devoted hours of each day. She would pick up any items of his still there. Maybe she would see something or hear something – anything – that might give her some answers.

Parking spaces were scarce in town, and they had no choice but to walk the rest of the way. His chubby hand was firmly gripped in hers. He plodded along, and she forced herself to match his pace.

Every so often, he stopped. Bending to touch the sidewalk, pick up a rock, or examine a bug. Arizona tugged on his hand and propelled him forward. The screams of the morning still vibrated in her ears. The toddler rollercoaster was too unpredictable. She hung on by her nails during each violent turn.

She held tight to his hand. Whenever she responded with a firm "no," he cried for his mommy in that soul-rending manner. She wanted to tell him it wasn't fair to pull the mommy card – to stab her heart repeatedly. But she had to remind herself none of this was a game; he was just a child, a bewildered little boy, thrown into a sea of confusion without the stable anchor of his mother.

They stopped a meter from the news office. He wanted to chase a cat slinking amongst the cars ahead. She pulled him to her safely and suddenly felt the syrupy stickiness of his hand in hers.

Oh, crap! She'd forgotten to wash his hands. Peering at him, she noticed a brownish stain at the corner of his face. Caramel coloring courtesy of the Pepsi. They stopped, and she dug in her purse but came up empty-handed.

Maybe Ms. Donkers, the receptionist, would have some wipes. The matronly woman would not blink an eye at this.

The weathered brick building rose before them, tall and officious. Double glass doors, polished to a shine. Just as they approached the door, she caught the reflection of Malcolm's hand reaching for the glass. She cringed, but before she could stop him, he smacked the hand against the glass and rubbed it. Sticky smears stared back at them.

"No, Malcolm!" she chided and immediately regretted it. Tears shimmered in his eyes. "It's okay," she quickly comforted him. "Just stay by me, okay?"

He sniffed and nodded.

Arizona sucked in a deep breath. She felt itchy and tired. One of Marc's brainy puzzles would be a lick compared to this.

Inside, a new girl sat on Celia Donkers' chair. She smelled of floral wash and cheap perfume, and the combination assaulted Arizona's hypersensitive nose. Small teeth, brilliantly white, of course, and a pert nose were set in a milky face. A baby face, Arizona decided; a woman not yet steeped in life's realities. No fatigue weighing down her eyelids, no age lines spoking outward from her eyes.

Fresh and unscathed.

She glanced down at herself. Her wrinkled shirt smelled off. Shoot. This one had come from the dirty pile and not the clean one.

"Hello." The woman's voice was polite but cool. "Are you looking to place an ad?"

"Hi. I'm looking for Celia Donkers."

"I'm afraid you're out of luck. I'm covering for her now," she said, working around the wad of gum in her mouth. She tapped her French manicure on the counter and looked down her nose at Malcolm, her neat brows raised in question.

Arizona shifted, her fingers cramping from clutching the small, tugging hand. Should she come back? "Do you know when she will be in?"

She shrugged. "About a week, I heard." A pink bubble

suddenly grew from her mouth. Malcolm stopped wriggling. The bubble popped, and her tongue slid out to pull it back in.

Malcolm moved closer to the counter.

Arizona hung on tighter.

At first, the girl paid little attention to him, but his wriggling was hard to ignore. Her eyes trailed over Malcolm, and Arizona saw it: that slight upturn of the nose at his disheveled appearance. That judgy look moms always complain about.

Arizona's shoulders stiffened. *I'm not incompetent!* she wanted to shout.

"Is there anything else?" she prodded Arizona.

"You know, I'll just come back another day." She made to leave the building.

The girl merely raised her eyebrows and shrugged her perfect little shoulders.

Malcolm managed to pull his hand from hers then and moved towards the door. Before she could say anything, he seemed to change his mind and turned to clutch her hand instead, pressing his little body to her legs.

Something softened deep inside her.

• • •

As soon as they walked up to the front door, she heard it.

The persistent ringing of the phone, a muted sound from outside but sharp enough to cut through her. Her heart began that familiar thud-thud against her chest wall. "Quick, Malc!" She pulled his hand. The wind plucked at her skirt, her hair, and shoved against her and Malcolm like a pestering child.

Once inside, Malcolm ran for a book, plopped on the floor, and shoved his sticky thumb in his mouth. The

Energizer Bunny had run out.

Arizona dropped her purse and dove for the phone.

Just in time.

"Mrs. Stuart?"

Her mouth felt fuzzy. An unfamiliar voice. Professional. She tried to place it. "Yes?"

It was Twin Coulees General.

Seraphina had passed.

• • •

Nora

The train trundled past, its large boxes rattling, the metal clacking on the tracks. And then it was gone, swallowed up, a speck on the horizon. The house still shook for a few seconds, and then, silence.

Nora dipped her brush in the paint. The hands. Paint the hands. She gripped the brush. A trembling hand approached the canvas. It stared at her. Cajoling her.

She watched her left hand from the angle of the mirror leaning against the wall beside the canvas. The fingers are fine, the skin smooth and unblemished. The brush touched the canvas. Her heart picked up speed.

Paint it. Suddenly, Adam was at her side again, his gentle hand at her elbow.

She remembered how they'd met. The little bell had tinkled merrily as Nora slipped into the tiny bookshop, Pages and Pages. The musty smell of well-loved books enveloped her.

"Hi!"

She searched for the friendly voice.

Then she saw him, kneeling on the floor, rearranging a few books on a shelf. He pushed his largish frame off the floor, his cheeks coloring with exertion.

"Can I help you find anything?" Dark, warm eyes looked at her, and she felt herself relax. There were tattoos dancing up his arms. Bold eagles and heroic tigers. She knew this kind of man. Rough on the edges, warm as pudding beneath. Blonde hair curled around his ears. His arms and cheeks were doughy, almost like toddler chub, sprinkled with a fine dusting of freckles.

She bit her lip. "I am looking for books on grief, actually."

He didn't skip a beat. "Sure. We haven't been here long, but I'll do my best to help you." He turned to a row of shelves. "Let's see. We have a section here." His thick fingers grazed the spines of a half-meter worth of books. "Self-help?"

"Yes, that would be a good start." Her hands still felt clammy. He smelled of manly soap and sweat. Just the right blend.

"I don't want to pry, but, if you are more specific, I can – " his voice trailed off.

"Losing a child." She swallowed past the lump in her throat.

"I'm sorry," his voice was soft. "I really am."

She simply nodded and moved toward the section of books.

"Take your time," he nodded. "If you need assistance, please, I will be at the counter."

She thanked him and knelt in front of the row of books. The bookshop was quiet. Fragrant notes of coffee swirled through the room. A soft classical melody embraced her.

"Excuse me."

Having been so entranced in searching, his voice startled her.

"Oh, I'm sorry, I didn't mean to scare you. Can I get you a cup of coffee?"

"Coffee?"

"Best there is," he smiled. "And fresh. On the house."

"Um, sure, that would be lovely. I think I have the books I need."

"I'll take them to the counter for you. Here," he said, indicating a worn couch under the window. "Have a seat. I'll bring it to you."

"It's been slow today," he called over his shoulder. "I think it's the nice weather.

The coffee was perfect.

He rang in her books and looked up at her. "Do you paint?"

"Yes, I do. Why do you ask?"

He smiled, the light reaching his eyes. "It's here." He lifted his hand to her face then pulled back immediately, his face glowing red. "Sorry, it's just by your jaw."

She felt her face grow warm as her finger brushed against the hard flake "Oh. I must have forgotten to wash it off."

He chuckled. "No worries; I do the same thing. I'm Adam Brighton, by the way." He handed her the bag and cleared his throat. "Paint it."

"I beg your pardon?"

He shifted awkwardly. "Your grief, ma'am." He paused. "The pain."

She blinked.

"It will help. I promise. It did for me." There was pain in his blue eyes. Pain for himself. *Pain for her.* And when they scanned her face, little could he know they seemed to reach far into her.

She nodded. "I'm Nora Clarkson. I really appreciate your help."

"Any time."

She walked home that day with a light step. The sky was filled with brilliant hues as if a child had dipped her chubby hand in a palette of paint and smeared it willy-nilly across a blank canvas.

She did paint Henry's portrait. She came back to the bookshop often, enjoying browsing the books, discussing painting, and chatting over a cup of coffee. She'd never made close friends. And with Reg in Afghanistan, well, she soaked in his friendship, the easy camaraderie between them. He seemed to understand her.

She stared back into the mirror. The scarf was off. The brush had traced the outline of her face. She sucked in a breath.

That obsession, that exploring the other side. The hidden danger, like sucking in water while under. To feel the explosion of pain as your tongue traces the contours of a canker sore. Doing it all knowing it will hurt, but also knowing you can safely withdraw.

She stared at her face in the mirror, at the wet brush, at the canvas. Before she really knew what was happening, the image on the canvas resembled the one in the mirror. Her brush dipped into reds, browns, and pinks, expert strokes forming the ridges that comprised the uneven terrain of her new face.

She stood up and lifted the still-wet canvas, moving to deposit it in the narrow space between the dryer and wall.

There, but unseen.

• • •

Arizona

"She's dead." The phone twitched in her hand as Arizona looked out of her kitchen window. It was quiet and cold. The wind chased wet, matted leaves over the pavement, branches dipping and swaying, powerless to do anything else. She thought that emptiness had to be the worst thing you could feel. Now, more than ever, she needed Marc.

There was no response at first, just a sharp intake of breath. "I just knew this was going to happen." Melody's voice was soft.

Arizona looked at Malcolm's closed bedroom door. She'd carried his sleeping body to bed to finish his nap there. The poor child had no idea his world had just collapsed. "I was hoping, trying to persuade myself –"

"I know."

Arizona pressed the cold receiver to her ear and wiped her cheeks. Her lips tasted wet and salty.

"Now what?"

"What do you mean?"

"Malcolm. What are you going to do, you know, with him?"

She swallowed. "It's me or foster care."

"Foster care, of course."

"I can't." She could picture Melody scrambling to her feet, her eyes wide.

"What do you mean, you *can't*?"

She looked at a small picture of Marc tacked to a bulletin board hanging in the hall. A camera was slung around his neck, and he was winking. At her. If she could just unravel time, somehow pop back into that morning when she last saw him, and find some excuse to prevent him from going to work.

"Ari, be sensible!"

"I can't abandon him, Mel."

Melody sighed, and Arizona heard the frustrated clinking of dishes. "No, I suppose not. But, Ari, you have – are – going through so much right now. Besides, he isn't just *any* child."

"I know, he's – "

"No, I don't mean he's Marc's son. He's been through who knows what kind of trauma. This child has baggage, Ari." She could picture Melody, hand on one hip, admonishing her as if she was one of her students.

"So do I."

"Exactly!"

Arizona bristled with irritation. "Why is it everyone's always asking if you're going to keep a child? Like it's an object rather than a human being?"

"I don't know. Maybe because your husband is – " She cleared her throat and started again. "You have been through enough already."

"So has he."

"How are you ready for this?" she demanded.

"I'm not." She drew in a deep breath. "Malcolm wasn't ready to lose his mother. Maybe I'm not ready to care for a child. Maybe we're never ready." She clutched the receiver tight. "If we wait until we are, it might never happen. Maybe, maybe, we can help each other."

"You are biting off an awful lot. You know, Ari, giving him up does not make you a terrible person. You can't save the world."

"And what will happen to him? Send him back to the slums? Cycle him through foster homes for the next fifteen years where he'll more than likely be passed around like a hot potato and then spit out when he turns eighteen?"

"I just can't believe Marc did this to you. Left you his child, never even told you, and then left you hanging. It doesn't seem like him."

"No, it's *not* like him!" Silence spread between them. She looked down at her small hand, at the simple gold band encircling her ring finger, remembering her mother's shock there would be no cluster of diamonds – not even one single one. "I told her I would take him," she added quietly.

"You promised her?"

"Yes." Silence once more mushroomed around her. "Mel?"

Melody cleared her throat. "Yeah?"

"I have to do this."

She expelled a long sigh. "I know." She paused then: "You know I'll support your new role as a mother no matter what, Ari."

"I know you will, Mel."

Mother. She whispered the word in the dark; it sounded discordant to her ears.

Later, the reality sank heavily on her, those simple words she had spoken to Seraphina in a burst of emotion. In the darkness of night, the fatigue and adrenaline rush of the last few days receded like a full tide pulling back and exposing the length and breadth of what she'd committed to. And in that moment, she dreaded the coming of winter, the expanding cold of the prairies, that graveyard feel.

• • •

Basil

"Who is she?" Basil searched Wally's face again, his heart speeding up.

Wally knelt beside her, feeling for a pulse. "Adele Laramie." He cleared his throat, nearly losing his balance. A soft wind moaned around them. Both looked quietly at the body. It was evident there was no need to rush. The gray, waxy skin spoke volumes. Blue eyes were open wide in astonishment and clouded over, the mouth slightly open in surprise. Wally just stared at the body, breathing heavily.

Basil knelt on her other side. *Looks like he's been sucker punched in the gut.* Finding a dead stranger is one thing;

finding the body of someone you knew is another matter entirely. Nothing like freezing conditions to skew time of death. She was in rigor, but how much of that stage was extended because of the climate? He was glad he wasn't the medical expert here.

Wally pulled down his non-detachment toque. "I guess we'll need to call an ambulance." But he did not move.

"Wally," he touched the large man's arm. "We need to call the medical examiner."

Wally merely nodded. Adele Laramie wore denim pants and a thick hoody, which was pulled halfway up and frozen to her skin. There was roughly a six- to nine-inch partial incision on the left abdominal region as if whatever had scratched or sliced had not quite penetrated through. It seemed to have begun healing, and there was no evidence of blood.

Wally stayed on his haunches.

Basil continued examining the body. If she had fallen where she lay, why was her hoody so awkwardly pulled up, even on the backside? Why was she not wearing a coat? Why was she lying with her arms spread out? "Can't see any cause of death. Or even a cause for the wound on her side."

In a suspicious death, such as this one, any police officer worth his or her salt would carefully look for bullet casings, exit wounds, even a gun or knife, or other clues. But a body in rigor with a superficial laceration would require a closer look by the medical examiner.

"Possibly natural causes," Wally stated quietly.

"Let's let the coroner figure that one out." Snapping on a latex glove, he felt in her coat pocket and pulled out a wallet. He flipped it open. "Can rule out robbery; ID, everything's here."

It was the norm for RCMP members to act as the long

arm of the coroner, their duties falling under the Coroner's Act. These duties included attachment of toe tags and fingerprinting, amongst others, and (as Basil liked to put it) babysitting the body until its removal. But with suspicious deaths, all bets were off. With unusual calm, Basil radioed Sergeant Ichabod.

He was grateful for winter. The combination of summer heat and humidity would allow bacteria to proliferate and smells to travel further and faster. Her icy tomb prevented this. Basil visualized tiny hair-like bacteria frozen in that same agape-like perplexity. Decomposition had been halted, and the body preserved. How long had she been lying here?

"There's no art to find the mind's construction in the face."

Basil stared at him.

"You know the rundown I gave on the other guys? Well, I'm Constable Death. Apparently, the rate of death increases when I am on call."

DAY 24

Marc

"So, has the seed taken root?"

Marc felt a fist squeezing his insides.

"Can I count on you?" He could feel eyes probing him for an answer.

Don't say no – buy time. "You'll get caught," he whispered hoarsely. "You know that, right?"

"The course of justice never did run smooth."

That smile. Marc thought again of the mutilated photo tacked on the wall near the snake cage. He could feel the brazen stare of the one-eyed woman. His skin crawled. "Who is that woman?" He pointed blindly in the direction of the photograph.

"None of your concern."

"If you want me to help you – "

He did not take the bait. "No general outlines his plan in detail to mere underlings."

"You hate her, don't you?" Marc pressed, aware he was

on an icy slope. "She is one of them, isn't she?"

"I said none of your concern." His voice was sharp, a hint of dangerous currents beneath.

"I need to know if I'm to help you," he insisted. His voice grew stronger. This man needed to be stopped. He had to find his weak point.

"Leave Peggy – leave her out of this." His voice was strained.

Peggy. The mice. "Your mice. They're all called Peggy. You feed them to the snake! Peggy is – was – someone who meant something to you."

He heard the man move towards him.

" – someone who *did* something to you."

"Enough!" His voice cracked like a whip. "You know nothing." The man had moved closer. Marc could smell his stale breath.

"I bet she looks just like you!"

The sharp sensation of a blow on Marc's cheek stunned him. His face stung.

Suddenly, the surface was placid once again. There was scraping and scuffling from behind him and then a terrified squeak. Footsteps moved a distance in front of him. Then rattling. The cage? Footsteps returned. The sudden tickle of breath on the back of his neck made him shiver.

Then, a quick tug on the blindfold knot and sudden light as it was torn from his face. At the same time, a large hand clamped the back of his neck.

"Look!" The man hissed from behind him, his fingers digging into Marc's neck to prevent him from turning.

He blinked as his eyes adjusted to the light. He stared at the cage in front of him. The vermin lay on its back in front of its predator, feet clawing air.

Marc swallowed. The snake was sliding forward in its

cage, its tongue darting in and out.

He closed his eyes and tried to stop his ears from hearing the terrified squeals.

"Watch!" The man hissed. "Look at Hercules. A snake who knows what needs to be done and does it."

Heart pounding, Marc watched the snake devour the mouse whole. His insides cramped.

"That," the man continued, suddenly calmer, "is how you can help me. Do as I say, and stop with the questions!"

"Help you?" He saw Arizona's face; he would never see her again. And his son. The hope that flickered dimly died. *Please, God, I'm not ready!*

"You don't have a platter of options. You've sealed your own fate no matter what you decide." Roughly, he secured the blindfold in place once again.

"What do you mean?"

"You wrote your own suicide note."

"I did what? How?"

"Oh, I did the courtesy of typing you one."

"You…you…how could you?"

He heard the snapping of a latex glove. "Your own prints were all over it. Damning evidence, I should think."

Rage mixed with grief flowed like hot lava through his trembling limbs and into impotent fingers.

"So, you see, your options are limited."

"I can't," he shot back, aware he was sealing his own fate.

"Justice will continue to happen, with or without you." There was no pleading. Snatching something from the counter, he stalked toward him.

Marc shrank. What was he going to do?

"I am priming a needle here," the man continued.

Marc cowered in his seat, his body tense and waiting, imagining the sharp point glinting with evil. "Stop!" Then, the sharp sensation in his arm.

"You will die. Slowly, your body will cry for food and water, and there will be none." Marc felt his legs shake. "You will join the others. Your body will break down, cell by cell."

"What others?" His stomach pitched.

With swift movement, the man slipped something over Marc's head.

Marc stared at the blackness. A hood? Why? A glimmer of light snaked beneath, but his thoughts jumbled furiously. His lungs struggled for air.

Suddenly, the man jerked him to his feet. Roughly, he shoved him forward and then sideways. There were steps. Hard. Probably concrete. His arm was held tight. The man yanked him down the steps.

"Please!" Marc begged.

They stopped. There was creaking and groaning. Something was being opened. Suddenly, a savage jolt, and he half pitched and half stumbled forward. The ground disappeared. A sharp drop in his gut. No hands to break his fall. His head smashed into something hard on the way down. Pain sliced through his skull.

He barely registered the thud of a door forced closed. The darkness of his grave engulfed him.

• • •

Arizona

She lifted the portable phone, looked at it with hesitation, then quickly put it down.

Coward.

She picked it up again and took the plunge. Shaking fingers pressed the buttons. With each ring, her heart beat faster. Shifting from one foot to the next, she cast a glance at the open doorway of Malcolm's room. She could not see him, but she could hear the banging of blocks as he babbled to himself. *Please, please*, she begged silently, *don't cry, don't scream.*

"Hello?" The voice demanded.

"Mom?" She twirled the phone cord and slipped a finger through the smooth coil, working hard to keep her voice calm and even.

"Arizona! How nice of you to call. You know, I have been looking at my phone and waiting. I'm worried about you. I've talked to Justin Sharpe – "

"Justin Sharpe? The realtor? Mom! I never agreed."

"How *are* you doing, Arizona?"

Her nails dug into the cord. "Quite well, actually, considering."

Like most mothers, Estelle could spot a fib in its embryonic stage. "Oh?"

"I have a son." The bullet left the gun.

"You're pregnant." Mother's voice was calm, trained as it was to remain unflustered in the face of indiscretion.

"Pregnant? No, not that. I have a son. Well, not really mine, but Marc's and Seraphina's, and she's gone; she died."

"I'm sorry, dear, but you're not making any sense."

She tried again. No sound. Not even a breath of life. "Mom?" *Say something. Yell. Lecture.*

"I knew it." There was conviction and a subtle air of triumph in her voice.

"Knew it?"

"That you needed to see a counselor. Grief does strange things to people – to their minds. I should never have left you there in that hick town."

"Mom, I actually have a real flesh-and-blood boy in my house." She glared at the portable in her hand and made as if to throw it at the wall.

"I see. So, just until other arrangements can be made, correct?"

"Actually, no. This is permanent."

Silence stretched out once again. Arizona sighed. This was painful.

"Raising a child is not a game," she finally said, enunciating each word with precision as if speaking to a toddler. Arizona could almost see the cogs of her mind spinning furiously as she tried to pick up the pieces and salvage what she could of the newest tear in Arizona's reputation.

"Of course it's not. I know that."

"I knew Marc had a checkered past, but this – "

"Mom," she began to pick at a loose piece of paint flaking from the wall, "our past does not define us."

"It's like a pebble in our shoe, isn't it?" Her voice trailed off with that faraway tone.

The sun slipped behind a cloud. Arizona pulled her vest tightly around her. "Mom?"

Estelle cleared her throat. "Don't forget Nana's birthday. You're coming by as usual?"

"Of course."

"Arizona? Please, don't take the boy."

"The boy?"

"Nana won't be ready for such a revelation. Not yet."

Nana? "Of course."

She pressed the "off" button harder than needed and sighed. A tiny sliver of her felt sorry for her mother. After all, was she not the errant daughter – the one who'd discarded her silver spoon without thought? She'd been taught to drape herself in the curtain of facades and mannerisms – to worship the peel of life.

But it'd begun to choke her. Maybe it all started in university, or at the beginning of a teaching career in Twin

Coulees. But then she met Marc, a drifter finally finding stable ground on which he could carve something lasting out of life's marrow. It was he who taught her to reveal her rawness and vulnerability. To trust in God rather than all the material trappings of her former life. That's when she found herself, and with it, love.

Malcolm had come out of his bedroom and was staring at her while tugging on his ear lobe, and she realized, to her horror, that she'd peeled the paint on the wall until it reached a cup size in diameter.

Taking his hand, she ushered him quickly to the kitchen. "We're fine, Malcolm; we're just fine." She swallowed the terror clamping itself on her throat and busied her hands with preparing lunch.

• • •

That afternoon, her doorbell chimed. It was her newspaper carrier, Reg Clarkson.

"Hi!" He smiled, lifting his baseball cap.

"Mr. Clarkson, how are you?"

"Oh, just call me Reg. I'm doing well, all things considered."

"How's Nora?"

A shadow crept over his face. "Every day is still a struggle for her."

"I'm really sorry," she said softly.

"Thank you. I think she will be alright." His voice sounded thick. "She's a fighter. Time, hey? It all takes time."

It was what all people said. Well-meaning words that spun round and round like a merry-go-round. But did time really heal?

He took off his cap then and played with the rim. "I'm really sorry, too, about Marc."

Arizona squared her shoulders and nodded. "Thanks." They all knew about Marc. It was, after all, a small town. She was now the object of pity and gossip.

"Did you hear? Mrs. Stuart's husband committed suicide.

"But no body. Strange. Very strange."

"They say he left her. Another family somewhere?"

"Odd mix, the two; she from high society and he from low."

But Reg did not have that one-up look. She saw that pain in his eyes, that paradoxical mix of grief and anger she herself felt.

Malcolm suddenly appeared beside her, pressing his head against her, watching but not speaking.

"Hey there, little fella!" Reg suddenly smiled, but not before Arizona noticed the flicker of pain in his eyes. He dropped to the little boy's eye level. "Wanna see something?"

Malcolm pressed his body tighter against Arizona's leg and nodded slowly.

The man placed two pennies between his fingers. "Okay, watch carefully. I have two pennies here." He rubbed his index and thumb fingers together, sliding the coins next to each other until only one penny remained.

Malcolm's eyes never left his hands. Suddenly, he piped up: "It's gone!"

Both the man and Arizona laughed. She could not remember seeing Malcolm's smile so wide.

"Neat, huh? My magic trick." He stood up again and straightened his cap. Malcolm watched him admiringly, a smile spreading across his face.

"I'm sorry to intrude on your day like this, but I've just started doing odd jobs on the side." He handed Arizona a card that read *Reg's Handyman Service*. "You know, things like lawn work, repair jobs, anything. I know most hard-workin' folks are pressed for time, and no job's too hard."

Arizona turned over the card. Marc loved yard work. She looked up to see rotting leaves and broken branches, courtesy of the last windstorm. Another man doing Marc's work? But then again, he wasn't just anybody. He was a man who had given for his town and country. Suddenly, another thought seized her. If her mother dropped by unannounced, as she was prone to, seeing a tidy yard would make it appear her daughter really was not unraveling bit by bit. And perhaps, she would back off.

"You know, Reg, could you perhaps mow and tidy my yard?"

• • •

Basil

Bats and owls are nocturnal creatures. When the rest of the world is supposedly ensconced in a deep slumber, hundreds of small animals are bustling with activity on the night stage.

But I am not a bat or an owl, Basil thought.

Chronic insomnia. A clinical designation for the endless nights of twisting and turning that resulted in bleary eyes and a throbbing head.

That is what you get when you forget your sleeping pills. It was 4:00 am, and he knew taking the pills now would give him that sleep-deprived hangover come shift time. Not a brilliant start to his first solo run in Twin Coulees.

The night started like most others on a sans-pill journey into slumber land: he wouldn't get there. Simple as that.

No, not *simple.* Chaotic, a beleaguered brain searching for sleep like hunting for a needle in a haystack. Or, more accurately, holding a slippery bar of soap that kept slithering from his fingers. He could *see* sleep. He could *feel* it. It danced mockingly in front of his eyes, jeering at him, flaunting itself, seducing him, and then laughingly twisting itself from the grasp of his tired fingers.

Sleep, get some sleep! But when he closed his eyes, he saw the wiper blades, the pelting rain, and felt the brakes fail. His eyes shot open.

At 12:02, his heart hammered wildly. At 1:32, he bunched his pillow and turned for the hundredth time. At 4:00, he called a stalemate.

Three hours till shift start. Was he ever going to be able to sleep like a normal human again?

This was it. If sleep wanted to cry wolf – if it wanted to tug at his eyelids, throw him into a trance of exhaustion, and make him see things that weren't there – so be it. Two could play the game. He would simply walk away from it.

He would be the bigger guy.

Zipping up his windbreaker and donning a pair of badly scuffed running shoes, he slipped into the night. It was dead outside. And bone-chillingly cold. Nothing moved, nothing spoke.

Suddenly, a loud clatter behind him.

Crap! He whipped around, his hand automatically falling to the gun belt that wasn't there.

Two shiny orbs peered at him from below. A cat tangling with a garbage lid. It meowed and then slunk away.

Coward.

A few meters onwards, in the curtain of light spilling from a thin streetlamp, he saw the broken body of a large possum cradled in a layer of snow. He stopped and leaned over the dead vermin with macabre curiosity. "Poor fella. Bet ya never stood a chance." A sudden helplessness washed over him. All at once, it was Jules and him delivering news of death.

The woman had responded by dropping the coffee cup

on the floor, shattering it. "I'm so sorry!" She dropped to the floor, her hands beginning to shove the porcelain shards into a neat pile.

"Ma'am, please be careful," Basil stopped her.

She pulled herself up without looking at him. "Of course. I'll get my dustpan. What a klutz I am."

They watched her as she swept the shards into the dustpan.

"Here, let me," Jules offered.

"No, no," the woman shook her head as she took the dustpan. "I've got this. It's all good."

Jules and Basil looked at each other helplessly.

She returned with a cloth and wiped the spot over and over, even after any trace of the spill was gone, as if there was some invisible stain that needed to come out.

Taking a deep breath, Jules moved in. "Please, Mrs. Stevens, sit down."

Carla allowed her to take her arm and lead her to a chair. But her eyes remained glued to the spot where the coffee had spilled. Her hand shook just a bit. "So clumsy of me."

Basil moved in front of her and crouched down to her level. He looked her in the face. "Mrs. Stevens – "

She pressed herself into her chair, moving her angular knees away from them as if they were contaminants. Her fingers pulled and twisted the folds of her skirt. "That was my nice porcelain."

"Sean is dead. The crash," he paused. "It was bad. He didn't have a chance. We're so sorry."

She suddenly turned to them, her eyes strangely unfocused. "Where are my manners? Coffee? I have more." She began to rise.

"Mrs. Stevens –"

"I know; I'm sorry about the mess."

Jules laid her hand on the trembling knee. "He is not coming back, Carla."

Suddenly, her body jerked as if she was waking up to a reality so hideous and unbearable. The cry that finally escaped her white lips was primal and soul-rending.

They had plunged the knife in that much deeper.

The distant barking of a dog jerked him back to the present. He picked the possum up by its tail and gingerly laid the animal on a scraggly patch of grass off the road. It was as dead as dead could be, but he had salvaged the poor critter from complete destruction. It was a futile, almost senseless act, but he just felt he needed to do *something.*

DAY 25

Basil

Basil was a tad breathless as he parked his bike in the detached parking lot. The tremors in his hands had started, so imperceptible that he felt them as if his limbs were shaking violently. He glanced at his watch: 6:58 am. He rubbed his face and inhaled deeply.

Wally and Lester were in the bullpen, a small square room with computers, but none were working on reports behind the computer. Lester was sitting with his legs propped up, hands linked behind his head. Wally was feasting on a sugary donut. He appraised Basil, raising his eyebrows. "Been running a marathon? One would think you'd been chased here by a dog."

The others laughed.

"A whole pack of them."

"Here, some sugar to help you recuperate." Wally offered him a donut, but Basil declined politely.

"Uh, sorry, too early for me."

"Too early? Look at this golden and aromatic form. This

is culinary art. If music be the food of love, play on!"

"Please," Sharon begged, throwing her hands up in the air. "Stick a spoon in it already. You gonna eat them, Wally, or rhapsodize about them all day?"

"Aw, man, I would've, but you've just effectively destroyed my appetite."

"Oh, really?" Sharon questioned, not at all concerned.

"By ripping the guts out of another cliché." Wally shoved the last bite in his mouth. "Well," he grinned, "gonna get outta here and fill the day's quota." He moved to the door, but not before Basil glimpsed the slate-gray eyes infused with pain.

"That guy's a font of optimism and good cheer, huh?" He noted as the door shut.

Sharon looked up from entering traffic tickets. "Hard guy to figure out."

"The call the other day seemed to really get to him. Major Crimes took it over from us, and I haven't heard anything else yet. Autopsy will take a bit."

"Guess some deaths shake you up, and some don't. Least, I've heard that."

"That's true." But really, he wasn't so sure here.

"Well, he's quite a closed book." She shook her head as if she couldn't figure him out.

"He seems to be an outgoing, friendly guy," Basil shrugged.

"Oh, he's got it down pat. You feel like you really know the guy after just a little bit, but he never talks about his personal life."

Come to think of it, Basil thought, *he asked about my life but never divulged any of his.*

•••

Arizona

She watched the simple wooden box being lowered into the ground. The wind, like a whip, snapped the hem of her skirt across her bare legs. Everything before her blurred. Her nose itched, but she did not move to relieve it. Her lips tasted wet and salty.

There was no ceremony. No entourage of mourners who wept at her death. Arizona's eyes slid shut, and she prayed for a young woman whose life was cut short. For the little boy who no longer had his mommy. For courage herself to go on.

She opened her eyes at the first thud. The earth had swallowed the coffin, and the men were scooping shovels of dirt onto it. She braced herself for each *whump*, keys digging deep into her palm.

The men wiped their brows, nodded at her, and left. Their task was done.

Shrouded in quiet, she walked to the fresh grave. For a long moment, she just stared at the rectangular mound. Then she hooked her fingers into a patch of soft earth, brought up a handful, and threw it onto the grave. *Dust to dust, ashes to ashes –"*

Around her lay the first covering of leaves still soft, winter's calling card. Soon, they would brown further, furl at the edges, and turn brittle. The ground was already cold, the warm pulsation of summer having drained away.

A few geese overhead broke the silence, and as she tilted her head back to catch a glimpse of them, she felt the wetness welling in her eyes. She blinked and sniffed hard, digging deep in her pockets. But they were empty. She swiped at her cheeks slick with wet.

Suddenly, she noticed something. A tiny purple flower. Still blooming. Still alive. "Feisty little thing you are," her voice broke as she reached to stroke the tiny petals. She hesitated, then bent down to the little flower and scooped it up, roots and all, and walked to her car.

•••

Basil

Basil began his routine by checking his duty bag. Forms, violation tickets, safety gloves, extra bullets, notebook, extra radio battery, field first aid kit, collision forms, and more. The list was long, but it was all there. So was the pelican case with roadside breathalyzer and digital camera and recorder. He had signed out the carbine C-8 rifle, as well as his taser, given it a spark test, inspected the cartridges, written down the serial number and expiry date of the cartridge. Everything but the kitchen sink. Myra used to jokingly add that his duty bag put her closet of a purse to shame.

He stuffed his lanky frame into the Crown Vic and updated his notebook by recording the shift start time of 7 am and noting his patrol unit, 2-Alpha-23.

He hit his first roadblock when trying to log onto the car's computer. When he inserted his PKI token into the computer port and entered his passphrase, he was denied login. He tried again. Same response. "Blasted thing!" He stared at the laminated card and his own unsmiling face. Carefully, he ran his thumb over the chip to remove any residue that might affect its use.

Without being able to log in, he could not access the Police Reporting and Occurrence System (PROS) to do his reports or access the Canadian Police Information Centre (CPIC) database. CPIC streamlined most information he needed. Everything from criminal records, stolen vehicles, and missing persons was provided in one complex database accessible by a few strokes. It was like swimming in uncharted waters with his hands tied. He punched his steering wheel lightly and sank back into his seat. What a great start to the day. He had cleared his transfer with IT and should have been ready to go.

C'mon, c'mon, please! He inserted the token once again, praying this would be the golden attempt. Suddenly, the login screen was replaced by the Microsoft home screen. He sighed in relief.

Plugged in and ready to roll.

There was a hesitant knock on his window. A grandmotherly woman peered in at him. He unrolled the window. "Morning, ma'am, can I help you?" The little lady reminded him of his Nanny Liz, with her perfect gray coils of salon-fresh hair and delicate, gossamer cheeks that looked ready to disintegrate under the touch of a finger.

"Excuse me, police officer," she began politely. "My name is Dorothea Cabrey, and I would like to report a missing person. How do I go about doing this?" She was poised and in control, but his discerning eyes picked up on the minute trembling of her hands.

"Come inside, ma'am, and you can give me the details there." Satisfied he was able to access his computer, he unfolded his frame from the car and ushered her into the detachment. She shuffled slowly and, once inside, gratefully took the chair he offered.

"Janey, sir, my granddaughter. She didn't visit me yesterday. She always does. I can set my watch by her. Comes, she does, at two in the afternoon. So punctual, just like my Arthur was."

"How old is Janey?"

"Twenty."

"Does she live with you?"

Dorothea shook her head sadly. "She moved out half a

year ago to stay with friends; said she needed her independence." She sighed. "I'm afraid she may have fallen in with bad company, even though it's not in her nature. Peer pressure, perhaps? I don't know. That's why I came here. I don't know who I can call; she never even introduced me to her friends."

"What about her parents?"

"She was orphaned at five. Bad car accident."

"Have you noticed anything different about her lately?"

"Pokémon," the woman smiled tremblingly. "Seems like the youth are so involved in this lately. She saw one in my kitchen, funny girl."

Of course. While world leaders are contemplating a third world war, our noble citizens are preoccupied with finding Pokémon, he thought.

It turned out that Janey McAlistair visited her grandmother every Saturday. The twenty-year-old worked at a little eatery in the seedier part of Twin Coulees to pay her way through college. Lately, she'd seemed very preoccupied.

"I never liked that part of town; women selling their bodies and the like. I'd feel much easier if it wasn't for them. We have a good mayor now, but things move so slowly." She jutted her chin out stubbornly. "Maybe if those women were gone, I wouldn't worry so much."

"Do you think she could have – "

"She's Christian!" Dorothea spat suddenly, but her pale cheeks colored, and she dipped her head in instant apology at her tone.

It wouldn't be the first time a Christian sold her body. But he did not tell her this.

"It's just me," Dorothea's voice broke slightly. "She is all I have, a real sweet girl, sir. I may not be up to snuff on these young 'uns, but –" she patted her heart gently, "I have intuition, and it tells me she did not simply forget to show up. I *cannot* lose someone else so dear to me." Her rheumy eyes began to water. "If you've ever lost someone, you would understand."

He felt a splinter, sharp and cruel, somewhere under his rib cage.

Basil extracted whatever information he could from her and promised he would look into her granddaughter's absence.

Dorothea pulled her knit shawl tightly around her shoulders. "Find her!" she whispered painfully, and then, in that elderly robotic shuffle, she joined the rustling leaves outside.

•••

Basil turned his car down Patterson Street, an offshoot of Main Street. Patterson was more of a service street for the many businesses that lined it. Small, dark alleys ran from it to Charleton Boulevard. Slightly gravelly, it was lined with industrial garbage bins and a chain-link fence studded with the detritus of human life. He turned onto Charleton and eased the car next to a curb.

He stepped carefully over broken needles that painted a landscape of despair. The RCMP would be merely a little band-aid to staunch the flow of blood from a gaping wound; the girls would just move on to a new patch. The decomposing leaves were soft and didn't crunch. A biting wind shrieked and moaned like a banshee, whipping around garbage and clattering signs. There would be no seamless transition between the seasons this year. Autumn, with its fiery colors, was rapidly being replaced by winter's icy fingers and frigid breath. Even the sky, with its gray palette, was pregnant with snow. Soon, mountains of snow-kissed by the warmth of a temporary Chinook wind would revert to messy slush as temperatures would rise drastically, making Twin Coulee's already narrow streets a nightmare. Then, of course, they would plunge again. After all, Canadian winters were no laughing matter.

Basil shrugged deeper into his coat, tucking in his chin. He was supposed to be a hardy Canadian, no stranger to weather extremes and fluctuations. "Suck it up, Princess," he scolded himself.

For a fleeting moment, he understood Ratford's 'Clean up the City' mission to beautify buildings, improve the landscapes, and clean up streets. Parts of Twin Coulees sported aesthetically pleasing landscapes, modern-styled buildings, and repaved streets; tax dollars hard at work. Charleton Boulevard, in the older section of Twin Coulees, was heading in the opposite direction, as it had all the makings of becoming a bustling red-light district. Here lived the destitute, bartering their one possession. And here was the apparent stomping ground of Janey McAlistair: The Red Fox. The little eatery sported a gaudy neon sign that flickered lazily. Inside, there were few patrons; the lunch rush had not yet begun.

"Can I help you?" A tall, skinny kid with perfectly coiffed hair and tight, preppy clothes found him immediately.

"Constable Andrews. I'm investigating. You have a Janey McAlistair working here?"

"C'mon into the back," the preppy beckoned him without looking back. "You're not good for business in these parts."

"Is that so?" *Cheeky bugger.*

"That's what my manager says." He shrugged, his pursed lips sucking noisily on his Pepsi. "Whatever, it's his business, so I do what he wants. So long as he pays me for my work. Besides, we need the customers, and you fuzz don't exactly make 'em feel welcome here." Mr. Preppy shoved a stack of papers over on the cluttered desk and perched daintily on its edge. "

"So, Janey McAlistair?" Basil prompted. The kid rolled his eyes knowingly.

"Yeah, she didn't show up for shift a couple of days ago. It's weird, man, like she's always on time." He chuckled. "We call her Janey-on-the-dot."

"Any idea where she lives?"

He shook his head. "She closed shop herself two days ago, and we haven't seen or heard from her since. Odd, you know? No phone call or anything; just left Ron hangin'. I never suspected she could pull a stunt like that. Ron's replaced her already. Can't wait for her to sashay back in when she feels like it."

"And you say she's dependable?"

"Yeah, but it's a steppin' stone for her. We've had others leave at the drop of a hat; no 'thank you, I'll give you notice,' or whatever."

Basil thanked him and made a mental note to stop in again when the manager returned. He made to leave, but not before he instructed Mr. Preppy to phone the RCMP if he heard from Janey.

"Yeah, sure." They walked to the dining area, and the kid began to wipe tables. Suddenly, he stopped. "Hey, just a sec. Not sure if this is important or anything, but Janey was always a real quiet chick. Not depressed or anything, just quiet. Lately, I don't know, but she seems so happy, like crazy excited about something. Seemed to be a light in her eyes and a bounce in her step. Maybe a guy or…who knows? Anyways, that just struck me." He shrugged his shoulders, satisfied he'd done his public duty.

DAY 26

Arizona

She stood on the sidewalk as one raw nerve, staring up at the gold script of The Twin Coulees Gazette.

Here, Marc had hammered out his dreams. Here, he had found his gift of words and climbed the career ladder, earning his own office as an up-and-coming journalist.

Her hand suddenly felt at her side. But there was nothing to grab. Of course. Malcolm wasn't there. She realized then how she'd come to depend on him, his small frame bringing her such comfort. There was the busyness of the last days, the mind-numbing exhaustion. Nightmares, the bedwetting, the interrupted sleep. But ironically, it had all filled the void.

It was then she saw him. He stood near her, looking into a window. The broad shoulders, the dark hair licking his collar. The long-fingered hand playing with the button of his shirt sleeve.

Suddenly, the busyness of the town melted away, and time stood still. It was just the two of them. "Marc?" Her voice came out soft and unsure, her heart quickening.

He turned away suddenly, and she hurried after him. He was turning a corner. *Quick, catch up with him!* she thought desperately, feeling as if she was trying to pin down a mirage that kept shifting out of reach.

There he was, trying to flag down a cab. Her stomach somersaulted. Hope flared. Two more meters. One. She moved closer on jellied legs.

"Marc!" Her voice came out part squeak, part whisper, "Marc!" He turned to look behind him, his eyes searching. Her heart shot into her throat. She got ready to shout, but the words died on her lips.

His gaze traveled past her. The hope died. A face marked by unfamiliar freckles and a stubborn cowlick. "Hurry!" he shouted.

She turned slowly.

The high-heeled woman jerked past her. "Thanks!" She pecked the man on the cheek and tumbled into the cab.

Then they were gone. She stood there quietly for a moment longer and then slowly turned to The Gazette, her legs trembling violently.

• • •

"Mrs. Stuart!" Celia Donkers smiled at her from the main desk as she entered. The baby-faced girl was gone. "I have, uh, his things here." She reached beside her and placed a cardboard box on the desk, her large bauble rings sparkling in the sunlight. "Just some of his things, you know." The stocky woman peered into the box, her reading glasses sliding from her nose. They came to rest on her large chest, suspended by a thin string. "Yes, I believe they are all here." Her hands flitted over the box like a confused butterfly while worried eyes seemed to probe the mental state of the widow in front of her.

Arizona took the box with still trembling hands and peered inside. A few knickknacks, a framed photo of Marc and her on a camping trip, a pair of worn winter gloves, and a travel mug. She picked up his mug and trailed a finger over his name engraved into the sleek, silver-like finish. She steadied herself against the desk. "Is this everything?"

Celia shrugged. "Other than his laptop, which you already have, this is it. I mean, he was neat, and – " Her voice trailed off as she gazed with concern at Arizona. "I am so sorry. This must be brutal for you." Her eyes suddenly misted. "We miss him here."

Arizona nodded, her own throat constricting.

Reg Clarkson walked by in a work shirt and denim pants, carrying a toolbox. "Mrs. Stuart. Hi!" he greeted her. "How's the little boy?"

"He's fine, thanks for asking, Mr. Clarkson."

"Just Reg is fine. Cute kid. I'll be by in a few days to help winterize the place. Sound okay?"

"Perfect." It really was a relief to know that she did not have to take care of that part of life.

He nodded and turned to Celia. "It's all fixed, Miss Donkers."

She gave him a thumbs up. Turning to Arizona, she wrinkled her nose: "Those toilets are always backing up." She gave a little shiver. "So, you, uh, planning a memorial, love?

Arizona stared at her blankly.

"Some form of closure for you and – "

"No! I mean, I need to see Dawson. Oh, here he is!" She shifted the box in her arms.

A bespectacled man appeared with two boxes stacked in his arms. Dawson Williams. Marc's nemesis. He wore a suit that seemed expensively tailored, and he sported perfectly tousled, highlighted hair. His face was pale and soft, childish almost, with no hint of facial hair. A flashy ring sat on one finger, the flesh puffing up around it.

Celia followed Arizona's eyes. "Bozo's movin' upstairs," she muttered.

"What?" Arizona asked.

"I'm sorry, dear." She was truly apologetic. "You know the news world; it doesn't sleep. People are getting promoted. Whether or not they've truly 'earned' it is something else." She lowered her tone suddenly. "And he's got this slimy, disgusting critter he keeps in a cage, which, thankfully, I won't have to see much anymore."

"Snake?" Arizona shuddered.

Celia nodded. "A python or something. "Thick and striped," she shuddered back. "I can just imagine this thing slithering over our desks at night. Oh, it's locked up, but you know."

Reluctantly, Arizona scurried after Dawson, leaving Celia standing there open-mouthed. "Mr. Williams?"

He stopped and turned in surprise. "Mrs. Stuart? Hello!" A reddish hue crept into his cheeks. "I am truly sorry about Marc." He set his boxes down on the floor and ran a hand through his hair. "Is there anything at all I, we, can do for you?"

She shook her head.

"We were all shocked beyond belief. I never knew he had, you know, personal troubles."

"He didn't! None of this makes any sense." Immediately, she felt contrite. "Look, Mr. Williams, was there anything peculiar about Marc before he disappeared? I'm trying to piece everything together. I really would like some concrete answers," she said more forcefully.

"Nothing I can recall," Dawson responded. "Look, Mrs. Stuart, I am truly sorry for your loss. The, uh, lack of closure must be hard."

"I am still in talks with the police."

"Police?" He looked alarmed. "I thought – "

"Like I said – it makes no sense. I can't just give up." She took a deep breath. "It's not over. We need to keep looking. Investigate. Search for evidence." She felt the pity in his eyes and turned away.

"I am so sorry, Mrs. Stuart. I know it must be hard, but I had no idea you were struggling so."

"I'm fine!" she flung back. She massaged her fingertips. "So, you say there is nothing you can think of?"

He shifted. "No, I'm sorry, Mrs. Stuart. I can't think of anything out of the ordinary. Look, I hate to do this, but I have to – " he trailed off, sneaking a peek at his watch.

"That's okay. I just wanted to see if –" She bit her lip. "Well, I should go. If you think of anything." She spun on her heels and, clutching her box, sailed past him while holding her head high. Suddenly, she needed to speak to Constable Kennedy again.

• • •

"The note. I would like to see the note." She still held her chin high.

Constable Kennedy rubbed his face. "Mrs. Stuart, you *have* seen the note already. I don't think – "

"Please!" Somewhere in the dusty bowels of the police records room lay her husband's words. She needed to see them. To burn them into her brain.

A tall police officer suddenly materialized at Kennedy's elbow. Arizona took in the shock of red hair and long, wiry frame. His friendly eyes lit up. "I believe we are neighbors."

He smiled at her, reaching out to shake her hand. "Constable Basil Andrews."

Of course! The man who had moved into her duplex next door.

"I'm sorry for your loss, ma'am," he supplied kindly.

"Thank you."

"Alright, ma'am," Kennedy conceded. "I will show it to you again. But I don't think it's helpful." He shook his head and disappeared.

She watched the tall constable turn to talk to someone else, and she waited at the counter, her mind going a mile a minute. How could they not know where Marc was? Probably death by drowning, they'd implied, to spare her the aftermath suicide invariably brings, or through some other means where a body is found to be "at large," as if lost or misplaced, floating somewhere in a state of perpetual limbo.

Constable Kennedy returned with the note in an evidence bag. So clinical, carefully contained as if it was some contaminant that would live out its life in the detachment basement. She reached for it.

"It needs to stay in the bag, ma'am," the constable cautioned her.

But it's my husband's – it's mine! she wanted to shout. But instead, she nodded silently. The typed letters leapt at her:

I cannot go on. I am sorry to everyone, but especially my wife, Arizona. I love you.

That was it. No real explanation.

She gathered courage. "Are there times, you know, when people leave notes and just disappear?"

"Yes, though rarely. We did discuss that," he reminded her gently. "But credit cards – "

"Of course, of course," she said hastily. For a moment,

she imagined Marc living a second life somewhere else, perhaps with a different woman. Quickly, she slammed the lid on that thought.

• • •

Basil

Wally sighed as Mrs. Stuart left the detachment. "She doesn't give up. She comes here every day almost."

"Really?" Basil watched her look both ways and cross the street, her black, curly hair half pinned back, a rose-colored winter jacket nearly drowning her small frame. Her large eyes reminded him of a wounded deer. "Some people are like that," he said. "The self-inflicted pain; I don't know, reminds them that they are not numb shells of their previous life, but still very much alive."

"I know." Something flickered briefly in Wally's eyes.

"I can see how difficult it is for her, though. No body. Nothing."

"Yep. Suicide note paired neatly next to his wallet. So," he paused, "I don't know, final. Only his prints on either one. We've looked at every angle, interviewed people, but," he threw up his hands, "no sign of the car, no signs of foul play, zilch."

"Security cameras?"

"They'd been acting up for at least a week prior. But I doubt there would've been anything there. See, he comes and goes at all hours. Was there that morning, but then he left, for who knows where? Didn't always say where he was going. Seemed happy, but quiet." Wally shrugged. "Nothing sticks out. Until we find his body, if we ever do, we'll keep looking." He looked toward the door. "Selfish act, though. She loved him; it is clear to see."

"What about his phone?" Basil crossed his arms and

leaned forward with interest.

"The number you have dialed is no longer in service," Wally quipped.

"Could it have been – "

"The wife?" Wally questioned. "We've explored that angle, and unless some damning evidence surfaces…" He shook his head.

"But he was unhappy."

"According to the note, but not his wife or friends. Apparently could be melancholic, as one guy put it. Moody. But that is just the thing. It often happens so out of the blue. They can hide it quite well. Then he told Basil about her new son.

He just shook his head.

•••

It was getting dark out. Some of the working girls would be out. Perhaps they had seen or heard of Janey, or worse, she might have joined forces with them.

He keyed the mike. "Control?"

"Ten-four."

"Alpha-23, I'll be out at Charleton Boulevard. Fifteen-minute timer, please." At least if he didn't get back to dispatch with an update, they knew where he was.

"Ten-four."

He walked through an empty back alley onto Charleton Boulevard and lingered in front of Chinook Antiques and Mox's Taxidermy. Up ahead, he noticed a tired laundromat that never slept. The buildings huddled tightly together, proudly displaying flickering neon signs. Gaudy advertising and wired windows gave evidence of the area's seedy nature and the dying heartbeat of old Twin Coulees.

A few meters down stood a nightclub tucked in between

the other buildings. The neglected building would soon pulse with life. Lone figures would emerge to be swallowed up by taxis. Soon, with the influx of corporate Christmas parties, the streets would be jammed with cabs.

Then he saw her. The faint light of the moon, coupled with that spilling from the streetlights, illuminated her tall figure. At first, all he saw was the outline of a long coat and heeled boots. Even in the faint light, she appeared big-boned. Like any other streetwalker, she would be on her guard, feeling for hostility and danger. She stood boldly under the lamppost with the casual air of one waiting for a city bus.

But the minute she spied him, she melted into the shadows around her. He could still feel her eyes on him.

"Ma'am?" He called out, walking towards her.

Slowly, she re-entered the curtain of light, this time pulling her jacket tightly around her. Her reddish eyes, framed by a bold clump of lashes, searched him carefully. Her platinum hair hid the left side of a heavily rouged and tanned face. She ran her hands vigorously over her arms for a minute and then began to fumble with a pack of cigarettes. "What do you want from me?"

"I'm looking for a young woman named Janey. Have you heard her name mentioned around here?"

"No." She lit her cigarette and drew in a long breath. For a moment, she reminded him of the decay he saw around them. She shrugged at his description of the missing woman. "Still never heard of the girl. I guess she might just be one of the smarter ones."

"Smarter ones?" he echoed.

She jerked her chin. "Look around you." Suddenly boldened, as if she'd scoped out the situation and found it relatively safe, she shot out: "You fuzz! All you care about is women other than us. We've had a few girls go missing in the last few months. No one believes us. Just par for the course, right? Risks of the trade."

"Which girls have disappeared, Miss – "

"Just Stacey." Her voice was suddenly hard and flat. "More than a few. And lately, Lola and Birdie. Louisa and Brigitta."

"How long have they been missing?"

"For days now. Okay, they both come and go often, but not gone for this long!"

"Have you reported them missing?"

She glared at him. "Of course not. The fuzz didn't lose any sleep over the first ones missing; they won't with these. Women are droppin' like flies. No one cares. We're disposable. Now that we have a dictator running this town, no one will even care anymore."

She looked at him carefully, some of the anger having dissipated, but it was back as quickly as it left: "You only care because a 'respectable' woman has gone missing, huh?" She flashed him an acidic smile and made to turn away: "I wouldn't touch me if I were you; I'm one of the pieces of garbage they're cleanin' up here."

"Ma'am," Basil tried to stall her.

"Can I go?" she asked impatiently, shifting from one foot to the other. "My feet are killin' me."

He turned to walk to his car, shoulders hunched. Closing the door, he peered at the building she had slipped into. The Silver Arms was a rundown hotel with a sagging roof.

Just then, a short, balding man emerged. He looked around quickly and then seemed to half-run, half-walk, hugging the shadows as he went, until he turned into an alley.

Basil blinked. Mayor Ratford? What was he doing here?

NORA’S MASK

DAY 27

Basil

"Alpha-23, this is Alpha-21. What's your twenty?" It was Wally wanting to know his whereabouts.

"Alpha-23, ten-seventy-eight.

"Meet at Mickey's?"

"Ten-four."

Basil entered the grease-laden atmosphere of McDonald's with a pleasant shiver, his tall body throwing off the last vestiges of an increasingly colder autumn.

"Whadya think of this town so far?" Wally was his usual jolly self.

Basil laughed. "Well, Sharon is interesting, and Ichabod? Let's just say nothing seems to get by him. I thought for a second there I was back at Depot, and he was gonna make me drop ten."

"A rainbow of humanity," Wally chuckled. "Sharon is an odd bird at times but an excellent resource. And Ichabod? Behind that steel complexion beats a heart of flesh. One day, you will be lucky to glimpse it. But it's there; trust me. On another note, here are some gold nuggets to keep at your fingertips: don't wear non-issued hats, including toques, when he's around (unless you're part careless and part set in your ways like me), and don't be skimpy with the ticket book. Oh, one more thing: he gives us a lot of freedom, but if you abuse it, you'll think a dog collar is less restrictive."

Basil detailed his missing person's case and Stacey's response. "She claims women have gone missing among the streetwalkers, and no one blinks an eye."

Wally sighed. "These complaints come in all the time. Don't tell me you didn't have this in Calgary? Mostly, they don't pan out. They see us as a bunch of thugs in uniform." He shrugged. "They're always in flux. Follow up on it, of course, but don't hold your breath."

He calmly unwrapped his burgers and arranged his tray just so. "All the world's a stage, and you and I, and everyone else, well, we're all just players." He scrutinized his burger closely, smelling it as if it were a fine wine.

Basil watched him in silent amusement. Shakespearean followers do not eat cheeseburgers from greasy spoons. They dine on fancy, five-course meals that have the character and flair of a theatrical performance. Or do they?

Satisfied, Wally attacked his burger with a vengeance. Such irreverence. He looked up to find Basil staring at him. "Watchin' my cholesterol soar?"

"You know that thing will kill you one day, right?"

Wally pretended he'd not even heard. "What you orderin'? A garden salad? Just a coffee?"

Basil sipped his coffee with great satisfaction. McDonald's had to have the best coffee on the planet. "It's just eleven. Besides, I'm watching my girlish figure."

Wally snorted. "It's twelve o'clock somewhere."

"True."

"So, speaking of rural areas, ever been without backup?"

"Yup. One time, responding to a theft in progress on one of the ranches to the east. Hard time getting reception when I was talking to the perp – a real jerk. I keyed the mike, pretendin' I was talking to back-up. One of the few calls where I was sure my heart would ping pong right outta my chest!"

Basil chuckled. "How long you been doing this for?"

"Ten years."

"Any aspirations to move upwards?"

"Nope. I like the front-line work and have no desire to touch anything bureaucratic if I can help it. What about you?"

Basil shrugged. "Have my eye on becoming a detective. I like to be able to own a case and see it down and out."

"Good for you," Wally responded. "You know how it works. Get yourself transferred from General Duty to the General Investigation Section once you've got your five years. Your third year, you said?

"Second."

"You need excellent memory and a keen eye for detail for the job. You'll be like a city detective, but the great thing is that your work is interestingly varied; you'll be looking into every call that comes in." His job would be to follow trends, such as people or vehicles repeatedly being checked in the same region. He would have to weed out the indictable offenses from the petty crime. "Alrighty, let's do a little thing here. Close your eyes."

Basil complied, wondering what Wally was up to.

"Okay, that man that walked in a few minutes ago. We both looked at him good. Now, tell me, was he wearing a ring?"

"Yep. Thing was larger than his knuckle."

"What was he wearing?"

"Pants of some kind," he laughed.

"C'mon, now you're just shootin'. Aim!"

"Okay. Uh, denim pants, quite worn, plaid shirt, mostly untucked, then, uh, shoes, wait a sec, runners, no...cowboy boots! Polished and sparkling. Stuck out like a sore thumb with his clothes."

"Eye color?"

"Really? Green."

"You sure?"

"Absolutely. His one eye does that lazy wandering thingy. They're green. No guess there."

Wally whistled, clearly impressed. "Not bad, not bad! Okay, open 'em up!"

Basil opened his eyes and looked right into the green eyes of the man he was describing. *Kennedy, you jerk!*

The man shoved his large frame into the remaining seat. "So. My clothes stick out like a sore thumb, huh?"

"Okay, look – "

"My eyes. Got abused bad as a kid. Face beat to a pulp. Retina detached. Endured tons of bullying, and here, you, officer of the law, no better than the rest!"

"I'm sorry, uh, Mr. – "

Then he saw it. Wally shaking with silent laughter, his face redder than a tomato. "Oh, Whip!" He barely managed to get the words out between bursts of laughter. "You shoulda seen his face!"

Whip?

In an instant, Whip's eyes crinkled with silent laughter too. "Yep, still a bit green around the ears. But I think he'll do nicely." He thrust out a large hand. "Winston Kennedy. Been called Whip since Wally managed to get out a few syllables."

"Brothers?"

"You could say that. Share the same DNA."

Before Basil could respond, they were interrupted by the static from their radios. This sound alone placed them both on high alert for the piercing tones that followed quickly after. It would be dine and dash.

"Twin Coulees RCMP, possible Sierra, possible 10-38."

Wally picked up his radio: "2-Alpha-21 responding."

Basil followed suit: "2-Alpha-23 responding." Only a few days and possibly body number two.

"Control, Twin Coulees Ambulance requesting an assist at 24 Maple Drive. Witness reports hearing a shot fired. Man assumed to be alone in house and threatening suicide."

Wally looked at his half-eaten burger with fleeting anguish and grabbed his radio. "Ten-four!"

Whip shoved the tray in front of him. "Go save 'em. Don't worry about your food; I got it covered!" And he dug into the tray with Kennedy-style appetite.

• • •

Wally got to the body first and immediately began performing CPR. Role reversal. This time, it was Wally who appeared to be in control.

For a moment, Basil simply froze, then heard his shaky voice: "Control, a sixty-four to our location!"

The victim, lying on the hardwood kitchen floor, was a stick-thin guy with bloodshot eyes that were rolling back in his head. Wally's body soon obscured most of his view, but Basil noticed the man's feet jerking with each pump of the chest, and a large crimson puddle spreading beside his body. The cracking sound of ribs breaking seemed amplified. Nausea pulled at Basil's gut.

"He's bleedin' like a stuck pig, man! We need EMS!" There was a trace of fear in Wally's voice. As cops, they could only do so much. His face was red, and he grunted with exertion.

Basil steeled his body, fighting the urge to puke. There was a sudden buzzing feeling…

Her eyes were pleading, green with the odd brown fleck in one of them. Heat slammed into him. Blood meandered down her face.

"Oh, man!"

Basil blinked and whipped around. The voice was calm and poised, unnatural given the situation. A leggy brunette craned her neck in the doorway, trying to look at the man on the floor. "Oh, yuck, what a mess to clean up."

"Please move outside, ma'am," Basil urged the woman. From outside, he could hear the piercing wail of sirens announcing the arrival of EMS.

"Look, I called it in. Least you can do is let me look."

Look? Was she nuts? What was it about gore and blood that thrilled people? What did she want to see? Brains splattered everywhere? She was like the ants at an afternoon picnic. "We'll need a statement, but let's move to the living room. Give the guy some privacy."

Pouting, the woman moved to the living room but not without trying to sneak looks over her shoulder. "I called it," she said confidently. "I called it. His girlfriend left him a few days ago. Just never came home again. It was his own fault. He was always slappin' her around. Told him one day she'd be gone. Coward. Can't own up to things. Shoots himself instead. Well, when I heard the shot, I just knew. Said he was gonna kill himself cuz she left him. I tried to stop him; called you guys, didn't I?"

"Yes, and we appreciate that."

"If you need me for anything, anything at all, officer, please let me know."

Still shaking his head, Basil looked up to see Wally standing in the doorway, gray matter and blood stuck to his uniform, his florid face red with exertion, moisture beading on his large forehead. "He's a goner." He then unclipped his radio: "Control, we have a ten-thirty-eight."

"Life's but a walking shadow," Basil's voice tapered off.

Wally smiled ruefully. "I see I'm already rubbin' off on you."

He managed a slight grin.

"You gonna be okay?"

"Yeah, yeah, I'm fine. Not my first one. It's just – I don't know. I always knew brains were gray, but splattered all over, they have that color of – " He shook his head, "I'm fine."

The last body was neat and preserved, rather than one large wound.

• • •

Marc

The stench was so powerful, like something rotting. His fingers fumbled with loose soil. He had to be in some sort of crawl space. Footsteps clunked noisily above him. He froze, hope and fear swirling in his gut. The footsteps faded.

He tried to move. His head throbbed in sync with his pulse. Images like distant flashes went through his mind, but there were too many holes for anything to make much sense. Soon, more painful sensations crept up his body as, nerve by nerve, they shouted their existence. Then, the metallic taste of blood as if he were sucking on pennies.

Ropes. He was tied. The air around him was suffocating and warm. He felt fabric covering his face, and he remembered the hood. His heart began to race once again. Moving his body, he ignored the pain that fed upon each square inch of him.

And then like a twin punch to the gut, it all came rushing back. His captor. The diabolical plan he was spinning. He moved again. The ropes – they felt looser. Wriggling, he found they were coming undone. Ignoring the explosion of pain in his left shoulder, he jerked himself to a sitting position and allowed the dizzying sensation to pass. Then he tried more forcefully to free himself. The rope was loosened, but it wasn't undone. His arms ached with each attempt. He pulled and jostled. Drawing in a deep breath, he gave a final jerk.

Suddenly, the rope relaxed and slipped from his wrists. Muscles screamed in weakness, and his arms shook as he lifted them to his face. Stiff fingers pulled the hood off his head. Darkness was replaced by more darkness. He smelled it now. Dirt. "God is our refuge and strength," his voice shook, "an ever-present help in trouble."

For a moment, light swept through the space from a small, grimy window across the room. Dark shadows danced and then were obliterated in the light as he took in the gruesomeness before him: skulls submerged in a sea of dirt, jeering, taunting.

"No, no, no!" He tried to scream, but bubbles gurgled in his throat. *This is my grave!* And he wept, helpless tears mingling with dirt. He had smelled death. And once you smell death, you *never* forget.

• • •

Basil

He saw the reflection of the whiskey in the mirror. It stood there brazen and seductive on the counter, taunting him. *Just one more drop. You can stop whenever you want to; you are the boss.* He steeled himself against the weakening inside him. It was battle. He tore himself away from it and stared into the eyes that looked back at him.

He felt the buzzing.

Suddenly, they were green, frightened, and pleading. He gripped the counter as the familiar buzzing enveloped him.

He managed to tear himself away and lunged for the whiskey. Ramming the open bottle against eager lips, the burning liquid slid down his throat in that familiar, pleasant sensation. Seconds later, the empty bottle fell onto the linoleum, and his body sank into the dips of the couch, powerless against the vestiges of a drunken sleep.

The bottle had won. Again.

• • •

He is driving along a dark road. Sheets of rain pound his windshield, and his wipers are working furiously to remove the cascading water. Suddenly, two pinpricks of light grow in the distance.

Another car.

Jules.

Mesmerizing, almost hypnotic, he cannot tear his gaze away as they grow larger until they are right in front of him. His fingers clamp the steering wheel, and a trembling foot poises above the brake. Beads of sweat grow on his brow. "This is the end!" His foot presses the pedal to the floor, but there is no resistance. The brakes have failed. Careening forward at top speed, he rushes to meet the rapidly growing lights. "No, please, no!"

Squealing tires, crushing metal, and splintering glass are followed by deathly silence. His face is pressed tightly against the warm leather of the steering wheel. Always his heart is galloping, but he is unhurt. Not a scratch. Not a bruise. Slowly, he lifts his head, knowing what he will see. The windshield of the other car is gone and is mere inches from his face, with the nose of each car mangled beyond recognition.

He does not want to look, but some invisible force propels him to. A pair of green eyes meet his. Jules' mouth is partly open, and blood meanders down her torn face. "No!" The scream tears from his windpipe, a sound otherworldly, almost primal, and ridden with unimaginable pain. A soft wind carries it to the hills around him, which, in cruel fashion, fling back the cry in an echo of mockery.

DAY 28

Arizona

The "little celebration" – as Estelle called it – was thrown in one of the activity rooms in Calgary's splendid La Vista Assisted Living. But it was a far cry from a little celebration. Over-the-top elaborate flower arrangements, streamers, soft music, and the woman of the hour: her beloved Nana.

Arizona's heart flopped in her chest. There were thirty-odd people in the room. Estelle's friends, Nana's friends, and others. People who would ask her about Marc. People who would rummage through her feelings, unasked, of course. Frantically, she looked for the nearest exit.

"Oh good, my dear; you're here!" The lines of tension melted around Estelle's mouth the moment she realized there was no little boy hiding behind Arizona's skirt. She paused only a moment from flitting around the room like a butterfly, satisfied things were in order.

"You didn't tell me there would be all these people!" Arizona hissed.

"If I would've told you," Estelle flashed a bright smile

at those walking past within earshot, "you wouldn't have come. And you *need* to get out." Bedecked fashionably from head to toe, she expertly balanced a silver tray with champagne flutes. "Holed up in that little town by yourself, withering away – "

"I'm not by myself!" she fumed. So long as she did not mention Malcolm, Estelle could pretend he did not exist. Desperate to keep her hands busy, Arizona grabbed a flute. "I can't talk to all these people, Mom! They all want to know how I am."

"Arizona!" A voice warbled from a few meters away. Marie Dunworth sat as a fragile bird in her large chair, a pastel shawl carefully draped over her stick legs. Her eyes brightened with joy. "Oh, Arizona, wonderful you could make it!" She leaned close and whispered conspiratorially, "I think your mother is really enjoying this. More than me."

Happy Birthday, Nana!" Arizona hugged the frail woman. "Yes, she's in her element," she sighed.

"Visit me in my room later, dear, then we can talk more." She smiled at her granddaughter before being pulled away by a latecomer.

Arizona sipped her champagne and thought of Malcolm with Melody. Part of her was glad she'd left him there. The questions – everything – would've been more unbearable. And she couldn't imagine the whispered glances swirling around them, the invasion of his little bubble as they would scrutinize him like something unwanted. She suddenly felt a jab under her ribcage. It felt weird being here without him, like she'd left something precious behind.

"Finally!" A voice at her elbow jerked her back to the moment. Heather Smythe from high school stood before her, as usual wobbling on heels much too high for her ample frame. "I am so sorry, Arizona!" she gushed. "How dreadful to lose your husband so young and not, well, having a body." She lowered her voice conspiratorially. "I mean, did he really kill himself?"

Arizona blinked. A hysterical thought popped into her mind. Before she could stop herself, she blurted: "Would you like to know how?"

Heather's eyes widened, and she leaned in.

Crazy laughter bubbling in her throat, Arizona thought of ways she could horrify Heather with tantalizing details. Why not? It was all a pantomime anyway. Marc wasn't dead. This was all a dream, wasn't it? Husbands didn't just disappear and end up dead, right? And then, no body. For one wild moment, she wanted to pick up the food and throw it at everyone, rip off the table linen, and create one terrible scene her mother would not be able to live down.

She settled for horrifying Heather instead. "Well, he took some rope – "

Heather sucked in her breath.

Arizona looked wildly around her. *What am I doing? What is happening to me?* "And then he – "

"Arizona." Estelle's timing was, as usual, impeccable. "May I speak to you for a moment?"

• • •

Worn out, she lay there neatly tucked in and surrounded by lace coverlets and satin sheets, two clawed hands frozen in arthritic rigor lying on each side. Arizona gripped one hand. "I am so glad you came, Arizona."

Arizona nodded quickly. "Me too, Nana."

"Our little tradition, Mother," Estelle smiled, satisfied the food had been perfect, arrangements beyond judgment. She flitted around once more, straightening the blankets, arranging the pink carnations in a crystal vase, adjusting the curtains, and making sure everything was neat and orderly.

"Ninety-two years," Marie Dunworth laughed lightly. Suddenly, the smile disappeared. "Lisette is gone."

"Lisette Farning?" Estelle questioned in surprise. "I thought she looked so good the other day."

"She didn't want to live anymore. Said the best had happened, and she was leaving with grace before the decay set in too far." Arizona shuddered. Assisted dying. It had finally come to Calgary's La Vista Assisted Living. "They all want to be in control, instead of God." Marie shook her head. She suddenly gave in to a coughing fit, her fingers clenching the edge of her sheet. "No one wants their body to slowly break down until all that is left," she drew in a shuddering breath, "is a decaying shell." She lay there spent for a moment. "Death hasn't banked this flame yet, but it's waiting quietly in the shadows for its orders."

"Shh, Mother, don't talk nonsense." Estelle's suddenly agitated hands attempted wiping the wrinkles out of the blanket, smoothing it over and over. The tense lines made a quick comeback, her spine suddenly stiff.

For a moment, Marie closed her cloudy eyes, and it was quiet in the room. Arizona gently picked up her hand again and traced the delicate skin. Thin, like parchment paper, she was afraid it would tear under her gentle strokes. Satiny with bruised patches, it reminded her of the petals of a wilting rose.

"You didn't bring your boy?"

Arizona startled. Estelle stood up like a deer ready to bolt. The air in the room was suddenly stifling.

Marie's eyes slowly opened.

"Mother?" Estelle scrambled.

"Sit down, Essie." Her voice was remarkably strong now that the coughing fit was over. Estelle obeyed. Arizona didn't know what to say.

"I may be old and holed away in this glorified retirement home, but I still have contact with the outside world."

"We didn't think you would be ready."

Arizona opened her mouth to protest, but Marie interrupted: "'We'? I think you mean 'I', Essie girl. Let me guess, you advised her to keep mum about this?"

Estelle blushed faintly.

"Why?"

"Your heart," Estelle fumbled.

"My ticker is just fine."

"Nana – " Arizona tried to get a word in edgewise, but Marie cut her off.

"Let me say my piece, dear. It has been beggin' to be said for a long time already. Life isn't – can't be – a neatly wrapped parcel. It's not about the outside, but how you've lived. One thing you learn near the end is that control was never yours in the first place, but God's." She struggled to sit up a bit, and Arizona quickly moved to arrange her bed pillows. Estelle glared at the window, her jaw wired tight. "Look at Lisette," Marie added. Her finger jabbed the air. She was like a dying fire that momentarily flares and shoots sparks before it lapses into the hot, glowing embers of decline.

"I just don't think it was wise of her." Estelle shook her head, struggling to defend herself. She walked to the window, her arms tightly folded.

"What? That she is caring for a defenseless child, or that your grandson is illegitimate?"

"My grandson – "

"Yes," Marie cut in. "He's *your* new grandson. How do you feel about that?"

"I think I made it clear."

"Concerning appearances, yes," she barrelled on. "But he's a child. Never mind how it looks. What *is*, is more important."

"Her husband is gone. She's raising a child on her own. She threw it all away!" Estelle's voice shook slightly.

Arizona wanted to run.

"No, I don't think she did," Marie smiled suddenly at Arizona. "No, she turned and embraced the life meant for her, Essie." Her mother stood by the window a moment longer, but the shoulders sagged, and she turned to the bed. Walking stiffly towards it, she carefully perched on its edge. "You know," Marie continued looking at both women, "it's not what happens that defines us, but what we do about it."

"Please, Mother, not now!" Estelle begged, her fingers gripping her knees.

"No, it's not my story to tell," Marie agreed quietly, "but you need to make peace with it. To take your troubles to God in prayer." She was seized by another paroxysm of coughing and sank into her pillows.

"You need to rest, Mother." A grateful Estelle jumped at the opportunity to take charge once more, fussing over Marie's needs. She turned to Arizona, "I think it is time we let Nana rest."

The spark of animation had left Marie's eyes, and they were once more dulled with fatigue. Turning to Arizona, she said, "Take my little great-grandson with you next time you come, you hear?"

Arizona smiled, her lips trembling. "I promise, Nana," and hugged her thin frame tightly for a moment, drinking in her scent and etching it into her memory. "He would love you," she whispered in Marie's ear. The woman's eyes closed as sleep was fast claiming her, and she merely smiled.

Turning at the door once more, Arizona watched her

nana sleep peacefully. A benign sky was pouring liquid oranges, pinks, and purples into the small room, giving everything an otherworldly glow. Even the water in her crystal decanter was liquid gold.

She left then, her head still spinning.

DAY 29

Basil

He drummed his fingers on the steering wheel of his new-to-him Jetta as he listened to CBC's "The Current". He was en route to Calgary to procure his "things" from the little fixer-upper he and Myra owned.

The panorama of his life was in the distance a serene green field; uneventful, even picturesque. The tragedies were merely distant blooms. But zoom in, and each bloom was a painful memory that seeped fumes of grief, of regret and helplessness. A landscape of tragedy and despair he could not flee no matter how he tried. And how he'd tried.

The drive to Calgary was peaceful, with no sign of the rush hour to come. The Rockies loomed to the west, topped with the fresh icing of snow and bathed in ethereal light. Alongside, the foothills proudly marched on.

Why does nature always seem to have it so together? he wondered, sipping his coffee.

Because God is behind it all, Myra's voice wormed into his brain. He shifted uncomfortably and pushed the thought from his mind.

Everything had a clearly delineated purpose. Winter knew it needed to gently prod the remaining geese south and to drape everything in blankets of snow. If a Chinook interrupted with its warm breath, winter allowed it to pass through. Spring knew its hands could clothe fields in green, and nudge bouquets of crocuses through a gentle birth. Fall had at its disposal colors in rich hues of crimson, green, and gold, and knew how to weave a breathtaking tapestry with an expert touch. And summer? It knew when to rest in the warm glow of lazy days.

But not him; he was like a rat in a maze.

The Andreas home was a green and white bungalow with a sagging front porch. In its tiny kitchen with white Formica cabinets, Basil and Myra had dreamt of their future, drawn up plans for renovating, and started planting roots.

He was not prepared for the sight of *their* home. It stood vacant and alone, its small windows casting bleary eyes onto a busy street. It seemed so depressed and defeated.

He walked up to the house and was surprised to find her there already. She must've walked, as her car was nowhere in sight. She stood on the porch, facing their little garden plot in the front yard, a smile straining her features.

Her eyes had always been diamonds of hope in a day dark with gloom, her smile a beacon of welcoming comfort and solace when his career felt like a ship amidst gale-driven seas. Patiently, she listened to his frustrations of judges who dispensed warrants as if parting with their life savings, bureaucratic red tape that was choking his cases, and the day-to-day drudgery of police work.

But now she stood rigid. Her once graceful shoulders were unnaturally lifted with tension. The wind, like a playful child, tugged at the hem of her skirt and teased the wayward wisps that escaped her ponytail. But the scene was anything but idyllic. Her lips were stretched thin, and her eyes reflected an ocean of pain. For a moment, he forgot his hurt and resentment and longed to reach out to her. What was home without her? She was the missing ingredient. But he couldn't – wouldn't – tell her this. *She'd* left him, had she not?

The ball was in *her* court.

He cleared his throat and tried to walk casually up to her, shoving his hands into his pockets. "Damning scene, huh?" He eyed the remnants of vegetables that should have been picked, left shriveled and half-concealed by myriad thistles and choke weed.

A small smile. "You never were the best gardener, Basil." She clutched her purse in front of her tightly like a shield.

Bull's eye. He cleared his throat. "Did you, uh, walk?"

"Yeah, I've kind of started walking more and more. It feels good." She chewed her lip and swiped a strand of hair from her eye. His stomach felt tight.

"That's good," he managed. "Weather is still nice." He looked at her. "No car trouble, though?"

"No. Car is fine. Hugo from work just checked the oil and all."

Hugo from work. Good ol' Hugo. Maybe he could weed this pathetic patch of garden. He rubbed the back of his neck, digging his nails into the skin.

Myra bent down and touched a purple bloom. "Feisty little thing, this one. Stubborn."

"Seems to be. Half-dead, but still has some color."

He watched her run her fingers through the soil and then pack it gently against the flower. She shrugged. "A few more days, and it too will be gone." Her voice sounded empty. "But it didn't give up."

He kicked a stone and watched it skitter across the grass.

"Are you wanting to sell?" Her voice was hesitant, as if she was trying to tiptoe around the inevitable.

"I – "

"Nothing wrong with this place," she suddenly blurted.

He looked at her peripherally, trying to read her face, something he was never too good at. His heart felt heavy. "Just thinkin' of renting it out for now. I wouldn't sell it without discussing it with you first, Myra." Who did she think he was?

"Are you giving up?" There it was. But this time, it was mixed with fear, or was it disappointment?

"Giving up?"

She nodded.

He kicked another rock. Hard. It flew over the grass. "I didn't throw in the towel, remember?"

She dropped her hand, her purse bouncing against her leg. "You did." Her voice broke slightly. "If it weren't for your mistresses."

"Mistresses?" As in plural?

"The alcohol. It's just a replacement, Basil." Her voice sounded strained.

Replacement. "For what? I don't know what you're talking about."

"Yes, you do. Jules."

Jules. Something sharp dug in his gut.

Her small hands were placed on her hips. She sucked in a breath. "You went to her. Always." She hugged herself. "Your successes, your hurts. Your disappointments." She worked her lip furiously. "Green."

"What?"

"You said they were green with," she paused and turned

away, clutching her purse close to her chest, "this thingy in them, a brown spot or something."

"What were?"

"Her eyes."

"Her eyes?" He stared at her.

"That – that tells me enough."

A dog barked in the distance. Myra turned to look intensely at him, her face a rictus of pain.

He got ready to justify himself, but she stopped him.

"Affairs don't need to be physical."

He sighed and ran a hand through his hair, frustration mounting. "She always understood me, Myra. I could talk to her. About things you wouldn't have understood."

"You never gave me the chance!" she said angrily. "I could've – would've – but you just – ." She closed her eyes briefly, her slender fingers now clutching the purse so tightly they were white.

He didn't want to talk about Jules. "I'm entering that program, Myra," he pleaded suddenly, his eyes never leaving the alligator-skinned bag.

"You already have, or you've good intentions?"

Man, could she ever pick at him like one would a scab. "I'm dealing with it!" he said severely, knowing exactly what a cornered animal felt.

"Because you have no choice."

No, he didn't. Strong suggestions on the part of the RCMP were often thinly veiled orders.

She moved her hand inside her purse. "You gave your work and Jules the best of you, and I got the rest. I was tired of the leftovers, Basil."

Suddenly, he heard the bark again, much closer now, followed by incessant barking. His pulse quickened.

A dog. No, a menace on four legs. The large brown

animal whipped into the yard and began a war dance around his legs. For a moment, he was taken back to his youth. The two-inch scar on the inside of his arm seemed to burn. "Stop!" he yelled.

But it didn't stop. The monster was all energy and muscle with a white underbelly. He swallowed reflexively, not wanting to move. It was barely noticeable, but the dog's hair stood erect. His slobbery lips were pulled back in a sneer, revealing white daggers; a sound so menacing, yet subtle, came from deep within his furry gut. The animal moved slowly around Basil – a predator circling his prey and sniffing for weakness. Prickles of cold danced over his body as if a chilly breath was near his skin.

Mustering his courage, he jerked his arm at the dog. "Git, git!"

"Basil!" Myra's voice cut through the roaring in his ears. "C'mere, Charlie." She crouched down. The dog ran up to her. She ruffled between his ears. The dog stopped barking and rubbed Myra's leg with a whine. "Go home, Charlie." The dog obeyed immediately.

How did she do that? "Charlie?"

"Leroy's dog."

He stared at her in confusion.

"He's had him for the past year, if not more."

Basil simply blinked, and words failed him. Myra opened her purse, and his heart began to speed up again. "My vows mean something to me, Basil." With that, her trembling hand handed him a stack of envelopes. "Just some of your mail I thought you might want."

And then, she was gone. He stared emptily at her retreating figure, aching for some sign of regret. Slumped shoulders, a quick glance back – anything.

The sheets on Leroy's wash line snapped sharply in the

cold air. Who in their right mind hung clothes out in late autumn? He wanted to reach out to her, to stop her, to beg for understanding.

But words failed him like they usually did when they were needed most.

DAY 30

Nora

She is running through dark alleys and streets, her heart racing, her feet lead.

Footsteps pound behind her. The ground vibrates.

Her lungs sear with pain, her legs feeling heavier. Suddenly, they are pulling weights. She can feel hot breath on her neck. A shadow grows before her.

Then something wet and cold bites her face.

A shrill sound pierces her dream, and she wakes up sweating.

•••

Reg grunted, slammed the snooze button, and rolled over to begin snoring again.

She lay there staring at the ceiling, waiting for her heart to slow down, her body enveloped in a sticky layer of sweat.

Reg's striped back slowly rose and fell with each breath. She turned with a sigh to watch him. *What does it feel like to be free? You get to be up soon, grab a coffee, and head out.*

You get to meet people, hold conversations with those other than your spouse; you get to live. She sat up suddenly. *You're jealous. What would you not give to see something other than these four walls and your white canvases?* "Girl with no face."

"What?" Reg's sleepy voice sounded out from under his pillow.

"Oh, time to get up." *I can. No one is holding me back. No one is telling me I must stay in this house.*

Reg rolled onto his back and turned to his wife. "Another bad dream?" He yawned.

She just nodded.

"What you just said," he began.

"It's nothing," she insisted.

"But it's bothering you, isn't it?" he probed, now fully awake, his hand reaching out to clasp her cold hand.

She lay down and turned away from him.

"I'm sorry, Nora. I know you're disappointed with me."

"Why would I be?"

"For wanting an end to the reporters."

She remembered clearly how naked and scrutinized she'd felt. "It's okay, I understand now."

"I didn't want the truth to remain hidden, Nora. The world needed to know. Honor killings must be revealed for what they are."

"I thought the price was too high," she remembered. "I hated being on everyone's lips, in everyone's mind. The reporters, they seemed so nosy and cold."

"I know." He pulled her to him and pressed his face to her hair. "And for that, I am truly sorry. For putting you through it."

"It's alright," she cut him off, patting his cheek. "I just need time, Reg."

"Take all the time you need, darling. I'm right where

you need me."

She felt a twinge of regret – for them – for their marriage. Their entire relationship almost had been reactionary in nature; the blossoming between two individuals had been stunted in many ways, with tragedy having wormed its way in a few times too many.

"I need to get going," he interrupted her thoughts. The bed springs sank. "I'm – "

She turned to him. He was staring at Henry's portrait on their shared dresser. "You put his picture here." His voice was suddenly thick, his back stiff.

"I didn't mean to do it without asking you. It's just –"

"Why?"

"We never talk about him."

He turned to her, his face a mask of pain. "It's a reminder – "

"So is my face."

The tables had turned.

"His death wasn't our fault, Reg."

His lips twitched. He turned away.

"We need to talk about what happened – about him." Her hand slid over the tight coils of his back. The pain was still there, more intensely than she'd realized. He'd grown angry and sullen when Henry died. But just as quickly it was gone as if it never existed in the first place.

"There's nothing to talk about. He was born with a congenital condition. He needed a transplant. He was denied."

"The mother didn't act out of spite. She loved her child. She couldn't bear – "

He shook his head.

"Reg – "

He stood up suddenly, the bed springs bouncing back.

"Reg," she persisted. "You can't bottle it all up inside."

"We need to look forward. Change what we can. Leave the rest." He collected his watch from the night table.

"But you can't if you don't deal with it."

"I *am* dealing with it. In my own way." He ran a hand through his hair and looked at her for a moment. "He could've been saved, but some mother changed her mind. End of story."

"Not really, Reg. You're hurting."

"Not you?"

"Of course I am!" Only for a few short weeks had he touched their lives. A congenital condition and then a suddenly denied transplant. It was like rubbing shards of glass in a raw wound – pain upon pain. At just four weeks old, his little body was interred at Twin Coulees Cemetery. Part of her had died that day. "But I've come to accept that she chose what she thought was best for her child – "

"Her dead child, Nora. Her *dead* child. She could've saved our child!"

"Even the doctors said it was a very slim chance."

"But a chance, Nora! A *chance*! He didn't have to die." He grabbed his robe off the chair and stabbed his arms into the holes. "Look, I gotta get going." Already, the thickness of his voice had disappeared. A muscle still twitched ever so slightly in his jaw, but then it, too, was gone.

She knew the moment was gone.

He didn't have to die.

He had uttered those same words when he left on his tour of duty. He'd set his battered suitcase on the conveyor belt, his mouth firm. Ready to solve the world's problems, though he had not solved his own. He'd dragged a hand through his hair, his face a rapidly changing landscape. He did not wear his emotions on his sleeve, but in that taut face, she could read a narrative of pain: the flicker in his eyes, the tightness of his jaw, and sometimes one emotion on the heel of another flitting across like the seasons, but easily restrained. They would suddenly disappear as if no longer existing.

But she knew better.

The pain had just gone underground.

Just like now.

Reg managed a sudden smile. He leaned over and pecked her on the cheek. "Papers to deliver and doors to fix. Oh, and I'm going to the town meeting today in between delivering papers and doing the odd job here and there. Support our mayor; fight for change."

That was Reg. A gentleman and a fighter. A fighter for honor, for what was right. For her. For their son. For their country. Though she felt dragged in front of the media then, she knew he was fighting for her. Just like he did as a soldier in Afghanistan.

The media had latched onto the acid attack with characteristic tenacity. Abundant articles were printed. People came forward with similar stories. Reg urged her to join a support group for female trauma victims. She couldn't say no. He even went with her that first time, the only husband there. And she knew then what others meant when they talked about shared pain. It was too painful to go again. And Reg, bless his heart, did not push her. He always gave her space.

She reached for her scarf on the side table. She jumped as she heard the bang of the shower door, followed by the rush of water. Or maybe it was her guilt that hung like an albatross around her neck. What had she been thinking with the affair? It hadn't been physical in any sense, but the emotional attachment had been there. A blot on her conscience she carefully hid, frightened he might pull the last rug of stability from beneath her feet.

She fixed her niqab and thought of Adam Brighton, glad she'd ended it when she did that day in Gemma's.

It was Valentine's Day. Reg had gone to Afghanistan, and she was with Adam. Music played softly. Classical overtures.

She was studying the smooth planes of his face, the artist in her imagining the colors on her palette. Smooth white, ruddy pink. Hints of browns and beiges. His smile was just right, slightly crooked. And the way those hands painted was magic.

But this evening was different. She couldn't really explain it. Maybe it was Jarvis' loathsome stare. The fifty-something busboy of few words often stared at her when she was not looking. She could feel his eyes burn into her neck.

She would turn and catch him turning his head just in time.

The man was a snake.

But maybe it was because it was Valentine's Day, and she was in a coffee shop with Adam. Reg was on the battlefield. She would be enjoying a latte; he was fending off bullets and shrapnel; she, enjoying light-hearted conversation.

"Penny for your thoughts."

But a waitress interrupted. She handed them each a pretty cup with thick foam shaped into a heart, and apple pie a la mode.

Reg's favorite.

"For you and your sweetheart," she smiled.

She wanted to correct the woman, but instead, her eyes settled on a safe spot: the velvety perfection of her coffee.

The room was full of happy, chatting couples. But she wasn't among their number.

"Nora?"

She dropped the spoon and stumbled to her feet.

"Is everything okay?" Adam reached for her hand and stroked her fingers, an archipelago of sunspots scattered over his pale skin.

She pulled her hand away. "I – we can't do this anymore, Adam."

He looked confused. "I don't understand."

"I am married, Adam."

"I know," he said quietly. "It's not like we're – you know."

Yes, she did know. But did it really matter? Not if her conscience was a worthy guide.

She stared into her latte. The heart had disintegrated in the foam.

"I need to go, Adam. I'm sorry – I really am."

She grabbed her coat and half-walked – half-ran from the room.

Outside, it was oddly chilly. The moon hung scythe-like – an arbiter of justice in the sky.

The crank of the tap jerked her back to the present. She imagined it running over the scar on Reg's leg. Remnants of a shrapnel wound that left him with a slight limp.

Her wounded soldier had come back to her.

• • •

Marc

The room was long and narrow, probably no bigger than twenty feet. He lay, a living one among the dead. From the daylight filtering in through the tiny box window on the far side of the room, and the light pooling in from under the door, he could make out a skull here and there, a femur bone, then a leg bone, probably five…six bodies?

Every inch of his body screamed to be let loose from his grave.

The window. It was his only hope. He had to get there

and somehow break through. But that was far from easy.

Sharp pain shot through his leg. He bit his lip.

And then he touched it. Something soft. He shrank back. It smelled putrid. His gut spasmed, and he retched.

He lay still, breathing heavily. *It's just a body*, he tried to calm himself. He sucked in a deep breath and closed his eyes. The dizziness passed. Opening his eyes, he turned to the curtain of light spilling in from the window. Two black orbs. Set in a dirty white skull. Decaying flesh hung in tatters from a skeleton. Tufts of blond hair on top.

Moaning, he dragged his frame back again and instinctively looked for that rusted pipe the way a newborn searches for a nipple; his salvation in this dark dungeon. With relief, his swollen and excessive tongue licked the thick condensation that was the step between him and the grave.

Gradually, the nausea lifted.

• • •

Arizona

Arizona tore a chunk out of her warm cinnamon bun and licked the sticky sweetness from her fingers. She looked again at the note lying beside her on the passenger seat: *Check out the silver spoon. All clues point there.* "Idiot!" she scolded herself. How could she have been so blind? There had been something concrete – some sort of explanation – at her fingertips all along. The sound of the rumble strip made her jerk her cruiser back into her lane. "Shoot! Sorry!" she called out to no one in particular. With a stubborn lift of her chin, she'd decided that morning she would try to figure out what he meant.

Melody had helped with this. "Look, Ari, if you need to find out exactly what happened, then do it."

Arizona knew Melody wanted her to realize she was

hanging onto a ship that had already sunk.

"You've done so much already." But the protest was half-hearted.

Melody dismissed the notion with a wave of her hand. "I said I'd support you."

She clutched the steering wheel of her silver PT Cruiser, her lips a thin line of determination. Come what may, she would doggedly persist. Marc was out there. Let them think she was a raving lunatic. The idea had come to her in the stillness of night. She'd jumped out of bed in nervous excitement. If it weren't for Malcolm and the fact that it was the dead of night, she would've raced out there immediately. How could she have forgotten? Of course, The Silver Spoon! A little café touting French-inspired cuisine in downtown Calgary. Her parents used to dine there on occasion.

A little voice nagged her: What if this Silver Spoon had nothing to do with Marc's disappearance? But then reason would assert itself: Where was he then? She *had* to take the plunge.

Behind her, Twin Coulees Meat Industries spewed out fluffy white clouds of steam that slowly disintegrated as warm air assimilated into cooler air. Before her, tumbleweed after tumbleweed somersaulted across the road, egged on by a shrieking and laughing wind. Bemused, she smiled at the weeds, her heart singing. In such high spirits, she could converse with a mere plant and feel anything but idiotic.

Once she entered Calgary, traffic was one giant snarl. However, when she got to Sixteenth Avenue, no matter how slowly she drove, or the fact that she drove twice down the street, carefully looking on both sides, she couldn't spot the little café. *Odd*, she thought in confusion. She knew it was there. Each time, she stopped in front of The Last Frontier Pizzeria. With a sigh, she parallel-parked and climbed out slowly. It *had* to be here!

The bald little man with dark, piercing eyes greeted her in a friendly enough manner. Gesturing at the still-empty little pizzeria, he said: "Well, Miss, once upon a time, there was a little eatery called Silver Spoon or something or other right where you're standin'." He scratched thin, gray sprouts on his head and sighed, "Musta been fifteen years back or so. Little French café it was. Quite a bustling little affair. Drew plenty of folks, especially those outta the top drawer, if you know what I mean."

She knew: People like her parents.

"I stumbled upon the space about five years ago now. It was long past its glory days. Boarded up and empty. Apparently stood like that for a very long time. Sorry, Miss, that I can't help you more."

She felt like a punctured balloon.

• • •

Absorbed in self-pity and a steaming hot chocolate a mere fifteen minutes later, the realization hit her: Dawson Williams had to know more. She'd taken him by surprise. Maybe he would've had time to think. Maybe he had an idea. There was a chance Marc could've mentioned the Silver Spoon to Dawson, despite the fact the two didn't always see eye to eye. It was the only option now, as far as she could tell. The notion slowly took hold until it was firmly entrenched in her mind. Chin up, girl! You are a Beckam, after all.

• • •

1974

THE BOY

"I'm sorry, my darling," she stroked his face. "See what you made me do? I can't help it I get this way. You need to remember to be less naughty."

The boy nodded silently. His arm still stung where she'd pinched him hard. Why couldn't he be good all the time? If only he wouldn't be so stubborn!

"Be a dear and bring me my cigarettes and bottle."

He quickly did her bidding.

The lid made a tinny sound as she unscrewed it. She lifted the bottle to her lip and closed her eyes. She always closed her eyes. He tried it once. But she just got mad. "Open your eyes! Wanna spill juice everywhere? I'll make you lick it up."

He watched her fat lips unable to seal the bottle properly. More than a few drops trailed down her face onto her shirt. Her pretty flower shirt. She took two sips then pulled the bottle away. "Life is good, kid. Life is good." She fumbled for a cigarette, and he eagerly lit it for her. "What would I do without you?" she crooned, shoving the stick between her lips. Sliding down her easy chair, she pulled up her legs.

His heart swelled at those words, and he began rubbing her back just the way she liked it.

"Mmm," she sighed in contentment. "What would Mommy do without you?" she repeated. Suddenly, tears pooled on her cheeks as they so often did.

"Don't, Mommy! Don't cry," he begged. In a moment, he knew, she would stop, sleep quickly claiming her.

He would watch the smoke drift around them. Her mouth would soon drop open, and the snoring would begin. Once, he crept close and looked in her mouth. There were gaps. He felt his own teeth. He had more than she did.

He would watch her for a long time. Something would burn inside him then, but he couldn't identify exactly what it was.

• • •

Arizona

"Nothing? Nothing at all?" Melody asked gently. Malcolm had fallen asleep on the couch, clutching a stuffed elephant he'd adopted from her collection of toys.

Arizona shook her head and perched on the edge of the couch. "Nada." She felt lost. She was sure she'd stumbled across something meaningful. Sure, she wanted to contact Dawson, but what would he think or say? He'd envied Marc and his journalistic skills. He wanted the limelight, not life in the shadows.

Besides, Marc was gone for nearly a month. By now, most would've accepted his suicide for what it was: unlike Marc in many ways, but not impossible. His case was now old news. The police had moved on – everyone had moved on. Except her. Could she really bear the whispers to start, worried looks cast her way, the speculation that she might be "losing it?"

"Arizona," Melody interrupted her thoughts. She pulled her legs from underneath her and sat up.

Arizona slowly looked at Melody. It *was* there: the slightest trace of doubt, that barely noticeable tinge of worry. "You think I'm nuts, don't you?"

"You have a very well-developed sixth sense; I won't deny that. I've always admired this part of you, but you can't go on like this."

"I can't just throw in the towel, Melody."

"You have Malcolm now. I know it's not easy, but *he* needs you. He is totally real, whereas Marc, well, I don't know. For all you know, your mind might not want you to believe he is dead."

"You told me I should go this morning!" Arizona rubbed her face. "You were completely on board with this."

"I wanted to support you; to help you find some peace.

Please, Arizona! She leaned forward. "The fact that you couldn't find the café is a sign that it probably had nothing to do with his death."

Her throat ached. "I just want *something*. Bloodied clothes. His body. Something!" Anything was more cutting, more real than nothing.

"Oh, Ari," Melody reached for her hand.

"Never mind; I get it." She dropped to the floor on her knees and began frantically cleaning up Malcolm's toys. "Grief has been playing tricks on my mind. I refuse to see reality for what it is. Maybe the looney bin is the best place for me, huh?" She waved a board book.

"I'm so sorry, Arizona. Your parents – "

"So, that is what this is! My mother has been talking to you behind my back?" She shelved a couple of books.

"She's worried!"

"She never liked Marc. She despised the fact that I would ever date, much less marry, a man below my social class. You *know* what she's like, Melody!"

"She might be a social snob, but she loves you, Arizona. In her mind, a layabout took her daughter away from a life of ease, married her into poverty, and then killed himself. Most people would be beyond the breaking point by now." She knelt by Arizona and helped her sort the toys. "Why did he kill himself? Who knows? You may never know. And if you wait until you find out, that moment of closure might never come. He loved you deeply. Your mind is trying to make sense of this grief, and in its own way, it's creating this idea that something else must have happened. Suicide is a difficult reality for loved ones to digest. It is not your fault, Arizona, and you don't have to find an alternate ending, either, to make sense of it all."

"There was no body!" she repeated. "Just a flimsy piece of paper found on his desk." Arizona picked up a scrap of paper from off the floor and waved it in front of Melody to emphasize her point.

"Arizona, there were no signs of foul play, no motivations for his death, nothing. Please, don't try to make something out of nothing." Melody moved to place a hand on her back, but Arizona pushed her away. She felt as if she were in a deep, dark pit with no way out.

"Please, Melody. I need to be alone."

"C'mon, Arizona, don't be like this. Don't push me away!"

She stood up. "Just go."

"Being alone like this – " Melody slowly stood up as well, her brows drawn together in concern, and decided it was pointless.

Covering her face with shaking hands, Arizona barely heard the door click shut. Malcolm shifted and played with his earlobe but stayed fast asleep. The quiet seemed stifling. Arizona held fast to the sobs that threatened to break loose.

She hurried to her bedroom. *Their* bedroom. His smiling face looked at her from the nightside table. She picked up the frame and held it at arm's length. "Why, Marc?" she whimpered as if he would suddenly pop out of the frame and answer her many riddles.

Suddenly, she hurled it across the room. It landed with a sickening crack against the closet door, the glass fractured in two places. Horrified at what she'd just done, she hurried to pick it up and carefully pressed it close to her. Tears stung her eyes.

She was alone now, truly alone. It was all over. *Where is your God, Marc? Is this how He rewards those who turn to Him?*

Bile rose in her throat at the overwhelming reality of it all. There were no answers; she would never have answers. There would never be closure; she would always feel like there was something missing. A journalist who had taken his own life. Had he crossed the line, ethically speaking? Had his investigations taken him a step too far? Had he done something he could not live with? Clasping the picture close, she rocked herself back and forth on the bed.

Outside, it was becoming dark and silent, except for the mournful hooting of an owl.

How could she raise a little boy while feeling as if she were spiraling out of control? One who looked like Marc, whose tender little face stabbed her heart daily? Her eyes brimmed with tears that threatened to spill over.

As she sucked in a shaky breath, the first tear slid down; she no longer held them back. She no longer cared to; *she no longer could*. Each drop reflected liquid pain, anger, and disgust. They slid down unheeded, silently at first, until her body convulsed, a gradual trembling that erupted so powerfully into heart-rending sobs as if her soul had ripped open, no longer able to hold the pain. The feeling was so powerful, so overwhelming, she felt she was drowning. Guttural moans seemed to tear her apart. They sounded unnatural yet sprung from beneath layers of pain. Her fingers dug into the carpet as she crawled on the floor, her lungs struggling for each breath. *Please, God, help me!*

The choice was no longer hers. The dam had finally burst.

When she was finally spent, as if all feeling had been wrung out of her, she sat up. Like the cleansing rain after a powerful storm, for the first time in weeks, calmness enveloped her.

It was not until then that she noticed a small form peering at her from the doorway.

•••

Still trembling, she pulled herself up from the floor. "Come here," she whispered, her voice thick and raw. He walked towards her, dragging the elephant behind him.

"Owie?" he asked concerned.

"Owie," she responded softly.

"Sing!" he suddenly chirped. Of course. When he seemed sad, or one of his many tantrums occurred, she would sing to him, and it almost always seemed to relax him.

She was drained, but there was something hopeful in those eyes that stared back at her. Taking his hand, she said, "Come, let me show you something." She took him to the leather chair and stopped. The cologne nearly undid her. She sank into it and pulled Malcolm onto her lap. She picked up Marc's guitar and held it. Malcolm's chubby fingers slowly moved to the strings and then stopped, as if he remembered the last time.

"It's okay," she whispered. "This was your daddy's guitar." Slowly, she began to pluck at the strings. "Amazing Grace, how sweet the sound, that saved a wretch like me..."

Malcolm melted into her lap.

• • •

After browsing Facebook long enough, she found Seraphina's page. There was raw beauty in her eyes before the illness set in, particularly in the way she gazed adoringly at baby Malcolm. She printed off the profile picture, glued it onto some scrapbook paper, and then inserted it into an old four-by-six picture frame. The print quality was not too bad, but she promised a sleeping Malcolm that she would get him a better copy. A peace settled in her heart as she placed the frame by her new son's bedside.

"Good night, Malcolm," she whispered hoarsely. "Tomorrow *will* be better."

DAY 31

Nora

Nora experimented with wrapping colored scarves around her head and face. Each time, she sighed in disgust. Either she looked like a clown, which, of course, was marginally better than looking like a monster, or she looked like a devout Muslim girl, which was not how she was trying to present herself.

She threw the fifth scarf down on the bathroom counter and stared menacingly at the mirror. "No more, mirror, mirror on the wall. If I remain concerned about who is the fairest of them all, I might as well go to bed and never get out again!"

Picking up her favorite scarf with soft, pink dahlias scattered over the thin fabric, she decided to try one more "look." She propped her cellphone on the counter and found a YouTube video of a woman trying on different scarves.

"Ta-da!" she sang airily as she found a style she would be comfortable in. "Now, just look at the floor. Everyone will be too busy to pay you much heed." *Hopefully.*

She picked up her glass of wine and looked right at the latticed skin, the small nose with oddly shaped nostrils, the shiny patches here and there, and squared her shoulders in determination. *You can do this, Nora!*

Heading for the front door, she noticed the bird figurine on the bookshelf. It was bold and black with a rainbow of color when the sun hit it just right. It perched on the shelf, its beady eyes following her.

"I found another collectible," Reg had declared with a sheepish grin that afternoon shortly after her attack. "I know, I know. I really need to stop collecting, but this one is not only for me, but for you. Look, honey, it's perfect." He lifted the porcelain bird to the light as its dark feathers suddenly sparkled. "Neat, huh? Goes from dark to bright." He grinned like a little boy in a toy store.

"Yes, it is lovely." She tried to sound enthusiastic. The dark eyes seemed to probe deep inside her, and she shuddered.

"It's a reminder, honey, that one day, you will be free again. One day, you will walk out of this house, confident.

She could not deny it was a lovely gesture.

Daily, its eyes taunted her, reminded her of her imprisonment – of what had happened to her.

But how could she tell him? He firmly believed that growth did not occur without discomfort. The last thing she wanted was to show fear of one more thing and to feel like she was going backward.

"Alright, Nora," she coached herself, "let's try to break out of your prison, then." Her heart felt like it would beat right out of her chest as she opened the front door and allowed the cool breath of autumn to caress the half-dead nerves of her face. For just a moment, and then she tightened the scarf around her face. She squared her small shoulders, sucked in a ragged breath, and felt guilty as sin. Trembling legs carried her to their detached garage.

Cold keys pressed into her hands as she turned the ignition. It felt so strange to be sitting behind the wheel again. The car roared to life, startling her. Exhilaration coursed through her.

The car sputtered along proudly. For a moment, she felt she was being followed. But a glance in her rear-view mirror told her she was imagining things.

• • •

Basil

"I don't know about Calgary, but here in our neck of the woods, political passion runs high," Wally noted. He and Basil had joined the masses in the town hall to hear Mayor Ratford's speech on the need to hit hard on the sex industry in Twin Coulees. Wally was, in true Wally fashion, totally enthralled with his burger, not at all fazed by the smidgen of mayo that clung conspicuously to his lip.

Glorious poster boy for the fast-food industry, Basil chuckled inwardly.

"Wonder how he expects to slam down on prostitution where so many have failed?" he said aloud.

Wally shrugged. "I think he wants to zero in on this issue – place it under our community's magnifying lenses and make it a top priority."

Basil scratched his neck under his collar in irritation. The room was very warm, what with nearly a hundred bodies packed in, no hint of air movement, much less AC.

"Thing's always failin' when you need it," Wally noted, gesturing a napkin toward one of the radiators then shoving it in his pocket. The mayo had disappeared from his lip. Their radios squawked simultaneously and fell silent as if not daring to interrupt a political gathering.

A hush fell on the room as Ratford stood up. The stout, round man with his bald head and large girth ambled confidently to the podium, a far cry from the man who had slunk out of Twin Coulees' seediest hotel the other day. His well-oiled smile slid easily into place.

Basil wondered whether touching the man would make him rock back and forth like an egg. His bald pate was so smooth and shiny; it sparkled like a well-polished mirror, plenty visible from their sideline view. His eyes seemed so frozen in perpetual astonishment that they nearly bulged from their sockets.

"He's a rising star in Twin Coulee's politics," Wally supplied mid-chew. "He's a piece of work, but an ocean of improvement over the last one to run this town. Now, that guy smoked weed in between meetings, hooked up with questionable women, and made decisions while marinated in whiskey. And the town bought it all hook, line, and sinker."

"Really? What a gong show! Wonder what makes people put up with that?"

"Family connections. Real charmer, too." Wally shrugged. "He knew what to say, how to say it, and by the time everyone figured him out, the guy was destroying their town one bad decision at a time while sloshed." The noise of the crowd dipped suddenly. "It was a bitter pill to swallow," Wally whispered. "They'd been had."

Basil frowned. "So, they came to their senses and voted him out?"

"Nope. Suicide. Just before he got voted out."

"Dear friends," a voice resounded from the podium. His dark eyes swept the room with intensity. "There is a contagion in our community." He walked away from the podium and paced in front of the crowd. "It strikes the unsuspecting."

He spread out his fat, little fingers. "It spreads its spores." The fingers wiggled. He was growing more and more animated. "This contagion, my dear friends, is crippling us all, creating vulnerable wounds where the disease of crime and drugs is rushing in with abandon." He scanned his audience. "And do you know, ladies and gentlemen, the spores of this quiet, creeping bacteria?"

There was only the collective silence of bated breath.

"Prostitution!" He slammed his fist on the lectern to rousing enthusiasm. "The men and women who perpetuate this trade; those who solicit it and those who sell it! We need to eradicate this disease – destroy it – obliterate it! Cut the disease out swiftly and thoroughly. Up the police presence, shut down the trade…"

Obliterate. What about social programs to help vulnerable women? He imagined his sister Paula's indignant outcry at such a simplistic solution – a band-aid solution – to a complex issue.

"Is this the kind of atmosphere conducive to raising children? We must protect them – shield them! The future of our dear children lies in the balance! Together, we can put Twin Coulees on the map! Make it great once more, a bastion of beauty and strength! Ratford's face glistened with exertion but shone triumphantly in the face of resounding applause.

Then Basil saw him. The cabbie sat there on the periphery of the crowd, his eyes following Ratford with awe and adulation. *So, he did survive!* Basil thought with relief and a flash of guilt. He had meant to check in at the hospital to see if the man had made it.

"There you have it," Wally sighed when the oration finally ended, and they were walking to their vehicles. "But to get from A to B won't be easy. Talk is cheap. His romantic ideals require manpower and money, both of which this town is short on."

"What about the women?" Basil asked, opening his car door. The cool air felt so good as it rushed about his face and body. "He focused on the immorality of it, of those who solicit its service, and on the increased crime rate prostitution brings, but he didn't touch on the plight of many of these women. It all seems like sanitary politics – emotionless."

"Politics *is all about* emotion," Wally asserted. "It's driven by it, just not necessarily the warm and fuzzy kind. Besides, if the male part of the equation is removed, prostitution will be history. It's not simple by any stretch of the imagination, but you gotta love his idealism."

"Idealism?"

"Okay, I know, I know, that's not the right word. Single-mindedness, maybe."

Basil knew the issue was, without doubt, a complex one. Targeting the johns and pimps was a good and necessary move and in keeping with the government's position on it in general. But what about the human side? Ratford mentioned nothing of the women – the pawns of the trade. These were women with children, women who were daughters themselves, women with souls.

But Ratford was no doubt seeing in black and white; empathy, apparently, was neither. And no one in that room had protested its absence. They were all drooling at the mental picture Ratford painted in their minds of beautiful Twin Coulees with stunning architecture and a beautified town landscape. The way he talked, one would think he was creating Utopia.

•••

Nora

There were hoodies everywhere. Different colors, designs, faces concealed. Nora melted into her seat. One hooded figure was absorbed with a cellphone. Another cuddled close with his girl.

Then, she saw him.

The man in the window.

Suddenly, everything seemed muted. Like a deer caught in headlights, she stared at him unmovably, most of his face concealed by his hoodie. Only the intensity of his stare finally compelled her to tear away her gaze.

She wondered if he had followed her. The sweat on her skin suddenly felt cold and uncomfortable.

Pulling her shawl tighter around her, she prayed for invisibility. The speech continued, but she no longer heard any word.

She had to get away.

• • •

Basil

Basil heard the strains of anger through the thin walls of Ichabod's office. He looked up to meet Sharon's questioning gaze and shrugged in return. Wally entered the detachment, a take-out cup of java in one hand and a sugary donut, aka cop kibble, enough to drive anyone's blood sugar through the roof, in the other. His characteristic grin, dusted with white powder, showed his contentment at arriving in time to hear the performance being played out in the other room.

"The rat, I take it?"

"Rat?" Basil questioned in surprise.

"Ratford."

"Thought you didn't mind our fine mayor?"

"Oh, I don't like him, just like him better than the last guy," Wally clarified. "If he delivers on his promises, I might just be coerced to like him a little." He chuckled. "He likes throwing superlatives around like confetti."

Sharon quickly came to Ratford's defense: "He has a vision and goes after what he wants. Ichabod can be such a brick wall."

Wally simply laughed in that carefree manner of his and tore another chunk out of his donut: "All the world's a stage."

Sharon rolled her eyes in mock exasperation and waved a nail file at Basil. "I don't know how you put up with him, Basil, with his flowery tongue and all."

"Ah, but it is an interesting and varied diet," Wally responded, "and he did have a vast knowledge of human experience. You should read him sometime. You'll see I was right."

"Well, I know I couldn't listen to this twenty-four-seven. Anyhow, those two are like oil and water." She shrugged and began to file her nails. "I don't know. I love this little town. It's my home. I want Ratford to succeed." She chewed her lip. "If he doesn't," she waved her hand dramatically, "this place is going to be a – " she scrambled for the right word, a bit flustered.

"You can do it," Wally egged her.

She glared at him. "Pathetic dump. Happy now?"

"Delirious." He popped the last chunk into his mouth.

"The drugs, the petty crime. People are tired of it. I get that."

Wally nodded.

"He is a bit extreme," she shot a glance at Ichabod's closed door. "I don't care for how he is going about it, but," she paused, "I think the only solution might be something drastic."

Basil shook his head. "I don't know – "

Sharon jumped in. "Okay, just so I'm clear, I don't agree with his approach. I'm just addicted to making this place great again. Getting rid of prostitution because it's some form of contagion? That's a bit over the top. Seriously, calling them spores, pores, whatever." She shook her head. "You gotta love that one." She placed her hands on her hips, satisfied she had everyone's attention.

Wally chuckled. "I gotta say, I do love the metaphors he tosses around."

Sharon turned to him. "Of course you do."

"I didn't say I agreed with his position," Wally clarified. "But we're spread so thin as it is, our resources, manpower. You know what I mean."

Sharon moved a stack of papers about. "I think Ratford should go at it from a different angle."

If she did not command all their attention before, she did now.

"Decriminalize it."

Paula, with her sociology degree, would probably agree, Basil thought, wondering where she was now. Rome? No, probably Scotland, joining one tour group after another, laughing gaily, and being vocally entertaining in true Paula fashion.

Basil saw Stacey standing there in clothes tight and uncomfortable, on heels too high for her, lines of fatigue and stress spoking out from her eyes. He remembered the depth of pain hidden in her angry eyes. The life of misery she had sunk to. She was one of many who loathed what they had been reduced to. Angered by those who preached the viability of choice when they had never stood in her place.

No one has a clue about these women.

"Ratford has passion," Sharon asserted. "I must hand that to him. He doesn't pussy foot around, and people appreciate that. Thing is, Ratford makes Ichabod look like an incompetent fool, and Ichabod, in turn, despises political posturing, and even more so, playing puppet."

"I could get used to decriminalization," Wally agreed thoughtfully, "if it would solve the drug problem here, the petty crime, the vandalism. We can stop siphoning tax dollars to it and spread our energies and money elsewhere."

"Why not deal immediately with the condition rather than merely the symptoms?" Basil jumped in. "Decriminalizing it just sends the message that prostitution is okay."

All heads swung his way.

"We need social reform, programs, assistance for these women, or we are right at square one again. We need to *care* for these women. We need to stop with this 'us versus them'."

At that moment, he was reminded of a conversation he'd had with Myra about the teenagers she worked with at New Beginnings, a Calgary youth outreach program: *If you want to truly help, you must do so in love. Otherwise, you simply widen the gap between you and the ones you want to help until it's unbridgeable.*

He sank into a nearby chair. *What about the missing women?* he wanted to add, but the low murmuring coming from Ichabod's office had escalated slightly.

Through the glass window on the door, Basil could see the two figures facing each other; Ratford waved his hands about, whereas Ichabod faced him stonily and unflinchingly, a man refusing to budge for anything or anyone. He was like a smooth, glassy lake with deadly undercurrents.

"I cannot put all my men on this problem!" Ichabod barked. "I will not subject myself to the vagaries of changing political whims." Neither one could make out Ratford's response.

The voices continued quieter for a few moments longer, and then the door suddenly opened. Ichabod stalked out, but in a calmer manner, Ratford at his heels.

"Ratford, let me introduce you to our new constable, Basil Andreas!"

Basil shifted uncomfortably. The heat of the argument was still palpable. But Ratford, being the politician, smiled widely, a grin that tried to reach his eyes and failed miserably. "Basil, you say? Interesting name." He appraised him coolly. "You sound very familiar. I can't quite place it."

Basil did not feel inclined to jog his memory.

"Where did you transfer from?"

"Calgary," he supplied grudgingly.

Ratford nodded expectantly but seemed to realize nothing else was forthcoming. "You're privileged to work in such a fine town and be part of history in the making. Your sergeant is a fine man with the ability to do much good here," he nodded toward a glowering Ichabod. "We all need to be on the same page and turn Twin Coulees into a fine town once again!"

And what a page-turner it will be, Basil wanted to interject. Out of the corner of his eye, he could see Wally raising his eyebrows at the rhetoric.

"Justice for one must be justice for all," Basil added quietly, and Wally, for once not supplying any comment, simply nodded.

Ratford floundered momentarily as he tried to make sense of whether Basil and Wally truly were on his side or not. Then, bidding them a good afternoon, he slipped out of the detachment.

Turning to face Ichabod, Basil was surprised to see a smile tugging at his lips. Ichabod rolled back his shoulders to relieve tension. "Well, that was fun!"

Wally raised an eyebrow. Sharon's pen paused mid-air. Basil stared at him questioningly.

"How does he know you?" Sharon whispered at Basil.

Basil felt his heart speed up a bit. "It's a small world."

Sharon blinked and looked as if she wanted to press further but then decided against it.

"Let him stew in his own juices for a bit," Ichabod was saying. "I'll tell him about the auxiliary program we have been approved for in due time."

"Auxiliary policing?" Lee Nygard wondered aloud.

Ichabod stroked his chin. "We need some more manpower. And this is a generous move by the head honchos. But I refuse to jump when he says jump."

Sanctimonious fool! Basil thought of Ratford. The man only cared about his public image and popularity. He was using the crackdown on crime and drugs as an auspice for ridding the town of these women, rather than truly helping them. He had his blinders on. His solution was far too simple for an issue far too complex.

• • •

Basil glanced over the '70s tan box house in front of him. A large white cargo vehicle with *Exotic Animals* declared on its side was parked near the curb.

After a series of business-like raps, the front door crawled open painfully to reveal a short, spindly man in tartan shorts with knobby knees that were scabbed over, and a stained white muscle shirt.

Once cleaned up, Basil had no doubt Bob Higginson was a handsome man, but like this, he looked like he had gone to seed.

"Hey man," he blinked a time or two. "Is everything okay, officer?" His eyes darted over Basil's shoulder and then landed on his face again. He shifted awkwardly. "Don't believe I got any outstandin' speedin' tickets."

"Constable Andrews. Mr. Higginson, we are looking for Janey McAlistair. Reports have it she was last seen with you at Gemma's."

"Janey." He snapped his fingers. "Oh, ya, Jane. That's what she called herself. Somethin' wrong?"

"So, you two dating?"

He laughed then. "Dating. Nah. She wanted to meet me for a quick coffee." He gestured at his work truck. "I work for Exotic Animals. She wants to buy one. Not just like any ol' pet. S'what she said. Had some questions. My phone number is on the truck, and she called me. That's it."

"And?"

He shrugged. "Nuthin. Didn't get back to me."

"When did you see her last?"

"Uh, last Tuesday, if memory serves me correct. She just stopped texting me. Asked me a lot of questions. I figured she'd be back for more. But, hey, just like she dropped off the face of the planet, you know."

"So, you haven't talked to her since, either?"

"Nope."

"You married?"

"Not anymore."

"So, do you just transport the animals?"

"We use them for outreach programs, uh, schools, exhibitions, you know, and the like. Keyless entry. I only know the code. Animals quite safe. People quite safe." He shrugged dismissively.

A man who covers all his tracks. "What sort of animals are your specialty?"

"Snakes, spiders, you name it. The dangerous sort intrigues me. The public are fascinated by them."

"What do you do with animals when it gets cold?"

The man looked at him as if he was dense. "Don't have animals in there all the time. If I do, park it in the garage at night."

Basil shut his notebook. "So, you are connected to a store?"

"Yup. In Calgary. Name is on the truck." He shifted impatiently and yawned.

Basil snapped shut his notebook. "Alright, thanks for your time, Mr. Higginson. Please, don't go away. We may have more questions for you, alright?"

"Yeah, yeah, absolutely. Where would I go?" He chuckled then and frowned. "So, uh, what exactly happened to the girl?"

"You tell me, Higginson, then we'll both know."

There was a sudden noise that seemed to come from the basement, and Basil stared past him.

"Just something overturning its cage," Higginson shifted, tugging at his ear.

Walking past the truck, Basil peeked in the passenger window. Papers and garbage were strewn on the passenger seat and foot areas. On the dashboard lay a trail of nebulous crumbs, almost like droppings. Mouse droppings? For a wisp of a moment, he envisioned the cages of violence held at bay.

• • •

Basil's heart sank to his toes when he saw Felicia Treboni enter the station upon his return. The muscles in his jaw flexed. Treboni was one of those human slivers that got deep beneath the skin. The last thing he wanted was to be part of some tiresome theatrical display. Perhaps she wanted in on the autopsy. Some people were like that.

"I know this is weird," she began. "But Ian Wenkins, the suicide?"

Basil remembered. He never forgot any case he worked. Some may have been reduced to mere skeletons, but they were all there in his mind's eye: organized, cataloged.

"Well, the girl he dated belongs to the same office I work at: H.W. Accounting. Took a few days' vacation, during which time she left Ian. Okay, I figured she'd left him; Ian figured so too. But she never came back to work. She's missing. No family here in town to speak of, but this isn't like her. You need to investigate this. I'm so sure she did not leave him. I think something happened." Her eyes were wide and frantic. "Look, I hated Ian and the way he treated her. But if she didn't leave him, *something* must have happened!" There was fear in her eyes this time, rather than the complacency she exuded only days earlier.

"Where does her family live?"

"I really don't know. The States, I think. But it's not like her."

It's not like her. A theme becoming strangely familiar. As a policeman, it was his job to look for patterns between cases or inconsistencies in a person's behavior, including missing persons. Behavior out of the ordinary could very well be chalked up to a simple reason, but it could also send alarm bells ringing like they were now.

Janey was missing, and now Britney, and not to forget, Lola and Birdie, and who knew how many others. As much as Treboni irritated him, he could not ignore the tragic picture that was forming.

Was it possible idyllic, small-town Twin Coulees was sheltering a killer? There was one glaring fact Basil could not deny: part of the equation was missing. There were no bodies, at least not evident.

Suddenly, an image of the Rat and the unconcealed dislike in his eyes as he spoke with fervor of the "prostitute problem" popped up in his mind, and he remembered the slinking form in the dead of night. What exactly had he been doing there in the seedy part of town?

• • •

Nora

Nora set the table with trembling hands, thankful the kitchen was not in view of the living room window. The milk jug shook, and the plates slid roughly out of slippery hands, clattering onto the table.

She heard the roar of the cab's motor. Then silence, followed by the slamming of a door. Reg was home.

She hoped he would be proud of her willingness to finally step out of her shell; perhaps something could yet be salvaged. She was like a morning glory dying the same day it bloomed.

He breezed into the house with a whistle. "Hi, sweetheart!" He pecked her on the cheek. "Smells good!"

"Sorry, the lasagna is a bit burnt on the edges. I just lost track of time."

He waved his hand dismissively. "It will still taste good."

"Why was it a good day?"

"The meeting at the town hall. Ratford is the greatest orator I've ever known. Talk about passion and a good sense of judgment. You really missed out – excitement, hope, a breath of fresh air! The pinnacle of history in the making."

She wished she had. "He doesn't quite like the streetwalkers, does he?"

Reg looked at her with incredulity. "*Like* is too weak a word. And why should he? They drag our town down."

"Yes, he was fervent, I will give him that. But a bit, I don't know, angry. No, more than that, spiteful." She knocked over a glass of milk. "Oh, sorry, so clumsy!"

Reg handed her a damp rag. "Fervent? What do you mean?"

"He seems to hate more than their actions, which would be understandable; he hates *them*. I was there." Silence stretched out between the two of them as Reg carefully weighed her words.

"In spirit, right?"

"No."

"You ventured out of the house?"

"I did. I decided I needed to, you know, come to terms with my new appearance. To stop living my life as a prisoner."

"That's great; that's really great!" Then with a nervous smile, "Just don't overdo it. One step at a time, okay?" He stepped closer to her and tugged gently on a tendril of her hair. "Had I known, I'd have taken you, honey."

"I kind of decided last minute. A quick gathering of what courage I had before it was gone again."

And it was gone now.

He took her hand. "You seem skittish like a newly born colt, Nora."

"I'm alright. It just was a big step."

Reg nodded. Nora dropped herself onto one of the chairs. He started cutting up the garlic bread. His calloused hands worked rhythmically, but there was a slight tremor to the wrist. He wiped his hands on the rag and then took the lasagna to the table. "It will get easier with time. Like I said, one step at a time." He looked searchingly into her face.

"I know, I know." Fingernails dug into her palms.

"I'm sorry, my little bird. It's a cruel world out there." He was quieter than usual during the meal.

Nora wept inside.

DAY 32

Nora

Mother stands in front of her, a beautiful smile on her face. Her silky fingers trace Nora's misshapen face.

"Why did Father hurt me? Why, Mother?" Mother just smiles and strokes her face.

Rani and Amir are together in the background in a deep embrace. "Aynoor!" They wave happily. *Rani and Amir – together?*

"For you." Mother hands her a little white box – so white, it shines.

Clumsy fingers undo the wrapping paper, and a little lid pops off the box. She looks inside. A small bottle sits there. She reaches for it, yet somehow knows she shouldn't. Suddenly, it grows tentacles and grabs her, pulling her in. Fingers swarm around her, reaching, grabbing. Then, a man wearing a black hood appears. She ducks: "Stop! Stop!"

Half-awake then, she finds herself part-ways out of bed, her hands grabbing for a bowl of knick-knacks on her bedside table. She gropes, slightly confused, and then, with a crash, knocks the bowl off.

• • •

Fully awake then, she sat up. What had she been searching for? Blinking, she spied the luminous digits of her alarm clock: 5:00. Why was she in bed so early?

Then she remembered. A splitting headache had sent her to bed late that afternoon. Pulling herself fully back into bed, she lay, heart thumping. For most people, waking up provided relief and rendered the dream impotent. But the reality of her life was not bound by the borders of her nightmares; it was fluid, with the only exception that in the dark abyss of night, his voice sounded clearer, his face so recognizable, his threats so near, as if he were whispering menacingly in her ear.

Shivering, she stretched her feet to Reg's side but found it empty and cold. *Get a grip, Nora!* Of course, he wouldn't be sleeping now. Besides, he was gone. He'd left the evening before on a two-day cab convention in Calgary. She sighed as she remembered how she'd clung to him. *Don't leave me here with this madman!* she'd thought in desperation.

She hadn't wanted to tell him. It would make it more real. But even more, he didn't need a wife falling to pieces every time.

Now, here she lay. With some madman lurking in the shadows outside, perhaps watching for her at this very moment, ready to strike.

The melodic chime of the doorbell interrupted her thoughts. She sat up, one hand on the coverlet, the other on the mattress.

There it was again. She could hide. But where? Then she stopped short. This was ridiculous. First a prisoner in her own house, and now in hiding? No. She had to see who she was dealing with – salvage some sort of control.

She slipped out of bed and tiptoed to the hallway. She waited a moment and then crept to the door.

The floorboard creaked. She stopped. It was quiet. She dropped to the floor before she fell and crawled the rest of the way to the door, where she pressed her curled body against it. Her hand left a wet handprint against the faded wood. She rose and gripped the lock.

The chime sounded for the third time. Her fingers felt numb and stiff from holding the lock in place.

It had to be the hooded man. There were only a few inches of wood between them. That and a measly lock. No deadbolt even. No kickplate. The door would be a poor contender for any swift kick. Could he hear her breathing? She exhaled. Slowly, she shifted her weight until she stood on her tiptoes to look through the spy hole. She squeezed her eyes closed. Soon, they would be face to face.

The ticking of her watch sounded loud in her ear. Muscles were hardened against the next chime. She slowly opened her eyes. There was no one there. Muscles untwisted.

She slid to the floor. Armpits itched with sweat. That was too close – way too close. Was he toying with her? Had it really been him? Maybe – just maybe – it was a prankster.

She sat, back resting heavily against the door, when she heard a soft clatter above her. She watched the brass lip of the mail slot lift, and a white envelope slowly emerge from its mouth like a growing white tongue. With a soft whoosh, it fell to the floor, inches from where she sat: a small, square letter. She closed her eyes. There was no noise, no departing footsteps. Had he been there all along? Hiding just out of line of the peephole? Was he gone?

Her hand shot out for the envelope. Clumsy fingers ripped it open. A small, folded paper dropped out onto her lap. Carefully, as if it were a dangerous substance, she unfolded it. Angry letters jumped out at her: **ADULTERESS**.

With a strangled cry, she leapt to her feet. She nearly tripped. Her breath came in and out in gulps. The ground started to sway. The phone. She half-ran, then stumbled. The sear of a carpet burn on her knee faintly registered, but all she could think of was getting to the phone. She reached for it wildly. The receiver slipped from her fingers and thudded against the floor.

"No!"

She reached for it again and then pulled back her hand. They would question her, rip open the painful memories of her attack. Scrutinize her face.

She charged for the back door – she had to get out!

The keys. She fumbled with the key rack. Feeling for the distinct square souvenir of Reg's keys, she knocked the other keys off. They fell to the floor. Then she found them.

Leaning against the door, she prayed for help. Carefully, she crept the door open. Coldness and blackness engulfed her. A few raindrops made her flinch.

Suddenly, she remembered the meeting. She'd heard the new cop in town talking to his partner. Tall, red-haired man. What had he said? He lived at Number 15, Wilson Drive? He didn't know her; maybe he would believe her.

She lurked in the shadows. She needed the courage to make a dash for the garage. Suddenly, she ran but bumped into something hard. She let out a terrified yelp then realized what it was. Just a fence post. A torrent of rain fell in powerful sheets, soaking her quickly to the bone. Half tripping, half falling, she made it to the car.

The garage door lifted slowly. Numb hands yanked the steering wheel. The engine roared to life. Like a madwoman, she plowed through growing puddles.

She saw it then. A familiar cab – Reg?

But it was just the same color: gray. It turned onto Prince Avenue.

Her heart sank.

• • •

Arizona

Arizona leaned against the counter, chewing her fingernails and listening to the weather report. She was ready to put Malcolm to bed and hoped he would fall asleep quickly.

Then she heard the banging. At first, all she could see out the living room window was the rain and moving shadows. The wind had picked up slowly that afternoon, but now it was howling, whipping around garbage cans, and severing the young limbs of nearby trees. The road looked like it was submerged under a small flood of water.

Anxiously, she picked up Malcolm and peered closer through the window. The fury of lightning unveiled a barrage of gunmetal clouds waiting to strike. She paced back and forth, talking calmly to Malcolm, who sat on her hip, his little fingers gripping her shirtsleeves.

Suddenly, the lights flickered.

Where had she put the candles and matches? In a few moments, they would be plunged into darkness.

She reached for the phone to call Melody. There was no dial tone. The phone lines were down. Not another flood! She thought back to the flood that destroyed High River only recently.

She was all alone with Malcolm. If motherhood was frightening in many ways, this was one of them. Now she had someone who depended solely on her. Perhaps if they both went to bed and slept, they would miss the worst of it. Albertan weather changed frequently. There was no sense in watching it and increasing one's dread. Taking Malcolm by the hand, she led him to bed. Trying to keep her voice even, she read him a short story and tucked him in. Surprisingly, he did not resist.

Walking into her kitchen, she fiddled with the kettle. A hot cup of chamomile tea would certainly calm her frazzled nerves.

It was just as she grabbed a cup and reached for the kettle that she saw it — a pale face pressed against the glass. Her hand shot to her mouth. The face seemed to melt with the rain dripping down the window, and she was unable to pull her gaze away. She looked closer. But it wasn't a normal face; rather something deformed – alien-like. She bit her fist to prevent a scream.

She finally tore her gaze away. For only a second. But when she looked up, the face was gone. The doors. Had she locked them?

Her feet refused to budge. But only for a second. She sprinted for the front door and threw the latch. She gazed around her imagination in overdrive, half expecting an intruder to crawl through some tiny opening.

The windows! They aren't locked!

Suddenly, she had to get Malcolm and herself out.

• • •

Marc

Marc blinked, his fingers groping in the dirt beside him. Dirt. That smell. Memory came flooding back.

He'd been out of it for a while and then sleeping off and on for long stretches as he fought waves of dizziness and nausea. He ran his leathery tongue over parched gums. His gut cramped. He felt his pocket for the fruit leather that had been in there since before his kidnapping, and which he'd been rationing in this dungeon.

The wrapper was empty.

Slowly, he turned onto all fours and then squeezed his eyes. Pain exploded through his left shoulder. He sat still for a moment, allowing it to slowly fade.

A sudden flash of lightning illuminated the window opposite him. He immediately crawled toward it, pretending there were no half-rotting bodies around him, pretending he was not embroiled in something heinous.

Lightning cracked again, filling the window with a flash. He glimpsed the torrent outside.

He paused when needed, to allow the dizziness to pass. Somewhere in his mind, he registered hard bones – a femur here, a skull there – interspersed with dank earth – but he pushed on.

Finally, his outstretched hand felt the cold, cement wall. There was maybe a foot between him and freedom.

He watched, mesmerized, as large drops of water slid down the grimy glass. The heavens were unleashing a heavy blow, but he couldn't wait to feel the wet against his skin. Rapidly forming puddles seemed to dance with agitated joy, overfed by the torrential rain.

He lifted his right arm and flexed his wrist. His fist exploded with red-hot pain, but he had not hit hard enough to break the glass.

When lightning momentarily spilled light into the room once again, he spied a chunk of concrete against the wall. He reached for it. He swung his arm back, ignoring the throb in his wrist, and threw the concrete slab at the window with all the force his weak body possessed. Shards of glass rained around him just as a flash of lightning cracked across the sky.

He lay there, cool air – fresh air – stroking his face.

Freedom lay beyond the shards of glass.

He could almost taste it.

• • •

Basil

His feet propped up on the cracked leather ottoman – one of his recent acquisitions – Basil stared at the whiskey bottle in front of him.

Just one more sip, he promised himself.

Famous last words. Empty promises. Every day again.

He rubbed his face as if trying to erase the fatigue that weighed heavily on his eyelids. It started as it always did, that niggling sensation at the base of his skull, throbbing in intensity, pulsing in rhythm to the beat of his heart, and then spreading over his scalp; iron fingers that pushed and pulled as if his head had the malleability of clay.

Outside, the wind moaned. Rain fell in steady sheets. Basil listened to the news anchor on his phone: "First terrible storm of the year; flash flooding expected and winds reaching speeds of up to one hundred kilometers an hour." It was strongly advised that people stay inside and off the roads. Those on the roads were recommended to pull to the side and wait out the storm. Emergency crews had their work cut out for them.

Shaking his head, he thought back to the High River flood of 2013. Nature had spoken with destructive vengeance then. Thousands were left displaced and homeless in a catastrophic flooding considered the worst in Albertan history.

But he was inside, sheltered from nature's blows. He picked up the bottle that beckoned for him. His long fingers ran over the length of the cool glass. Liquid courage. You can stop whenever you want to, it counseled.

He poured a small amount.

He looked out the dark windows. The burning liquid touched his tongue and slid readily down his throat. He felt the heat in his belly once again.

Plopping into his chair, he closed his eyes.

Then, somewhere in the distance, a voice, pleading and begging for help. It sounded so far away, and was soon joined by others: "Help, help!" He stood up and tried to run towards the voices, but his feet were lead. Suddenly, the images of three women stared at him with pleading eyes: Britney, Janey, Stacey, and then a crowd of faces in deep anguish swam into view. Hundreds of hands reached desperately for him, their voices screaming in terror. He tried to reach out for them, but his fingers fell just too short. It was like a whirlwind sucking them away. He tried to reach further, but the invisible force kept a tight hold on them.

"Please?"

It was one voice again, this time clearer. He sat up, rubbing his eyes. He looked around him. He must have fallen asleep.

He sank back into the chair, blinked, and then scrambled to his feet.

"Who are you?"

• • •

Arizona

She saw the shock on the man's face. "Constable Andrews? I'm sorry, your door wasn't locked. Can we please stay here till the storm passes?"

The tall man with red-tinged eyes nodded. "Um, sure!" His pale face sported fine stubble as if he had not shaved for a while. Arizona's hair dripped. Her teeth were chattering, and her back was soaked. Malcolm, thankfully, was huddled under a small blanket, at least dry.

"I, there was a – " Her lungs strained to catch each breath. Beneath her canvas shoes, a small puddle was forming.

"Wait here," he ordered. He returned with an extra-large towel, which he draped over her trembling shoulders. "Let me get you something to warm up." He gestured at Malcolm. "Is he okay?"

"I kept him dry. His name is Malcolm. Can I just set him down on your couch?"

"Yes, of course, go right ahead." He moved some laundry and papers over.

"I woke him. He was just sleeping." Arizona softly stroked his face and wrapped his blanket tight around him. His large eyes flitted from Arizona to the tall man, and his little fingers worked their way from the blanket and found his ear lobe.

The man reached for a glass from the cupboard, took a bottle from his counter, poured it quickly, and pressed the drink into her hand, his brows knotted in concern. "Drink this; it will warm you up quickly."

She nodded her thanks and drank. She winced as the liquid went down. Not one for hard liquor, Arizona nevertheless felt its warmth in her belly and began to feel half-human again.

"Thanks!" she finally managed. "I'm so sorry to barge in like this. There was a face at my window. And the phone lines are down. I guess I just felt terribly isolated."

The man peered outside. "That's understandable. No need to apologize." The rain had suddenly stopped, but the wind was still a force to contend with. Brief bouts of lightning lit up the prairie sky, but other than that, it was black darkness punctuated by streetlights that shone like little stars. "Terrible night to be out for anyone. Look, you're still shivering." He seemed to be feeling for words. It was apparently not every day that a woman was in his house. "I don't have clothes that fit you, but there is a robe in the bathroom. Go put it on. You'll get the chills this way." The red hue of embarrassment began staining his pale cheeks.

She looked at Malcolm, but he did not make a peep. In the bathroom, she felt mortified as well. Here she was, stripping down to her undies in this strange man's house. She heard his mobile ringing and a muffled voice. Snuggling deep into his terry robe, and feeling quite weird with this whole situation, she noticed a uniform hanging from the bathroom hook.

Of course, he was a police officer. She knew that. For a brief, irrational moment, her wrongs flitted across her mind. *Okay, seriously, get a grip!*

The man did not look like a cop, even when she'd met him at the station wearing his uniform. Tall, red-haired, with reddish eyes. And that smell of alcohol. He had been drinking. For a moment, it slightly jarred her sense of equilibrium; cops were good people. They were law-abiding, tee-totalling, completely honest and upstanding citizens, even off-shift.

Okay, but they are human, too, she reminded herself.

The place was scattered with take-out containers and whatnot. She quietly snuck open his bathroom drawer, feeling a bit guilty for prying into the life of another. Irish Spring soap bar, nail clipper, ear plugs, Q-Tip...a ring? She gently turned the simple gold band in her hands and then placed it back.

Divorced, separated? Maybe she left because he drinks. Some people didn't value relationships. She was starting to feel angry. What if he hit her? Not all cops were on the straight and narrow.

She heard cupboards banging softly in the kitchen, and she pulled her hand out of the drawer like a child caught stealing in a candy store. No one could see her, but she turned a deep shade of red nonetheless. Here she was poking around in someone's things and judging them when she didn't know a thing about them. *I am so pathetic!* she thought.

She emerged slowly from the bathroom, suddenly even more self-conscious. Wait until she told Melody.

"Making coffee," the man called from the kitchenette. He chuckled. "I've got a pair of eyes keeping tabs on me." He gestured towards Malcolm. He appeared with a freshly brewed cup. "Phone lines may be down, but my cellphone is working fine. Apparently, I won a million dollars, two cruises, and a partridge in a pear tree. Uh, sorry, this place." His hand half-heartedly swept the room. "My housekeeping is not up to par, I know."

She laughed nervously and sank onto the couch next to Malcolm, pulling his little body against her. "My cell is broken; perfect timing, huh?"

Constable Andrews smiled. "Murphy's law. Off-duty now." He plopped into his recliner and gestured for her to sit down on the faded loveseat. His dark eyes pinned her to the couch. It felt as if an invisible hand was pushing her against the fabric. He was not physically imposing, but his eyes more than made up for this. They were brooding eyes that seemed to have lost their sparkle, if they ever had any. There was something there, something Arizona could not articulate readily. And yet, she felt this fortress of a man was cracking. Beneath his calm, amiable manner was a crumbling wall of emotion. Only someone experiencing the same could really observe this in another. It was there in his brooding mannerisms. It was his weak spot. If she were the enemy, this is where she would direct her attack.

For a fleeting moment, it all felt wrong. Two emotionally vulnerable people in a house together, but only for a moment. The frisson of panic was still there.

Suddenly, the lights flickered again and died.

She pressed her body deep into the couch and pulled Malcolm close to her.

"I've got candles, left by the last renter, I presume."

A few moments later, she watched him over the violent trembling of the flame. Shadows slid down the wall as thick drops of rain continued to pummel the windows.

"It's actually Basil," his voice intruded on her thoughts.

"Beg pardon?"

"My first name is Basil. You can call me that instead of constable, if you like. We're neighbors, after all."

"Basil?"

He smiled then and glanced at the bottle of whiskey on the counter. Tearing his gaze away, he asked: "Ever been to Moscow?"

She shook her head.

"It's the home of the famous St. Basil's Cathedral. Place consists of nine chapels, each epitomizing a successful battle. It's a grand and vibrant landmark."

"Is this what you're named after?"

"Nope. My mother was just partial to the name."

"Oh." That was anti-climactic. "Ever been to Moscow?"

He laughed. She suspected he rarely let it out. "No. I have this description memorized from one of the books my father left me. I think it sounds more canned each time I use it. What about you?"

"Oh, Arizona Stuart." *Okay, now you're a bumbling idiot on top of everything else.*

"Arizona. Arizona," he repeated slowly. It was not a question. His voice was softer now as he rolled the name along his tongue, feeling its nuances. "Singular. There must be an interesting story to go with it," he prompted.

This time, it was her turn to laugh. "Sorry, no more dramatic than yours."

"I think we've both had a mother partial to unique names."

She found his smile to be personable and warm and felt herself relax. Should she ask him about Marc? Her mouth felt suddenly dry. Maybe he would show more interest, more enthusiasm, than Constable Kennedy. Maybe he had an idea, some fresh take on it all.

"I'm sorry about your husband," he said.

She murmured her thanks. Here he was, making the perfect segue for her. "I don't understand it all," she began.

He nodded his understanding.

She moistened her lips. *Can you look into it for me?* she wanted to ask. But then lights exploded, making her jump. Blinking digits. The microwave, the stove.

Basil's body stiffened as he glanced at the living room window. The apparition, the melting face in the window, was back. Without a word, he covered the distance to the door in a few strides and flung it open. The strange face had disappeared again, but not before Arizona had noticed its panicked stare. She found herself trembling all over. "Not sure what to make of it," Basil said, looking puzzled.

"Did you see the face? So strange, almost like someone wearing a mask."

"Not closely; it was too quick. I just hope it's not someone in distress themselves." He turned to her. "Would you like me to walk you back?" The rain had stopped, and the wind had noticeably died down.

"In this?" She looked down self-consciously.

"Unless you want your wet things on again?" he responded pragmatically. "It's dark out, and only a short distance to your door. You can return the robe whenever."

She collected her clothing, thanked him profusely, and scooped up Malcolm. Drowning in Basil's large robe, and Malcolm huddled in his blanket in her arms, she half walked, half ran to her front door as if the deformed face was nipping at her heels.

• • •

Marc

He felt blood dripping from his wrist. He must have cut it on a shard of glass. Looking around, he searched for something to bandage it. Spying a hole in his shirt, he dug his fingers into it and ripped a section off. Then he wrapped it tightly around his bleeding wrist.

It throbbed, but the blood would soon stop. The laceration did not appear too deep.

He lay back again, watching the rain pelt the ground. Bolts of lightning snapped across the sky like a fireworks display.

A few times, he reached his good hand out the window and savored the cold air. As soon as the storm subsided, he would make his breakaway.

Soon, he promised himself, *soon*.

• • •

Nora

Nora sat back in defeat against the cracked leather seat, soaked to the bone. She was exhausted from running, her hands red and sore from knocking and banging against windows.

A normal person would have knocked on a door or rung a doorbell. But not her. Oh no, like a chicken without a head, once she'd spotted the figure in the first lit window, she'd made a mad dash for it, banging and knocking like someone possessed.

Shadowy figures moved behind curtains like a silhouette of slow-dancing puppets.

Was it Number 14? No, wait, Number 15? When no one was forthcoming with the first window, she moved to the next one. Just her and the mad torrent of rain, her cries muted by the thunder.

But no one came. Of course not. She was an idiot!

The car's heater was blasting in her face, but soothing warmth snaked around her. Her heart was still galloping at full speed, and she angrily berated herself. *You are such a coward; you badly frightened one woman and then bolted like some wimpy raccoon!*

She was a fool. Tears stung her eyes. Now she was out in the middle of the night in a violent rainstorm, no closer to any help. The car rocked like a ship on gale-tossed seas, rain like angry fists pummeling the windshield and bathing the small car in a steady deluge of water.

In that moment, she felt her prison extended beyond her home. She was separated from everything and everyone.

She craved the warm sanctuary of her home. But where was the stranger? Had he left when she did? Was he waiting for her return? She pressed her head against the warm leather of the steering wheel, her skin itching terribly from the damp clothing, her teeth chattering.

Maybe he was waiting for her in the shadows, the hunter waiting for his prey. Tears fell unheeded down her cheeks. She could not remember the last time she felt so scared and alone.

Pressing her body into the seat, she pulled up her legs. Her eyelids felt so heavy, and the constant heat felt so good. Slowly, the chattering stopped as the blast of heat thawed her chilled limbs.

• • •

She jerked awake at 3 am, her heart racing once again.

What was she doing in her car? And then it hit her: she'd fallen asleep. Slowly, painfully, she stretched her stiff legs, muscles screaming in agony. Damp clothing was plastered to her skin, making it itch terribly as if hundreds of insects were crawling underneath. There was a relentless pounding sensation above her eyes from the continual blast of warm air into her face.

She rubbed dry, burning eyes and peered into the blackness outside her window. The rainstorm had finally abated.

Home! I need to get home! She craved a hot shower and a dry, warm bed.

Slowly, in the wee hours of the morning, she crept home. Alone. Defeated. Like a dog with its tail between its legs.

DAY 33

Basil

Basil found Wally at the local Timmy's, enjoying an extra-large coffee, his hulk dominating a small chair strategically placed against the north wall.

The man has definite presence, Basil thought, *and dark eyes that can pin a perp to the wall just like that.* But there was something else. The way he held himself in moments of brooding. A darkness, when no one was looking, that lurked behind his ready smile.

He smiled when he saw Basil and flipped him the ripped edge of his paper cup. "Please *pay* again," he intoned with humor. Tim Horton's roll-up-the-rim cups sometimes won a free coffee or donut, or rarely, a new car. Basil had only ever received ones with 'please play again.' This rim was blank, though.

"Nice try," Basil chuckled. "That's a spring promotion."

"Glad that storm is over," Wally mused.

Basil looked at the still-gray sky outside and nodded. Suddenly, he saw Exotic Animals lurch around the corner.

I keep it locked, resounded in his head. Something about it bothered him like a throbbing tooth. "Did you read the preliminary autopsy results on Adele Laramie?" he asked.

The smile slid from Wally's face. "Yeah, I did. Briefly." His voice was guarded and even.

Basil watched him closely. Wally's thick fingers played with his cup. He cleared his throat. He wanted to ask Wally how he knew Adele, but there suddenly seemed to be an invisible line he would be crossing.

Wally tapped his fingers on the table and sighed. "Results are inconclusive, though."

The "inconclusive" results left Basil stymied. "Are you not even slightly curious about their findings?"

"Pathologists are like bloodhounds when an otherwise healthy person dies. Even if it is like looking for a needle in a haystack, they are tenacious to find that needle. Besides, was there anything on the report that indicated what she may have died from?"

Basil nodded. "Well, she was fifty-five years of age. It mentions the natural aging of the body; some arterial plaque build-up, a large fluid-filled cyst on the kidney, slight graying of the lung tissue as evident in a casual smoker, but nothing that clearly or definitively points to a direct cause."

"Natural causes, Basil, just like I thought." He waved his hand dismissively. Or rather, he'd been hoping. "I believe they say about two to five percent of autopsies are inconclusive." He obviously did not want to entertain the possibility of murder.

Basil frowned. Something was off. There was a certain incongruity between the superficiality of the cut and the finality of death. It jarred him. Six to nine inches of careful precision. Clean and exact. Methodical and intended.

Wait a minute, where did that come from? How did he know? But there was this feeling. It didn't come out of thin air. The thought hadn't dropped suddenly into the deep recesses of his brain. Ever since the scene of death, the incision bothered him. And intrigued him. Even the way she'd lain there, arms spread out, shirt and hoody hiked up. There was something so staged about it all. Forensics would have noted this, but if there was no cause of death evident...

Wally rubbed his face. "I think that we sometimes connect dots that shouldn't be connected."

Is that it? he wondered. *Am I just trying to distract myself?* He thought of Myra.

"Your mind has no brakes. Sometimes we never discover the exact reason. But in this case, murder isn't one of them." His voice suddenly had an edge to it; a warning to back off. Wally parked his elbows on the table and folded his large hands in contemplation, his dark eyes piercing. "Sometimes, we need to be satisfied with an: 'I don't have the foggiest idea.' Who would have killed her, and why? She basically kept to herself, other than enjoying her yearly escapades to the tropics. Let's say she was murdered. *Hypothetically.* It would have to be very carefully planned, as the scene showed no signs of foul play, and the body bore no signs of homicide, either."

"But the cut – "

"Superficial and clean. No evidence of blood. Do you see a perp cutting just the top layer of her skin and then cleaning the cut afterwards? Besides, it was already healing." The tone was becoming accusing.

He's building armor around himself – losing his objectivity. Or is he? "Well, no – "

You are clutching at straws, chasing shadows. Do you see a perp cutting her and then changing his mind as to an alternative? And the report mentions the cut being made pre-mortem, so no evidence of overkill or savagery either. There are myriad reasons for such a cut, particularly for one hardly deemed serious. The cut didn't kill her. No one killed her. End of story. It was her time to go."

Basil knew he could be a persistent bugger, but he also knew when to back off. Why did he want him to leave well enough alone? Had he known her? If so, how well?

A silence hung between the two men. Staff Sergeant Michaelson's voice seemed to whisper in Basil's ear: *Listen to what the scene is telling you. Unclutter your mind and look again. Free it of all thoughts; be present, be mindful.* It was a skill he drilled into his men. There were so many unanswered questions, missing women, Laramie's inexplicable death, the plight of the streetwalkers.

Wally refused to categorize Laramie's death as anything remotely close to homicide; Basil felt the need to examine his current cases with absolute fastidiousness. Was he chasing shadows? Possibly. But who'd be the women's collective voice? Who'd keep going until there were answers?

Besides, his mind needed to be kept busy. The guilt needed to be quieted. It was tethered to him like a heavy weight. Sometimes the rope was slack, other times taut, but it was *always* there. And the only thing worse than its painful presence was the need to keep it hidden.

• • •

Back at the detachment, hoping to catch up on paperwork, Basil was beyond astonished to see the familiar face of the cabbie he'd rescued. He noticed the man had a slight limp.

"Newest member of the Police Advisory Committee," Sharon introduced him casually. The Policy Advisory Committee of Twin Coulees was intended to relieve part of the burden of policing but also to create a working relationship between the RCMP and community. The committee's role was to provide community feedback to the detachment commander on policing and public safety matters, but also to assist in community outreach.

The cabbie smiled warmly and ceremoniously handed a heavy paper bag to Basil. "You saved my life, Constable – "

"Andrews. And there was no need to go to such lengths." He peeked into the bag and spotted a bottle of whiskey.

"Now, wait until you're off duty," the cabbie added cheekily as if sensing Basil's desire to partake of the bewitching liquid immediately. "Don't want to make an alcoholic out of you."

Everyone laughed.

"Thank you kindly, uh – " Basil had only ever known him as the cabbie.

"Reg. Reg Clarkson. And no need to thank me. You guys do a fantastic job keeping this community safe. Just glad you were there at the right place and at the right time."

Guilt tugged at Basil. He felt as if he should've visited Clarkson in the hospital or made some sort of contact with him. He'd saved this man's life. Didn't this create some sort of connection between them? "Glad to see all turned out well. Still cabbing?"

"Picked up a route delivering papers. Doing some odd jobs for people around town. A bit of maintenance for people in our community, aside from the one I already have at the newspaper office. Still driving cab part-time, but my doctor strongly suggests exercise." He shrugged with a smile. "Nice change of pace, lots to see, quite relaxing. Get to see the nooks and crannies of this town. And still get to make a dime on the side."

"Good for you," Basil said. "That was one close call. I'm certainly relieved to see you're up and at 'em again. Welcome to the advisory committee too. This joint effort between police and community is a welcome change. We've got a full plate here."

"This is a great community, and we need to look out for each other," Clarkson nodded. He paused for a moment, shifting awkwardly from one foot to another. "Say, not sure if this is something you do, but is it possible for me to go on some ride-alongs?"

"Well, I don't see why not," Basil responded. "See what policing is like from our side of the fence."

• • •

Marc

He opened his eyes to sunlight streaming into the tiny window. Cold air whipped around his face. He lifted his head and felt the throb in his wrist.

Suddenly, he remembered. The thunderstorm. The cut to his wrist. His heart picked up speed. Today was escape day! The storm was over, although the wind had only taken its drama down a few notches.

Perhaps it was morning. Or afternoon. Time was fluid and irrelevant in this dark hole. But that would end soon.

Every part of him wanted out. Now. But he cautioned himself to slow down. There was a way out now. The window was ground level and recessed into the side of the house, away from the front entrance.

He waited until the sound of a motor started and slowly faded. The man was gone. He left often, although he always came back at unpredictable times.

Now was his chance.

He'd packed mud on the window's ledge to create a soft barrier for his body to snake over. Placing his sore wrist on the new ledge and gritting his teeth, he moved in a serpentine manner over the ledge until he was outside.

For a moment, he lay there, sharp gravel cutting into his flesh.

For the first time in weeks, he was out of his prison. He lifted his body until he was sitting and turned his face to the wide expanse of sky. He drank in the fresh smell around him and smiled as the wind ran her fingers through his hair and stroked his face.

Then he saw it. Two large black bags were positioned against the house near the corner of the front side of the house.

He stared at the lumpy bags and felt a sudden emptiness in his stomach.

Food.

Moving slowly once more, he crawled to the bags.

Exhausted, his weak fingers groped at the plastic, long nails leaving jagged striations in the tough black skin. It was the barrier between life and death.

He licked his sore lips. His stomach groaned.

Suddenly, he pounced on the bags, hands like paws, slashing – tearing – as if into flesh. Tissue paper, empty bags, and food waste began to leak from the wounds. A half-empty ketchup packet tumbled onto his lap. He brought the plastic to his mouth, his tongue licking the congealed sauce.

An explosion of taste, and then pain in his salivary glands, but he continued to lick away at it like a dog.

Then he spied half a bun.

It was a kingly feast.

For a moment, he held the white bread in his mouth, feeling the rough texture. Then he swallowed a few bites.

His stomach heaved, and he felt the familiar cramping. *No more*, he told himself. *Slow down*. He'd read too many stories of malnourished people eating far more than their weak stomachs could handle.

It was then he spied the gutter. He crawled to the corroded metal pipe and placed his ulcerated lips to its edge, blinking as the sharp metal cut into his lower lip. But he ignored the pain, drinking the scant water that had pooled at its mouth.

Suddenly, he heard a motor.

The man had returned.

• • •

Nora

When Nora came home, she made a beeline for the shower. Like dull needles, the high-pressure water stabbed her back until her skin felt numb. Gradually, her muscles unclenched, and she felt herself relax for the first time in hours.

Until she entered the living room.

On the floor lay a ripped envelope. A half a meter away, a wrinkled paper. She didn't have to pick it up to know what it was.

The wind rattled the windows and played at the door. "Betrayer, betrayer," it whispered.

Mustering courage, she scooped up the papers and balled them in her fist. She carried them to the sink and dropped them into the basin. She grabbed a lighter from the drawer. She tried igniting it, but her finger slipped. She tried again. Nothing.

She wiped at the moisture forming on her brow. Her thumb stung from each attempt. Finally, on the fourth try, the red canister spit out a fiery plume. Without hesitation, she held the trembling flame to the papers, watching as it devoured her sin.

Then, just ashes. But she must not leave a trace. She ran the faucet, flushing the remains down the drain.

Reg must never know.

• • •

Marc

Marc drew his body into a compact ball, pressing himself against the side of the house. All the man had to do was turn the corner, and it was over. *Please, God, hide me.*

If he gave himself away, he would be like the corpses on the other side of the wall.

The man dawdled on the front porch for what seemed like eternity.

Suddenly, the wind, in one of her devious moods, took a bright yellow hamburger wrapper and pitched it meters from where he lay. His stomach dropped, and he squeezed his eyes closed, praying again for invisibility.

Just then, the door creaked and banged shut. Relief washed over him. His muscles slowly unglued.

Move, Stuart, move!

Beyond him, the road stretched like a ribbon of freedom. So close and yet so far.

Every part of him screamed to make a run for it.

But he knew impulsivity would kill him. He needed to regain his strength to endure his escape.

He turned then, even though every part of him rebelled against this move, and slid his body back into his grave. Peace settled over him such as he had not experienced for so long.

• • •

Basil

Basil cradled the bottle between his legs the entire short distance to his pad. His heart was beginning to race in anticipation, and the thirst was building quickly and intensely. Really, it had been building all day; it always did until it reached a fevered climax of longing that obliterated all other thoughts.

He drummed his fingers impatiently on his steering wheel. *C'mon, turn green! Why is it that when you hit one red light, you hit them all?* With his foot of lead, he careened his car into the driveway and then suddenly slammed on the brakes.

Immediately, his hand dropped to his service revolver. His front door was ajar. Someone was in his house. No wind could open a locked door.

He turned off his ignition and quietly exited the car, gently closing its door, his body on alert. He crept slowly from the vehicle, careful not to alarm the intruder. He pressed his body against the wall next to the house door and glanced at the unscathed doorknob. Someone had carefully picked the lock, leaving no scratch marks.

"Hey, Red!"

Basil jumped at the sound of the voice. Even as his heart was still beating wildly, his brain registered its warm familiarity. Paula. Globe trotter extraordinaire. "What are you doing here?"

She emerged from behind the door, all six feet of her, the crown of her head tinged with streaks of gray. Her skin hung sharply on her frame like a thin garment on a wire hanger, shoulders angular under her gray cardigan. "You know, for a police officer, you can be a total idiot." She waved about his silver door key, totally enjoying her little play of power. "I know you longer than a day. You still keep this thingy in your downspout. You are so predictable!"

"Idiot? That happens to be a pretty nifty place, considering most people don't think of it. But now that you've broadcasted it over the neighborhood with your loud mouth."

"Oh, please, Red."

Red. It'd been ages since someone had called him by that nickname. "And what's wrong with predictability? If it isn't broke, don't fix it."

He followed her into the house, questions swirling in his mind. Paula had been backpacking through Europe with some friends over the past half-year and pioneering social programs as an extension of her university work. Their contact had been minimal. And now she was here, trying to rearrange his life.

Just like when they were kids.

"I've actually been here for the past hour," Paula explained as Basil's wide eyes took in the unfamiliarity of his clean home. "You know, these disgusting things can actually be redeemed for something." She held up one of the whiskey bottles with her forefinger and thumb, wrinkling her nose in disgust. "It's called recycling."

"Paula, please. Aren't you supposed to be traveling the world or something, doing some sort of social work?"

"Charity begins at home."

He glared at her. "Charity?"

"You. My lil' brother is tightly shackled, and I've come to help."

"Oh, give it up, Paula. We're not kids anymore." She was clearly on a roll. He had to get out of his monkey suit before he could deal with her "sisterly" love. He changed into a pair of denim pants and a t-shirt and returned with a beer, plopping into his chair in defeat. "Alright, Paula, dish it up and serve it hot. Fix me." He popped the tab from his beer just as Paula plucked the can from his fingers.

"This is the twenty-first century, Basil. You don't need a crutch to get through life."

His mouth dropped open, and he looked from his empty hand to Paula as she continued to invade his home, removing take-out containers and mopping and wiping with a vengeance, the older sister in charge. Silver hair had woven itself proudly into the thick rope of hair that licked her waist. It jerked defiantly with each movement, as if it too felt frustrated with him.

"Do you mind?" he asked, finally managing to find his words.

"Look at this place, Basil." She swept her hand over the room and raised a pencil-thin brow. "A mirror image of you."

"What?"

"I *know* you, Basil. For what? Nearly four decades? Life knocks you down, and you retreat into yourself like an animal licking its wounds." She perched on the edge of a chair, and he noticed new lines spoking out from her eyes – lines that had not been there before. For a fleeting moment, it was Mother sitting there, her grayish brown braid slipping over her shoulder, wisps of hair crowning her forehead, the same gray-green eyes making him squirm. He blinked. Paula was getting older; *they* were getting older. But that bossy look of an older sister would always be there. "I heard you moved here."

"Not that bad of a place. Boxy, musty, but – "

"What happened to you, Red?"

He shook his head. "Forget it. I don't want to go there." He looked at the living room window and imagined the cold wrestling its way through as it often did. Perhaps he could re-silicone the frame.

"That Dutch stubbornness. C'mon, Red, I'm your sister, not your enemy."

He turned back to her and shifted. "She walked out on me."

"Oh, Red, why didn't you tell me?" There was a glimmer of pain in her blue eyes. He was still the little orphan brother she felt she needed to mother.

"Wanted to get my bearings first." He rubbed his face. "Look, she couldn't fix me, couldn't align me with her ideals, and threw in the towel. That's all there is." He sat up and looked towards the kitchen.

She leaned forward. "You don't need any of that stuff. Look, Red, that can't be all. Talk to me. It's eating you alive."

He flinched. "I don't know what you're talking about. I don't need a therapist." His jaw ached, and a menacing headache spread like a band over his forehead.

She nodded and sank back against the cushions. "Alright, I'm sorry. You know me. How's your new job?"

He eyed her for a moment longer, then sat back and crossed his legs. "It's good, actually. I kinda like the small-town feel. It's less busy than Calgary, of course. But – "

"But what?"

He chewed his lip. "Remember the *Highway of Tears*? Those murdered women in northern B.C.?"

She nodded. "Yeah, I do. Powerful documentary. Awful. Those poor women. Why?"

He shrugged. "We might have a missing women problem."

Paula sat up straight. "Murdered?"

He held up his hand. "Okay, I'm not sure what is going on." He relayed Stacey's accusation, careful not to divulge confidential information. He relayed the meeting with Mayor Ratford and his extreme approach.

Paula frowned. "That new mayor of yours sounds like a fanatic. Going about it all wrong."

Basil nodded. "Yeah, that's my feeling too."

"Treating them like a disease is not going to solve anything. Understanding the root problems would be a better place to start. So many enter it because of poverty, poor mental health, their inability to find work to support their family – well, the list is endless. This us-versus-them moralizing creates a dichotomy that no matter what 'side' you are on, nothing gets solved."

Stacey's defeated face swam into view again.

"This is good, actually," Paula added.

"What do you mean?"

"You dealing with this. It'll give you focus. You can fight for the women, Red."

He stared at her.

"The little brother I know wouldn't settle for anything less than justice for all. Besides, it'll be a good distraction from everything else going on in your life.

His back stiffened slightly.

She played with the end of her braid. "I think, Red, your drinking is a convenient scapegoat."

"What do you mean?" he demanded, sitting up. "I drink. So? It doesn't affect my professional life."

"Even so."

"Ok, Paula, spit it out."

"It's a front for much deeper pain."

He stood up. "Look, this is just psycho-babble – "

"Her eyes – "

He felt the familiar buzz at the base of his neck.

" – Jules' eyes."

"No more." His voice stretched taut like a rubber band.

"Basil – "

"I mentioned it once, after – " He ran his hand through his hair. "I told her about this nightmare of sorts I had." He plopped back into his chair and drew in a deep sigh. "She fixates on things, she – never mind." He picked up an open book beside him, shut it, and tossed it on the table again. On the counter sat his bottle of whiskey. Two – three meters away. His skin tingled.

"I think those eyes have a different meaning for you," she said quietly.

He rubbed his face with both hands. "I don't want to go there."

"I know. But you have to, even if it's painful. You must make peace with yourself, Red. I can help you – I *want* to help you."

His legs twitched.

She stood up and walked to the window. For a moment, she said nothing. Then: "That aspen tree looks scraggly. Remember climbing our apple tree?"

"Yep." He remembered their backyard scattered with rotting apples, the aging limbs of the giant tree perfect for climbing, the long grass that was never mowed, ideal for playing hide-and-seek and other adventures, the long, rotting fence fun and daring to climb. He saw Paula, arms outstretched, practicing her balance walk.

Those were the days. A neglected yard. A child's paradise.

She turned back to him. "I don't want you turning out like Dad."

The shutter that had inched open slammed shut.

Dad. His spine was suddenly rigid. "I'm not like him. I don't hit the bottle like he did. Wasted and abusive. I'm nothing," he bit off through clenched teeth, "like Carl Andreas."

Paula looked pained; she knew she had gone too far. "Basil, I – "

"Leave it!"

"C'mon, Red. I am your sister. I'm all you've got. Who is going to steer you in the right direction and kick you in the butt occasionally, huh?" She desperately tried to turn the conversation around by infusing it with some humor.

But it was a bit too little, too late. Anger coursing through him, he attacked the bottle with a vengeance. It was either Paula or the bottle. Downing a few large swigs, enough to wet his palate and burn into his stomach, he stormed out.

"Basil! I just got here. Please, be reasonable!"

Reasonable? Without it really registering, he'd grabbed his bike and found himself pedaling furiously down Main Street like a man desperately trying to outrace something.

DAY 34

Basil

The next day, every nerve was still on high alert. His fists ached. The pent-up rage unsettled him. Thankfully, Paula was sleeping when he got home and sleeping when he left.

A call had come in of a drunk stumbling along Main Street, shouting obscenities and causing a public disturbance. "2-Alpha-23," the radio chirped.

Basil picked up the mike and held it close to his lips. "2-Alpha-23."

"Two-three, clear for a call?"

"ten-four."

No sooner had dispatch relayed all the necessary information than Basil knew instantly who she was referring to: Mulligan. Some guys like the inside of a holding cell so much they feel the need to revisit the place frequently. Mully was one of those harmless drunks who infrequently gave in to violence, but nothing over the top. Normally, it ended up being a situation where he was read his rights, cuffed, and hauled off to detachment to dry up.

Today, Basil was irritated more than usual. Calls were being stacked, and it was only noon.

He saw Mully stumbling along. Driving his cruiser a few meters ahead to gain distance on him, he parked. From his rear-view mirror, he noticed Mully coming closer. Stepping out of the car, he easily covered the distance until he stood square in front of him. Crazy-eyes Mulligan, clothes smelling like rotting flesh.

"Ain't doin' nuthin' wrong, Mister Policeman," he drawled jauntily.

"You're drunk and causing a scene, Mully," Basil objected.

He laughed and swung his right arm aimlessly, his left clutching a whiskey bottle. Suddenly, he tripped on a rock and fell. The whiskey bottle hit the pavement and broke, spilling amber liquid everywhere.

For a moment, both looked at the dwindling liquid in alarm; Mully's precious stash of booze was quickly being absorbed into the crevices of the sidewalk. Basil, already sporting a headache, gazed longingly at the disappearing alcohol. "Git up!"

"I can't," Mully whined like an overgrown toddler.

"Do I need to take out my crayons and draw you a picture?" Basil snapped.

Mully paid no attention to the escalating anger in Basil's voice and laughed. "Yoush funny, man, yoush funny!"

"I'm not playing games here, Mully!" He wanted to throttle the man.

Mully dipped his finger in the small puddle of whiskey that remained and held it up tantalizingly. "Want some? Dis is good stuff."

Oh yes, he wanted it! The entire bottle. And now the precious liquid was gone. With his head busting and everything else colliding together in his brain, seeing Mully sitting there taunting him was the pebble that caved in the house. Pulling Mully by his arm, he dragged the man upwards and stood him on his feet.

Mully glared at him. "You can't touch me!"

"You're nothing but a filthy drunk!"

"It takes one to call one."

Basil blinked.

"You wanna have some of the good stuff, hey? You no better than me, huh? Yoush got a spiffy uniform. All sparklin' like some hero, huh? Underneath, you just like me! I see the look in yer eyes. You wantin' that stuff bad as I do. A rose by any other name is still a rose."

Basil saw red. In one instant, his long fingers grasped Mully's neck in a tight vise. He could feel the jugular straining against his thumb. Mully's eyes locked with his. *Go ahead*, they taunted, *I dare you to!*

In that moment, he knew. He could kill this man.

Yet, somewhere in the fuzzy distance, a voice warned him not to cross the line. His toes were already over. His body ached to squeeze the man's neck harder. Trembling fingers ached to put all that anger, frustration, and pain into that squeeze. Black eyes cajoled and jeered at him, seducing him to cross over.

Would he have? He would never know.

"Constable Andrews!" Wally's rich baritone sliced the deadly silence, effectively severing the dangerous magnetism of the man's eyes. The death grip released, and Mully fell to the ground, gasping for air.

In that gap of time, he hadn't heard his radio. He hadn't heard Wally pull up in his truck. Perhaps Wally had merely driven by at that precise moment. He didn't want to know.

"You okay?" Wally spoke in calm, measured tones. But he knew. An officer of the law had crossed the line. He was sensing Basil's emotional state and deciding whether he needed to continue to intervene.

"I'm good," Basil lied. "I'll bring him in. Thanks for backup."

But he was far from good. Mully would probably not remember once he came out of his drunken state, but Basil would remember. He would never forget the moment he came close to killing a man.

• • •

His heart thumping with exertion, his anger had cooled down somewhat. The weather was a balmy five degrees for early winter, and he was sweating. He hardly noticed the houses growing wider apart and the rapidly melting fields of snow stretching on either side of him. Ranch country. Wide open and free.

In the distance, his eyes landed on a long, sleek white frame. Like a majestic eagle with a breathtaking wingspan, it rested motionless on the large, snowy expanse. Near it stood a forlorn and dilapidated hangar badly in need of a face-lift, its wide-open doors stiff and unyielding like outstretched arms in rigor mortis. The hangar stood near a run-down shack of a house with blistering white paint and a sagging front porch. Despite the layer of snow, the grass grew wild and long, strewn with a rusty bathtub, tractor parts, and other metal pieces, aging relics of a bygone era. Sunlight glistened off the smooth form of the bird, a jewel amongst the trinkets scattered near it.

Suddenly, it moved ever so slightly. Then, with a few unsteady jerks, it moved straight and then arched upwards, soaring with graceful flight into the crisp blue sky. Cleanly slicing a few low-hanging clouds, it disappeared for a few moments and then hovered between heaven and earth.

Noiseless and graceful. The stuff of boyish dreams. Dreams that never died.

There, Basil thought, *you're estranged from troubles. There in the alien skies, suspended amongst the quiet fluff of clouds, worries and guilt fall away.*

He turned around then, but not until his eyes blurred from looking into the sun. He would be back. There was something to be found in this quiet little place of snow-covered hills and the graceful flight of the glider.

There was a desire growing in him – a need to be up there in that quiet expanse of sky, away from the noise in his head. For the first time in days, the desire was for something other than the intoxicating liquid that held him in a stranglehold.

DAY 35

Basil

“Can you give me a hand?” Wally’s voice sounded hectic on the phone, like he’d just completed a 5k marathon.

When Basil arrived at his small white bungalow, he was surprised at the sight that met him. Snow drifted lazily from a late Saturday afternoon sky onto what used to be an RV. The 2000 Coachman had been stripped to its bare bones; wall paneling lay on the concrete driveway, sawdust lay coated in white powder, and a vast array of tools were spread out. The gutted, naked trailer understandably raised the eyebrows of passersby.

The trailer shook slightly, and the large form of Wally appeared. He grinned when he saw Basil. “Leak in the back corner; part of the wall and flooring moldy. Crappy timing, but I hate a project waiting.” He popped the tab off his can of coke and took an indulgent swig. Sweat ran murky trails down his large face. “Gonna strip this thing to its skeleton and work up from there.”

“What about bringing it in?”

"What, and have someone else mess with it? Nah, it's a good little thing to keep me busy without burning holes in my wallet." He let out a satisfied belch and dropped himself on the neatly stacked woodpile beside the trailer. "You know, it's hard to soar with eagle's when you're workin' with a bunch of turkeys."

"Thanks." So like Wally to throw a wrench in the conversation. But it worked for the perps they interrogated on a regular basis. Blindside them. Effective little tool.

Wally laughed. "I wasn't exactly referrin' to you. Rather, Ratford. Joined Ichabod in his glass castle the other day. Again. This time, Ichabod's on board. We've a john-nabbin' quota to fill. You know, perhaps he needs to invest in soundproof walls. But, hey, I'm not complaining."

Basil laughed. "Perhaps he poked too many hornets' nests?"

"Hmm. Not like him to tow the political line."

"Wonder what changed his mind? We're stretched thin as it is, and even as mayor, he cannot dictate how RCMP services are allocated."

"Trump card."

"Really?"

"I'd put my money on that."

"Let me guess, though, you didn't exactly summon me for this?"

Wally chuckled. He threw Basil a crowbar and a can of coke. "They say a good sweat is good for the mind; empties it of all the crap that's living rent-free in there."

Basil stroked the crowbar with exaggeration. "Hasn't anyone ever told you I'm not exactly the jack-of-all-trades type? You might end up with something other than an RV."

"I'll risk it. Not much expertise needed with just rippin' the guts out of this thing." His own crowbar found traction on the wall paneling, and he pulled. "There is something about destroying things that feels good."

"Alright," Basil agreed, "here goes nothing." With satisfaction, he ripped apart paneling, rotting wood folding into itself. He felt almost like a truant schoolboy beyond exhilarated with the art of vandalism.

For a long while, they grunted alongside each other. Wally finally paused and took another sip of coke, crumpled the can in one fist, and threw it into a cardboard box filled with more of the same. He cracked his hammer against a wooden beam. "So." He paused. "You drinking?"

Basil's shoulders tensed. Of course. Mully. "Yeah, a coke." He chuckled and reached for his can.

"You know what I mean." The hammer cracked against another beam.

Basil pulled hard at a slat. Wood splintered around him. "Socially. Nothing crazy. It's under control." The crowbar slipped in his sweaty palm. He grunted loudly. Hungrily, it latched onto the lip of another panel, and he craned and pulled, allowing the cracking sound to fill the trailer. He surveyed the mangled wood and drywall around him.

Like a crumpled car.

Wally rubbed his neck. Basil shifted on his feet, Mully's face superimposing itself on the discolored walls. He glared at it. "I don't, you know, stumble around like *someone* we know. Cause bar fights or neglect my work, or you know, engage in domestic violence." He watched rusty water bead at the top corner seam of the wall. His hands shook. The water swelled suddenly, and then a languid drop broke off and hurried down the wall.

Wally cleared his throat. "A rose by any other name," and with a shudder and groan, his wall released a thick, rusty nail. "I don't care what people do on their own. But look,

Basil, it's affecting your work. That incident with Mully," he wiped the sweat from his forehead. "What was going on?"

"Nothing. It's all good."

"Just, if you need help, I want you to know that I'm someone you can talk to. I'm not your superior, Basil. Just someone you can unload on."

"I'm not some little experiment – "

"No, you're not. You are an alcoholic." A splintering crack and a skeletal frame stared back at Wally. "And probably a drunk more often than you would like to admit."

Basil clenched his jaw.

"But, c'mon, Basil," he kicked a two-by-four lying at his feet. "You're a good cop. Stop letting this beat you. One day, you might go too far."

Basil picked up a screwdriver. His arm ached to throw it, to smash something hard. He swallowed and sucked in a ragged breath. His fingers relaxed, and he allowed the tool to clatter to the floor. His teeth ached, and his shoulders burned. "Gotta go." He walked out of the trailer.

•••

Nora

Nora heard the cab in the drive and squared her shoulders. She wouldn't show fear; she wouldn't show him that she slowly unraveled each time he was gone, and that this time she'd quite nearly gone off the deep end. But she was relieved.

Okay, relieved was a gross understatement. She felt her anxiety melt away. She was now on top of her game. His newspaper was neatly folded and waiting for him, a stack of letters on top. Mozart played softly in the background. The house was neat as a pin. Just the way he liked it.

"Hi, my love!" He pecked her on the cheek and then pulled her into a one-arm hug. "How's my little bird?"

A ball of emotion suddenly crowded her throat. Hot and thick. She pressed her head against his chest.

"Got your favorite chocolate," he grinned, pulling a pretty white package with a red bow from behind his back.

"You didn't have to." She smiled through misty eyes.

"Is everything alright, Nora?" He gently held her from him, his eyes probing her face.

"Just happy you're home. I missed you."

"Me too," he smiled and traced the contours of her face as if he was learning Braille, with slowness and deliberation, lingering on the uneven ridges.

She eased his hand away. His helpless little wife, naïve, frightened, a little bird clipped of her wings. No more. She no longer wanted to be so vulnerable. She straightened her spine and jutted out her chin. He mustn't find out. "Did you have a great time?" *You didn't call me; you didn't check in.*

She heard his muffled voice as he moved to the bedroom to unpack his things. She continued to fold towels on the kitchen table. "...saw Lane again....he says 'hi'...shoot, where did I put my book?...what did you all do to keep yourself busy?" His voice grew clear and loud again as he walked into the kitchen.

"Oh, I just puttered around. Time went fast, actually. We had a terrible rainstorm." *And I spent half a night in our car, soaking wet. Oh, and banged on a few windows like a complete idiot.*

"Really?" His eyes probed her deeply as if he was examining her very soul. "Everything went okay?"

"Fantastic. Really." *Liar.*

"I'm relieved, Nora; was a bit worried. See, you *can* do it!"

Then why didn't you call? She gave him a strong smile. Okay, tried to; her lips quavered slightly. He walked up to her, and for some reason, she felt unsettled. He took the blue towel out of her hand, gently, purposefully. "I think you've folded this one enough already – three times, to be exact."

She lowered her eyes. "That's me, daydreaming."

"Got some laundry; can I just stick it in the washer?"

"Oh, here, I'll just – " her nose twitched at the acrid smell. "What's that smell?"

"Oh, these? Spilled a cleaning solution on them. Don't touch them; I'll dump 'em in myself."

"Alright." She shrugged. She heard the banging of the washer lid and the rush of water.

When he came back, he saw it. She saw him flinch.

Of course. She'd taken the painting and impulsively hung it in the hallway when he was gone. It was one way she felt she could lash out at the world – at her family, the hooded man. Bold slashes with the brush. Raw. Violent, in-your-face colors. It was no coherent visual to the unpracticed eye.

It was the vomit of her soul on canvas, the contempt she felt for herself.

Reg moved past but did not say a word.

She was thankful for that.

She set the table, carefully, precisely placing the forks and knives, commanding her fingers to stay still. As they sat down, she took in his strong, relaxed shoulders. He said grace and then dug in with a hearty appetite.

She placed a bite into her mouth.

"Perhaps I can go more often," he suddenly stated.

She sat up straight, a sudden fuzziness in her mouth. "Sure," she squeaked, forcefully cleared her throat.

"Oh, and some good news here. Got accepted onto our town's police advisory committee!"

She forced a smile. "Wow, Reg, really?"

"Yep. Get to see how it's all done up close." He was proud; his eyes shone. "The guy that saved my life, he just transferred to our town."

"That's really great, Reg. I'm very happy for you."

"So, bills, bills, and more bills, huh. This it?" He picked up the envelopes and shoved them aside with his newspaper.

"Yes, that's it." She cleared her throat again and lifted her glass of milk to her lips, the liquid sloshing into her mouth. From her seat, she saw the metal lip of the mail slot, and she clutched her fork tight. Her face suddenly hot, she jumped up. "Mind if I open the window? It feels so warm in here." She didn't wait for his response.

"It's cold out there, Nora. You okay? You seem on edge."

"No, I mean, yes, I'm okay. Not on edge. Just excited you are home." She jerked the window open. Suddenly, Ratford's face swam into view. It was twisted in contempt.

I will not stop at anything to eradicate this contagion.

Her fingers started to buzz. How far would he go? There was something about the little man that unsettled her.

"Nora?"

A blast of cold wind rushed around her, and a black-capped chickadee flew onto a branch outside the window. It stared at her with its beady eyes. Then, with a loud whistle, it flew away.

"Nora, please close that window. It's cold in here."

It *was* cold. She closed it and sank into her chair, trying to shrug away the heaviness that weighed on her.

Reg reached over suddenly and took her hand in his. "I'm glad to be home too, Nora." He suddenly flipped her hand over and slowly examined her fingertips, concern in his eyes. "Are you biting again?"

She pulled her hand back as if she'd touched a hot surface.

•••

Arizona

"Kitty! Kitty!" Malcolm danced, his eyes sparkling. He was running after Melody's cat, dodging the garden of plants in macramé baskets, and skipping over the colorful rugs splashed everywhere.

Melody laughed. "This is Sir Arthur. I think she really likes you." She turned to Arizona. "He's such a delightful creature. Look how he loves Sir Arthur."

"I'm getting a cat flap put in." Arizona smiled at the boy's enthusiasm. They had stopped by Melody's house, where Malcolm instantly branded the feline as his.

"You mean – "

"I thought a kitten would be therapeutic for him."

"I think it's a great idea!"

Arizona dropped into a chair. "I asked Reg Clarkson. He's been doing stuff around the house for me. Winterizing and the like."

"Well, you picked a good person to do it. He's meticulous and organized." She moved to her cupboard and pulled out a bowl of lollipops. "Can I give him one?"

"Mel," she groaned.

Malcolm squealed in delight.

"Everyone needs some sugar, or life is too bitter."

"That's one way of looking at it." If only candy took away pain.

Melody laughed. "You know, he did a presentation at our high school last year."

"Reg?" Arizona knelt down to stroke Sir Arthur's fur. The kitty purred and rubbed its furry body against her legs. Malcolm threaded his fingers into the plush carpet and was thoroughly enjoying the feline's antics from where he sat on the floor.

"Yep. About his tour in Afghanistan. He didn't want to," she laughed. "Nora signed him up, devious little lady. But it was good. He was a natural with the kids. Guy's got a real passion for justice and loyalty; good for the kids to hear."

Arizona played with the wedding ring on her finger. "It feels weird to have some other man taking care of things around the place."

"But if it helps you," Melody offered.

"Just for now." Arizona stood up abruptly.

Melody wisely held her tongue.

She would not tell Melody, at least not yet, that she had a list of private investigators ready on her kitchen table. She would not give up on Marc, even though everyone else had. If only she could unravel time; if only she'd known that with the click of her front door, her life would march away. He was the half-full glass to her relentlessly half-empty one.

He was the man who had it all together.

• • •

Marc

His body hugged the dank earth as violent shivers tore through him. Face against the dirt, he tried to absorb whatever heat he could. A lancing pain tore through his head.

Suddenly, another bout of nausea overpowered him, and he vomited. Again.

When the painful retching subsided, he slid his body away from the foul puddle of bile studded with half-digested food. The very food he hoped would give him strength had likely poisoned him.

The little window seemed so far away now. It was blurring before him, moving from side to side and then spinning and spinning. He closed his burning eyes.

His last thought was that he was going to die. He had tasted freedom for a few precious moments, but like everything else, it slid away.

• • •

Basil

He felt lonely. Paula was still at his house, acting as if she owned the place. His feet had propelled him to the large expanse of field, to the strip with the glider and the sorrowful house with dismembered parts strewn around it. Standing by the barbed fence, he could not shake off the loneliness, even though his heart told him to come here.

"There's no trading for a place like this." The voice strong in timbre, and commanding authority, took Basil by utter surprise. He turned around. The old man's appearance contrasted oddly with the voice. Startling blue eyes reflected an ocean of wisdom. His face was benign, and even the leathery, cracked skin and sagging earlobes could not quench the fire that still seemed to burn fervently. Wild hair like tattered moss barely covered his scalp, giving him the Einstein effect. "Now that," his liver-spotted hand pointed at the majestic white form with its one wing tipped skyward, "takes you away from the busyness of our world."

"Yours?" Basil asked.

"It is."

"It's like a majestic bird," Basil noted.

"It takes you to a place of nothingness. A place all of us need from time to time," he added quietly, his piercing eyes seeming to ferret out the pain in Basil's soul. He suddenly thrust out his hand. "Name's Jake Sullivan."

Basil introduced himself.

"Come on, I'll take you up," he smiled. Without waiting for a response, he walked toward the glider. It was as if he knew Basil would not object.

And he didn't. He followed the man as if he were the Pied Piper of Hamelin, through the barbed fence and a few yards until he reached the glider. It was pulled out of the dilapidated hangar and shone even whiter than snow. "Can you really fly at this time of year?"

The man pointed at a few birds soaring peacefully above them. "Perfect thermals. Just like a few days ago." He gently slid his hand over the pristine surface of the glider. He knew Basil had been here; he'd seen him. If he noticed Basil's surprise, he didn't let on. "Spring is most favorable. Once the sun reaches a great enough angle so that it will produce enough heat variance on the ground to form thermals and cumulous clouds, the stage is set. But gliding in the winter is not impossible so long as conditions are right. We use a winch to launch the glider."

They walked up to the yellow winch, which was slightly pitted with rust. "Thing pulls in three thousand feet of cable and can give you a much higher launch than a tow plane. Ever been in a glider?"

"Not a glider, just a Cessna."

"Well, then you're in for a treat. My son, Bryce, is due here any minute, and he can operate the winch."

"Looking forward to it. You sure?"

"It's an experience you don't want to miss."

Bryce showed up minutes later, a short, stocky fellow of few words. Soon, headgear on and strapped in the plane, Basil found himself seated in the front.

"Ready?" the old man asked.

Basil gave him a thumbs-up. Suddenly, the glider jerked and moved forward with great speed and then ascended sharply. The negative vertical acceleration produced a stomach drop akin to a rollercoaster, and Basil caught his breath. Adrenaline surged through his body.

The world tipped to the side, and then they were perfectly vertical and suspended high above the earth, tracing a circular path. Up here was the perfect arrangement of sky and trees and endless prairie. A rush of stillness filled him. The old man did not speak. Basil was glad. He wanted to savor the moment for as long as it lasted. He looked around and below, but when he started feeling slightly dizzy, he leaned back and closed his eyes. All tension melted away, and he felt one with the sky. Up here was a pure sort of freedom that only birds feel.

"So, what do you do for work?" Sullivan suddenly asked.

"I'm a police officer – RCMP."

Sullivan whistled. "Good for you!"

"What about you?"

"Used to be a carpenter. Retired. This here is my hobby. Bryce and mine."

The flight lasted twenty minutes before they began the descent. "Every flight is different," the old man smiled when they had landed. "If the glider can't generate enough lift to stay up there, it's done."

"Up there, I felt like I was by myself," he grinned. "Thanks again!"

The old man nodded happily. "Glad to have taken you. You can join me anytime. I fly out of here at least a few times a week, provided conditions are favorable."

Bryce returned from the winch with three beers and offered one to each of them. It was strange; Basil didn't really feel like he needed one.

DAY 36

Basil

Sergeant Ichabod did not agree with Basil's theory. He didn't think something menacing could be to blame for the working girls' disappearance. His attitude strangely compounded Basil's feeling of being alone. "If I didn't know better, I would think Ace's been spoon-feedin' you."

"Ace?"

"Big-time pimp, remember?" He raised bushy eyebrows.

Yes, he did remember.

"We are increasing pressure on the women to move on and clamping down on the trade. This is the best we can do for now. Everything else, at best, is conjecture. Pouring money into any investigation must be done with caution, as you very well know."

Had the Rat been playing the trump card? "What if we're missing something?" Basil persisted. "What if there's a connection?"

"We *will* look at each angle – we *have* to. But I'm not holding my breath. Let's not place a minority under the media microscope in that sense. Ratford doesn't just breathe down my neck anymore – he releases noxious fumes."

"I thought we don't dance to the tune of the municipal government?" As soon as he spoke these words, Basil flinched, fully expecting Ichabod to rake him over the coals.

A muscle jumped in Ichabod's jaw, but he remained calm. "I know. We are federal. But the last thing I want is a community divided. *Again*. Taxpayers pay a bundle for our services; they understandably expect a certain level of policing. I don't want a division between this town and the Force. Like I said, I am not dismissing your theory, simply prioritizing."

Basil could not deny that everything was conjecture at that point, and that theories abounded like weeds with the occasional fact thrown in. The truth was elusive and seemed to constantly slip just beyond his grasp.

One woman disappearing, two, okay. But there were also the other women missing. What if the disappearances were connected? What if something more sinister lay behind it all than merely moving on or disappearing of one's own volition? And Laramie. A death that seemed natural but jarred him enough to make him feel they were missing something.

Ratford claimed if there was anything with the streetwalkers, Ace was behind it all. Why? It didn't make sense to Basil. Why get rid of those who bring you bread and butter? Were these women who'd cheated him? Or was he simply a red herring? There was only one way to find out.

• • •

The Boy

TWIN COULEES, 1970

He felt the warmth spread down his legs, into his socks, his shoes, and burning humiliation on its heels. Without looking, he knew there was a puddle at his feet. His heart hammered wildly. He didn't dare move. It was coming. It always did.

"You're disgusting!" Mother yelled. His knees began to knock, and he wanted the earth to swallow him. Her crimson lips twisted into a sneer, and sinewy arms planted themselves firmly on her hips. "You fat pig! What if your friends see you? A grown baby!"

He slid to the floor and covered his face, his head. There would be no cloth, no help. She would make him sit in the pungent urine for an hour until the folds in his doughy legs would itch terribly, the damp sticking to his flesh.

But he was thankful. Today, she'd not rubbed his face in it.

DAY 37

Basil

Like vultures, they circled around her. Scavengers of death, despite the biting cold. She was clearly dead, but the entire scene was puzzling to Basil. The young woman lay serenely on her front side, hands to her side and hair neatly framed around her head as if she had laid down on the sidewalk and gone to sleep. Unsettling was the fact that she wore no coat, and her feet bore no shoes. There was no obvious blood or needles to be found either.

The jogger who had alerted passersby sat beside the scraggly bush where the woman had been found, shaking and weeping quietly. Her first impulse, strangely, had not been to call 911 but to alert another pedestrian until a small circle had formed quickly. Only then had emergency services been hailed. It was clear to them all she was beyond saving.

That morning, Clarkson had shown up for his first ride-along. "Thanks again for taking me."

"No problem at all. Gives me someone to talk to as well," Basil grinned. "There might not be anything remotely exciting happening today, though."

"No worries. Interesting to see what it's like from the other side, you know?"

When the call came in, Clarkson sat up straight. "Well, that was quick! Wonder what the matter is."

"Well, we know it's a body, so obviously a death. Likely an overdose, as it appears to be a young person. I don't want to speculate too much until we get to the scene. I have to keep my mind open and my professional hat on." He scanned Clarkson's face. "Would you like me to get another officer to bring you home?"

"No, no. I'll be fine." He fell silent for a moment. "I've seen my share of death."

"Really?" Basil was surprised.

"Toured in Afghanistan for a bit. Saw some ugly things."

"You fought all the way out there?"

"I was in the Canadian reserves." He lifted his right foot. "Shrapnel wound. Healed nicely, but the limp is here to stay. I'll stay out of your way, but only if you don't mind me sticking around."

"Not at all."

They arrived at the scene to see a crowd having formed. "Look at 'em! Can't get enough, can they?"

Basil shook his head in irritation. *Irksome vultures!*

The body was a mottling of purple and blue. He heard the excited drone of voices as he emerged from his vehicle. Wally had just arrived and left his Tahoe running with a quick, "Hate having to reboot the computer when I start up again." *Just like Wally to live life on the edge*, he thought. Good thing Ichabod was not present.

Basil knew death changed everything. Suddenly, an invisible wall separates the living from the dead, and an "us versus them" mentality emerges. To view the deceased as an object – a mere body – is to strip the person of any identity and link to the living as a way of protecting oneself. Even more so is to begin intense speculation as to the cause of death.

"Clearly a druggie," a young man offered.

"Or homeless," another quickly added. "Probably high on something. It's got no coat or boots on! I mean, who goes outside without those in this weather?" *It.* Effectively stripped of her humanity.

"Poor lady. Oh, yuck, look at the skin!" Repulsed and intrigued.

And so, a clear demarcation is forged. *We are not druggies or homeless, and so this fate can't possibly befall us. We are safe from a similar fate and, even more so, safe to speculate.* Basil shook his head and sighed.

"Perhaps we need to give out tickets to the latest outdoor show," Wally shook his head and sighed, a yellow roll of *Police Line Do Not Cross* tape in his hand.

One of the spectators was a doughy, brown-haired girl who'd just shown up with loud colored clothing and an even louder voice: "Oh, man, get a load of this, Fred! It's a *body*!" Gesticulating wildly, she pulled her cellphone from her jacket pocket. "How awful!" But she neither shrank back from it nor covered her face.

Enter the selfie and "post-it-all-on-Facebook" era.

"And it starts," Wally sighed. He moved closely behind the woman, whose partner was nudging her, none too discreetly.

"Clara, quit it! The cops are here. Put that stupid thing away."

"Put that away, ma'am, or there'll be a warrant put out for it," Wally ordered.

She whirled around. "We've got rights!"

"Not to satisfy voyeurism," he shot back.

"C'mon, Clara, let's go," The hippie prodded her.

Glaring at Wally, she bit off one more time, "I've got rights!"

Basil looked at her in disgust. "What about the rights of the deceased, ma'am?"

"She's dead! She doesn't care."

"Around here, we still respect the dead."

Clarkson chose that moment to step out of the cruiser and wave people aside. "Alright, people; you've had your fill, let the police do their work. Move on!" Basil gave him a thumbs-up.

"Do you know the victim?" Wally asked Clara, not willing to let her quite off the hook yet.

She shrank back, horrified. "No!" Clearly, the last thing she wanted was to be linked to the deceased. That was too close for comfort, even for her. She glared at them and finally allowed her partner to drag her off, but not before Basil heard her grumble under her breath as she sank sulkily into the car: "Bunch of idiots. Look at that tall redhead; can you believe he is a cop?"

• • •

"Lower left quadrant. Roughly seven to nine inches?" Wally peered closely at the incision on Jane Doe's abdomen.

Basil felt a shiver go up his spine. *A coincidence?*

Wally merely shook his head. "Just a coincidence; likely a recent surgery. Not a strange location for one."

But what were the chances?

A few reporters had already stationed themselves behind the barricaded crime scene, the intrusive noses of their cameras clicking at random intervals, trying to capture the best angles. A Global News truck slipped next to the curb. There was an excited murmur as more people gathered despite the RCMP waving them off. Clouds of vapor formed above heads. Until the body was skirted away, there was no chance of the crowd dissipating. They were, after all, waiting for the encore.

The tall man moved nimbly up beside Basil as he moved to the barricade. "Reporter, D. Williams, sir." He snaked out a manicured hand. Basil couldn't help but notice the ornamental ring on his pinkie finger as he carefully adjusted horn-rimmed glasses on a soft, round face. A biting wind plucked at his tie, but his crisp hair was a trooper in it all, bold and stiff; it would not give in to nature's whims. Basil couldn't figure out if it was amateurishness or a kind of practiced condescension that set him apart, but he felt an immediate irritation with the man. "Sorry, we're not done here yet."

Wally shook his head. "Everyone wanting to make a buck; one person's fate another's paycheque." He looked at the back of the retreating reporter. "Most know to wait till we're done here."

"I wish they would just leave those scanners be for once," Basil groused. His feet were starting to feel numb, and he felt lightheaded from not having had much breakfast. "*Elucidate* – who uses that word? Excuse me, sir, but what have you been able to elucidate from the crime scene," he pantomimed.

Wally chuckled. The cameras whirred and clicked. For one bizarre moment, Basil wanted to grab the equipment and smash it. The woman, whose life was a piece of meat now, was too big for even the widest lens; their snapshots would merely capture a nebulous lump of body under a sheet – the shell of her existence.

•••

"Those crime scene guys are sure meticulous, huh?" Clarkson commented later. Once at the scene, he'd been told to stay by the car. As amiable as he was, the last thing the crime scene guys needed was a curious civilian underfoot.

"They have to be," Wally noted. "Cause of death is unclear. Might be natural, but for someone so young, you especially want to make sure you leave no stone unturned."

"Wonder who will be next with this guy – with this perp?"

"Whoa!" Basil laughed. "Let's not get ahead of ourselves. Being presumptive will just cloud our judgment. Besides, this is not the stuff of sensational fiction. I sure hope it is a one-time thing!" His gut told him otherwise.

Wally interjected. "Andrews is right. Speculation can be dangerous. Besides, women can be just as violent.

•••

That evening after shift, Basil joined Lee Nygard and Bill Smith for a drink at Shorty's,

"No Kennedy again?" Nygard asked, sipping the foamy head of his beer.

"I asked him," Smith noted. "But he said he'd somewhere to be."

"For the past few weeks," Nygard said as he put his glass down. He shrugged. "Maybe taking care of his pet."

The men laughed. "Never heard of a pet," Basil probed.

Nygard leaned forward. "Large cage in the back of his vehicle the other day. Empty, but he's got some sort of critter alright."

"What kind?"

Nygard lifted his shoulders. "Dunno. Reptile by the looks of it."

"The death we went to a while back really shook him up," Basil said as he fumbled with his napkin.

"Yeah, thought so too," Nygard agreed. "Every case impacts us differently." He leaned towards the men, lowering his voice. "I think he needs a woman in his life."

They all laughed again. Basil did as well, but it fell flat. An uneasiness settled on him that he couldn't seem to shake off.

DAY 38

Arizona

The rap on the door was soft and tentative at first, then sharp and demanding. Estelle stood there, book in hand. "I was just passing through. Here's the book you wanted to borrow from Nana." She peered hesitantly over Arizona's shoulder as if she was looking into a deep, sinister cave.

"You want coffee? I'm just going to put some on."

"Coffee? Well, alright."

"Malcolm is taking his nap."

Estelle suddenly swept inside. "Nana remembered you wanted to borrow this book. Her mind," she clucked, shaking her head. "Like a ball of yarn I feel I have to chase after and roll up again to make any sense of it, and then it just unravels as quick again."

Arizona moved to the kitchen and stopped. "Just cream, right?" When Estelle said nothing, she turned around to see her staring at Malcolm's clothing half folded on the kitchen table. "Mom?"

"I can't believe you told Nana about Malcolm," she said quietly.

"I didn't, remember? Someone else did."

"Gossips!" she spat suddenly. "They twist and skew things."

"Actually, they got the story pretty straight, Mom. Besides, Nana was not even upset about it."

"She's started speaking very strange. Senile wanderings, I call it," Estelle shook her head again as if she'd not even heard her daughter.

"I thought she was quite sharp."

Estelle huffed. "Of course you did."

What exactly had transpired between her mother and Nana the other day? "Caffeinated or…?"

"Caffeine. Please." Out of the corner of her eye, she noticed Estelle reach out to touch the neatly folded pants and shirts, fingering the soft material. She jerked her arm back when she saw Arizona watching and cleared her throat. "Nana is fading. And now I have to deal with a child – a *grandson*." She rubbed her shoulder. "It's not like I'm trying to be uncaring." She paced the kitchen.

"You don't need to deal with anything if you don't want to." She grabbed the can of coffee from the cupboard, suddenly needing something between her and her mother. "We're fine here."

"It's just that I'm not ready." She sighed. "I can't believe Marc did this to you."

"Do you think *I* was ready? And Marc *didn't do* anything to me. They don't know much surrounding his disappearance; a lot of it's speculation. I can't even wrap my head around it all most days. And what did you expect me to do? Throw his child into the street?" She set the can down hard on the counter.

"Of course not! But he's really thrown a wrench into your life."

"No, Mom. He's thrown a wrench into *your* plans for *my* life." She grabbed the coffee pot and held it in shaking hands. "You think I always take the easy way out? That I'm escaping my responsibility?" She took a damp rag and began wiping the counters down furiously. "Responsibility to what? Attend lavish society parties and look pretty? I don't want the cake or the whipping cream! I want substance – meaning – real love." She threw the rag into the sink. "To work for my worth. To face life. I haven't been running, Mother! Here, in this hick town, as you call it, I am in the trenches, in real life. Raising a child who's suffered more than you and I combined, and he's only three! And when I go to bed at night, I feel like I've done something more than just look polished."

Estelle looked pained. "I just want…I don't know."

"What? What do you want from me, Mother?" She realized with horror that she was yelling.

"I don't know. Yes, I do: to *need* me!" Estelle shot back.

Mouth agape, Arizona tripped. The coffee pot with morning brew slipped from her fingers. Shards of glass and cold coffee lay strewn over the floor.

They looked at each other. Mother and daughter. The kitchen clock ticked loudly.

"I do need you, Mom," she finally burst out, the energy suddenly drained. Wearily, she bent to pick up the shards. "But I'm still an *adult*. And besides, you don't want anything to do with Malcolm."

"I just can't." Estelle stood there limply. Suddenly, she blinked and made for the sink. "I'll get the teapot and put on water. Then I'll mop up this mess."

"No, I'll do it."

"Let me at least wipe it up," she replied, grabbing a damp rag. "Please."

Arizona nodded quietly and watched the prim woman dispose of the glass shards and mop up the cold coffee.

Malcolm was suddenly at her side, pressing his body against her. "I'm sorry, Malcolm," she apologized. "I didn't mean to yell and wake you up." She quickly scooped up the little boy and found Estelle staring at him, her face pale.

Estelle quietly moved to a chair and perched on its edge. "So, this is he?" She gave him a wobbly smile. "Hello," she said tentatively.

"Go play!" Malcolm squirmed from her arms, not in the least interested that someone else was in the house with them. It was a testament to his lessening anxiety, for which Arizona was grateful.

"How do you do it?"

"Do what?" Arizona finished making the tea and poured it into two cups.

"Look at him. Daily. He's Marc all over."

"It was difficult at first. Like a knife through my heart each time. But I have to."

Estelle stared at her pensively. "So independent you are, Arizona," she sighed deeply, then gave a short laugh. "It's what all parents want their kids to be. Then feel like a duck out of water when it does happen."

"I guess I'm stubborn, huh?" She suddenly laughed too and dropped into another chair, Malcolm having gone back to play. It felt weird. Were they really sharing a normal conversation over a cup of tea?

"Don't get me started. But your father blames me for that one." There was a haggardness around her eyes and mouth.

Father.

Malcolm walked into the kitchen again. "Kitty meow."

Estelle raised her eyebrows, "What's he saying?"

"Ask him," she encouraged.

"What kitty?" She asked with a tinge of uncertainty.

"Kitty," Malcolm pointed to Estelle's embroidered sweater.

"Oh!" She chuckled with relief, her hand clasped to her chest. "Yes, my sweater has a kitty. Nice to meet you, Malcolm. My name is – I'm…Grandma," her voice wavered.

Malcolm stared at her with huge eyes, a smile breaking across his face, and then he ran off once more.

Estelle stared after him for a long moment and then stood up abruptly. "I need to go. Thanks for the tea, Arizona. I – " She suddenly shook her head, having changed her mind, and pecked her on the cheek.

Of course, a new coffee pot arrived in the mail the next day: *Williams and Sonoma*. Arizona merely shook her head and laughed.

DAY 39

Basil

Basil was placed as lead investigator on the case of the murdered woman. Wally had taken off for a couple of days, but Basil didn't mind; he was eager to take on the challenge.

Sergeant Blake Jarowicz of Calgary's Major Crimes unit nodded slowly at Basil's suggestion of a link between this woman and Laramie. Ichabod had called in the big guns. As Twin Coulees was a small detachment, it did not possess adequate manpower to fully investigate a string of murders. "This cut is definitely deeper and stitched up, I might add, but there is something haphazard about it. The last body had a superficial cut. Let's not get ahead of ourselves." They'd examined her closely, but there was no ID. "Cases of missing women?"

"Man," Basil responded.

Jarowicz looked at him curiously.

"Well, two with names," he suddenly backpedaled. "The streetwalkers claim they have been missing women over the past few months."

"Prostitutes?" Jarowicz puzzled. "Perhaps, but that's a transient group to begin with. They come and go and often resurface later. At any rate, according to Ichabod, there is latent tension there. They think law enforcement is out to get them; not the first time we've heard such an argument. He also specified that each missing person's report was carefully followed up, but no leads. Many were runaways who not only were estranged from their family but changed their names. Not a whole lot to go on. Are there any recent cases of missing women in general?" He probed.

"Two women: a Janey and Britney. One with no family around here, and another whose grandmother came to file a missing persons report. None are streetwalkers, that we are aware of."

"See if you can figure out who she is. Let me know as soon as you've found something."

•••

Preliminary autopsy results indicated Jane Doe was a healthy female in her early twenties with no obvious cause of death. She was missing her left kidney, but all other organs were intact. Basil knew it was not common procedure to remove a kidney. Besides, the stitching lacked a professional touch.

To cover all their bases, every available member was placed on the case. Constable Nygard was tasked with visiting Twin Coulees General to see if they'd had a patient in for recent kidney surgery fitting her description, but he reached a dead end. Broadening his quest to include Rockyview, Foothills, and Peter Lougheed hospitals in Calgary turned up three women in a similar age range, but none fitting the necessary description; one was Hispanic, one Black, and another Asian. The Asian woman turned out to be a transplant surgery.

Basil dragged himself to Dorothea Cabrey's home. She'd been unreachable for a bit, and it was a couple of days later when he finally got hold of her. The last thing he wanted was to cause her grief, but they needed to know. Would she be able to handle identifying a body? He was reminded again of the difficulty of dealing with death on the job. It wasn't necessarily the gruesome sight of a dead or mangled body, but rather dealing with family.

He was shocked at how frail she appeared. Janey's disappearance had taken a definite toll on her. "Constable Andrews, good afternoon," she greeted him quietly without preamble. "I know why you're here."

"You do?" She was calm – too calm. *Make her sit down; she is in shock.*

"The news. I may be old, but my mind is sharper than a tack. And no, I don't need to sit down; I won't collapse on you. I *know* it's her."

"Look, Mrs. Cabrey – "

She shook her head. "Here," she pressed a thin, veiny hand to her chest, "is where I feel it. My *heart* tells me she is gone. Please, take me to identify her body. I want this over with."

Basil nodded.

At the morgue, Dorothea looked for a long moment at the dead body. "It's her," she breathed at last. "Precious child," her voice wobbled. Wiping her eyes quickly, she held herself strong and poised, drawing from an invisible source of strength somewhere deep inside her. She turned to Basil, and her eyes held him piercingly. "God will avenge her death. You *must* find who did this, Constable!" Her cold hands suddenly clutched both of his, and he was surprised at their strength. "Promise me, Constable!"

Basil promised her solemnly that he would leave no stone uncovered. “Mrs. Cabrey, there is one other thing. I’m not really sure how to say this, but we need to know. Did Janey have a recent operation?”

“Operation? No. Why?”

“She is missing a kidney. I’d thought – or rather, hoped – maybe she’d had recent surgery, some reasonable explanation. There are no hospital records at Twin Coulees General that suggest she had a procedure done, and none in Calgary, either.”

“Kidney? Janey was a healthy girl, Constable! Last I saw her, there was nothing wrong with her. Are you sure? This can’t be! What happened to this poor girl?” No longer was she calm and sure but wringing her hands.

“Don’t worry, Mrs. Cabrey, we’ll get to the bottom of it.” But what if he couldn’t find what happened to her? A second perfectly healthy woman had died. There had to be a reason – one that was looking very sinister indeed.

Two incisions. Was there a connection between Adele and Janey? But Adele was not missing a kidney. And yet, two healthy women whose cause of death remained a mystery. According to the autopsy results, the incision was considered unprofessional, although neat. A back-alley surgery of sorts? An amateur operation gone wrong? The interesting thing to note was that neither an infection nor blood loss had killed her – a twin-edged sword with back-alley operations. Why was she missing a kidney if she didn’t have an operation? And what had really killed her?

Basil remembered the Ted Bundy case that gripped the nation in the late ‘70s. Bundy did not fit the stereotypical image of the serial killer at the time. Was the killer right in front of them? Was he blending in like a chameleon, sitting under their very noses?

Basil shivered.

Suddenly, he sat up straight. *Bob Higginson*. Ever since talking to the thin man, there had been a niggle in his gut – something didn't quite fit right. He was likely the last person to see Janey alive. He'd been cooperative – polite – but still.

Exotic Animals was one of many pet-related emporiums in Calgary. He dialed the number and found himself talking to a chirpy little thing.

"Bob Higginson. Oh, yes. He worked for us."

"Worked?"

"You bet. Left around three months ago, I believe."

"Fired?"

"No. He just left. Found other career interests, I imagine. Not uncommon."

He thanked the woman and hung up. Why was Higginson still driving that vehicle with the company's inscription? No, back up, why had he lied about who he worked for? An image of women hog-tied in the back of the van flashed in his mind, and his pulse sped up. Could it be the crime scene? He'd likely been the last person Janey had seen while alive.

He paced the room then, dread climbing his stomach. He kept his van locked and his phone in there. Too convenient. For all he knew, there hadn't been a single animal in there at the time. He smacked his forehead. He should have asked if he could look in the van the first time. Right when he had the man in the palm of his hand. At the very worst, Higginson would have demanded a warrant.

Now, he would have no choice but to get one.

• • •

Arizona

She walked into the Gazette, past the giant yucca with its sharp, reaching arms. Reception was unusually quiet. She tapped her fingers on the counter's edge. Phones rang in the background. A murmuring of voices. A toilet flushed.

She massaged the back of her neck, digging her fingers into the ropey muscles. She glanced at her watch and decided to do it for herself. She knew where Marc's office was.

Timidly, she rapped at the door. It was partially open. For a moment, she was startled. The simple space with a few scattered knickknacks had transformed into a showy office. "Come in!" a voice ordered.

She obeyed immediately. He sat there like a sparkling trinket box, ornamentally trimmed but empty. A rounded chin rested on perfectly manicured fingers steepled in contemplation, a mere pretense on a man whose waters apparently did not run deep.

But the façade crumbled when he saw her. Two crimson spots suddenly bloomed on his cheeks, and he jumped up, sending the chair behind him spinning wildly. "Mrs. Stuart, how nice to see you! I'm sorry," he gestured behind him. "This must be hard. I just wanted to make the place my own. I hope you understand."

The wall behind him, formerly bare, was festooned with certificates and mundane, run-of-the-mill prizes highlighted in ostentatious gold frames that bespoke a man attempting to rise higher than his intellect justified. One frame held the Award for Journalistic Excellence for an article on dog breeding from the Kennel Club of Southern Alberta. Gold-toned bric-a-brac perfectly matched the large gold ring on his pinkie.

Then she saw it and jumped.

A large cage stood on a simple wooden unit. Inside, she glimpsed the smooth, striped flesh of a large snake. Its scaly skin shimmered in the sunlight streaming into the window. It seemed to hug the bottom of the cage, a soulless, monstrous beast, and she imagined the venomous power and speed held coiled in its never-ending body.

He followed her eyes. "Oh, this is the office mascot. Sleeps most of the day."

"Mr. Williams," she said, her eyes never leaving the cage. "I am only here hoping, maybe, since my last visit, you might have remembered anything that might explain Marc's disappearance."

The beast suddenly lifted its head and began undulating. Arizona's breath caught in her throat. A forked tongue darted out as if tasting fear in the air.

"You know, I did find some things; placed them in a drawer." He suddenly seemed to relax. "Things not needed tend to lie forgotten, don't they?"

Like Marc.

He zeroed in on a tall filing cabinet diagonally placed in one corner.

"What do you feed the snake?"

"Oh. Mice." He finally pulled open a tightly closed filing drawer at the bottom of the cabinet and pulled out a dictionary and fountain pen covered in dust.

"Mice?" *Alive or already dead?* But she dared not ask that.

He also pulled out a small notebook. "Supplies all their nutritional needs."

"Oh." She looked at the books and pen. "Is this *all*? No paperwork, works in progress, or anything else?"

"This is it, I'm afraid. You were thinking there was something more?" His neat brows arched in question.

"I don't know. Did he have any notes or articles he was working on?" She knew she was grasping at straws, and tears stung her eyes. This was it. She tried to swallow past the stone in her throat.

He reached for his bottle of water. "Technically, all those items you mentioned would belong to this office. But I don't believe he was."

She refused to give up quite yet. "Has Marc ever mentioned a silver spoon to you?"

The bottle stopped at his lips. "Why do you ask?"

"I am trying to piece together Marc's last days. I found some things he'd written down. Look, I *need* some form of closure." *Don't make yourself look so needy!*

"Silver spoons? Kind of seems odd."

"Silver spoon. He had the words scrawled down on a note. It must mean something." She leaned forward, her fingers digging into her knees.

He scrunched his brows in contemplation and lowered himself to perch on the corner of his large, wooden desk. "You know, he liked pulling the extraordinary out of the banal. Probably some garden variety piece he was working on between serious articles, no?" He watched her carefully.

It's not like Marc. What if Dawson knows more than he is letting on? Marc's voice echoed in her brain: Give out tiny bits. Feel around. Use just the right amount of bait.

"A clue, he said."

"A what?"

"The clue lies in finding the silver spoon."

"I see." His body straightened up, a hint of a glimmer in his eyes. "Mrs. Stuart, Marc and I did collaborate on sensitive subjects at times, certain works in progress. Did he leave any other paperwork lying around?"

Arizona frowned, then shook her head.

"Well, I'm sorry, Mrs. Stuart, that I can't be of any more help to you. What I have here is all there is. I realize that grasping at something is helpful or, at the very least, comforting. But please, spare yourself the pain of digging for something that never was. It will just exacerbate your loss."

She wanted to beg him for help, but she was no groveling fool. She left the room clinging to the one thought that dug like a deep hook in her mind: there was a thick layer of dust on the dictionary and pen, common with items that have laid undisturbed for a long time. But there was no dust on the notebook. The items had all been sequestered together in a drawer.

She opened it. There was no writing in the notebook – but wait. She hastily flipped through it, noting the uneven tears of pages ripped out. What exactly had been written in that notebook? Who had torn the pages out? Marc? Dawson? Why did mention of the silver spoon pique Dawson's interest so much?

• • •

Basil

Clarkson leaned back in the cruiser as Basil took him down the rural roads of Twin Coulees. "Nice and peaceful. I love this little town. Lots of backroads. Away from all the big city rush."

Peaceful, Basil thought, *but don't scratch too deep.* Instead, he said, "Comin' out here probably costs them an arm and a leg, no?"

"You pay by the kilometer."

Basil laughed. "Trust me, I know."

"Thanks for still paying your fare the other day, although you sure didn't – "

"It all happened quite near the end of my trip," Basil waved his hand dismissively.

Reg nodded quietly. "That was a close one."

"Enjoy being a cabbie?" Basil changed the subject.

"I do. Get to see all the faces of humanity. See and hear it all, kind of like you, but with a difference."

"How so?"

"Well, with police officers, folks subtly, perhaps without realizing it, align their actions with that of the well-behaved citizen. You don't get to see people as they truly are."

"No, you're absolutely right." Basil swung the car past the Laramies' vacant farm and felt a sudden heaviness in his heart.

Reg was looking at the place with interest as well. "Nice little farm," he commented suddenly. "Looks pretty quiet."

"Yeah," Basil nodded quietly. "So, you find your customers are less subtle?"

His gaze lingered with interest. "Kind of feel like a hairdresser. They spill their troubles to a complete stranger."

Basil laughed. "Sometimes they need a listening ear, I imagine. You're a safe audience. Small talk really passes the time."

"Might be small, but it can sure reveal big things. You know, it's how I met my wife."

"Oh?" Basil was intrigued.

"Yep." He turned to look out the window then. "She was the perfect one for me. Such hopes and dreams we had." His hand shook slightly. "Life can sure change in an instant."

"*Was?*"

He frowned at Basil. "Oh, no, we're still married. She was the victim of that acid attack. Entire face disfigured."

"I'm sorry," Basil said. "I think I remember. It was in all the papers."

Reg nodded and rubbed his face. "Her family. They destroyed her, you know? Took away her self-esteem, her confidence, and reduced her to a pitiful shadow of her former self. And now she's a prisoner in her own home. A bird with clipped wings." A muscle twitched in his jaw.

Basil ached for what this family had gone through. How could your own family subject you to something so monstrous?

Reg fell silent then and stared out of the window. Finally, he spoke. "You know the irony of it all?"

Basil shook his head.

"I went to Afghanistan. Fought against cultural wrongs. Fought to make the world a better place. And then it happened here in my own home. To my own wife. When I wasn't there to protect her."

Basil felt that familiar buzzing. He gripped the steering wheel. "I know about beating yourself up," he added quietly.

For a moment, they fell silent. A few patches of long grass danced and bowed in gentle rhythm at first, and then in frenetic moves like orchestra players imbued with bursts of energy and movement at the direction of their conductor.

"Guilt can be misplaced," Reg offered quietly. "And people aren't always what they seem."

Basil turned back into town just as Wally's Tahoe drove by. Something wormed around at the back of his mind, and he tried to reach for it just as it slid away.

Reg leaned back. "I think we've both seen things too horrific to forget. But I've learned we can all make a difference one way or another. It's why I joined the advisory committee. We need to look forward; move forward."

Move forward. Easier said than done.

• • •

It did not take Basil long to procure a warrant for Higginson. He waited until evening to approach Higginson's house, when he would most likely be home. But when he arrived, the truck was gone. The little house with its closed blinds seemed lifeless. He rapped insistently on the front door. And then again.

But no one came.

He noticed then the blinds in the window next to the door were slightly open. He peered inside. It was dark. Frowning, he lifted his flashlight and peered inside again.

His stomach dropped to his feet. Just as he'd suspected. There was not a lick of furniture in the tiny house. Striations in the carpet were the only indications that furniture had been in the room only recently. Higginson had cleared out and disappeared.

But why?

The guy had masterfully woven a web for the RCMP, and he had willingly stepped right into it. Higginson's smug face floated into his vision, and he punched the wall of the house, ignoring the searing pain that sliced through his wrist. How stupid could he have been? Like butter, the man had slipped through his fingers.

And he'd simply let him.

For all they knew, Higginson's vehicle did not contain animals of any sort but was a convenient place to hold kidnapped women or, at the very worst, commit murder. It wasn't such a terribly ludicrous notion to believe that he was behind the murders.

After all, he'd had a connection with Janey McAlistair. And now he'd vanished even though he'd been asked to stay put in case the RCMP wanted to ask more questions.

Blame shot through every vein in his body. *Nice tip off, Basil!*

Now, they would have to trace the whereabouts of Higginson. They had his license plate, but he had days on them and plenty of opportunity to hide or dispose of his vehicle.

Speaking to a middle-aged couple living next door, Basil learned they felt the same way about Higginson. "He came and went at the oddest hours, too. No surprise he's gone. Something odd about the guy."

Higginson had royally duped them all.

• • •

Arizona

It started after supper. He was lying on the couch, complaining of his tummy. She tucked him in with his stuffy, not sure what to do. She'd never dealt with a sick child. She placed a bucket beside him and rubbed his head. Restless, he finally fell asleep.

She was in the kitchen, preparing something to eat, when she heard him wake and groan. Quickly, she went to him and then stopped dead in her tracks.

He looked at her with eyes that seemed hollow and suddenly gave a laugh she did not think it possible to come from the mouth of a toddler.

A sickening sense of panic rose slowly and steadily. His cheeks were crimson flowers, and his eyes held a glassy hue. Somewhere deep in that maternal side of hers, she knew something was terribly wrong. More strange laughter came from him. It sounded eerie, almost. He had become this little monster, some hideous fragment of her imagination.

She walked slowly towards him, pretending his odd stare did not bother her. She felt his forehead, his chest. A burning oven. She pulled back fingers as if scalded. Fever! She pulled away his blankets as if they were a roaring fire. "Malcolm, what's wrong?" she asked.

He pointed to the wall behind her. "Balloons! I want a balloon!"

She slowly turned around, a blank wall staring back at her. Turning to him, she walked backward for a moment, tripped over a toy, and froze. She looked around then saw the phone. Mother. She had to call her mother.

Gripping the receiver, she sucked in a deep breath to still her heart. It flopped around dramatically, like some spastic animal.

"I'm coming right over. I'm in High River at the moment. Give me ten minutes. Get any clothes and blankets off him if you haven't already done so."

She paced the floor. Then she checked and rechecked Malcolm's forehead. Finally, she moved to the window. *C'mon, Mother!* she begged.

Then she came. No doorbell, no knocking.

"We're in the living room!" Arizona's words stumbled over each other.

Estelle took one look and was at Malcolm's side. She ignored his strange utterances and felt his forehead. "Tylenol or Advil in the house? He's delirious."

Delirious? "Um, for adults, not kids!" She realized it with horror, wringing her hands. How could she not have prepared for this? What kind of mother was she?

"I'll run and get some."

"No, Mom! You can't leave. I'll get Melody to bring some."

"Never mind. Run a cool bath. Not cold, not warm, *cool.* This is the way we did it when you were little."

Arizona stared at her mother. Her legs felt rubbery, her feet glued to the floor.

"Arizona, look at me!"

She obeyed.

"Take a deep breath and do what I say. Run cool water in the tub. Now!"

Shaking fingers fumbled with the faucet. Hot water, freezing cold. Cool. Okay, it's cool. *Stay calm!* she thought. Mother was at her heels, holding the naked boy. She lowered him into the tub. "It'll take time to cool him off." She ordered Arizona to get a cold washcloth ready, and she carefully placed it on his forehead, splashing cool water onto his body – his armpits, his groin.

• • •

Estelle cradled Malcolm in her arms, rocking him slowly. Her own face was flushed, and the perfectly curled hair had fallen limp against her forehead. His gentle breathing and cooler skin were proof the fever no longer held him tightly in its grip.

"I've messaged Melody to please bring some fever medication in the morning," Arizona whispered. "Can I get you some tea?"

Estelle simply nodded. She was too busy studying Malcolm's sleeping form, a look of tenderness in her eyes. Arizona watched her for a second longer, a strange feeling washing over her, and then quickly obliged.

• • •

Basil

Sleep was difficult to find that evening, but he finally managed to chase it down with the help of a sleeping pill. After repeatedly tossing and turning, he fell into the embrace of a pleasant dream.

But a knock on the door ended this rare moment. Without immediately registering the sound, he knew sleep was fleeing from him, and reality was thrusting itself through.

The knocking grew more intense and persistent. Suddenly, he was wide awake, his eyes searching the fuzzy red digits of his alarm clock: 3 am. Who on earth would be seeking him out at this hour!

Wrenching himself from the warm confines of his bed, the sweet taste of his dream lingering in his mind, he padded across the cold floor to the front door. Opening it, he was startled to see the familiar face of Stacey.

"How many more of us have to die?" Her crimson lips were an angry smudge; hands placed defiantly on her hips portrayed a sense of bravado, but they were trembling.

"It's the middle of the night!" His brain still felt fuzzy from sleep. "How did you find out where I live? Has something happened?"

"Yes, something happened!" she snapped, her voice rising. "We're dying in this town, and no one's doing anything! We're not getting answers at your fine police establishment. A woman is dead on the street, and *now* you finally care? Oh, wait a minute…" She looked at him mockingly. "… she is not a whore, huh? So, *she* matters. But all the other women? Transient garbage!"

"Stacey – " He grabbed his coat and slipped out the door so as not to wake Paula.

"*You* need to do something! You're our only hope – our *last* hope!" Her anger had faded somewhat, and the severe glint in her eyes had changed into desperation. She folded her arms tightly. "I hate groveling."

"Stacey, we're following every lead possible. Our manpower is slim." He huddled deep into his coat, cool air nipping at his nose and ears.

"Oh, give me a break!"

Basil rubbed his face. "These women are all classified as missing persons; their files are open. But at the moment, we have our hands tied. Until new evidence surfaces, we have no proof these women have been killed."

Her eyes darkened. "These *women* are my friends." Her voice was calm but frozen around the edges. "And they're dead alright."

"Wait a minute!" He raised his hand. "We are not sure of anything at this point."

She stared at him for a second and then gave a short laugh. "You're not sure of anything? Really?" She glared. "They can't all have fallen into a black hole and disappeared."

"I got that, Stacey. I am not treating their cases with any less care and concern than I treat the others."

"Right!" She jerked some photos from her purse and laid them roughly in front of him. She stabbed her forefinger at each photo. Basil peered at the colorful photos of three women grinning widely, arms thrown around each other's necks. "Do you see the dreams and hope in their eyes? Lola wanted to be a doctor someday. And Birdie? She dreamed of opening up a home for troubled women. They are not statistics. Look at them; look closely. Let their images burn themselves into your brain! You think we enjoy being groped? Standing in the cold like meat for the taking? Self-righteous pigs," she bit off. "No one *really* cares. If we're dead, you can nicely wash your hands of the problem."

"Stacey, please – "

"Who is next, huh? I *knew* these women; we were close like sisters. And we're dropping like flies. Someone, for once, needs to be on our side." Stacey ran the zipper of her jacket up and down. "To protect us from the Rat."

Or Higginson. The man was still at large. RCMP detachments in a wide radius around them had been alerted to his vehicle description and license plate. "The truth does not scare me," Basil replied quietly. "I will help to uncover whatever happened to those girls, this much I can promise you. I will explore every avenue," he promised quietly.

She looked at him hard and nodded slowly, but not quite convincingly. "Mind?"

He shook his head as she pulled out a cigarette, flipped it slowly in her fingers, and then clamped it between her lips. She peered into the carton again, shrugged, and then offered him one.

Taking the box, he peered inside. One measly cigarette. He graciously declined.

She sucked the life force out of her cigarette as if drawing some form of strength from the white stick.

"Wait a minute, you've got that; at least let me get my fix." He slipped into the house and returned with a couple of beers. Sleep would not be happening anymore. "Want one?"

She looked at it with disgust and wrinkled her nose. "It's too cold."

He shrugged. "Suit yourself."

They sat there, she puffing, him drinking, the silence between them oddly comfortable. "You know, he assaulted a woman once."

"Who?"

"Ratford."

"Ratford?"

"Yeah, guy apparently has a non-existent fuse. Just blows up when he's pushed too far, or someone doesn't tow his line."

"How do you know this?"

"I have my sources." She dragged on the cigarette again. "It don't matter anyhow."

He looked at her questioningly.

"He was 'exonerated'," she mimicked. "Never formally charged. She apparently chickened out. Don't blame her. But the guy got out of a criminal charge just like that." She snapped her fingers.

For one moment, he imagined Ratford sending out his henchmen to deal with the town's "contagion" and wanted to laugh.

A porch light down the street suddenly blazed for a second and then died just as quickly.

A heavy feeling draped over him that he couldn't seem to shake off.

Stacey stood up, stubbing out her cigarette. "I need to go." Turning to him one last time, she begged: "Find the proof; it's out there. I know it is!"

"Wait!"

She turned back.

"Why me?"

She shrugged. "You're new here. Besides, there's something about you. I saw it the other day. It takes a broken soul to recognize another one."

• • •

He finally returned to bed. He must have drifted off, for the next thing he knew, his alarm clock showed 6:00 am. When he padded into the kitchen to make coffee, he spied the note lying on the counter.

Paula had left, having slipped out early.

Dear Red, the note began, *I am going to say this as truthfully as I can, hoping I don't hurt you further, so here goes: You are having an affair with alcohol; you've given it your heart and soul. You have shut Myra and everyone else out with that hollow 'You wouldn't understand.' But you don't give anyone the chance to. You don't let anyone in. Alcohol is your bona fide mistress. That is not what marriage is about; it's sharing your joy and pain. Your memories are more than the reality ever was, Basil – it is for everyone. You cling to this farcical notion. Strip the gold, the feelings. Will you love as dearly what is left?*

I love you, Red. I'm your big sister, now and always. I figure you might as well get this from the horse's mouth. Love always, Paula.

He crumpled up the letter and threw it in the garbage. On second thought, he walked over, pulled it out, and shoved it into his pen drawer then shut the drawer on it.

DAY 40

Arizona

Melody came bearing a bouquet of yellow roses and a small bag of medication. "Arizona," she breathed happily. "When I saw that text – "

"I felt so dumb sending it in the middle of the night; no 'hi' or whatever."

"No, no, don't say another word." She pressed the flowers into Arizona's arms. "Here's to 'I'm sorry' and second chances, and to friendship. Please?"

Arizona beamed. She had already forgiven Melody. And besides, no one could stay mad at the bright vision in green and yellow, complete with floral pumps. "Oh, Melody."

She pulled Arizona into a tight embrace. "Where is the little sick kiddo?"

Arizona gestured towards the living room. A bleary-eyed Malcolm sat on the couch, playing with a toy car. He smiled when he saw Melody. "Look how fast my car goes!" He zipped it along the couch cushions.

"Wow, Malcolm!" She turned to Arizona. "Oh, you poor dear. That must have been some fever, huh?"

Arizona shuddered at the memory of last evening. "It was positively frightening, but you know who came to help me?"

"Your mom."

"How did you know?"

Melody shrugged. "She might be oil to your water, but she still has a heart."

Arizona smiled and nodded. Then she told Melody about the last few days.

"You dropped the coffee *and* broke the pot?" Melody gasped, her eyes growing large. "You don't do things in halves, do you?"

Arizona nodded. "That's me. I've never seen her so speechless." She told her about the new coffee pot.

"Williams and Sonoma, and you are not using it? Where is the thing?"

Arizona laughed. "In the cupboard. Don't tell me you want it?"

"Seriously, the thing needs to be displayed and used. You are such a blockhead sometimes!"

"Admit it, you want it."

"One day, when your mom has forgotten, and it's under a thick layer of dust, I will come for it. Just, turn the other way, okay?" She threw her head back then and laughed gaily. "Oh, for a million bucks, I would've loved to have seen the coffee fiasco!"

• • •

Basil

The streets were dark and quiet. But not everywhere. Charleton Boulevard held its own when it came to nightlife.

The gaudy neon signs winked as if to say: "We don't sleep. C'mon! Let's party all night long."

Ace. Basil needed answers, and he wanted them now. Was this elusive character truly responsible for the missing streetwalkers, as Ratford so boldly accused? He needed to help Stacey. He had failed enough women in his life.

"You going rogue on me, Basil?" Wally's voice echoed in his brain.

"Yes, I am, Wally. I have to, and no one will stop me," he spoke quietly and boldly to the star-studded sky. He shivered at the element of danger surrounding him. He crept quietly. It was all cloak and dagger. There was no uniform to set him apart, to present himself as the man who walked with and for the law. The playing field was level; nothing must draw attention to him, although his senses were police-sharp. He had parked his Jetta a street over and walked here on foot. Charleton was not a very safe place; here was the apex of the drug trade in Twin Coulees. He was going into the lion's den as an outsider. The only protection was his police-issue semi-automatic, a Smith and Wesson model 5946.

Two roads diverged in a wood, Wally, and I don't have the foggiest idea where this one will end up.

Are you stark-raving mad? Acting outside of work parameters? Perhaps. He knew what he was doing was irresponsible, reckless, and dangerous. Investigations were meant to be conducted on duty only. If caught, he would be brought up for code of conduct. Perhaps he could kiss his hopes for a detective career goodbye.

But he was beyond second-guessing. There was a restlessness inside him that could no longer be contained. Perhaps he wanted to be caught. Perhaps he wanted something bad to happen to him. God only knew that he felt terribly deserving of this. Nothing so far had been able to assuage his guilt.

No snow fell, and temperatures were holding steady at minus fifteen Celsius. He saw the occasional woman when she moved into the bright light of the streetlamp, no doubt shaking from the cold in her thin fishnet stockings and miniskirt. He saw the furtive movement of a car sliding quietly up to the curb like a yacht easing into harbor, the clandestine murmurs as the woman peeked her head into the window, looked both ways, and then jumped into the car, whisked away.

Hidden in the shadows of buildings, he felt invincible, even for just a brief moment.

Alright, Basil, what exactly are you intending to do?

I am not sure.

Do you have a plan – any plan?

Not really. Talk to Ace. Lure him out and demand answers from him.

Really, and how exactly do you plan to draw answers from him?

"Hey." The low, husky voice took him off guard, and he turned to look into Stacey's face. "What on earth!" she whispered when she recognized his face. "Are you undercover?"

"Nope."

She looked at him closely, her dark eyes unflinching.

"I'm helping you."

She raised her eyes in question. "You need to leave. I shouldn't have come to you."

Then he saw it. A small mark, like a tattoo, on the side of her neck near her collarbone. "Hey, is that a tattoo?"

She shrugged.

"He marks you, doesn't he?"

"It's just a tattoo," she bristled in defense.

"A *barcode* tattoo."

"So? Why on earth would he kill his own?"

None of the deceased women presented with a tattoo.

"And why would he mess with another pimp's women? It would be a death sentence."

His women.

"Go! You can't help anyone *here*."

"Stacey," he hissed and suddenly grasped her arm. "You need to get out of here; you could easily be next! We don't know *who* is behind it. There is still a strong possibility it is Ace. He doesn't care about you women. So long as he gets his money, your lives are not even worth a farthing to him!"

"It's too late for us." Her eyes grew wide, and her mouth formed the word 'no!' at the same time as he felt a crushing impact to the small of his back. Concrete came rushing up to meet him, and the next thing he knew, he was lying on the freezing ground, tasting blood. For all the carefully honed skills drilled into him at Depot, he never saw this one coming.

Like a rag doll, he felt himself being flipped expertly, an alligator shoe pinning him tightly to the ground.

Ace. A bloodless face with thin lips and dead-like fisheyes set deep in a severely pocked face loomed over him. "What's your business here?"

"Ace. You can't. He's – " Stacey's voice trailed off in fear.

"He's what?"

"Um, a paying client. We just had some words."

"What are you doing in my territory, assaultin' my girls?"

"I wasn't. Just looking for information."

"Infomashun, huh?"

"You are Ace, aren't you? All these women who are disappearing – "

He suddenly laughed in derision. "Client! You've just officially met the town's pharmakos."

"Pharmakos?"

"Sacrificial goat of the town." He smiled, revealing an even row of predatory teeth. His face remained taut. His nose was inflamed, probably from coke. His appearance was a startling paradox; a sour smell emitted from him, and yet he wore an expensive shark suit and flashed an equally expensive diamond watch.

Basil laughed and then winced as fiery pain shot through his middle. "And I'm the son of the world's first father."

Ace raised a thin eyebrow. "You've got nerve." Without warning, he kicked Basil sharply in the side, knocking the wind further out of him. He writhed in pain. "Shut your face and pay up. Or get out of here!" He spat a few inches from where Basil lay.

Basil had to get to his feet. "I work for the newspaper. I want to hear your side; get the facts straight."

"Oh, really?" He threw his head back and laughed. Apparently without really realizing it, he had withdrawn his foot from Basil's chest.

Basil knew his perfect opportunity when it glared him in the face. He moved his body down, his left hip inside Ace's right foot. His leg swung outside. Bracing it on Ace's right hip, his right foot came up under his bottom. Ace's right ankle was pulled forward. He pushed forward with his hips. The tables were turned. Ace was on the ground.

Ace glared at him and roared: "You cretin!"

"Please!" Stacey suddenly cried, and for a split second, Basil turned in her direction. A knife glinted inches from his face. Then, a sharp sting on his wrist. Blood spurted from the wound. He clasped his wrist. It was warm and wet. Blood oozed from between his fingers. Ace jumped up, still wielding his knife, and held it inches from Basil's heart. Taking a step back, Basil tripped and landed once again on his back.

All noise seemed to float away. His gaze locked with the dead eyes. This was the end. It was all over.

Suddenly, an arm snaked around Ace's neck. He slumped to the ground, his knife clattering to the pavement.

Sullivan!

"Quick!" Sullivan motioned. "You got this side of thirty seconds. Move!" Pulling Basil, he directed him through a dark door and quietly closed it without turning on the lights.

• • •

"Where are we?" Basil whispered.

"The Little Woodshop right off Charleton. No lights yet in case he's looking for you."

"How did you know how – "

"Where you were, or the carotid control technique?"

"Both, I guess."

"Heard the commotion when closing shop. Worked late. As for the latter, I'm a Korean War vet. What on earth are you trying to do, messing with this guy?"

"I'm a police officer."

"You working undercover?"

"Actually, no."

"Ah, one of those."

"What is that supposed to mean?"

"Working off the grid; either you're an expert in vigilantism, have a score to settle, or paying retribution."

"Retri – what?"

"Retribution."

Basil slumped down on a chair near him. Sullivan peered out the window and decided to flick on a backlight.

"Simple workshop." His liver-spotted hand swept the room. "Do some carving, some custom work, and the like."

Basil nodded mutely and suddenly noticed blood staining his wrist and clothes.

"You've been cut," Sullivan noted matter-of-factly. Despite Basil's protests, he found some bandage and wrapped the wrist carefully. "In a woodworking shop, you're bound to get cuts of yer own. Handy keeping this stuff around."

His piercing eyes scrutinized Basil carefully, and he handed him a cup of steaming tea. "Drink up. This will restore some of your spirits." He finally flipped on a front light. The soft glow illuminated a neat and orderly shop filled with woodworking tools, wood projects in progress, and even finished work.

He didn't need to be asked twice.

Sullivan picked up an unfinished miniature wood canoe he was sanding, and slowly and methodically his hands moved back and forth – large hands with bulbous, calcified knobs.

Basil sipped his tea, feeling the warmth spread through him. The smell of cedar filled his nostrils and brought him back to his boyhood days camping. "You do lots of woodworking?"

Sullivan lifted the canoe this way and that, closely inspecting its surface. "Yep. Carving, sculpting; it's relaxing work. Clocks, shelves, little do-dads. The smaller and more intricate, the better." He worked again quietly for a few moments and then said: "This here is burl wood. Most beautiful wood around. Trees that undergo fungal infection or injury of some kind often produce these growths." Basil bent over to look closely, noting its bold colors and beautiful patterns, his back aching where Ace's painful blow had landed. "Sometimes, it can destroy the tree, but mostly, out of its stress emerges true beauty like this."

Sullivan ran his knobby fingers over the smooth wood. "The tree could give up and die, but it doesn't, instead producing these lumps and swirls of color and design. Kinda like people. Some push through the pain and become stronger and better people, and others find refuge in pills, the bottle, you name it."

Basil stiffened.

Sullivan kept carving and sanding.

Clearing his throat, Basil managed, "You one of those?" His fingers tightly gripped his teacup, even while his brain was telling his mouth to shut it.

"One of what?" he quietly probed.

"Uh, a pill-popper, or," he cleared his throat, "a drinker."

"Was. An alcoholic, that is."

Basil nodded and placed his cup on a shelf near him. He shifted on his feet, his eyes searching for the door. He needed to go. This was too close – much too close for comfort. "I drink, a bit here and there." What was he, some sort of idiot? Why was he flapping his lips? "Never stumbled around like a drunkard." He gave a forced laugh. "Tastes good that stuff; it can warm you deep inside. So long as you can stop when you want to, you know what I mean? Relaxes one, you know, work stress, personal stress. Now, if you see some of the drunks I do, stumbling around, can't hold a job, get violent – "

"It takes one to know one."

Basil's head snapped towards Sullivan as if a live wire had touched a raw nerve. He felt the blood rushing in his ears. He opened his mouth, but no words came out. The man had flipped him inside out and could see right into his soul.

If Sullivan was aware, he didn't let on. The old man moved the canoe away from him, his arm outstretched, and carefully inspected the carving. "What made you tangle with that man?"

Basil exhaled slowly. He mentioned the missing women and his feeling that there was something more sinister behind it all.

Sullivan nodded thoughtfully. "These are women with souls. We don't need to agree with their lifestyle, but we need to realize that all human beings are the same on many levels." He laid the canoe down then and peered intensely at Basil over a pair of spectacles he had put on. "The Bible is the great equalizer, you know that?"

"How so?" Basil questioned.

"God is no respecter of persons. Being addicted to one substance or another is no different to God than selling one's body. Simple as that."

Basil's shoulders tightened again, his eyes frantically searching the dim room.

Sullivan placed a hand softly on his shoulder and shook his head. "I don't have any of that stuff, son."

Basil slowly sank back down.

Stretching the kinks out of his back, Sullivan continued: "...and the evil that lives in the heart of a killer lives in the heart of yours and mine."

Basil looked up, startled. Had he heard the man correctly?

"We want to believe evil lies outside of us – that it is some force aimed at us; sadly, this is light years from the truth. The evil comes from within; it resides inside us. We can never escape it entirely."

"You are not evil, and neither am I!" Basil said defensively. "We're *nothing* like the man carving up these women with medical precision. *We* are fighting evil – we're the good fighting the evil!"

"You know the Bible?"

Basil conceded that he did, but not that he had left it and church behind when Myra and him parted ways.

"Then you know the *Book of Genesis*. Then it follows that this is not such a ludicrous notion at all. Most people have never seen the full panorama of evil; most have never even fathomed its existence. Usually, it is tethered securely, and much must occur to loosen it. For others, the connection is tenuous at best, and little influence is needed to untether it. But it lives in us all."

It lives in us all. A roaring filled Basil's ears, and a sickening feeling rose in his gut. He barely heard Sullivan: "The same heart that desires evil desires vengeance."

Mully's contorted face and bulging eyes swam into focus. He shook his head violently, forcing the image from his mind. He had to get out of there!

• • •

The Boy
1971

He watched her leave. Suitcase in one hand, limp cigarette clamped between heavily rouged lips, tottering on heels much too high.

She didn't wave goodbye. She never looked back. The future was before her. And he was not part of it.

Simple as that.

"You've gone to seed, Horace!" she'd yelled.

"You've driven me to this!" The man raised his beer. "Waltzin' in and out as ye please with nary a care in the world."

She rolled her eyes. "If this is marriage, I want no part of it. Fat, lazy husband and good-for-nuthin' kid!

My dreams all gone. Poof!" She threw her hands in the air dramatically.

He made as if to rise, but she waved him down. "Don't worry, I ain't taken one red cent. You can have the house, the car, and the fat brat."

The boy clutched his ratty Shakespeare, his precious find at a garage sale.

"Ye can't leave your son!"

"Watch me!" she spat.

Pressing his nose against the cool glass, the boy watched her until her image was wet and blurred. His dirty finger picked the blistering paint on the sill over and over and over.

A car gunned impatiently at the end of the drive. She threw her head back with laughter and pitched her suitcase in the back. The car swallowed her as she banged the door on her former life.

The man stood up and ruffled the boy's hair. "She ain't got time for us, son. It'll be just you and me."

He swallowed. The car motor faded beyond the trees. A lone dog whined. "Mother," he whimpered, pressing his body against the wall.

• • •

Arizona

He was gone. One minute, it was the kitty he saw on the sidewalk outside of the window. The next minute, he was not there. The front door was open.

It was the kitten. He had followed it. Children do this all the time.

He wasn't really gone.

It wouldn't happen to a person twice. Lightning doesn't strike you twice.

He was probably hiding. Mischievous streak. He definitely had one of those.

A thought flashed in her mind: if he was gone, she couldn't do life again. She inched along. He was so little, so helpless. It was getting colder. And darker.

She imagined gray lips and pale skin. A body void of life. The police summoned once more to her home. She would have to pick out a coffin this time. A little suit. The questions. The long, lonely nights. It would be Marc in the coffin at the same time.

Only a short while ago, she held a pair of scissors in her hand while staring at Malcolm's tousled hair. She could cut it short. Buzz it even.

But she couldn't fill in the cleft in his chin or straighten the downturn of his mouth. She could not take Marc out of the child. But she no longer wanted to. He was all she had of him – all she had left.

And now her little boy was gone. *Please, God, protect my little boy!*

She picked up her pace. The street was empty. Parked cars. No life. Just a gray strip of nothingness.

Then she heard it. Soft. A meow. The striped cat emerged from the underbelly of her car, stretched lazily, and sat there, licking its paw. She held her breath. He would come scrambling out too. Cherry red cheeks. Begging for a drink. Or a snack.

Nothing.

She dropped on all fours. Hard. Her cheek scraped pavement as she eyed the space between the vehicle and pavement. Nothing.

She turned her watch. The metal was cold. 4:30 pm. A few more minutes of daylight.

She rubbed her chest in agitation. What if she went back inside again? Maybe he would just reappear.

Then a sound. She turned. Malcolm was standing in the doorway.

Suddenly, the world stopped. She ran, scooped him up, and squeezed him in her arms.

Her son. Her little boy. She pressed her face to his hair, something burning deeply within.

• • •

Arizona stroked the thin stem of the purple flower she'd rescued. It sat in a little pot on her windowsill. And still bloomed. *With the right conditions, anything can grow.* She looked to Malcolm's closed door.

DAY 41

Arizona

Arizona was pushing Malcolm on the swings at the playground when she noticed a sleek, silver Jaguar pull up like a boat in a harbor, the faint outline of a man staring at her. Her heart missed a beat, and with cup in hand and fingers tightly gripping the stroller handle, she pushed forward, coffee sloshing over the rim. "Crap!" Forced to stop, she turned her head again, this time staring harder and longer.

Father?

As far back as she could remember, Clanton Beckam had never visited her in Twin Coulees. In fact, she barely saw him with his business ventures abroad. When was the last time she'd seen him? He'd popped up like a jack-in-the-box, something he'd done ever since she was a baby.

"Hi!" he called out with a wide smile, his long legs easily covering the distance between them. "Zonie," he smiled, tugging a lock of her hair. "Haven't seen you in a long time."

She stared at him. Funny how he could just roll into her world again with such ease. He wore a Ralph Lauren business suit and expensive cut and cologne, the well-heeled businessman. "I haven't seen you in a while." Her cup shook.

"This the little man your mother was talking about? Cute guy." He dropped to one knee and looked Malcolm in the eyes. "Hi there, fella."

Malcolm did not smile back and merely leaned towards Arizona.

"He doesn't do well with strangers."

"Touché," he replied with a slight grin.

His face was all angles and planes. His hair was grayer, but the skin was still chiseled and smooth. Money could do that.

She worked up her courage. "Haven't seen you since Marc's – no, wait, you didn't make it."

"I tried, Zonie, remember? Emergency abroad."

"Right. Something about recovering lost assets or *burying* a bad business deal. More important than family.

"Zonie, please!" He gave a short laugh then. "The apple does not fall far from the tree."

"What's that supposed to mean?"

"Look, can we stop by your place for a coffee? You know, catch up?"

"No. Um, a coffee shop would be better."

"Okay. How about you and the boy ride with me, Zonie?"

Zonie. The name he had given her affectionately when she was little. A pesky lump formed in her throat.

"We'll walk. *Malcolm* has no car seat here."

He shrugged. "Suit yourself."

He reached out and touched her chin. "My rebellious spitfire. Good to see you again." Like they were old acquaintances, ships passing in the night, not father and daughter.

Clanton Beckam was quite different from his wife. He was not a master manipulator, at least not overtly. He was more a shapeshifter, morphing in and out of roles when needed; a peg soldered to fit a specific opening, Estelle had chiseled him to fit her agenda.

He was like a puppet.

But then again, not really. That was the beauty of it. He was no one's puppet. Rather, he could blend and twist, rising to the occasion when needed, giving the impression he was a limp noodle next to Estelle. A master at knowing what was needed and when, while temporarily suspending his needs to ensure Estelle looked perfect, he contributed to her artifice willingly and superbly. On the flip side, when he was on business trips, he had a "get out of jail free" card. They were a master team.

Fifteen minutes later, they sat in a booth at Gemma's, sunlight highlighting the years of excess, red-eyed flights, and business stress that left their narrative on his slightly bent frame.

"Got you a coffee."

"Thanks." She didn't really feel like another one, but she wanted to keep her hands busy. "Why are you suddenly here?"

"Can't a father visit his only daughter?"

Arizona tore at her napkin. Malcom chattered in his stroller and paid them no regard.

"Look, Zonie, I know I haven't always been there for you. Marc is gone. I know I never gave him the time of day, and I am truly sorry for that, but this…this limbo you are living in has to end."

She balled the napkin in her fist.

"I wanted to do for you what my father never could. Give you what material things I could." He covered her small hands with his large, manicured ones, but she pulled away as if burnt.

"Time, Daddy!" The words leapt out, her napkin suddenly forgotten. "Your money doesn't matter. Being there for birthdays, graduation, not some stupid, gold-embossed card or expensive trinket."

He rubbed his face and sighed. "I'm sorry you feel this way, Zonie."

Oh, so he was going to make this about her. She gulped her coffee, nearly choking on the hot liquid.

"I tried, Zonie. I screwed up, I know that. But I truly did try."

She kept silent, fearing that if she spoke, a cascade of tears would come as well.

"Come visit us in Calgary. I'm home for a longer stretch now. Do Christmas with us. You and Max, Mom and I. She needs – "

"It's *Malcolm*."

"Yes, Malcolm. Sorry." He popped the boy gently on the nose and laughed as Malcolm giggled.

He suddenly looked serious and rubbed the back of his neck. "I do have news, actually."

Arizona stared at him with a frown.

"Mom has cancer. Breast cancer."

There was a buzz in her ears. "What – how?"

"Stage three. There will be chemo and radiation following a – "

"No!"

" – a mastectomy."

"She can't – she can't do that!"

He looked at her gently. "Arizona – "

"It will kill her. You know that. Her body. Her looks – "

"She is tougher than you'll ever know, Arizona. She

didn't want you to know yet, so let her break the news to you herself. I'm just trying to prepare you."

Arizona sank back onto her chair. She rubbed Malcolm's arm and pulled the stroller close to her. "She looked done the other day."

He nodded and stared quietly out of the window. Arizona noticed the fine wrinkles that ran out from his thin lips. "She's dealing with this all in her own way."

"With everything under lock and key."

"Yup. I know she has this need to orchestrate your life."

Her brain spun.

"But she has this inner pain that no one can touch."

"Why?"

"She won't let anyone near it."

Malcolm started fussing, and she pulled him onto her lap, letting him play with her empty cup.

"She doesn't always have a delicate touch, Arizona, but if you understand some of her motivations, you'll see why she does what she does. Just give in to some of her demands; smooth the waters a bit. She'll come around. You'll see. She is her own worst enemy."

She nodded silently again.

He signaled for the bill. "You know what? I think you should stay with us for a while. Don't look so shocked. I hear there's a killer on the loose here."

Arizona shook her head, "I'm a big girl. Besides, I'm not ready for that." *You give an inch, and they take a mile.*

He looked at her intently for a long moment. "Please be careful, Arizona." He paid for their bill, kissed her on the cheek, ruffled Malcolm's hair, and then was gone.

Like a jack-in-the-box.

She sat for a long time, her head still spinning, until Malcolm tugged at her sleeve.

•••

Basil

Basil was on Milner's Road, ready to turn northbound, when the call came in of a red van going southbound from Okotoks. It was clocking at over 160k and refusing to pull over.

"2-Alpha-23 ready to exit Twin Coulees," Basil informed dispatch.

A Highway Patrol unit quickly informed dispatch that she was free to respond from Nanton, a small town situated further south. The traffic car had a spike belt that would hopefully work if she could lay it out in time, and provided the van did not take any side roads.

"...no license plate visible on vehicle," dispatch continued.

"Standby, Alpha-23," Ichabod's voice came over the radio." The chasing car, Bravo-8, would have to keep the pursued vehicle in sight. With traffic sparse, and the weather dry, the chase would continue without threat to public safety. Basil felt adrenaline pulse through his body.

It was only minutes later when Bravo-8 came on air to inform them the van had crashed. It had indeed taken a side road without slowing down and rolled several times. In one anticlimactic twist, a life had possibly been snuffed out. He immediately requested EMS and Fire and the assistance of another car.

Over the wail of his siren, Basil gave a clipped 10-4 to dispatch's request, his heart racing wildly. High-speed crashes were often fatal.

The van lay on its roof, the body crumpled like a piece of aluminum foil, its now motionless wheels sticking out like the limbs of a dying animal, underbelly completely exposed. His stomach lurched. There was no way anybody could survive that.

Opening his door against the cacophony of sirens, Basil noted the red paint on the mangled body of the truck. It was dull – the job of an amateur. Something registered in his mind then.

The short constable of Bravo-8 walked towards him, shaking his head, his breath making little clouds in the air. "He's gone." His face was white.

"ID?" he asked over the grinding sound of the jaws of life.

"Soon as they can get to it."

Basil nodded, pulling his toque solidly over his ears, impatience building.

It seemed to take forever. "A Bob Higginson," Constable Peters scrutinized the license card carefully once he procured it.

Basil's heart slammed in his chest.

"Say, wait a minute, is he – "

"The vehicle of interest. No license plate, run-of-the-mill paint job. We need to see what's in the van." He felt the coils of tension in his shoulders as he jogged to the firefighters and the twisted wreckage. Glimpsing at the driver's side, he saw the arm dangling out of the window, twisted at an odd angle.

Higginson. The buzzing began at the base of his neck, and he gritted his teeth. *Focus, focus!*

He quickly instructed two of the firemen to gain some sort of entry into the back of the vehicle, and they quickly obliged.

A loud crack reverberated through the air, and the mangled back doors fell onto the frozen grass.

All at once, it was the moment he was waiting for. He braced himself, hardly feeling the cold, and peered into the back of what was left of the cargo van.

• • •

Constable Peters whistled as he peered over Basil's shoulder. Broken wires, glass, electronic parts, and smashed-in computer monitors littered the floor.

It was relief and disappointment rolled in one. The hastily repainted vehicle had been a convenient holding tank for the spoils of obviously more than one robbery.

Basil shook his head, his heart still galloping furiously. It was back to the drawing board again. Higginson might be out of the game, but they weren't short on players.

DAY 42

Basil

Then the crap really hit the fan. Another body showed up. Another woman. No obvious cause of death; no blood, no noticeable wounds.

Basil reached for the zipper on her leather jacket. *Please,* he prayed, *please, let it not be her!* But it was – the tell-tale incision on the lower left quadrant. Jagged and uneven suturing, the obvious work of an amateur.

He stared at the open, glazed eyes and the parted lips. *Talk!* he wanted to yell in desperation. *Who did this to you? Help us so we can put him away for good.*

Another nameless woman; no ID was to be found on her person. Then he remembered something.

It took him some time, but he found Stacey, who positively identified the woman as one of the missing streetwalkers: "Louisa. No, I don't know her last name; we all just knew her has Lola. I told you! Here is your proof," she cried bitterly. "Now don't you see?"

He wished he could say, "Score, we got it!" But they needed more. Where were the other missing women – women missing over the past few months? These victims were recent. The connection between these women and the others was tenuous at best. If only he could find them, dead or alive, this would be the missing piece of the puzzle. Well, one of them, really. There was still the dilemma related to the missing kidney.

"If another kidney is missing," Jarowicz noted ominously, "we might very well be dealing with a black market in kidney organs. I have a feeling that whoever is behind this is not quite done. These women have been singled out for some reason, and we have to find what it is if we're to stop this."

Clarkson stopped by to see if he could join a ride-along that day, but Basil politely turned him down. "Now is a bad time; mind taking a rain check?"

"Not at all. I understand. Here, brought you a coffee. I know you guys are busy."

"A coffee, I can always use," said Basil, thanking him.

A shadow appeared on Clarkson's face. "There is a murderer on the loose, isn't there?" He whispered. "That woman – there are more, aren't there?"

"Very possibly," Basil reluctantly answered. Last thing he wanted to do was instill unnecessary fear. A town in the grips of hysteria was one nightmare they could all do without.

Clarkson nodded slowly. "Coward, cutting into women like that!"

"Most killers are cowards," he agreed. "But we're on it, and hopefully we can nip this in the bud!"

Best you don't know yet, he thought, *that very soon you may be delivering news of a serial killer on the loose, and a warning for women everywhere to take caution.*

• • •

Ratford burst into the detachment and headed straight for Ichabod's office, his face an angry scar, dark eyes bulging. Ichabod was just stepping out of his office at that moment. "*The Globe and Mail*!" He spluttered." What's next? *CBC*? *National*?"

"Look – " Ichabod began.

"This is our first publicity in who knows how long, and look at this!" He stabbed the article. "You need to stamp this out. There needs to be some sort of media blackout here. We are going to be in the grip of hysteria before the day is over! This sort of news does not put us on the map!"

"Unfortunately, it does," Ichabod responded with a deadpan face. The tables had been turned. No longer would the streetwalkers be so demonized if one followed the vein of the news; they were helpless victims of something large, something fearful, and something possibly predatory. Everyone was in it together. And apparently, Ratford didn't want them to be considered as one of them.

"Two deaths do not mean women are dropping like flies!" Ratford took out a hankie and mopped his red face.

Basil pretended he was busy typing a report, but he found his peripheral vision to be in excellent shape.

Ichabod shrugged and rearranged his piles of paper. "You can thank the press for that one," he waved a hand. "You give them an inch, and they run a mile."

"There needs to be some sort of wall that restrains them. Information should not be siphoned out!"

Ichabod sighed in exasperation and folded his arms. "No RCMP member has fed the media undisclosed information. We've not released any information, but word gets around. If we censor the media, there will be a far greater outcry and accusations of covering up."

He wields the sword of politics with the clumsy aim of a toddler, Basil thought. But then he remembered Stacey and what she'd said about his non-existent fuse.

"You are stirring up a hornet's nest here," Ratford said, changing tactics. "You've taken an interest in the 'plight' of the prostitutes, but they don't need *a voice*."

Basil flinched.

"We've not stirred up anything," Ichabod asserted.

"I think, sir, we are failing to protect society's most vulnerable," Basil suddenly interjected.

Ratford turned slowly to face him. For a moment, Basil saw Jules' green eyes, and Mully's brown ones, bulging in the throes of death.

"As mayor, it is my duty to protect *all* citizens. You want to speak of our most vulnerable? What about our youth, a prime target for drugs? And the businesses – mom and pop shops – that are affected?" Ratford turned to Ichabod. "I know you and your men are professional and able, but don't you think Ace should be your goal?"

"If we can actually find Ace, the women will just become the property of another pimp." Ichabod's tone was hard and flat.

Ratford shook his head. "Ace could be the murderer. It wouldn't be the first time one of the women tried to cheat her pimp and fell for his revenge."

"You do realize that you are suggesting these missing women have been murdered?" Ichabod asked quietly. "Something you initially denied. If so, you also realize we must investigate this angle. No one is suggesting these women are the only victims, but rather possibly part of something larger. But they're still human beings; individuals who need our help, not to be the target of some personal vendetta."

Ratford looked at them stonily, but something flickered in his eyes.

Basil's cellphone began to spin on the table in front of him, then stopped as if it had changed its mind. Just like that one day…

"Look!" Ratford sputtered.

Basil startled but realized Ratford wasn't speaking to him.

"I just don't want our town being media fodder for the gossip rags. You *know* the media; they will spin their threads of deception. We're a small town; we shouldn't even be having a prostitute problem!" He took out a hankie and mopped his red, sweaty face.

Ichabod ran a beefy hand through his hair. "Hate to drag stats into this, sir, but small towns are actually the perfect place for those escaping detection in larger cities, and Twin Coulees is certainly not any less immune to this. We'll have to feed the media a generous morsel rather than a few crumbs if we want to ensure correct facts and prevent hysteria."

• • •

Numbly, Basil walked outside to his vehicle. He saw crazy-eyed Mully walking erratically on the opposite sidewalk. He listened distractedly to the ditty he slurred off-key:

"Mary, Mary, quite contrary,
how does your garden grow?
With piles of bones, and dirt-filled skulls,
and broken bodies all in a row."

In that moment, he envied Mully. The man was a homeless drunk, but surely he wasn't hitched to a cart of guilt. He could lay his head down at night, whether on a soft pillow or the cold hardness of a rock, and sleep peacefully.

• • •

Standing in front of his bathroom mirror, he opened his button-up shirt. The disfiguring scar stared at him with its thick redness and jagged borders – the only physical reminder of that fateful day.

He'd agreed to meet Jules. She had some information on a suspect they were tailing. Finally, the breakthrough they were looking for. He'd been off duty then, waiting for her alongside the street. She'd turned the corner faster than normal and lost control, hitting a pole. He would never forget the sudden burst of flame, the intense heat, the desperate eyes of a woman on the cusp of death.

"I tried. God knows I tried to save her," he whispered at his blurred image in the mirror.

He had gone after the drug kingpin with animal savagery raging in his blood. His detachment proclaimed him a hero, and the newspaper sang: "Cops Praised for Uncovering Drug Kingpin."

But there were always some who wondered. Had he left her there to die so he could bring home the gold?

Plopping down onto the couch, an undertow of exhaustion pulled him into the murky waters of sleep.

Evil lives in us all.

He woke and sat up in broken sweat. Suddenly, he needed air.

The late afternoon sky was whitish gray, signaling snow and temperatures holding steady at minus two. The blast of cold air made his sweaty body shiver.

• • •

Wilson Street was at the edge of town. A long, brisk walk, and he would be at the strip. The majestic bird would be perched in her nest, one wing tipped silently skyward. But here, he'd felt the only peace he'd known in months, and like some starved animal with singular focus, he wanted to run there.

The words continued to burn inside his head; they crawled around in his brain like a terrible itch he could not get at.

Before he knew it, he spotted the old hangar. All was silent. Somewhere in the deep recesses of his brain, he'd known he was chasing peace like an elusive mirage.

He inhaled cold, crisp air and noted the lone poplar standing near the hangar. Around its base, the snow had slightly receded. Its craggy arms stretched heavenward in a sort of desperate plea.

Then he noticed it. An odd, brownish lump. He peered closely and then walked towards it. Even from a few meters away, he saw the tufts of gray hair, scraggly and sparse. His heart sped up.

A body.

• • •

Sullivan lay forward on the snow. For one wild moment, he imagined Sullivan as the next murder victim. The first *male* victim – a change in the killer's M.O.

"Sullivan?" His voice broke. He moved quickly, dropping to his knees beside the still form. "Sullivan!" There was nothing. The thin man hugged the ground as if he were asleep. He slapped the pale cheeks roughly. "Sullivan!" Was it a heart attack? Was he dead?

He grabbed his mobile and dialed, his numb fingers barely moving. His words slid over each other as he tried to communicate with dispatch.

A muffled moan.

Relief swept through him, and he pulled off his coat, draping it over Sullivan. "Are you hurt? Where are you hurt?" He couldn't move him for fear he had broken his neck. Suddenly, he noticed the roots of the tree rising from the soil like the bulbous fingers of some groping skeleton. He must have tripped over them.

Sullivan turned his head side to side weakly. "My ankle. I think I broke it." He winced as he turned his body, and Basil carefully used his strength to turn him over, noting the pain etched on the old man's face.

Just his ankle! Immediate relief washed over him. "Help is on the way. Glad I found you here. It's getting colder." Sullivan's face blurred in front of him, and something stuck in his throat.

• • •

Basil sank weakly into a sitting position, the sky stretching above him as a white canopy of nothingness. In the distance, he heard the fading wail of the siren. He watched as the black night swallowed the ambulance. Snowflakes fell softly around him, and he stared, transfixed. Sullivan might be old and held together by sagging skin and rusty joints, but he was like a diamond in the rough.

DAY 43

Basil

Jarowicz stood in Ichabod's office, face creased in concentration. "Kidney missing alright. Louisa's autopsy report eerily mirrors that of Janey McAlistair. Except for a missing kidney, she was in good health. She did have scarring from a past infection, but similar to McAlistair, there was no clue as to what killed her. Despite the fact that the suturing was a pathetic 'hack' job, it must have been done in relative sterility as there were no findings of septic or bacterial infection often found in someone who dies of systemic infection."

"Doesn't congestion of organs often suggest an overwhelming illness prior to death, sir?" Basil asked.

Jarowicz nodded. "Sepsis opens up capillaries and causes organs in the body to swell considerably. Neither report indicated congestion nor swelling of any kind."

Ichabod scrunched his face, his bushy eyebrows wriggling like caterpillars. "Usually, trafficking occurs in hospitals with doctors who are performing these operations illegally. There's usually money involved and some sort of system. But this feels different. Even back-alley organ pilfering doesn't usually end with a body left in plain sight to be readily discovered."

Basil noted, "From everything I have read, China seems to be a top contender for organ trafficking, but Canada? You usually hear of people waking up in bathtubs filled with ice, not dumped in plain view on the street."

Jarowicz nodded. "Think about it; we can search meticulously, but in cases like these, the traffickers are long gone." He paused a moment. "Okay, back to the drawing board; let's lay the facts on the table. There are a few common threads." He scribbled on the whiteboard in front of them, his writing worse than a doctor's prescription. But Ichabod and Basil followed his train of thought easily. The visual before them reminded them they knew little of what was going on. "All are women, generally young. Laramie's body has a very similar incision, but it's superficial. It's a slight anomaly only, like a hesitation cut of some kind. They're all missing their right kidney, except Laramie. I hesitate to add her to the roster of women for now. If not drug trafficking, why take their kidneys? It's unclear exactly how these women died. It's perplexing; I mean, preliminary reports cannot find a specific cause. If this isn't some organized process, these women did not die of infection. So, either the perp or perps practiced sanitation, or the kidneys were extracted post-death. But this begs the question: what exactly killed them?"

"Why these women? Why no men? Why leave these women for dead and dump them in public places?" Basil queried. "And the missing streetwalkers? They could be part of the puzzle." *It's not Ace.* But he couldn't tell them that.

"Leave the missing streetwalkers out of the equation for now," Jarowicz said, and Ichabod nodded in agreement, annoyed almost that Basil was picking at this thread once again. "Look," he added, seeming to note the concern on Basil's face, "I'm not disregarding it; I've just placed it on the back burner for now. As soon as it fits in somewhere, I'll entertain it."

At least they were on his radar. "What about Louisa? She was a streetwalker."

"And that may be her only connection to them. Have we found her family?"

"Picture is posted on our website."

"Alright, I've tacked a photo of each woman onto the board." Three grainy photos of women lying peacefully on autopsy tables were displayed before them. Quiet and serene in death.

"Do you see similarities?"

Two heads shook slowly. Adele's hair was grayish, Janey had platinum blonde hair, and Louisa had dark black ringlets. Janey was tall, but Adele and Louisa were on the short side. Even eye color differed. If the killer had targeted them due to any physical characteristics, it was certainly not obvious exactly what the similarities were.

"Okay, let's dig a bit deeper. First one: Adele Laramie."

"No family in Alberta," Basil supplied. "No parents. A sister she was estranged from living in New Brunswick. She's been contacted but refused to fly down for the funeral. Some bad blood there."

"Janey McAllistair."

"Her grandmother has been notified. Janey was missing in the days preceding us finding her body. Higginson was the last to see her alive, but there was nothing suspicious surrounding it."

Jarowicz chewed his lip in contemplation. He turned his troubled face to Ichabod. "We might not know what the motivations behind these deaths are, why kidneys are missing, or what even killed these women, but we're dealing with a serial killer. This does not feel like organ trafficking. I tend to agree with Basil; we have a deliberate placing of bodies." His mouth was stitched in a tight line. "I'm going to tighten the screws on the medical examiner to rush the full workups."

Once in the briefing room, he instructed Basil, Wally, and Nygard to return to those they'd interviewed and see if anything else could be obtained. "Retrace your steps," he ordered. "See if anything, no matter how trivial it might appear, has been missed."

"We have our work cut out for us if we are looking for a serial killer," Constable Nygard noted worriedly. The label was on everyone's lips. "He or she is clearly taunting us."

"All right, gentlemen," Jarowicz said, waving his hand. "Let's not get ahead of ourselves. One thing I would like to make clear. Forget the stereotypical view of killers. Most are not dysfunctional, or loners, or even social misfits. Why are they so difficult to pin down? They blend with the rest of society."

"Anyone of the populace of four thousand in Twin Coulees could be a killer," Wally noted.

"Why were their kidneys taken, if not for trade?" Basil questioned aloud. "Why kidneys? Why these particular women?" Suddenly, he wanted a stiff one badly. Just one drop...

"Thankfully, it's the dead of winter..."

Cold and strong to drown away all this pain.

DAY 44

Basil

The baby-faced reporter was waiting for him, a smug smile plastered across his face. Today, there were no horn-rimmed glasses. He wore a crisp suit and brightly colored tie. "Constable Andrews," he greeted, thrusting out his hand.

Basil frowned at the hand, then indulged him for the merest of moments. It was limp and soft. "More interviews?"

Williams smiled pleasantly. "Actually, yes. Not the recent murders, though."

"Oh?" Basil glanced around. The detachment was quiet.

Eyes sparkling as if he held a treasured secret in his hands, Williams suddenly leaned in. "I recognized you the other day." He stepped back with a nod.

"Really?" Basil's heart kicked up a notch.

"I did a stint in Calgary when I was just getting my feet wet. That horrific crash involving Constable Marguiles – the one where you left the scene."

Basil recoiled, a sour taste in his mouth.

"Can I do a feature piece on you?"

"No."

"Look, you're newish here. Show the public life after a tragedy; how well you're fitting in here. The local hero. You did get the guy by the jugular, so to speak."

"Forget it!"

But Williams didn't. "Something different from the depressing news going on right now. I will spin it in a positive light, of course – a bit of an accolade, if you will."

"As opposed to what light?" Basil clipped. He felt the moisture in his palms and under his collar.

Suddenly, there was a buzz. William's mouth moved, but there was no sound. His hands gestured, and his face contorted. Basil saw again Jules' eyes, suddenly green and pleading. He homed in on the fleck, accentuating her desperation. The blast of heat slammed into him like a concrete wall. Angry flames licked insatiably, shoving him backward. "I gave in."

"What?" The man looked perplexed.

Basil startled. Had he just spoken? What had just happened? Williams. He had to get him out of there. "You know nothing about my life or what happened. It's closed, you hear, closed!"

Williams' eyes grew wide, and he stumbled over his words. "Sorry, look, if you reconsider at any point – "

The man was like a painful itch. "I won't."

" – then, um, you know where we are located."

"I have no interest."

"Please," he walked backward, thrusting out his card.

Basil reached for it gingerly. Williams fled.

He balled the card in his fist and shot it into the wastebasket.

It was the red hair. *Always* the red hair.

• • •

Nora

Reg came home late that day, rubbing his leg.

"Is it bugging you again?" she asked.

He sighed. "This colder weather really settles around old wounds." He dropped into a chair. "Can you get me a paper and pen?"

"Sure, whatever for?"

"I have decided to write a letter to the editor. It isn't right how the police are being treated in light of these murders, as if they are somehow responsible."

"That's a good idea."

"I hate it when blame is pointed in the wrong direction." His face was a spasm of frustration, even – to her surprise – anger. He sat there, pen scratching the paper, the glow of the lamp highlighting the bulge in his face where his tongue pressed against his cheek.

He looked at her suddenly, pen hovering over the paper. "Please keep the doors bolted, Nora," he begged her. "No one seems safe anymore these days."

"I will," she responded, a catch to her voice.

Finally, he was done. "You know what? I think this perpetrator is after certain women – just not sure what his motive is. But then," he shook his head, "neither are the police."

There was a buzzing in Nora's head. She rubbed her arms and glanced at the bird on the bookshelf.

• • •

Arizona

She sat in their heated sunporch, staring at the grayness all around her, hunched over in a bright terry robe like a wilted flower.

"Mom?" She felt a sudden impulse to hug her.

Estelle turned around to see Arizona and Malcolm. "He told you." The voice wasn't accusing, simply couched in defeat. "Oh, Clanton," she sighed, shaking her head. "You've enough on your plate now, Arizona!"

"Mom, I needed to know this. You need support!"

Estelle's head dipped. "I haven't exactly supported you." She twisted her hands on her lap.

"This is real life, Mom. What you're going through, what I've gone through. We can help each other."

Malcolm walked to her. "Kitty?" His face was confused when he did not see the shirt with the kitty on it. Estelle tensed. It was like she'd never helped nurse the fevered child or hugged him tight. She'd unlocked a part of herself that night. But now it was locked again.

For the first time, Arizona noticed the lines around her mother's mouth, how they dipped into a slight downturn on each side of suddenly thin lips, the slight sag of skin that was becoming more porous. It was amazing how immediately time-worn the face's canvas could look when the layers of commercial beauty were stripped away. Today, there was realness and rawness there.

"You have cancer. Say it, Mom," she said. "Own it, just for once. Don't try to run away or hide from it." She sat down in a white wicker chair and leaned forward. Malcolm had skipped unperturbed out of the room, searching for her father.

Estelle looked at her. "I don't run from things, Arizona; I face them." But her voice held an edge, and Arizona glimpsed the shimmer of tears in her eyes. She stood up. "I don't want pity, Arizona. I can't abide all this ridiculous fussing over nothing!"

"Nothing? Mother, it's cancer! Not some little infection."

"Sometimes, it's easier to go through things alone." But the trembling of her lips showed she did not even believe it herself.

Arizona took a deep breath and barrelled on. "Like what Nana was hinting at?"

Estelle turned away. "That was nothing. No one's concern. Besides, her mind, you know."

"Please, Mom? I think I need to know. I think *you* need me to know."

Estelle clutched the robe around her, her mouth firmly set. She stared out the sunroom windows at the somber sky. "Even your father doesn't know," she finally whispered.

"Actually, I do."

Estelle turned to him. "Clanton!"

"I have always known, Essie." Clanton stood in the doorway, hands shoved into the pockets of his slacks, his voice calm and gentle.

She faced him, mouth agape.

He walked slowly towards her. "The blue booties, the little sailor outfit folded up. A little different each time. I know you touch them, look at them."

She shook her head. "No."

Arizona sat in shock. What was her father suggesting? "Mother?" she asked timidly.

Estelle walked to her bookcase and ran her fingers over the books as if she were drawing some comfort from the luxuriously bound volumes. She turned around and then faced the books again.

"Mom!"

She pulled out books halfway and slammed them in again. "These aren't in order. I told Leah, alphabetical!"

"Essie, please!" Clanton begged.

"We shouldn't have to chase after her. The dust, it's like layers." She ran her fingers over the exposed shelving, over and over.

Essie!"

Estelle suddenly whipped around. "No!" She shook her head.

"Please, darling."

"Why are you cornering me? I can't – " She was like a trapped moth, wings banging against the wall.

"No more running, Essie," Clanton stated firmly. "For your own health and peace of mind, it has to stop."

"How did you know, Clanton?" Her voice broke.

"When you live with someone as long as I have, you just know them."

"I didn't want to."

"I know, Essie." He took hold of her shoulders.

"I was young, I was afraid," she whispered, her eyes wet.

"Oh, Mom." Suddenly, like pieces falling into place, it all made sense. Marc. Malcolm. She reached for her mother's arm.

Estelle faced her daughter. "You kept a child, not your own, and I killed my baby boy." Her voice was thin and erratic.

Arizona felt the wind knocked out of her.

"He would've been Marc's age. And little Malcolm. It's all shoved in my face; my sin pointed at me day after day!"

Arizona withdrew her arm as Clanton pressed Estelle to him, trying to calm her agitation. She walked backward, nearly stumbled, and exited the room. Goose pimples popped up over her flesh as she watched the one predictable presence in her life become unglued. She felt a strange sensation in her stomach that made her want to cry and run at the same time. Instead, she softly closed the sunroom doors. Estelle sat crumpled on the floor, all poise and control a distant memory, her husband crouched beside her, picking up the pieces.

Arizona found Malcolm staring out the dining room window, watching an excavator at work. His little face was pressed to the window, his eyes mesmerized. He unglued his face when he heard her and banged his fist against the window. "Look at the truck!" he shouted gleefully.

Something danced inside her as she watched the glow on his face. Suddenly, she saw it. The rain had stopped, and a beautiful rainbow was arcing across the sky.

• • •

Basil

Basil sat in his recliner, deep in thought when the doorbell rang.

It was Myra. He blinked twice. She was still there. Smaller than he remembered, like a feather that could blow away at any moment. Her hair was freshly styled, flipping in with soft edges. She wore a navy peacoat and brown leather boots that nearly reached her knees. She was a character out of a new book; confident, glowing. He swallowed a lump in his throat.

She smiled at him, and it twisted like steel in his gut. "Um, can I come in?"

"Uh, sure." He quickly moved so she could enter. Wild thoughts ran through his mind. There were dishes everywhere, laundry piled up, garbage not taken out for days. Did the house smell stale? He watched her carefully, but she did not look past him.

His heart dropped.

"I got this letter in the mail." She pulled out a legal-sized envelope. "They want to tear down our house. Development." She cleared her throat. Small, delicate fingers adjusted her purse strap.

He stared at it as his mind raced. *Our* house. Their dream plans; their renovations. Vaporized!

"Look, can we meet for coffee tomorrow sometime? To discuss things."

Discuss things. Now, there was a loaded statement. Numbly, he agreed. His stomach contracted. It was happening, really happening. This was the perfect time for her to make things formal. She left swiftly, like a ghost.

He watched her like a peeping Tom from an obscure opening in his blinds. She looked twice, crossed the street to her car, and was gone. No backward glance.

DAY 45

Basil

She was sitting in Shorty's the next afternoon when he got there. A white cardigan sat like a glove on her small frame.

"Hi," she greeted him with a quivering smile. "I ordered us coffee."

"Thanks." He folded and unfolded his hands underneath the table. Her face was pale, and a fine sheen of moisture lined her upper lip. She played with her hands, and he watched the smooth skin, the delicate fingers – fingers which he once upon a time intertwined in his own. He shifted uncomfortably. She reached under the table to pull up her purse just as a teenage waiter brought their steaming drinks.

Basil felt he was on a tightrope, ready for the fall. His wife was about to serve him with papers. Over coffee. How classy.

But she didn't open the purse. Just clutched it to her like a shield. "Nice little place," she commented casually.

He stretched his legs out. "Yes, it seems to be." As if this was a new place for him, as well, and not his local watering hole. His right foot touched her leg, and an electric current rushed through him. He carefully pulled his foot back and sat up straighter.

"So," she hesitated. "What do we do about the house?" Her eyes searched his face.

For a moment, he did not answer. What should they do about the house? "How long do we have to decide?" he asked calmly. His gut churned.

"A few weeks. Though they do want a timely answer." Myra had always been the one doing the bills. The one on top of things.

She suddenly pulled out an envelope and laid it on the table. He noticed immediately this envelope was different from the one he saw yesterday. He tried not to show his surprise. Act cool – act nonchalant. Carefully, he raised his mug and gulped too much, too quickly. He felt the blood rise to his cheeks. His tongue suddenly felt raw. There was a sudden, feverish air about her. The glow – it was back. There was a fire in her eyes. He played with the tablecloth that hung onto his lap and dug his nails into its thin waxiness.

She cleared her throat, took a sip of her own coffee, and gently set it down.

"What are your thoughts?" he asked, running his index finger over the smooth porcelain of the mug handle.

"Well – " She touched the white envelope for a second.

Here it comes! he thought. *She's going to slide it my way.* He analyzed the envelope. How many pages were there? Was he to read the papers in front of her?

"I don't know how to tell you this," she offered a wobbly smile.

As quick and pain-free as possible, he thought with sudden desperation. He didn't want to decide. A ray of sunshine pierced him from a nearby window. The sky was a brilliant blue. He could be gliding far above all this. Myra and life could be mere dots below. He glared at the envelope, wishing it would disappear. Decisions. He hated them. "I haven't even entered any program yet," he said, clearly aware the word "yet" gave a subtle air of hope.

"Oh," she was taken aback. "I never – "

"Please, let's not drag this out."

She blinked, confusion spreading across her face.

"You've made it clear; the ball is in my court."

"Stop," she said. Her fingers picked up the envelope.

He sat back, arms folded, his lips pressed tightly.

"I know we're in a mess."

He rubbed the back of his neck, muscles corded with tension. He watched the man at a nearby table lift a bottle of beer to his lips. Inside, he panted like a dog.

"Here. Open this. Please."

It was happening. This all felt surreal. He wanted to push his chair back and make a quick exit. If she expected him to sit there while she dished it out for him…

Coward! he told himself. *You want to run away from this like you've done with others.*

From Myra.

From Paula

From Sullivan.

From *everyone.*

"Okay." His throat felt raw. He rolled his shoulders to shake out the tension. Pretend he was calm and collected. His hand shook slightly as he took the warm envelope. He noticed the stains of sweat where small, clammy hands had grasped it. He played different scenarios in his head. He could crush this thing. Walk out and leave her spluttering. Or he could apologize. Admit he was a fool, a slave to drink. He felt her eyes on him. Expectant. Waiting. His stomach clenched.

Trembling fingers unflapped the envelope. A series of thin sheets fell out – carbon-like paper. He picked up the first one. A black-and-white image stared back at him. An ultrasound image? A white, round head. A tiny, balled fist. The ache settled under his ribcage.

For a long moment, he stared at it, his heart pounding.

A baby. *Their* baby?

A roaring filled his ears, and the slip of paper fluttered from weak fingers.

DAY 46

Basil

As soon as the Chinook hit Twin Coulees, Basil jumped at the chance to take to the skies with Sullivan. His ankle was healing nicely, encased in an air cast.

A dizzying rush of air, and he was airborne. It was a cold day, but the sun shone brightly, comfortably heating the glass enclosure.

Looking at the white fields below him, a familiar tune crept into his mind: "Mary, Mary, quite contrary, *where* does your garden grow?"

Garden…? Wait a New York minute! he thought. "Sullivan, do you mind landing this thing? I have to do something urgent. Please."

Sullivan looked at him in surprise but obliged immediately, pulling the spoilers to begin landing the aircraft.

He had to get to Mully. He was off-duty, and perhaps Mully wouldn't cooperate, but who knew? If Basil appeared without his uniform, it just might loosen Mully's tongue a bit, if the alcohol had not already beat him to the game.

• • •

Mully was lazing around his favorite hangout, Shorty's, nursing strong whiskey despite the high noon hour. He stared at Basil with vacant, unfocused eyes, the same sour smell emanating from his body. If he remembered Basil's long fingers choking the breath out of him, he didn't let on. "Whaddya say, join me for a drink, huh? I could yoush some company."

"Alright," Basil responded. "But hold the drink for me."

"Ah, c'mon. Yoush no fun!"

"Too early, Mully, too early. Gotta keep my wits about me a bit longer. Say, Mully, I could really use your help." He leaned close and talked in a conspiratorial tone. "You get around, Mully, and I know you probably see much that us regular folk never glimpse, huh?

Mully raised a scabby hand and interjected proudly: "This town is my backyard. Know the cracks and crannies of this place!"

"Rumor has it there are bones and skulls half buried in this town. My friends and I made a bet: they say no such place exists, but I say it does. You're the man to ask, to settle this bet. Whaddya say I buy you a few drinks, and we put our heads together and see if we can come up with something? Help me win the bet, huh?"

Mully's drink suddenly stopped cold in front of his lips, and he stared at Basil as if horns were growing out of his head. He jerked halfway out of his seat. "Dead bodies? You shootin' a line of something or what? Memory's not so good, but I dunno nuthin' about bones or bodies!" He started shaking all over. "You darin', you know that?"

"Slow down, Mully!" He'd hit a brick wall.

"There's a killer round these parts, and I sure don't want my kidney pilfered, no sirree!" He made a slicing gesture to his neck and stood up. "Lookin' to get yerself killed, are you? Well, you ain't takin' me down with you! Talkin' of dead bodies, you gonna end up as one soon enough if you ain't careful." His voice had started to rise, and the few occupants in Shorty's looked their way, puzzled.

Irked, Basil stood up as well, adopting a nonchalant manner to hopefully deflect any attention headed in his direction. "Thanks for your time, Mully! See you around!"

Muttering and staggering to his feet, Mully slunk out of the pub, casting petrified glances over his shoulder as if he couldn't get out of there fast enough.

Bad memory or not, Mully knew something. Basil needed to find out where his stomping grounds were. He probably meandered all over this town, but somewhere, he had seen something – something that could add one of the missing puzzle pieces to this case.

• • •

Feeling even surer they were all barking up the wrong tree, Basil formulated a plan. He would deal with Mully later, but first, a phone call was in order. When one door closed, it didn't hurt to knock again. He tapped his fingers on the steering wheel as he listened to the dial tone.

"Wendy Wainwright," the soft voice responded expectantly.

"Mrs. Wainwright, this is Constable Andrews, calling from Twin Coulees, Alberta." He watched a few children throw a ball on the green across the street.

"Why are you calling me?" The voice was suddenly clipped and tense. "Is this about Adele? I've already talked to the police. Haven't seen her for ages or even talked to her, for that matter, and I did not come down for the funeral."

"Mrs. Wainwright, as you might be aware from the news, we are in a tough situation. Your sister's death might be connected to other deaths we have in our area. Please, I could really use your help if you could just answer a few questions I have for you."

She sighed. "Fine. I'm doing this for the others, not Adele."

Basil winced.

As if able to read his thoughts, Wendy went on: "You must think I am a monster, Constable. But that is because you probably know Adele as a friendly woman who met a cruel end. Am I right?"

"That's all I know with the limited information I have." An elderly couple walked past arm in arm, and he shifted in his seat.

"Of course!" she spat. "Narcissists always seem to garner an audience for their side."

"Look," Basil continued. "Is there anything about her that would help me with this case? Anything about Adele you might not have mentioned earlier?"

She was quiet for a moment. "I've not told the police before. Hate to speak ill of the dead, even if it does concern her. Where do I start? Let's see. I won't bore you about our childhood, although with her machinations, it was far from boring…in a bad way. The straw that broke the camel's back was her stealing my fiancé. And then she married him. What else do you want to know besides the fact that she is a cheater, betrayer, and thief?"

"You say she stole your fiancé?"

"That is *exactly* what I'm saying. And it only gets worse. I know she was dating another man *while* married to Harry. Oh yes, she loves them married too; something about wanting what others have, if you get my drift."

"Do you have any proof of this?"

"Proof!" she snorted. "Yeah, I got proof, living with her for too many years. You get to know a person a little too well for comfort sometimes. Actually, had a friend still living back there at the time who confirmed Adele was seen frequently with a married man and Harry absolutely clueless.

"What was this particular man's name?"

There was a brief pause on the other end. "I don't know, Constable, I don't even think my friend told me. Does it matter?"

"Well, it would be helpful so that we can follow any leads."

"Sorry, I can't help you."

"Well, thanks for your help, Mrs. Wainwright."

"Don't see how I really helped you. Constable, uh, Andre?"

"Andrews."

"Yeah, whatever. Um, good luck finding the killer. No one deserves to be murdered." The line went dead.

Basil held the phone a moment longer, his heart plunging to his toes. What should he tell Wally about his theory that Adele was perhaps the first victim? How was he going to feel when Basil told him what Wendy had said?

His fingers tapped the steering wheel. He gazed at a man walking, one child on each side. They were laughing gaily. A sudden image of his baby flashed in his mind. Something bubbled inside him then.

• • •

He spied the beat-up F150 with its peeling white stripe parked alongside a quiet road just outside of town, and he slipped behind it.

He'd seen the truck before. But where?

He snapped his fingers. Of course – it belonged to Wally. He remembered spotting it when helping him to tear apart his RV.

The ground rose up beside the road before sloping down slightly and then evening out. He moved out of the Jetta to the grassy area and climbed a few steps. A small cemetery slid into view. Far in the distance, he saw a man crouching in front of a tombstone. He glimpsed a bouquet of red flowers – roses.

Wally.

His stomach felt heavy. He hated graveyards. But then, who didn't? He walked back to his car and ducked inside.

Wally walked back to his truck, his shoulders rounded forward, his step slow. Just before he opened his door, he looked towards the Jetta.

It was there again. That liquid pain in his gray eyes.

• • •

Heidi

Heidi Jennings leaned back in the driver's seat and placed a Player's Light between her lips. "I owe, I owe, it's off to work I go!" she hummed quietly. She didn't quite feel like turning on her radio. Death was on everyone's lips. "Kill joy!" she groused. "Doesn't even feel like Christmas this year."

But her cashier's job at the local grocery beckoned her, and bills still needed to be paid. She'd only driven a few miles when her vehicle began making funny noises. "Shoot!" she cried, slapping the steering wheel. "I can't afford this!"

Her rusty car began to slow down. Pressing the gas to the floor failed to speed the vehicle up. Slowly, it sputtered and ground to a halt, the engine groaning like a maimed animal. She peered at the gas gauge, thoroughly puzzled. "I filled this tank up just a day ago. It can't all be gone! How is this possible? C'mon, ol' Betsy, you can't quit on me now! Not here!"

Heidi stared out the car window at the howling wind, tears pricking her eyelids. She didn't have a mobile after hers went down the washer a few weeks back. Who hadn't she told? Her hairdresser, mailman, and oh man, she couldn't remember who else. She thought it was hilarious that she'd accidentally washed it, sharing the story over and over and laughing with others at her own stupidity. Until she needed it desperately. Now she was miles from anywhere with a dead car. Just great.

Pulling her windbreaker closed, she was relieved she'd packed her mittens and toque. It was going to be a long, cold walk to work. Opening her car door, she suddenly spied, in her rear-view mirror, a car slowing down behind her. Relief splashed over her as she recognized it, and she jumped out of her car. Her knight in shining armor! How was this for timing? She beamed.

He walked towards her with a calm smile.

"It's you! Awesome, so awesome! I can't thank you enough for stopping here!"

"Your car has died." It was a simple statement delivered in a deadpan manner.

"Sadly, yes. And it's deathly cold out."

"There's a puncture in your gas tank."

"What an expert! How could you know it's a puncture?" She loved confidence in a man.

He smiled. "Because I put it there."

She laughed. "What do you mean?" She scratched the back of her neck. This guy had a crush on her. This was his 'I've run out of gas' moment. She was sure of it.

He walked closer. His smile never wavered. There was no blushing. "You should get in my car."

"You are a bold one, aren't you," she smiled, something tugging in her gut.

The smile slid off. "It really will be easier this way."

She frowned and backed away. "What do you mean?"

He moved closer and reached for her arm.

A cold shiver enveloped her. Her hip bumped the edge of her car, and she stifled a cry as pain shot through her. Why was he acting so strange? Her friend Raquel's words flitted through her mind then: "If you don't like the guy, stop being so polite. Just brush him off."

He grasped her arm, and she pulled away desperately, but he continued to hold onto her sleeve.

It all clicked into place then. She opened her mouth to scream, but no words came out. A few more tugs, and she allowed herself to be propelled to his vehicle, her leaden feet seeming to drag. It was as if she knew any fight, any measure of defending herself, would ultimately fail.

Maybe if she cooperated, he would let her live. A painful lump began to form in her throat. Where was he taking her?

DAY 47

Basil

He grasped the cool handle of the community center's door. He could turn back. Forget the circle of attendees no doubt gathered in the back room. Forget the curious faces that would probe his, wondering, guessing.

Then it was as if he stood before him.

The red-eyed, human volcano.

Father.

His fingers slid off the handle.

Right hand stuffed into his pocket, he felt the thin carbon paper. His hand tingled. *His* child.

Suddenly, he saw himself stumbling around, his little child cowering in a corner.

Never.

He lifted his chin. Wiping his palms on his jeans, he grasped the door handle once again. It was now or never.

Twenty-odd faces looked at him expectantly when he entered. He cleared his throat and mustered up courage. "Hi. My name is Basil, and I'm an alcoholic."

Nothing momentous happened.

No fire.

No thunder.

No earthquake.

No one laughed or ridiculed.

The roaring in his ears dulled. He sucked in a shuddering breath. All eyes on him, warm and inviting.

"Welcome, Basil!" The response was a coalescence of warmth and acceptance.

His heart stopped ping-ponging. The world had not ended.

•••

He slipped into his Jetta. Sunlight draped over the hood of the car. He pulled out his phone. It shook in his hand. His heart thundering, he typed the message:

Hi, Myra, just to let you know, I've been to an AA meeting.

He chewed his lip. Then: **Hope you and the baby are doing well**. His finger hovered over the letters for a second, and then he added: **From Basil**.

He frowned and deleted the last two words. He massaged his temples. Love, Basil? Then, simply: **Basil.**

He stared at the message and swallowed. Then pushed Send.

Should he have written, 'Love, Basil'?

Should he have written at all?

Too late.

He leaned back against the seat, exhausted. It was gone. Into cyberspace. Into Myra's inbox.

DAY 48

Basil

"...we need to stand united rather than divided," Basil finished reading Reg's op-ed early that morning. The wind suddenly scattered a handful of gravel at the window.

"It's a good one," Wally noted. Basil had asked him to join him for coffee at Gemma's, only a few other patrons scattered around them. "He's attempting to pacify an agitated public. And we need the public on board."

"Definitely a lot of rumors circulating," Basil noted. "Black market in organ trade. People being pilfered from their very beds and ending up in bathtubs with ice, sans kidneys."

"Stuff of urban legends," Wally sipped his coffee. "But Jarowicz is suggesting it could be someone turned down for a kidney transplant, no? Perhaps a female patient received a kidney instead of him or her."

"Yeah, he has some constables following up on this thread. But you know, the danger here as well is a public lashing out. Perhaps these dead women associated with streetwalkers, or worse yet, sold their own bodies. It must be the 'other' woman. If not, they could be next."

"The killer is most definitely harnessing the public's fear for his or her own agenda." He looked out the window with a shake of his head. The reflection of the rising sun made the sky look like a festering wound.

Christmas loomed on the horizon, but the joy had been sapped out of the season. Some half attempt had been made to decorate the town and induce some Christmas spirit, but the streets were empty, and the greatest decoration was the all-too-familiar yellow police tape. Riots and protests were carried on the wings of hysteria. He thought of Wendy Wainwright.

"Alright, what is it?" Wally probed, turning to study his apple pie with characteristic scrutiny.

Basil sighed. "I'm not sure how to tell you this, but I called up Wendy Wainwright the other day."

"Wendy Wainwright? You're gonna have to jog my memory a bit here."

"Laramie's sister."

"Adele's sister? Whatever for? Did Jarowicz task you with this?"

"Nope. I just had this gut feeling, this theory I wanted to explore."

"What theory?" His eyes were now firmly pinned on Basil, searching, questioning, his body on high alert.

Apparently, Harry was Wendy's fiancé; she stole him and married him."

"Blast it, Basil! Can't you leave things well enough alone? What does Adele have to do with the other bodies?"

"Who was Adele, Wally?"

"What do you mean?" Wally stabbed his pie.

"Who was she to *you*."

Wally slowly laid down his fork. "I knew her. She and Harry would sometimes hang out with Michelle and I."

"I'm sorry," Basil said. Of course. The cemetery.

Wally looked at him. Basil knew he'd seen him there the other day. "Michelle was my wife." He toyed with his fork. "The Laramies were family friends." Wally's voice was quiet and guarded.

Apparently, every November, when the air began to bite, and the trees looked especially lackluster and sad, Adele began scouting bargain stores for leftover summer merchandise on steep clearance and packing her travel bags while other folks began preparing for Christmas; at least the past couple of years, now that Harry was dead. When he was alive, she'd reason to stay. A tiny reason, she'd argue. Simply because Harry enjoyed the bustle of Christmas, the caroling, the lights, and the benignity folks dished out liberally at this time of year.

Each intermittent Chinook was like a jabbing finger reminding Adele of what lay south. Life's too short, she'd argue, to spend it shivering, shoveling, and bundled up while driving on precarious roads. And so, she'd flee with the first whispers of snow and return only when winter's frigid fingers had lost their power and grudgingly withdrawn.

The irony was that she was a robust woman of pioneer stock, built to endure the cold Canadian climate.

Wally cleared his throat. "Michelle died of breast cancer a few years back. This month's been hard. I visit her grave near daily during the month of her death and have done so for the past couple of years." He shook his head. "It's supposed to get easier. When Harry died shortly after, I would often check up on Adele. Fix up odd things at her place. But she went south frequently, and I hadn't been by her place a lot lately. If I had – " he shook his head.

"I'm sorry, Wally." Basil set his cup down. "You can't blame yourself for this." He paused and then trod carefully. "Look, I know Adele was an intended victim just like the others." Wally was like a calm river with a carefully concealed undertow.

"Your mind has no brakes, you know that, Basil?" He slammed his fist gently on the table.

"If we don't at least consider it, we're not being fair to her either. Sooner rather than later, Jarowicz will explore that angle too."

Wally's mouth was stitched in a straight line. "Alright, spill it."

Basil told him the entire gamut of the conversation with Wendy, leaving nothing out, including her scathing resentment of her sister.

Wally shook his head. "I was always more drawn to Harry than Adele, but she *was* good for him. Anyhow, he did follow her; everyone has a free will to some extent. Besides, you've only heard Wendy's side of the story. What proof besides hearsay does she have that Adele was dating a married man while married to Harry?"

"True, but although we can't verify facts with Adele, we also can't let this go. Each of these women was involved with married men."

"Well, for the sake of justice and truth," he grudgingly conceded.

"Look at it this way," Basil gathered steam. "All of these women do share some common thread here, don't they?"

"Yeah, they do," Wally replied reluctantly and then sat up straighter. "You know, they all appear to have dated married men. It's a long shot, but there's nothing else really to go on."

"Go a step further. The missing streetwalkers."

"Wait," Wally held up his hand. "They are not linked to the murdered women. I mean, they might be, but we've no real evidence, do we?"

"Louisa was a streetwalker. She might be the link, albeit tenuous."

"But Ace – "

" – likely did not do it."

"How do you know?"

"I talked to him. Off the record."

"Basil." There was a warning in Wally's voice. "Tell me you did not investigate on your own."

"I did."

Wally looked at him and whistled. "You *are* crazy, Basil."

"I had to."

"Why?"

"I promised Stacey I would look into this."

"Stacey?" Wally was now bent forward. His coffee sat cold and untouched, his apple pie mostly uneaten.

Basil filled him in with as much detail as he could. He told him about the barcode tattoos, his altercation with Ace, Sullivan helping him out and more.

"I've never met a member like you, Basil, you know that. On the one hand, you're a breath of fresh air; on the other hand, you're one crazy rogue! Again, *why* did they ship you this way?"

Basil shook his head as if to say, *You are not going there with a ten-foot pole!*

Wally ran a hand through his hair and moved his large frame off the chair. "You'll obviously need to let Jarowicz in on this theory." He shook his head and shoved his chair under the table. "I don't know. I am still feeling Ace as the one here."

• • •

Jarowicz nodded and moved forward on his chair. "Good work, Andrews. It's a connection, perhaps a weak one, but the first we've really managed to find amongst all the victims. The question now is, who knew these women intimately enough to be able to garner personal details from their lives? And how do the missing kidneys fit in?"

The press, of course, knew where the good pickings were and wasted no time sharing this information. "Adulterous Women Killer's Target?" the headlines shot out, not so innocently.

•••

Arizona

She lay there pale and quiet, her nose in a book. Since when had she picked up reading? "How's she?" Arizona whispered to her father.

He smiled wanly. "They're trying a new treatment for stage-three patients. They're hopeful and hitting her with all they've got. As you can see, it's flatlined her."

"How's she feeling about this?"

"Arizona!" Estelle spied her from the doorway and struggled to sit. "You two whispering about me?"

"Hi, Mom! You look great."

"Great?" She raised a pencil thin eyebrow. "*This* is not great. This is skin and bones. You don't look much better; you eating at all?"

"Mom!"

Estelle waved a bejeweled hand as if to dismiss the idea. "Sit down. Right here." She pointed to a white wicker chair next to her bed in the oversized living room. "Father wanted me in bed, and I did not want to miss any action, so we compromised."

Compromised? Mother?

"Where's Malcolm?"

"I left him with Melody."

"Whatever for?"

"I'm not sure. I just thought it would be too busy for you."

"Nonsense! Next time you take him, you hear?"

Arizona assured her she would, still feeling slightly off-kilter with her mom as of late.

DAY 49

Basil

He stared at the snow swirling at his windshield. It was dizzying. He blinked and drew in a deep breath.

Still no email.

Give her a chance, he counselled himself.

He eased off the gas and squinted through the blowing snow.

It was then he saw the car. It was slightly tilted off the road and layered in snow. He parked his patrol car behind it.

Car trouble. "Control, Alpha-23, RO check, please."

"Alpha-23, go ahead."

"Alberta plate, T-Tango, P-Papa, O-Oscar, 413."

TPO 413. Standby," said the dispatcher. In twenty seconds, she replied, "Alpha-23, ready to copy?" Registered Owner of the vehicle was a Heidi Jennings, thirty-two years old, no criminal offences or outstanding charges. He thanked dispatch and went to check on the vehicle. At the end of shift, he could enter the details into PROS as a street check. It would not be the first car to be left abandoned on the side of the road. Cars broke down all the time, especially in wintertime.

Wrapping the vehicle in lovely yellow police tape, he tried her phone number. It simply went to an answer recording: "Hi, you've reached Heidi Jennings. Sorry I missed your call."

There was something about this car that niggled at him. Donning a pair of latex gloves, he walked towards the vehicle and carefully opened the unlocked door. Who knew how long it had been sitting there? A piece of paper lay on the driver's seat with a sentence typed in capital letters:

I AM AN ADULTRESS.

The killer.

He wasted no time informing dispatch of his find. Soon, other constables, GIS, forensics, as well as Ichabod and Jarowicz would descend like a pack of hungry wolves. This was palpable evidence, really the first, something everyone had been desperately searching for. *And it seems to align neatly with my theory,* he thought with just a hint of satisfaction.

• • •

Things in Twin Coulees began to heat up quickly. Once word leaked out that the victims indeed shared one common detail, the often-hidden part of human nature came glaringly to light.

"Evil has slipped his hand into the glove of greater good," Wally quipped, pulling another quote out of his inexhaustible supply. "Someone is taking his or her moral zeal to spectacular heights."

Ichabod nodded. "We need to be careful. Tracked animals can be quite dangerous. And this person is no idiot. He'll harness the fear of the town, play on people's emotions, and cause even more mayhem. He's got the whole of this town in his iron grip!"

• • •

Marc

He lifted his head and looked out of the window. A few streaks of light still lay on the horizon.

He felt strength flow through his body. Like a faint flickering, almost, but just enough.

For days, he'd lain there hovering between life and death. Finally, the fever had broken.

It was now or never. Like some pathetic creature, he'd moved back and forth between the window and the bags of garbage to pilfer enough food scraps to help him regain some strength, and to the gutter to drink like some baby animal from the teat of the house.

The man had hopefully left for the evening. There'd been a few times – always unpredictable – where he stayed all night or until very late.

He crept outside the window. His legs threatened to buckle underneath him, but the open road beckoned. Before him lay the cold prairie, streetlights flickering far in the distance like fireflies.

Behind him lay his grave and the rotting corpses of murdered women.

There was no time to waste. He had to stop the man. He had to stop the carnage. Cold air rushed around him, and he shivered in his ragged t-shirt. It was below freezing.

Adrenaline carved a path through his exhaustion. There was no turning back.

Gritting his teeth, he slid into the black abyss of night.

• • •

Nora

"There isn't just any killer attacking women; there is a serial killer on the loose," Reg announced.

"Serial killer?" A tremor ran through Nora.

Reg took her shoulders in his strong hands and looked into her face. "Listen, Nora. I know you've been worried. He's targeting certain women."

Certain women? "Reg?" Her voice was suddenly dry and hoarse.

"Yes, Nora. Certain women. It's terrible enough, but you don't need to be as scared as you've been. Listen. The police have zeroed in on his motive."

"Motive?"

"He's targeting cheating women, including the prostitutes in this town. Women who've been going behind their husband's backs." His tone was meant to reassure.

Fingernails bit into her palms.

"The police at least know *who* the target is. He pulled her into his arms. "I'm sorry if I've frightened you. Women everywhere are on edge. I just want you to be careful and stay inside the house at all times. You just never know. Here, you are safe; here, there is no threat of any kind. No one is targeting you."

No threat? A chill wrapped itself around her. She thought of the letter, the night of the storm.

He released her with a quick peck on her cheek and retrieved a couple of wine glasses from the cupboard. He poured a Merlot and handed her a glass. He seemed more relaxed now that he believed she was not a target.

But her own spine tightened. *Cheating women.* Her hand shook as she took the wine glass from him, a few drops sloshing over the edge. She set the trembling glass down and fetched the dishrag. She commanded her voice to be even.

"How does this serial killer come to know this information about these women?" She cleared her throat. "Does he deliver letters to all his victims?"

Reg fingered his wine glass slowly. "I don't know. But usually, people who want something find a way."

"Are they close to catching him?" Desperation filled her voice.

Reg set down his empty glass and settled comfortably into his recliner. "The police? Hard to tell; they are tight-lipped and all. But he's one swift-footed bugger. Seems to be one step ahead of the police."

She tried to rise from her chair, but her legs would not move.

"Proof," Reg suddenly added. "Proof is always necessary."

She stared at him, the word jarring her suddenly.

DAY 50

Sheila

Sheila Albright locked her car and then began a repetition of touching her toes and straightening her body in an attempt to warm up before her jog. Fog hung like a funeral shroud around her, but the temperature had been hanging steady at plus one that morning. She'd prayed fervently that the weather would hold until she was done.

She loved her peaceful jogs away from town and in the crisp morning air. She loved the way her breath mushroomed out in small clouds of vapor, reminding her of puffing on twigs, as if they were real cigarettes, in her childhood. Reaching her fingers to the sky, she stretched out every kink, imagining her muscles to be elastic bands that could stretch and stretch. Soon enough, she would be cramped in a classroom desk in her biology class.

Then she saw it. Dark and low to the ground, something crawling out of the mist like a slowly undulating caterpillar, except magnified a thousand times.

Some animal ready to pounce.

Sheila quickly scouted the area on either side of her. Short, scraggly bushes, no trees. Coulees. Nowhere to quickly conceal herself or place herself out of harm's reach. She could turn back, but then it'd go after her even quicker. It was toying with her, deciding on the perfect moment to attack. *Okay, girl, think, think!*

Keeping her eyes on the slow-moving form, her fingers fumbled for the cellphone in her back pocket. Out of range. The form moved again, still very slowly.

Suddenly, a gush of relief rushed through her. It wasn't a dangerous animal; it was injured or sick. It was moving so sporadically like it was writhing in pain.

And then it hit her like a blast. The form was long, a head slowly lifted. The nearly inaudible moans were not animal-like at all. *It's…a person!* Someone was crawling towards her, someone badly hurt.

"Help!" The voice sounded weak and strained and filled with pain.

•••

Arizona

She was putting Malcolm down for a nap when she heard a noise. She stilled herself, listened, then went back to snuggling him in the blanket. Malcolm had been cranky and uncooperative. The tiredness that followed as a result of being ill made for a whiny, demanding toddler. Arizona reminded herself that motherhood was no walk in the park, and this too would pass. She'd drawn the blinds and turned off the lights throughout the house. Malcolm's room was cloaked in darkness to encourage him to doze off. Nap when your child is napping, she'd been told. Well, today she would definitely not argue with this.

She heard it again. The rough sliding of the patio door. Her fingers clutched Malcolm's blanket. She turned to the doorway and then back to Malcolm, who was snuggling under the covers. Should she go look? Or close the door and put a chair against it? But there was no chair in his room.

Taking in a deep breath, she tiptoed to the doorway, praying the floor would not creak.

Suddenly, she felt it. Her cellphone. In her hoody pocket. Clumsily, she pressed the digits for 911. A ring. *Hurry, hurry!* she begged.

"Stay where you are!" a flinty voice sounded.

"Put it down, you fool!" Another voice. They were both so familiar.

The cellphone slid from sweaty fingers onto the carpeted floor.

"911, what is your emergency..." came from the darkness below.

She dropped to the floor and felt around wildly. The phone – where was it!

"I wanna go out," Malcolm started.

"Stay in bed, Malcolm!" she whispered.

"No!" His little feet inched towards the floor.

She had to stop him. Keep him in bed – keep him quiet. The closet. They could go in there.

But suddenly, Malcolm ran, arcing past her, just out of her reach. "No bed, no bed!"

"Malcolm!" She tore from the bedroom and caught up with him, just as she glimpsed the man with a gun.

"Hold it!" Dawson Williams ordered sharply.

Before she even realized it, she grabbed Malcolm and threw herself onto him.

"I said gun down!" A voice from the patio resounded.

Reg Clarkson. *Oh,* she thought with sudden relief, *Thank God!*

• • •

Basil

Basil heard the call come in. "Car closest to Wilson and Douglas." He responded that he was on Douglas Road, close by.

"Okay, Alpha-23, report of a loud disturbance, maybe a domestic at fifteen on Wilson. ETA?"

Fifteen? Right next to where he lived! "Alpha-23, less than one minute."

Wally said he would cover. "Be there in five."

Basil stopped in front of the duplex and gave his 10-7. He heard the commotion through his open car window. The blinds were drawn in the front window. A woman screamed. The whimpering cry of a child could be heard as well.

Arizona and Malcolm! He banged on the door. "Police – open up!" The unlatched door immediately gave way. In the dim light, Basil could see the outline of two bodies in stranglehold. Arizona lay on the floor, shielding Malcolm. She was crying softly now, relief flooding her eyes as she spied them.

"Cover me!" Basil ordered Wally.

When his eyes adjusted, he was astounded at what he saw. Clarkson was struggling with the reporter, Dawson Williams, a gun lying at their feet. His arm was cutting off the man's airway, and they were both red-faced with exertion, oblivious to the officers. Basil pulled his gun from his holster and trained it on the men in case one of them got the upper hand and reached for the gun at their feet. Guns were pulled with the full intention to shoot. It was no simple matter; once a gun was pulled, the officer was committed. "Police!" he yelled for the second time.

Suddenly, it was over. Clarkson immediately released his arm and stared at Basil in surprise. "I am so relieved you guys are here! This man was trying to break into this lady's house."

"Liar!" Williams spat out.

With Wally's gun covering him, he slowly moved forward and kicked the gun away from the men. "You're under arrest!" He grabbed the man's hands, cuffed them, and then read him his rights according to the Charter.

Wally gave their 10-70 to dispatch. The situation had de-escalated, and no other members needed to respond.

"You were here before me, trying to open the door!" Williams threw back.

Clarkson shook his head sadly. "Really? Two people with intentions to break into the same house? Highly unlikely." He turned to the officers. "I pulled him away from the door and he pulled his gun on me." He turned to Arizona. "Just came to measure for the flap. Didn't see any car home."

"It's being serviced for a few days," Arizona responded shakily.

"I wouldn't have touched a hair on their heads," Williams responded angrily, "I just – "

Arizona stood up slowly. Clutching Malcolm to her, she pointed to the man: "He came in with a gun!" She related the entire story: she'd been ready to nap Malcolm when she heard the patio door. He'd trained the gun on her and Malcolm when thankfully Clarkson had intercepted him.

"Glad you were here, Mr. Clarkson," Wally noted.

Williams ducked his head. "I never meant to pull a gun, Mrs. Stuart. I just wanted the papers."

"What papers?" Basil demanded again.

"Marc was working on a story about something hidden in the silver spoon."

"Silver spoon?"

The man sighed. "We worked at the newspaper together."

"You wanted to get your hands on Marc's papers; I knew it!" She was obviously fighting back tears.

"What is this silver spoon?" Wally echoed.

Dawson shrugged his shoulders. "I don't know; that is what I was searching for. I just know it's something big, something he didn't want to share in detail with me. He died before he could finish it. When Mrs. Stuart came to see me, I just knew I'd stumbled onto something possibly big. I couldn't have this just languish in his desk drawer; I knew it had to be somewhere. It wasn't in his old office!"

"You could have asked me!" Arizona cried, sudden anger replacing her fear.

"I had no idea whether or not you would've given me the papers. I wasn't going to take the chance to have you know how important they are and hide them from me!" His eyes suddenly blazed. "How could anyone ever rise to the top with that man around?"

"He would've shared with you!" Arizona retorted. "But you refuse to work for things; you expect it all handed to you on a silver platter and then slap your name behind it! Besides," she continued, "I haven't seen anything other than that note I told you about. I looked myself and haven't found one other scrap of paper! Whatever amazing thing he discovered will never come to light," she swallowed, "because he's gone!"

"Okay, everyone, calm down," Basil interrupted. He turned to Dawson. "Maybe you can write an interesting feature on *yourself* from a jail cell."

They took down Clarkson's statement, and that of Arizona, and then escorted Dawson Williams to the police vehicle.

DAY 51

Nora

She watched Reg close the door. There was a bounce to his step, despite the persistent limp.

Man of the hour.

Local hero.

She poured them both a coffee as he pecked her on the cheek. "I framed the article."

"Article?"

She gestured to the frame on the wall next to the bookcase.

"C'mon, Nora. That's just silly. Not on the wall. In a drawer is fine."

She placed his cup on the table. "I leave the bird on the shelf. You can leave your article on the wall." She took a deep breath.

Reg walked toward her and gently lifted her chin. "Why don't you tell me what's really bothering you, Nora."

She jerked her face away and instantly felt remorse. "Nothing. You're the new local hero. Single-handedly you stopped a would-be thief."

"Anyone would have done the same thing. What would you have preferred me to do?"

She turned away and busied herself with wiping the counters down.

He gently took the rag from her hand. "They're already shiny and spotless."

"You – you left me."

He stared at her. "I don't understand."

"After Henry. You left. I was so alone, Reg. I guess it bothered me then, but – "

He nodded slowly. "And every day, I leave you alone to help others."

He'd hit the nail on the head. She dropped her head.

Silence spread between them. She saw the muscles working in his face. The shadow in his eyes. "I took Henry with me in my heart," he whispered.

"Why couldn't we...grieve together?" She tugged on his arm.

He sighed deeply. "If only I had. I should've stayed." His jaw suddenly corded tight. "I *really* should've stayed."

She shook her head. "No. Those people needed you more. I just – you're enjoying your life. Being active and able. And here I am. Alone." There. She'd said it. But a heaviness draped over her. *I'm being so petty and selfish!* she berated herself. "I'm sorry, Reg. I shouldn't feel sorry for myself. It all just came to a head, I guess." She brushed back wisps of her hair.

His jaw suddenly untensed. "If only grief came with a manual, huh?"

She managed a laugh then. "I *am* proud of you, Reg. You likely prevented something terrible from happening, you know? That was so close for that poor woman."

"Yes, it was," he nodded. "And that little boy." A muscle jumped near his mouth. "He's so little, Nora. Maybe two – three? He reminds me of – "

"I know." She moved to place her arms around him. She felt the tremor in his arms, his chest. A man who held everything so tight inside.

"There is yet hope for this town, Nora." His breath was warm and comforting on her head. "People need to know that justice will persevere. They need hope right now, especially coming from the media."

Nora nodded. People devoured this positive slice of news with the desperation of starving people who had not eaten in days. Here, it could be seen that murder was not the only rule of the day in Twin Coulees.

He held her away from him and peered intensely into her eyes. "You don't like the bird, do you?"

She wrung her hands. "It just stares at me all day. Reminds me of my prison."

"I shouldn't have bought it," he said softly. "I just wanted to give you something special." He looked downcast. "We'll just…put it away."

"No," she suddenly burst out, surprising herself. "It stays." She would be brave. She would look forward.

• • •

Office of the Medical Examiner

Calgary, Alberta

Dr. Halverston, the Chief Medical Examiner for Alberta, was carefully examining the latest corpse to land on his table. Preliminary reports could not pinpoint the cause of death, but this was too much. "This is the third body with no detectable cause of death," he sighed to his Assistant

Chief Medical Examiner, Dr. Clarke. "All kidneys have been removed post-mortem; that much we can establish. This in itself plays a significant role in the absence of infection of any degree."

"We've collected tissue samples and saved them, at least," Clarke responded.

Halverston nodded slowly, deep in thought. "All toxicology reports are negative." Toxicology reports often took the longest to come in. They'd saved samples of urine and blood, as well as vitreous humor – liquid from the eyeball – and tissue samples from the liver. No drugs were found in either system, with the exception of alcohol.

"Yes," Clarke noted, "the main blood vessels in each of their legs contained alcohol, but only at moderate concentrations. They were all imbibing alcohol at some point before death."

"And there was a low concentration of beta-hydroxybutyrate in the fluid of the eye; it would be much higher if they died from alcohol-induced hypoglycemia."

"You know the weird thing?" Clarke noted. "Whoever did this knew exactly how to remove a kidney. Suturing isn't bad either." When Halverston did not respond, he asked: "Halverston? Did you hear what I said?"

"Wait a minute, Clarke! I want to re-examine her body under bright light with the magnifying glass."

"What are you thinking?" Clarke asked, intrigued.

"Looking for hypodermic injection sites; maybe we've missed it."

"Injection sites? But we've ruled out drugs!"

"Think, Clarke! We've been talking about hypoglycemia, and it reminded me of something I read a while ago. I've never come across this before, not homicidally speaking."

"Insulin overdose?"

"Yes, exactly. Death by insulin!"

"Glucose generally disappears from the blood after death, and any level measured after death is unreliable, but – "

"If we find any injection sites and remove tissue around these sites – get me the magnifying glass – then we can analyze them more specifically."

Together, the two carefully combed over the body. But there were no noticeable injection sites, not on the arms or legs, or even the buttocks. Halverston wasn't about to give up; it was there – it had to be! Four bodies with no clear reason as to cause of death jarred him; it upset his equilibrium as a meticulous doctor given to extreme perfection.

"Between the toes!"

Clarke looked at him with incredulity. "Between the toes?"

But Halverston had already taken the magnifying glass with the aid of the bright light and was looking carefully between each toe."

"There it is!" His tone was triumphant. "Trial of Maria Whiston, 1996."

In 1996, Nurse Maria Whiston was accused of killing Eric Lloyd by injecting him with insulin; although she never did inject him between the toes, she did threaten her former husband, Robert Whiston, with this because she believed (wrongly so) that it could never be detected.

"Well, I'll be," Clarke whispered. They were tiny, but the punctures made by a hypodermic needle were there. "More than one!" He realized quickly. "When one injection was not enough, the killer just injected her again, and again.

DAY 52

Marc

He woke up with a start, his head throbbing as if someone had banged it with a steel pipe. His mouth was so dry, and his body ached all over. Moving slightly, he peered through half-open eyes. The lights were so bright. His eyes burned, and he quickly closed them as the room started to spin. An antiseptic smell permeated his nostrils.

Dirt. His fingers dug into the bedsheet. He had to get out of here. Where was the window?

Beside him lay a form with an open mouth threaded with tubes. It was thin and fleshless, like an open claw. His fingers snaked around the bed rail. There were corpses everywhere. That cloying smell of death. His muscles quivered as he tried to lift himself. But they betrayed him, and he fell back down. A moan came from the open claw, and he lifted himself once more.

"Shhh, try not to move. Here, suck on these." Her brightly colored scrubs soothed him. A few ice chips were gently placed between his blistered lips, and he sucked weakly, savoring their cold relief. He was so thirsty. And so tired. The soft voice of the nurse comforted him, and with a moan, he sank back into his pillow, other voices swirling around him.

"No idea who he is...been out of it for a bit...some jogger notified the ambulance...found crawling along a gravel road...no ID."

Crawling on the road? Who was he? Why was he in a hospital? "Where am I?" he suddenly rasped, trying to sit up. He pulled at the IV lines threading out of him.

"Lie down, sir! You are too weak to sit."

"Please!" He grasped her sleeve. "Why am I here?"

"What is your name? When were you born?"

His tongue suddenly felt thick as he tried to speak. Just before he closed his eyes, he spied a needle lying beside him. He shook his head while pointing at the needle. "No!" He pulled his legs painfully up to him and turned away from the menacing tip that sparkled beside him.

He did not see the questioning looks of the nurses around him.

• • •

Basil

"Insulin?" Basil questioned.

Jarowicz nodded. "The Chief Medical Examiner suggests that insulin may have played a role in the death of all four women. These women may have died from insulin overdose, *intentionally*."

Basil whistled. "Murder by insulin. "So how does the perp have access to it?"

"Well, either he is diabetic, or he has access to insulin that the average person does not have."

"This is gonna be a tough one. It could be a relative of a diabetic, or a pharmacist, nurse, doctor, someone with diabetes; really, almost anyone!"

"Someone with access to their personal lives," Jarowicz added. "Someone they were comfortable sharing details of their lives with. We need to move quickly. It might already be too late for Heidi Jennings."

Basil thought of Heidi in the hands of a killer, frightened senseless, waiting, praying, for the police to rescue her.

DAY 53

Arizona

Arizona paced the length of her small living room, the chatter of the radio in the background. What was Marc working on that was so important? What was this silver spoon they all kept referring to? Did it have anything to do with his death? She'd told Basil all about Marc's suicide, how out of character it was for him, and her desperate attempt to find out what work he'd been involved in prior to his death. Basil listened, mystified, but like any other police officer worth his salt, he was limited by concrete evidence.

She moved to Marc's vast bookcase. He loved classic literature. Books by Jane Austen, James Joyce, Dostoevsky, Milton, and other literary greats spanned the bookcase. He'd been a voracious reader.

"...looks like we are officially into winter," the meteorologist was saying.

Suddenly, an idea leapt at her. What if Marc had hidden something amongst the books – concealed it between the papers of one of his beloved novels? It wouldn't hurt to look; she'd nothing else to go on.

Pulling out book after book and quickly skimming its pages, she ended by shaking each out carefully. Some books released small papers that had been carefully placed between the thin pages; notes elaborating on ideas, commentary about theories different writers put forth, and so on. Post-it notes clung to other pages. Marc had definitely been an active, engaged reader.

Returning the last of these books to the shelf, she spied a rather thick-looking volume that sat a bit crooked on the shelf: *The Riverside Chaucer.* She suddenly remembered, with painful nostalgia, Marc trying to read a few passages of Middle English to her. It had been gibberish, but he immensely enjoyed the challenge.

"...amnesiac with full beard, curious marking on back of neck..." Arizona turned to the radio and frowned. Something fluttered in the corner of her mind. She shook her head as if to clear it.

Wait a minute! she thought as another thought took center stage. There was another book just like this a few shelves down. Abruptly, she dropped to her knees and found a similar-looking title on the bottom corner shelf beside a row of *Readers Digest.* It was odd. He was so meticulous about grouping books according to author and genre.

She lifted the large volume off the shelf and was surprised at how light it felt compared to the other book. Opening the cover, she discovered the book had no pages; it was merely a compartment box. Inside the box were a few carefully placed papers: notes and old news clippings, aged yellow from the passage of time.

Arizona took the box to the kitchen table and began looking through them, her heart aching as she took in Marc's familiar handwriting.

She spread the news clippings and notes on the table. The hum of the radio faded into the distance as she carefully read each one.

Apparently, the late Emma Watson had concealed precious gems in her home. These gems had been in her British family for a few centuries. Her hope was to give these to the town of Twin Coulees upon her death. She didn't want to give the gems to her rum-swilling layabout of a son, and as he'd no children to whom she could pass the gems, she eagerly sought to bequeath them to the town that had treated her so well and where she had found a place she loved. She didn't trust banks and hid them carefully. Years had passed since her will was made, and her lawyer, Eric Sierston, was charged with embezzlement. With Twin Coulees' famous Egeton Street fire, Sierston's office was destroyed, and with it, Emma's will.

Arizona knew how Marc loved their little town and how much he despised the way Mayor Jason Wheeler was destroying its finances. It did not surprise her one bit that he wanted to find the gemstones to help bring financial stability to Twin Coulees, and even more, to help salvage the tatters of its reputation. Marc was sure she had a copy of the will somewhere, but even more so, he believed the gems were hidden in the silver spoon.

Arizona sighed in frustration. The silver spoon. Likely some ornate spoon with a hidden compartment. A needle in a haystack.

DAY 54

Basil

It was 2:00 am. Basil paced the floor of his home. Even sleeping pills had not been able to mitigate the busyness of his mind lately. The progress they were making in the investigation had suffused him with so much adrenaline that, come nighttime, he lay awake for hours. He was, of course, no stranger to sleepless nights.

He thought of the women who had been so mercilessly killed to fulfill some personal vendetta. Insulin poisoning was a remarkable move if you wanted to cover your steps, but according to Dr. Halversten, it took a long time to kill someone through insulin overdose and the subsequent hypoglycemic coma, which meant he had the victims for a few days to ensure he killed them. He shuddered at the terrible nightmare these women had gone through. What savage animal inflicted such pain – such terribly misguided *justice*?

Heaving a sigh, Basil decided to attempt his nightly wrestle with sleep again. Pulling the covers to his chin, he glanced at his phone on the night table.

Heart picking up speed, he threw back the covers and grabbed his phone. It shook slightly in his hand. He opened his inbox and scrolled through. Work stuff, a bank notice, an article Wally wanted to share ("This *Could* be Happening at your Workplace"), and, of course, junk mail and more junk mail.

That was it. Still nothing.

He tossed his phone on the night table. Maybe tomorrow.

He lay back and closed his eyes. Even if for just a few uninterrupted hours, his brain needed some downtime in order to function come morning.

At 3:00 am., he must have dozed off, although at first, he felt as if he were in a washing machine – back and forth, this way and that. He dreamt of Myra. Then the missing women problem, his brain wrangling for answers.

At 5:00 am., he gave up. He got up and poured milk into an empty bowl and then stared into its whiteness as if an answer would suddenly, magically, surface.

Nothing came.

• • •

At the office that morning, Sergeant Ichabod informed Basil he wanted him to take on an unknown person investigation from another constable who was suddenly out on medical leave. Twin Coulees General had just admitted a severely malnourished patient found crawling on a gravel road, close to Milner's Road. A bulletin had already been put out to locate his family.

Basil hated the sterile smell of hospitals and their drab whiteness. Everything seemed so impersonal – so clinical.

Joe Doe lay in a private room of his own in Unit 4. IVs snaked from his skeletal arms, and machines beeped intermittently. He was a pale shell of a man. His body was a narrow lump under the tightly made sheets, his long arms narrow spindles tucked beside him. He looked like death warmed over.

The nurse gestured toward her patient. "He's on the mend." She caught the surprised look on Basil's face. "I know, I know, he looks bad, but believe me, he was a lot worse coming in; he's been through the wringer. On top of this, his memory seems to be erased. He's no clue as to who he is, where he lives, or even what year it is. But it's weird –"

"What is?" Basil questioned.

"He keeps saying the words 'silver spoon' over and over. I mean, one of us actually got him a spoon from the cafeteria, but he just pushed it away and repeated, 'silver spoon.' He sounds so desperate, so frightened."

Silver spoon? What was it about this silver spoon that seemed to interest so many people?

"Oh, and he's terrified of needles; I've never seen an adult shrink back so much from a mere injection. It takes us a while to calm him down." She shrugged. "He'll be ready to leave here soon, but where's he going to go? If we don't know his identity, well, I don't know. His memory can come back, maybe in bits and pieces, or maybe not at all." She shrugged sadly. "It's heartbreaking not knowing who you are."

A sudden thought seized Basil. *This man is Marc!*

• • •

Basil had just finished up at the hospital when the next call came in: "All cars, all cars, assault in progress, gun possibly involved, Fas Gas, 400 Charleton Boulevard. 2-Alpha-23, I believe you are the closest unit. What would be your ETA?"

"Control Alpha-23, I'm about one minute away," he responded into his radio. He left his half-eaten sandwich and noted the time – 14:00.

"Ten-four," dispatch replied. "Advise when you arrive and wait for backup. Be cautious."

Basil felt that familiar surge of adrenaline once again.

"All cars, this is a confirmed assault, one suspect. Descriptions follow. Cars, copy?" she asked.

Three patrol cars replied, as well as Sergeant Ichabod. He said he would be there as soon as he could and requested Basil give him a situation report as soon as he could, and then instructed dispatch to go ahead with the rest of the information.

"All cars. Further information. One suspect armed with knife. One victim down. Suspect described as tall and covered with tattoos and quite disturbed. Copy?"

All replied, "Ten-four."

Charleton Boulevard? He'd stake his reputation on it that it was Ace!

When he heard this, Sergeant Ichabod interrupted, "Andrews, what's your location now?"

"Just turning onto Charleton. No sirens used."

"Good. Wait for backup. Copy?"

"Ten-four, Sarge."

The airwaves went silent. Everyone felt the gravity of the situation clearly. One man was down, obviously knifed. Was he dead? Other police cars arrived and placed themselves advantageously around the gas station parking lot.

The victim was not down. Ace held a barrel-chested man with his left arm while his right arm held a knife tightly pressed against the victim's thick throat. For a split second, Basil wondered if this was the same knife used on him.

Sergeant Ichabod took the lead as the other men covered him. He shouted: "Police! Drop your weapon, or I'll fire!" They needed to move cautiously. Ace was a known junkie, probably on a high and, therefore, unpredictable.

Ace looked at the officers before him and laughed. "It's what you've all been waiting for, huh? Kill the pimp. Hey Ratford, you coward, where are you hiding?"

Ichabod repeated again, "Wheeler, drop your weapon!" His gun was unwaveringly aimed at Ace.

"He's gettin' what's coming to him!"

Basil's eyes zeroed in on the shiny knife blade that must have already made a superficial cut to the man's neck. The vision of knife cuts to the bellies of the deceased women came to his mind. For a brief moment, he thought of Ace cutting them and removing their kidneys. Was it possible?

And then it happened quickly. Ace moved the knife just a fraction, but at the same moment, a 9mm bullet left the muzzle of Ichabod's Smith and Wesson in a cloud of smoke. As if in slow motion, Basil would remember how Ace's eyes widened for a split second, his body twitching as if electrocuted before he sank to the ground. It happened so quickly. One minute, he was taunting and making the decision to kill another, and the next minute, he was dead.

With the situation under control, paramedics, who'd been staged nearby, rushed in to attend to the knife victim, who lay in a pool of blood. Later on, Basil would remember the acrid smell of gun smoke and the heavy breathing of the men around him during the climax of the scene; the senses were that much more heightened when danger existed, and tensions ran high.

With nothing more to do, the men returned to their vehicles to make room for the special sections to complete their work. Like a well-oiled machine, all the cogs would work together. The coroner would come in to pronounce death and attend to removal of the body. General Investigative Services, as well as the Alberta Serious Incident Response

Team, would come to figure out what happened and to speak to witnesses. The Identification Section would remove the knife and dust for fingertips and take photographs of the scene. A man had been killed by the police. Due diligence had to be followed.

• • •

Basil listened in frustration at the busy tone on Arizona's phone. He left a brief message telling her to call him back. He needed to figure out if she could identify the man as her husband. His body buzzed with nervous energy. Imagine seeing someone you believe to have been dead for weeks – someone you've already grieved over – someone you may have already closed a chapter on.

Ace was out of the game. Ratford's convenient scapegoat was dead. Another pimp would move in to claim territory. Unless the girls wanted to leave the trade, the cycle would perpetuate like it had for centuries. Unclear and ineffectual laws and limited police resources would ensure the trade would continue to flourish, and a fertile bed for crime and drugs would persist.

At the same time, the killer was still at large.

Every available constable had been placed on the case, as well as a few from Calgary. They interviewed anyone who may have known the victims, but it always ended the same: they didn't necessarily know anyone in common, and if there was a person more than one of them knew, they interviewed him or her extensively, always coming up empty-handed.

We're groping in the dark, Basil thought. He was dimly aware of Wally walking into the bullpen and Jarowicz talking to Ichabod. He watched Sharon roll her eyes at something Wally said, and heard the distant sound of phones ringing. Clarkson walked in. He said something to Sharon, and she smiled. Mindlessly, Basil lifted his lukewarm coffee to his lips, watching Clarkson's lips move in conversation.

The phone rang, and Sharon snatched the receiver once again.

Wally was biting into a sandwich, wiping his mouth with the back of his hand. Clarkson reached into his shirt pocket, pulled out a few pieces of what looked like candy, and threw them into his mouth.

Basil slightly envied the man's ease of fitting into different settings – the laid-back way he had of conversing with anyone, and the way he really was present with whomever he conversed with. Here was a man who seemed to really get him.

Suddenly, Clarkson was aware of Basil watching him. He raised his hand in a slight wave. "Good morning!"

"Hey," Basil responded, trying to infuse some enthusiasm in his voice.

"I have to run. More of the media's speculation to deliver." He shook his head. "Well, not gonna stand in the way of you guys catching that slippery eel!"

Wally moved beside Basil, still stuffing his face. "I think his wife was the one injured in that acid attack a while back."

"You didn't handle that one?"

"No. I was off work for a while then." A shadow crept over his face for a second, and then it was gone.

"Rumor has it she's housebound. Terrible anxiety and all."

Wally shook his head sadly. "Can't blame her there!"

Basil only thought, *And he stuck to her like glue all along. Did you know that, Myra? He stayed with her even though it must not have been a walk in the park!*

He thought of the email then. Still no reply. Reasons tossed in his mind. She'd always been slow checking emails.

She'd been too busy. She didn't know how to reply, how to gently let him down.

Again.

DAY 55

Arizona

Arizona walked into the kitchen and noticed her phone slightly off its cradle. *Malcolm.* She shook her head and smiled, nudging the phone into place.

Melody had offered to take Arizona, Malcolm, and her little niece to Zoo Lights at the Calgary Zoo late that afternoon and maybe even have them all for a sleepover. Not feeling up to it herself, she welcomed Melody's idea; it would be so good for Malcolm to have an outing in light of what had happened. He was comfortable around her.

She walked to the sink, filled the basin with hot, soapy water, and shoved her sleeves up. She stared for a moment into the soapy bubbles that rose higher and higher as if some clear plan was laid out in detail in the foam. She sighed and stretched her upper back. Normally, she loved this time of year despite the biting cold and howling winds. There was an ethereal quiet when snow fell, insulating the little town from any hustle and bustle, a dormancy in nature.

But she couldn't relax. Every task she did, even something as inane as washing dishes or getting the mail, felt like she was playing a part in a script, an attentive audience watching her every move. She would have that prickly feeling as if eyes were pinned to the back of her head, only to turn around and nothing and no one would be there.

Was she going crazy? Was this all part of the process of grief?

She flipped on the radio to listen to the news, pulled her robe around her, and opened her patio door. Crisp, fresh air nipped at bare ankles, and she shivered. "... Police are seeking any information the public might have regarding this unknown individual...suffering from amnesia... found crawling along a back road...malnourished...odd marking on the back of his neck at his hairline..."

Some lucky family, she thought, not without a twinge of jealousy.

Then, the realization slammed into her. The scar on the man's neck. It wasn't a scar. It was a *hemangioma*!

Marc!

She gripped the edge of the sink. She knew it as sure as she could breathe.

Then, a scratching sound coming from the door, as if someone was gently turning the knob.

Melody. She must have forgotten something. *Oh, I have to tell her!* she thought, then stopped herself. What if she was just being crazy?

But no door burst open. No apologetic Melody rushed in.

A prickly sensation danced over her skin then, and her heart jumped into her throat. Why didn't she lock the door? With everything going on in this town, she was such an idiot!

The hideous face from that stormy night suddenly flashed in her mind. White knuckles clutching the dish brush, she crouched: *Drop to the floor and crawl! Get to your bedroom and lock the door.* But she was rooted to the spot. *Move, move!* she told herself. But she couldn't. Every muscle rebelled.

This time, she heard the knob being released, slowly, carefully. She heard the kitchen clock. It sounded so loud – exaggeratingly loud: "Tick, tock, tick, tock." Her breath was pent up, held tight, waiting. She released it in short, shuddering gasps, trying to be silent.

The door creaked softly. Cold air rushed in and around her.

And then, as if someone had picked her up, she dropped to the floor and crawled into the hallway. *Get to the bedroom! Hurry, hurry!* Legs trembling, she dove for her door. She turned the lock and slid her back against the door until she was sitting against it. Her legs were shaking. *Breathe, Arizona, just breathe! You need to keep it together. No time to feel. Just act.*

But that was much easier said than done.

It was quiet now; eerily quiet. Moments stretched. She heard a car rush by, her back cramping against the door.

And then, footsteps. Creaking floorboards. Her heart rate spiked once again. They knew she was in here! She cast her glance around the bedroom in desperation. A chair!

But there was none, just a heavy oak dresser. Her mind raced. How could she move that in front of the door?

Then she heard it: heavy breathing on the other side of the door. Biting her lip, she tried to stem the flood of hysteria building within. *Scream! Alert the neighbors.* But she couldn't. Soft, pathetic moaning escaped her lips.

Then, a scraping. A turning of the doorknob. Quickly, she dove beside the dresser. She shrunk as much as possible into the corner between it and the wall. Like a hunted animal, she waited quietly. Some more noise, jiggling of the knob, and then the soft whoosh of the door on the carpet.

He stood there looking at her.

"Oh, it's you!" She felt her cheeks hot with embarrassment as if she'd been caught with her fingers in the cookie jar. She scrambled to her feet on rubbery legs. "Sorry, you just frightened me. I don't normally, you know – these last few days. Well, you've come to my rescue, again!" She moved out of the private sanctity of her room, the man close at her heels. Crouched like a frightened bird. So stupid! "You've come to put in the new flap, of course. Here, I need to show you. Um, you measured it, right? And –" Words slid over each other in a confused garble.

"No flap."

Somewhere at the fringes of her mind, she wondered why he'd walked right in. No knock – no doorbell. The faintest hint of panic began to stir deep inside.

"Oh? Okay. Um, some issue with the mail, or Nora?" She rubbed her elbow.

"I've come for you." His voice was deadpan, his gaze raking her.

"I don't understand." She laughed awkwardly, her lips tingling. She could feel wetness in her armpits and at the small of her back.

"I've come to take you," he enunciated each word carefully as if she were a child.

"Mr. Clarkson?" A buzzing sounded in her ears. "You're confusing me."

"Reg, remember?"

This is the part where he says, "Just kiddin'" and laughs his belly laugh. The part where Malcolm dissolves into giggles. But there was no smile, no humor twinkling in his eyes. Instead, his piercing eyes propelled her backward until she was tightly pressed into the corner.

"If you scream, Malcolm will not live another day," he threatened quietly. "It's over."

"You wouldn't hurt him!"

He smiled at her. "I never like to hurt a child. But sometimes, the price of justice can be high."

Justice? Then it hit her. She slid down as her legs began to shake again. Her fingernails clawed the carpet, feeling for traction. Nausea climbed her gut.

He continued to smile.

She closed her eyes. Reg Clarkson. Cabbie, newspaper deliverer, handyman.

The killer.

"Come with me," his voice cut through her.

"Where are we going? My son!"

His face blurred, and he started swimming. She squeezed her eyes closed and took in another lungful of air. Slowly, she opened her eyes. He stopped moving. Focus, Arizona, focus! You need to outsmart him!

"You know too much."

"What?"

"Marc."

"You hurt him?"

"The silver spoon. You are Marc's wife, aren't you?" He smiled ingratiatingly.

An ache centered under her rib cage. Marc had come back, and she was going to die.

"He's dead," said Clarkson.

A hysterical laugh bubbled up into her throat, but it died suddenly. Wait. He didn't know Marc was alive. She had to make sure he didn't find out!

He moved closer to her.

"No – " She wanted it to sound like an order; the command of a woman in control of her destiny, but it came out soft and pleading. Her throat constricted, and tears welled up in her eyes. She'd just found Malcolm – her little boy – her son. She'd just discovered Marc was alive. Now she'd never see either of them again. *God*, she prayed in desperation, *please stop this madman!*

He reached out gloved hands. *Latex*. She froze, unable to move.

This was no ordinary kidnapping. It was the end.

"You will walk out with me," he ordered her quietly. "If you scream or pull away, or do anything to draw attention to us, I will kill Malcolm."

No, not my baby!

He gripped her arm, his fingers digging in deeply, yanking, pulling. Her legs twisted and flopped like limp noodles. Her entire body vibrated, and she barely felt her feet touch carpet.

I have weapons! she thought. *Blood-curdling screams and nails that I can scrape till raw. I can go for his eyes.*

But she couldn't pay that price.

• • •

Reg

He sat back in his chair and ran his finger up the stem of his wineglass. Just him and the two women. Alone in this large house. He swirled the blood-red liquid and sipped it carefully. His nerves still sang with the thrill of the catch. It was a buzzing that began at the base of his neck and then spread like an electrifying tingle down his spine.

He flipped the dial on the radio and settled back in his chair. "...found crawling on gravel road. Unknown patient still suffering amnesia..."

He frowned and turned off the radio. A disquiet settled over him. He stood. Walked to the stairs leading to the crawlspace and stared hard. It was locked. He chuckled and threw the last of the wine down his throat.

Walking back to his chair, he lowered himself into it slowly. But the thrill was gone. He twisted the wine glass in his hand a time or two, his leg beginning to tremble. He jerked his leg outward and stared hard beside him. The mice were squeaking. His head pounded. For the shortest of moments, he felt powerless.

He was there. The boy. Staring at him with fear in his eyes. A large, yellow puddle grew underneath him, and he twitched in fear. He read the label on the boy's shirt: Reginald Clarkson. He sat up straight and tore his gaze away. The tremors started through his whole body. He stood up, half-stumbling, and looked down. The boy was suddenly gone. He lifted his arm and threw the glass. It smashed against the far wall, pieces shattering all around.

He saw her leaving, the smug eyes that bore through him with all the disgust in the world. The irritating noise from the box grated on his nerves until it became like a second, throbbing pulse deep inside him. He grabbed the closest mouse and squeezed, the loathing and hatred rising to his nostrils. His eyes closed. The noise stopped. The body grew limp. His body quivered with release.

With penknife in hand, he stalked over to her and slashed the portrait to ribbons. She hung there tattered; no smile any longer taunted him, no eyes saw through him. The anger slowly drained. "Goodbye, Mother."

DAY 56

Basil

He sat in the bullpen, organizing paperwork. He stopped, looked at his phone. *One more time*, he thought. *I'm a sucker for punishment.*

He opened his email. Two pieces of mail. One was junk.

One was from Myra.

His heart thudded. He put his phone aside. This was where she'd reject him. She'd finally gathered the nerve to do it.

C'mon, stop being a coward, he berated himself. He picked up his phone again. His finger hovered over her email. Then he clicked it.

Hi Basil. We are both doing well. You have no idea how happy I was to read your message. Sorry it took so long. Love, Myra.

Love, Myra. He drew in a deep breath and sat up straight. *Love, Myra.*

Love. Something bubbled inside of him.

Suddenly, his radio jumped to life: "Alpha-21, your twenty?"

Basil heard Wally respond with his location.

"Possible kidnapping at 15 Wilson Drive. Time 11:29. Your ETA?"

"Control, I'm about ten minutes away."

Basil jumped up. "Control, this is Alpha-23. I am five minutes away. Available to respond as well." He shoved his phone into his pocket. *Meet you there, Wally!*

• • •

Arizona's door was wide open, and a tall blonde woman stood there, a little boy held to her hip, her eyes wide and confused. "She's gone!"

It turned out that the tall blonde – Melody – had just come home from a short trip with Malcolm to find the house dark and deserted, and the door unlocked.

Basil felt he'd been punched in the stomach. He heard Wally's Tahoe in the drive. "Okay, ma'am, an on-duty constable is here. Everything will be fine."

Wally came in, talking into his radio. "What do we have here?"

"Not exactly sure," Basil responded. "Open door. Arizona Stuart is gone."

"Whoever it is has taken her!" Melody cried. "Please, please, don't let her be next. She has a little boy." Malcolm sat tightly on her hip, his eyes wide.

"Hey there, fella," Basil crouched to the boy's eye level. "You're gonna be okay. We'll find your mommy." The boy just pressed closer to Melody, his fingers white from clutching her shirt. Basil looked at Melody. "We don't know for sure if she's been kidnapped, ma'am."

"It's not like her to just leave!" Melody asserted.

Milk on the stove was cold, a grayish skin puckering the surface. The dishwater in the sink was cold, soap residue clinging to the sides of the basin.

Looking around, Basil noticed something nestled between the thin fibers of the living room carpet: something small, white, and circular. He frowned, took out his cell, and snapped a picture. He'd seen this before, but where? He could not take evidence from a crime scene, so he'd no choice but to leave it for forensics.

Before he left, he phoned Ichabod and shared his theory about the nameless patient. Security would have to be provided immediately for the man in case his life was in danger.

• • •

Ms. Jeffries lived in Number 16 with her cat, Ollie. She was the only one who answered the door and was only too happy to assist the police in their inquiries.

"Don't have the best eyesight anymore," she apologized. "Mrs. Stuart left the house with a man in the evening. That's new, but not strange. I mean, poor lady lost her husband weeks ago."

"Can you describe the man for me?" Basil cut in. "Anything at all, no matter how strange or insignificant."

"Well, it were kinda dark and all. He wore his jacket hood. Black or navy? Normal height, normal build. Kept his face down and towards her. I'm talking a wide hood that didn't give away hair color or nothin'."

"Was there anything about the two that seemed strange to you as they were walking to their car? I mean anything at all, no matter how insignificant it may appear. Their behavior and all."

"Not really, like I said – wait a minute! Yes, there was. Silly girl still had on her bedroom slippers!" She threw her head back and laughed. "She's got her head in the clouds already, forgetting to put on her shoes!"

"Did they appear happy together?"

"Sure, he was laughing. She, I dunno, never really smiled at him. Wait! He did seem to be tugging on her arm. Remember thinking he wasn't really chivalrous.

"Can you describe the car they got into?"

"You know, Constable, I ain't no detective, but I did raise me some boys. They were always talkin' about cars."

"Please, ma'am, we're in a hurry here," Basil prodded.

"It was silver or gray, a Honda Civic. That's all. Oh, and four doors."

Gray and four doors. A Honda Civic. "I guess it's too much to hope for that you caught a partial of the license plate?"

"Nope. There was none."

His heart sank. There was a good possibility she was taken against her will.

But there was something more. He could not shake the feeling that the killer may have struck again.

• • •

A BOLO was placed on the gray Honda Civic. But with no license plate to go by, they were shooting in the dark.

But if there was one thing Twin Coulees had going for it, it was its relatively small size. The bulletin put out on the car found surprisingly quick results.

"All cars, location of silver Honda Civic confirmed at 56 Harrigan Rd. No license plate."

Basil's heart jumped in his throat. Were they really that close? Was the killer so dumb as to park his vehicle in plain view? But then again, he might not realize they were on to him. Good thing the old woman was astute enough to notice the absence of a license plate.

That familiar feeling of adrenaline rushed through him. He wanted in on the action; he wanted to be there and help bring down this man.

Wally was the closet unit, a mere two minutes away.

"Ten-four," the dispatcher replied. "Advise when you arrive and wait for backup. Use extreme caution."

Two other patrol cars responded, of which one was Basil. Ideally, the Emergency Response Team would go in. Who knew how the killer was armed? But they were six hours away in Edmonton. The RCMP would have to make do with what they had.

Sergeant Ichabod cut in: "Kennedy, what's your location now?"

"A few yards from the driveway. Not using my siren."

"Okay. Wait at the side of the road until backup arrives. He's likely armed."

"Ten-four, Sarge," Wally replied confidently, and not without a smidgen of exhilaration.

Wally, Nygard, and Sergeant Ichabod arrived soon after each other, placing their vehicles strategically alongside the road. Soft flakes of snow drifted lazily from an icy, gray sky, and Basil pulled on his toque and gloves. With the absence of lights and sirens, hopefully they could use the element of surprise to their advantage. Ichabod pulled in behind Nygard and got out, crouching as he ran to the front door.

Wally was prepared to stake out the back door when suddenly the front door opened, slowly and casually.

Ichabod jumped up and trained his gun on the opening. "Police! Hands up!"

Basil did not know who was more surprised to see the sleepy, mussy-haired teenager standing in front of them, his mouth agape and blinking sleep from his eyes as he took in the dramatic scene before him. His hair was dyed purple on one side, and a round loop earring protruded from his nose. Slowly, as if he wasn't quite sure of what was happening, he put up his arms. "Whaddya all doin' here? I didn't do nuthin'!"

Was *this* the killer? Some scrawny, knobby-kneed kid?

"Who else is in there with you?" Ichabod snapped.

"I dunno. My dog, Boggs." He was clearly confused. As if to prove his owner's point, a black and white dog quietly appeared, rubbing his muzzle against the scrawny kid's bare leg.

"You live here all alone?" Ichabod persisted.

"No," he dragged out. "Pops works up in the oilfields, so he ain't home till next week. My ma's dead." He shrugged his shoulders.

Was the kid telling the truth? Maybe. But it was a chance no one would be taking.

Ichabod informed dispatch of the situation. He would enter the home, and Wally would cover him. Basil would watch the kid while Nygard would watch the back entrance. The killer's car was parked in the drive; there was a good chance the kid was covering for him.

A few tense moments, and Ichabod called it: "All clear; no sign of anyone else."

Basil stood inside the tiny kitchen, looking out of the dirty lace curtains. The place was filthy, with dishes covering every square inch of the countertop.

The skinny kid was Paul O'Brien. According to him, some strange man had asked if he would trade cars. "Said he had a hankering for orange and felt lucky that day." Shrugging his shoulders, he said: "My car's a piece of crap compared to his. I ain't got a license to drive it yet; belonged to my ma, but there ain't no way I was gonna turn him down!"

"And it didn't seem odd to you?"

His skinny shoulders went up again and then down. "Don't look a gift horse in the mouth, right?"

Ichabod glowered. "Is it under your dad's name still?"

"Nah. It ain't registered; it ain't even insured yet. Weird guy. My car is – was – an orange clunker, a Datsun. Thing limped along poorly. Dad was gonna try to get it runnin' smoother, but the guy didn't care. Don't get it. This car is in a whole lot better shape, even if it does got a bit o' rust on it."

Ichabod sighed in that long-suffering manner of his. "So, let me guess. No license plate, either?"

"Nope. But I'm sure the guy woulda put that all on, no?"

"No." Ichabod bit off angrily. "No, he wouldn't."

They'd been duped, simple as that.

"Keys, please," he gestured to O'Brien.

"Keys? But that car is mine!" The kid yelled suddenly. "You can't take it from me!"

"Sorry, kid, but it is involved in numerous crimes, probably the scene of these crimes as well. It's evidence."

The kid looked dejected. Basil felt a teensy bit sorry for him. A teensy bit. Anger was still roiling in his gut. Precious time had been wasted on a dead-end lead. They'd been foiled again.

Tails between their legs, they all slunk back to their vehicles.

Score one for the killer.

Zero for the RCMP.

• • •

"Wait a minute, sir!" Basil turned to Jarowicz. "I have this idea. It might sound crazy, but hear me out; it's a long shot but a shot nonetheless."

Jarowicz nodded. "Go ahead."

"It's something I overheard Mulligan sing awhile back: 'Mary, Mary, quite contrary…piles of bones…dirt-filled skulls…broken bodies all in a row.' I asked him if bones were buried in this town. He saw something; I just know he did. He denied it and got pretty frightened."

Basil tensed, assuming he'd be laughed out of the place. But Jarowicz was right on board. "Okay, bring him in. We might just need to tighten the screws on him and get him to talk. Obviously he knows something, inebriated or not."

Surprisingly, Mully did not resist being taken to the station for questioning. "Probably safest place in town these days," he noted seriously. For once, he did not seem intoxicated, his unfocused eyes moving this way and that. "I wouldn't mind sleeping here." He looked around, almost desperate. "Stick me in jail. I ain't fightin' you."

"Mully, we need to ask you some questions. You are in a position to help us."

Mully looked at Jarowicz warily. "How so?"

"We are looking for a place where a lot of bones are to be found. Something tells us you know exactly where this place is."

"A cemetery!" he chuckled nervously. "What do I know about bones?"

"C'mon, Mully! We need your help to catch a killer."

He shook his head. "Forget it! I will be dead by morning. There's evil here; I can feel it. I saw a bit of it, and no more. No more!" Restlessly, he got off his chair and walked circles in the room, his eyes large with fright. "I shoulda never slept there – never!"

"Mully, what did you see? We won't take you there, just describe where it is. The lives of other women depend on this – on you!"

"I just looked through a window. There was dirt in there. And bones! Evil lives there; evil lives there!" He shouted loudly. He wrung his hands pleadingly. "Let me go, please!"

"Where, Mully? Where did you see these bones?" C'mon, Mully, we're so close!

"I don't know." His normally shifty eyes were wide and blinking rapidly. "It was getting dark. Gravel road."

"Gravel road? Where?"

But the shutter had slammed shut, and no amount of cajoling would get him to open it.

• • •

Basil slid into a booth at Gemma's and ordered himself a strongly brewed coffee. He surveyed the few bodies scattered throughout the pub. His fingers drummed rhythmically on the table as he watched couples converse, the occasional boisterous laugh, and the waitresses weaving expertly among the tables, their eyes ever scoping out that one overlooked patron, that one shifting body signaling an impatience for the bill.

Then he saw him.

The Rat.

He sat hunched in a back booth with a tall blonde, his thick-fingered hands lying in front of him, quiet and a bit excessive in relation to her twig-like frame. Every now and then, they would twitch towards her – imperceptibly almost – reminding Basil of some swampy creature lurking in the shadows. She threw back her long neck, snorting at something he said, and Basil waited for her drink to exit her nose. She was a vulnerable, fluttery thing – a twig easy to snap, but infused with an electric energy of one who utilized her entire body to speak. Her hands fluttered like two hyperactive butterflies.

The Rat shook his head slowly. He laughed, his voice sounding canned. Slowly, his large hands inched forward like stealthy tentacles and silenced her hands. She pulled slightly, her eyes blinking, and then dropped her shoulders in defeat. He said something, and she gave a forced giggle, pulling once more to retrieve her imprisoned hands. Undeterred, and with flair, she popped a cherry from her drink into her mouth. He looked at her intensely for a long, drawn-out moment, shook his head, picked up his knife, and slowly, carefully sliced into his steak that had just arrived.

Why would anyone cut into the women like that? The words dropped unbidden into Basil's mind.

• • •

He followed her. She stopped, readjusted her jacket, and pulled out a cigarette. It was then she noticed him.

"Here, let me." He no longer smoked but kept a lighter on him for moments like these.

She accepted and then inhaled deeply, looking at him long and hard. "I saw you in the restaurant. Staring at us."

"I'm sorry. I never meant to be so obvious."

She swayed slightly, and his arm shot out to steady her. She laughed. "I'm a cheap drunk." She lowered her voice. "You looking for – ?"

"Actually, no, nothing like that."

She shrugged and eyed him sharply. "What is it you want?" Her voice suddenly held an edge, and she backed away, nearly falling again. "You're a reporter, aren't you?"

He slipped her a fifty. "I just want some information. Not looking to hurt anyone. Please."

She stared at the bill, disgust playing at her lips. For a moment, it looked like she would decline, but she shrugged and plucked it out of his hand. "What do I have to lose? Might be the easiest bill I ever earned."

"You're dining with the mayor. Seems like a nice thing of him to do. Not a bad restaurant."

She threw her head back and laughed. "Shoulda known. The mayor. Why would he dine with someone like me, right? C'mon, I've seen and heard it all."

"I don't care about that."

"Yeah." She shrugged her thin shoulders. "No one does." She sucked hard on her cigarette again. "Best meal I've had in forever, though." She lifted frizzy, bleached hair and scratched a scab on her neck.

"It was nice of him. Getting to know this town, its constituents." He stood there tentatively as if he were perched on eggshells, afraid she would cut him off on a whim, money or no money. She was like a loose spark.

"I like that. A constituent. I could live with that label." She laughed again and huddled into her coat. This was like a little game to her now. "Mayor," she spat. "Everyone's scared of the little guy, huh? There's a thesaurus in his mouth, ya know. He paints little castles in the sky, and everyone laps it up. They always have. Little bobble-headed idiot."

"You still dined with him," Basil pointed out.

"People like me loathe his neatly packaged theories." A spark of fire flashed in her dark eyes. She shrugged. "A free meal. A couple of glasses of wine. Persuasive conversation. At least he thinks it is. He's always been like that. The good boy. The oh-so-wise one," she mocked, spreading her arms dramatically.

"Always? You know him quite well?"

"Oh yeah. Everything always has to be to his song and dance." She rolled her eyes. "Oh, Irene, why did you marry a Bollinger?" she mimicked, hands on her hips. "Why'd you have to lower your standards to that of society's sewer pipe?" She rolled her eyes and spat. "But tonight, I've got him like a string on my little finger." She lifted her chin in triumph, but he could not fail to notice how worn she looked. Her eyes held a perpetual sadness.

"Oh, really?"

"If he could fix me, he would. Change me. Make me socially acceptable rather than the thorn in his side that I am." She scuffed a high-heeled boot, and he glimpsed a hole in her stockings on her lower leg. "I woulda, you know. I woulda done anything for him if he would have looked inside." She threw her cigarette butt into the gathering darkness. He watched the little spark die on the cold pavement. Winter had sunk its teeth in deep like a hungry beast that would not let go. It was a dry cold that made the insides of one's nostrils feel like they were icing from the inside out.

Basil opened his mouth to ask one of the questions that had started clamoring in his head. But then, a car swerved around the corner, its passengers swaying like a pendulum from side to side. Music pulsed from its rusted frame as glaring headlights momentarily sent the darkness scurrying where the pair were standing. Then it was gone, throbbing music fading, darkness rushing in again.

The moment was gone. "Look, I gotta go," she shifted on her feet. "I've already said too much." And just like that, she dissolved into the darkness.

How did she know Ratford? What business did he have with her?

Irene Bollinger. He made a mental note. He was not quite done with her.

DAY 57

Basil

He slammed the door of his cruiser back at the detachment and threw back a mint into his mouth. Freshness exploded in his mouth. He held another mint in his hand and suddenly studied it. *A round little tablet…* His radio gave a crackle then.

The night crew came up empty-handed. The BOLO on the silver car was removed, and they were now solely focused on an orange Datsun with no plates and no registration.

There was a chance the killer would put fake plates on his car. Either way, every orange Datsun encountered would have to be pulled over.

The killer was smooth. He knew they were on his tail, and he seemed to be one step ahead of them all.

"He's playing with us," Wally said angrily, "like a cat toying with a flippin' mouse."

The RCMP seized the car and delivered it to forensics for fingerprinting. Just as they'd hoped, the fingerprints of all the missing women were found in the car. Even Adele Laramie's.

Wally and Nygard were combing the gravel roads while Basil would follow up on Bollinger.

• • •

He surveyed the weathered row of ground-floor apartment houses. He'd traced Bollinger to Unit 11. The salmon stucco was stained brown in many places, a tidied-up hole. Number 11 was huddled in tightly, a layer of red paint blistering on the door, a sheet of ice serving as a welcome mat.

Conscientious landlord, he thought.

He pressed the doorbell. No melodic chime responded. Shrugging, he rapped his freezing knuckles on the weathered wood. "C'mon, Irene. Please be home."

He heard footsteps, scraping, and then the turn of the knob. She opened the door slowly, a few inches only. "Whaddya want?"

Unobtrusively, he wedged his foot between the door and jamb. "We talked the other night."

A flicker of recognition. "Oh yeah. I had a few. Told you all I know. It's 7:30 in the morning. What gives?"

He held out a hundred-dollar bill. Information wasn't cheap.

She chewed her lip for good measure, pretended to ponder the matter intensely, and then snatched it. "This is it. Got it? You aren't going to mess this gig up for me."

"Absolutely."

"I'll take this over standing on a corner, freezing my butt off."

The artificial light of the place was hard on the eyes. The blinds were still pulled shut. He noted the ripped sofa, take-out containers strewed all over the place, and the piles of dingy laundry. A row of stiletto heels sat by the door, a fur, and other getup that barely covered a body.

She perched on the armrest of the sofa as if there was a rod shoved alongside her spine and pulled out a cigarette. Her face was puffy with sleep and age and who knew what else. "What do you need to know?" She picked at a loose string on her jeans, rubbed her nose, and then began tapping the cigarette carton against her leg.

"Just want to put a few rumors to rest, filling in the gaps."

She stared at him hard, not believing him for a second. "Alright," she said, standing up for a moment. "But if you do me in here – "

He cut right through the threat, lifting his hand. "Scouts honor. No publicizing whatsoever."

She shrugged then, perched herself on the couch again, and slipped the cigarette between eager lips. "He'd probably come after you. That's the way he is."

"Not a nice guy, huh?"

"If you don't scratch the surface. Doesn't want to be linked to someone like me. Self-righteous pig." She picked up a beer can and took a swig. "Blech. Stuff is warm and flat."

"I just have one question, really."

A rude series of knuckle-rapping made Basil jump.

She gave an exaggerated sigh. "Can't a body have any peace?"

Basil rose as well.

She opened the door slowly and then swung it wider. "Oh, it's you. And what a fabulous hour."

"Who does the car belong to?"

"Really, you stopped by for *this*? What is this, my twenty-four-hour surveillance?"

"C'mon, Irene, I just happened to see it when I stopped here. Just want to see how things are."

"Fine. Nothing has changed in the last so many hours."

"So, you have a guest?"

Basil shifted. The voice sounded familiar.

"I'm not stupid, Ian. And if I say I'm gonna do something, I do it. I'm not a politician."

Ian?

"Can I come in?"

"Fine. Whatever. Just don't give me the third degree. I have a *guest*," she spat. "I'm not in the mood for it."

Basil nearly fell backward as Mayor Ratford walked in.

"Constable?" His eyebrows lifted in surprise. "What brings you here?

"Doing my job and trying to solve a murder case."

"Wait – " Irene backed up. "You're a cop?"

"Look, I'm sorry. Presenting myself as a cop would have slammed the door in my face."

"You bet it would have!"

"What does Irene have to do with the murders?" Ratford interjected, his hand raised.

"Nothing. But part of my job is to ask questions and see where things lead."

"What things?"

"About my lovely brother. Man of the hour," Irene spat, still fuming.

Thanks, Irene, Basil thought.

"Me?"

"Wait a minute. You're Irene's brother?" Suddenly, it all made sense.

"I am."

Basil cleared his throat. "There's been talk of assault – "

"Assault?"

"Rumor has it you were involved in an assault on one of the street girls. No charges laid, but where there is smoke – "

Ratford rose slowly, his face pale. "Assault?" He repeated. "I've never laid a hand on any woman!"

"Assault?" Irene echoed, her voice suddenly feeble. "That's what you were rootin' around for?"

Ratford turned to Irene. She still had the decency to turn a lovely shade of red. "Well," she stammered.

"Irene?"

"Okay, okay!" She stood up, hands on her hips. "It was me, alright? I was crazy mad at you!" She turned to Basil. "I never pressed charges because there were none to press. Let me guess. You talked to Stace?"

Basil affirmed this.

"Why, Irene?" Ratford demanded.

Her eyes sparked. "I hate the way you look through us rather than at us. We're not *parasites*, Ian. We're not some disease you have to clean up," she spat. We have feelings… hopes – "

Ratford sank onto the couch and rubbed his face with a sigh. "I only did this all because I care."

Irene glared for a moment longer, and then it all drained away, and she sank down on the couch near him. Basil noticed a mist in her eyes despite the firm tilt of her jaw. "I want out…I really do…I can't…I just *can't*!"

"Can't?" Ian probed. "Whatever obstacle stands in your way, Irene, I will help you." He took both of her hands in his. Irene, please, please, let me help you."

"Ian…"

But he'd turned to glare at Basil. "What does this have to do with your murder investigation and the missing prostitutes?"

"Like I said, I have to follow every lead."

He suddenly jumped up, shaking his head. "You think *I* am the one responsible?"

"Like I said, I follow leads. I go where evidence points. Even just a rumor has to be checked out."

"A lead? This is such a flimsy and ridiculous theory if I ever heard one!" He waved his hands angrily. "Irene, I cannot believe – "

"Ian, of course I don't believe this!" Irene jumped up in protest.

"Sir, as much as you might not want to entertain a connection between the missing streetwalkers and the murders, we have to fully explore it. You've read the papers. I saw you a few weeks ago – "

Ratford stood still, like an insect with twitching antennae.

" – leaving the seedier part of town one evening – "

He sank back down onto the couch, still shaking his head.

" – trying to avoid being seen. I know you have an extreme dislike for the problem our town is facing. Then I hear of an assault. You tell me what any cop worth his salt would do."

Ratford shook his head again, this time calmer. "Fine. Fine, I get it. But don't waste your time or resources looking at me." Suddenly, he stood up again. "I dislike prostitution; no, I *loathe* it! I have *good reason* to."

Basil looked at him questioningly as Irene stood trembling. "C'mon, Ian," she begged.

"No, the cat might as well come out of the bag." He looked squarely at Basil. "My mother was a prostitute." He let the words sink in. "I won't paint a picture of the squalor Irene and I lived in, what we were all exposed to, but I vowed that when I became mayor, I would eradicate it if it was the last thing I did!"

"What about social reform?"

"Reform!" he spat. "Nothing worked for my mother. It was an abysmal failure. Detox, rehab, a hand up. She turned her back on it all. We need *decisive* action."

"You're helping Irene."

"*Trying* to," he replied, calmer now. "She's..." His voice was suddenly thick. "She's my little sister."

Irene's face crumpled. "Oh, Ian – "

"Reform didn't work for your mother, but for others, I think it would," Basil continued quietly. I disagree with prostitution too, but there are more effective ways to deal with it."

"You know, Andrews, we might have different opinions, we're two totally different people, and we have each our own approach that we think works. I am a fair man, and I care about this town. No one can ever say I don't care about its citizens." He sighed. "I will take what you said into consideration. Like I said, I'm a *fair* man." He stood up. "Dig to your heart's content, but please – "

Basil lifted a hand. "I've no desire to rake someone over the coals of the media." He walked out then and softly closed the door, hoping and praying that Irene would allow her brother to help her pick up the pieces of her life, all the while knowing it would be far from easy or simple.

• • •

Arizona

Arizona struggled at the straps that were holding her body and arms firmly to the cot. She tried to move her position to stem the gastric fluid that was welling in her throat. She felt so nauseated and so lightheaded. What had he given her?

Closing her eyes, she remembered the needle he jabbed into her none too gently. Right between the toes, a sharp sting that burned for awhile.

The room she was in was large, a sort of kitchen area on the one side and a large open space on the other as if a wall had been taken out in between the kitchen and living area. The room smelled acrid.

The man was nowhere in sight.

Managing to lift her torso off the bed, she recoiled at the sight before her. The long counters were filled with containers holding some kind of liquid. A row of scalpel-like knives, needles, syringes, and bottles were positioned neatly and orderly.

A fresh wave of panic engulfed her. All hope that maybe he would keep her alive, that maybe if she obeyed him and did not scream or fight back, he'd release her. But the hope was in vain. He'd been planning on killing her all along.

She bit her lip until she tasted blood. Suddenly, the headline, "Killer Pilfers Women's Kidneys" swam into view. *He's going to take my kidney*, she thought. *God, please don't let them take my husband away from me again – and my son!*

The acrid smell worsened. Then she noticed it. Grayish clouds.

Smoke. Something was burning.

She needed to get out. Feeling weak, her upper body collapsed back onto the cot. White walls loomed over her, shutting her in. The room felt airless and stifling. Everything began spinning. Objects began multiplying. Two windows became four, the needles doubled, her vision blurred. *I'm losing it*, she thought desperately. *Breathe! In, out; in out; out, in; in…*

And then she saw it. Smoke was drifting from a space heater along the wall near where she lay. Tiny sparks shot out from between the slats.

Fire. I'm going to burn alive!

•••

Basil

Wally had been quietly pacing the room when he suddenly snapped his fingers. "I know where it is!" He stood up excitedly.

Jarowicz turned to look at him expectantly. "The Datsun?"

"His hideout. I'm sure he – Mully – was talking about the large, run-down house on the gravel road off Milner's. Used to be an old folks' home, and before that, I believe, a bed and breakfast. It's so tucked away – forgotten rather. I'm sure it used to be called – "

"The Silver Spoon!" Basil interjected excitedly.

"Exactly. Can't believe I didn't put it together earlier. Quite a story goes along with that place. Used to belong to an Emma Watson; apparently, her cooking was out of this world. Best crepes around! She drew quite a crowd. Place fell apart after her death. Some folks bought the place to turn into an old folks' home. Was starting to be quite the place, but the rug was pulled out from under in that venture. Place's been empty since then, I believe. I wonder if the killer's operating out of this house?"

"It is a possibility," Jarowicz responded, "If so, it sounds like he picked a well-concealed spot."

"Out of sight; it's on the edge of town, really, in the middle of nowhere," Nygard added. "Place could be booby-trapped up to the hilt. Guy's deadlier than an asp and smoother than a chameleon. He knows exactly how to get what he wants without drawing attention to himself."

"He's been playin' us all along!" Wally said, his face wreathed in sudden anger.

Jarowicz held up his hand. "Time is of the essence. If he has victims in there, it might already be too late for them."

Basil swallowed.

The next course of action was to close in on his hideout. Having undergone renovations, the home was bound to have quite a different floor plan than the original. However, still not a hundred percent sure what they'd find, the tactical team would need to be called in for a high-risk takedown.

The only caveat was that they were six hours away in Edmonton.

Time Arizona did not have.

• • •

Nora

Nora opened the blinds for the briefest of moments when she saw him move towards her house, slinking up the drive. The thick cord slid from her fingers, and she shrank against the wall.

He was coming.

She pulled her robe tightly about her, feeling the heavy weight in her right pocket. She should have felt relieved she was prepared, but her body moved as if weights were attached to her limbs. Clumsy fingers grabbed at the door to ensure it was locked. Like an agitated moth, she flitted around, panic rising.

She looked again and then froze. He was moving closer, glancing furtively over his shoulder, crouching near a bush. The dim form crept closer, and then – it was one with the shadows! Her skin crawled. She felt the sweat tickle and itch over her whole body.

She peered out the window. Nothing. Where was he hiding?

Then she sensed him. The large cedar bush by the front door. A shadow cast to its side. He was there, sitting, waiting. Icy fingers choked the canister in her pocket, the cool metal slicked with sweat.

Suddenly, she heard a motor approaching. Reg.

Relief washed over her, pushing her to her knees. A sob caught in her throat as the door opened. Shaking, she drew herself up on jellied limbs.

"Nora? What are you doing on the floor?"

He shut the door, and she pounced on it like a feral cat, sweaty fingers slipping and then gaining traction as the lock slipped into place.

"Nora! What is going on?"

She sucked in a ragged gulp of air. "He's here."

"Who's here, Nora?" Impatience threaded his voice.

"The killer." She fumbled over the words.

"Killer." His eyes pinned her against the wall. "At our house?"

She nodded. "You said these women –"

"What women?"

"The ones," she cast a nervous glance over his shoulder, "who've been murdered."

"Ah, those."

Time was running out. He was coming. For her. Fingernails bit into her palm.

"He – "

"Nora?"

" – is coming," she could barely talk, her lungs burned as she desperately tried to get more air, hysteria building, "for me. I –" she wanted to shake him, to slap his face, to wake him up. Didn't he see? Did he imagine she was dreaming this all?

"Nora. My frightened little bird. Why would he target *you*?"

"Reg, please don't!" A sob caught in her throat. "Don't mock me; it's not a joke!" Wide eyes searched his face, begging him to believe her, to get it.

"No, it's not." A muscle twitched in his jaw.

Confusion filled her. "Then why…?"

Suddenly, she saw it. The dim form, moving behind the blinds. Her fingers felt again the bottle in her pocket. Her sole weapon.

"He's there!" Her voice shook, and she pointed at the blinds.

Reg turned slowly, his eyes never leaving hers entirely. "Who?" he asked softly.

The shadow moved. A soft scraping at the door. The knob turned slowly.

• • •

Basil

Sergeant Ichabod, Nygard, Wally, and Basil made for Milner's Road.

For a long time, the airwaves remained silent; no one spoke, faces creased with worry and concern. What would they find?

Announcing their arrival to dispatch, the men walked along the front of the house. They needed to be ever watchful. Ichabod and Nygard went to check the back. Sudden sleet, like hundreds of tiny knives, cut into their numbing skin.

In the gathering dusk, the light from Wally's flashlight bounced off the bottom layer of the house and settled on one of the crawlspace windows. Except for a few sharp pieces of glass still clinging to the surrounding wooden frame, a large hole yawned from the window. Shards of glass lay scattered on the ground. Wally bent down suddenly. "There's blood on the glass." Basil crouched low as well, intermittently scanning around him. "Blood's dried," Wally added. "Definitely not fresh at all."

"You thinking what I'm thinking?" Basil prodded.

"Someone broke the window and crawled through."

"The man in the hospital!"

Basil aimed his flashlight into the darkened area and pulled back in horror.

"What is it?" Wally queried and then, without waiting for a response, shone his flashlight into the room as well. In the combined beams of light, a most gruesome scene met them. It was a sea of dirt filled with bones, skulls, and even partially decomposed bodies.

Basil reeled backward and tried to quell the queasy feeling growing quickly in his gut.

"Sarge, we have bodies in the basement crawlspace just before the back door."

"Ten-four," Ichabod responded. "So far, all clear here."

The knob squeaked slightly, and with a groan, the door swung open. With both hands on his Smith and Wesson, Basil cleared every inch of space before slowly moving forward, Wally covering him.

The door led into a large foyer. Splitting hardwood floors were stained and rotting. There was a short flight of stairs leading up to the main floor where Basil was sure the main action had occurred. Peeling paint adorned the walls, including some large oil portraits of prominent-looking figures staring defiantly down at him.

Suddenly, he spied smoke wafting in from the slightly ajar door, which most likely led to the kitchen.

"We've got a fire!"

Wally immediately requested dispatch to send for the firetrucks. EMS was already staged at the scene to be called up if, and when, needed.

Ichabod and Nygard met them at the doorway. "Rest of the house is clear."

Heart hammering, Basil entered the kitchen. If anyone was still alive, they needed to get them out immediately. The open door was the only doorway that led into a large room that masqueraded as part kitchen, part laboratory of evil.

Along the far wall was a long counter, and in front a white island. Books were propped open on the counter, a neat row of scalpel-like knives, and big, square, opaque containers that were filled with some form of liquid emitting a sharp, pungent odor. He could barely make out the shape of the objects that were in the containers. Small vials sat upright, and an equally neat row of syringes and needles. It was a scene from a horror novel; diabolical and yet orderly.

He heard Wally suck in his breath as he peered over his shoulder.

Alongside a far wall were two cots occupied by two pale-faced women. It looked oddly serene as if they were peacefully sleeping. Large leather straps held the women tightly to the beds. One of them was Arizona. Had he killed them already? Flames were shooting from a space heater near the cots.

The room was very large, as if the previous owner had removed the wall between the kitchen and dining areas. Everything was orderly and medicinal, almost like a hospital.

"Wally, throw water on the fire," Ichabod barked. "Basil, check the women! Control, we have a possible ten-thirty-eight, and the place is burning. Send in fire!"

For a brief moment, Basil felt paralyzed. His eyes were drawn to the dancing flames, and he thought of Jules, her wide green eyes, pleading desperately for help.

"Basil!" Ichabod shouted.

He sucked in a shuddering breath. A rope of tension knotted along his spine. He blinked hard and steeled himself. He had to get to her this time.

Water sloshed everywhere as Wally, having grabbed some empty containers from the counter, desperately threw water out of them at the flames. There was no time to retrieve the fire extinguisher from the cruiser. "We have to get this fire out. This place could be a tinderbox with those liquids on the counter!"

Basil felt the first waxen wrist. Heidi Jennings. A flutter. "Jennings is alive!" Nygard was at his heels and scooped her up. Basil reached over for Arizona's wrist and felt a similar flutter. Both were alive!

Firefighters rushed in. One of them took Jennings from Nygard and made for outside.

"Hypoglycemia!" Ichabod continued to bark orders. "They've likely been poisoned with insulin. Possible removal of kidneys!"

Basil reached to lift Arizona off the cot just as the fire seemed to explode. It licked insatiably. Maniacal flames danced from wall to table and beyond. They roared and crackled. Gray clouds of smoke rolled through the room.

"Basil!" from somewhere far away, he heard Wally yell.

He felt tightness in his chest – a terrible suffocating feeling. The buzzing in his head. Green eyes pleading – that fleck of brown. The familiar heat slammed into him like a brick wall. Metallic babble around him, flashing lights…

His feet were rooted to the floor, the flames reaching out for him.

Far in the distance, muted voices. "Basil! Basil!"

• • •

Nora

The door was locked.

Then she saw it. Reg had lifted the black hat of the hoody he was wearing onto his head.

Her mouth dropped open.

He glided towards her.

She stared in growing horror and moved back. She bumped against the bookshelf. Something hard fell onto the floor. She heard it shatter into pieces.

His eyes darkened.

Her stomach clenched, the air rushing out. Her mouth tried to form words. Fingers squeezed the bottle. *No, it couldn't be – it mustn't be!* Her mind raced, groping desperately like panicked fingers searching in the dirt for that one possible explanation. She tried to swallow the dryness in her mouth.

Instinctively, she covered her head with her arms.

The hand went up – and then the burning pain.

The floor moved under her feet. Arms flailed, and she caught the edge of the bookcase, her knees buckling, sweaty fingers grasping desperately for traction.

"What did you do, Nora?" He enunciated each word carefully and moved slowly toward her.

Panic clawed her throat. The man before her was a stranger. Her knees were shaking so badly. She moved backward, gimp-like, her feet barely feeling the floor underneath. "Why, Reg?" she whispered.

"You were unfaithful, weren't you, Nora?"

"Our vows – "

"You broke them." His voice cut off scissor-sharp.

How did he know she'd been visiting that man? "But I didn't actually – "

"You cheated." Jaw muscles tight as violin strings.

"I only talked to him. We never – "

"You cheated on me." He was calm, but anger clearly boiled beneath the surface.

She felt sick. He reached out and stroked her scars. She pulled back with horror. "You – " She lifted clammy fingers to her face.

"I did." Eyes swelled with anger. "My artwork. My little caged bird," he said bitterly, his composure slowly unraveling.

Caged bird – *caged.* He'd caged her all along. Her mind struggled to keep up with everything. "I got this note – "

"I know."

Her own husband. Her fingers clawed the carpet desperately. She wanted it to be just a nightmare – to be over. "No – no!" she groaned.

He stood over her.

"Why?" The word wrangled itself from her.

"Why?" he mocked. Spittle formed on his lips. He turned and paced, running a hand through his hair, making the tufts stand up straight. Suddenly, he turned around, eyes blazing, and swung his one arm outwards, knocking the lamp off the table.

Nora instinctively ducked her head.

"Why?" he roared. "You cheated on me!" He covered his face, his voice cracking. "First, losing my boy. He was going to be perfect. Perfect!"

"Your boy?" Pain dug deep. "He was my son, too!"

Straightening up, he raged, "They denied him life – she denied him life – *women.* Betrayers, like my filthy mother! All you cheating women are the same!" Suddenly, he was quiet. He turned around to look out the window, oblivious to the shadow lurking.

Nora shook violently, watching his simmering form.

"I made them pay." The whisper was soft and deadly.

Cold prickles danced over her body. "You killed all those women?"

"I did. Someone has to vindicate all those men. Take, take, take! *I* stopped them."

She stared at the stranger in front of her and clutched her stomach. "Why did you take their kidneys?"

"They took the one meant for Henry. He died because of that mother. Because of women like her. All those cheaters – *I made them give back*." His voice was triumphant.

Reeling, she envisioned Reg cutting open a dead body – calmly and methodically, like everything he did.

He suddenly laughed at the horror on her face. "Nora, my little bird."

She turned then to see what had fallen. The bird.

Its beady eyes were gone.

My little bird. A sudden calmness settled over her. She would fight. She would no longer be helpless prey. A little bird with clipped wings no more. All those women –

She had to stop him.

Everything moved in slow motion, and she watched herself as if floating. Fingers slid over the smooth surface in her pocket, her heart thumping wildly. *Act! Act!* The lid unscrewed easily.

In the back of her mind, she heard the scratching at the door.

She moved her hand from her pocket, slowly, her entire body vibrating.

He made to lunge at her then, as if he knew she was going to do something, his eyes blazing.

She would forever remember the shock and horror mingled on his face – the face that would be no more.

Do it, Nora! Now! A few more seconds, and it'd be too late.

And she did.

Later, she would remember it all in a blur: the blind fumbling, the sudden boldness undercut with fear and panic, the amazing accuracy and precision of her actions despite everything else.

The bottle slid from her fingers then, and she watched in horror as he screamed and writhed in pain. She saw herself laying on the floor, the terrible burning of her face, the masked man looking down at her wordless – Reg standing over her body as she thrashed in pain. She heard animal-like moans slowly build into a crescendo of high-pitched screaming – raw and primal.

It was coming from her own mouth.

Her legs buckled, and she sank to the floor, unaware of the door splintering open.

• • •

Basil

Suddenly, he looked into her face. The eyes opened.

They were not green. Brown.

There was a rushing sound in his ears. He picked her up, commanding weak arms to move. "I got you, I got you, I got you."

Her eyes grew terrified, her mouth moved. He stumbled slightly. But he never dropped her. He inched towards the door. Fiery flames like an iron fist shoved him backward. He saw the outline of firefighters; he heard the sizzle of water on flame. The barking of orders. A hard jerk as hands pulled him to safety.

He stumbled. She spilled from his arms like a rag doll, and instinctively, he dropped on top of her. "I got you, I got you!" He yelled this time.

Hands pulled at him. She stared at him. Her eyes desperate. "Re – Re – "

"Basil!" It was Wally. He grabbed Basil's arm to steady him as Arizona was pulled from underneath him. He felt himself being lifted and carried down a flight of stairs, and then a cold blast of air. He gulped it in like a starved man.

He looked into Wally's soot-covered face lit up by the strobes of lights around them and grabbed his sleeve. "I got her, Wally!" he yelled over the cacophony of men and sirens behind him. The night sky was filled with cracking and splintering, walls groaning under the fire as if they could no longer hold in the evil. Flames devoured, and thick hoses like angry serpents were uncoiled, unleashing clear venom. It was battle, both sides fighting valiantly. There was the occasional sizzle as tendrils of water snaked into its seams and cracks, but even the latest fire equipment was no contender for the flame's wrath.

"I know, Basil."

"I didn't leave her to die!"

Wally hunkered beside him, his large hand on his shoulder. "You didn't leave Jules to die, either," he added quietly.

Basil simply stared in shock. He wanted to speak, but suddenly, he coughed uncontrollably. His lungs felt singed. An oxygen mask was pushed at his face. "Re – Re –" sounded in his mind.

It hit him then like a volt of electricity. *Reg Clarkson!* Frantically, he pushed the mask off him. They'd been examining the veins of leaves, as it were, rather than the contours of the forest – the bigger picture!

• • •

"Sarge!" he managed, just as his radio crackled.

"All cars, all cars, 24-1 Cedar Drive, one man down, possible ten-thirty-eight!"

Ichabod barked into his radio and then turned to the men. "Alright, guys, we gotta go. Forensics and fire can finish up here. Suspect still at large."

Basil struggled to his feet.

"All cars, this is a confirmed assault, one suspect. One man down. I repeat, one man down! Descriptions follow."

"Nygard, let's go! Basil, you stay behind."

"...apparently house is owned by a Reginald and Nora Clarkson..."

No! Basil thought with growing horror. Like butter squeezing through their fingers, he was remaining one step ahead of them. "It's Reginald Clarkson."

"That's what dispatch – "

"No! Yes, I know, but the killer is Reg Clarkson; Arizona tried to tell me that inside."

Ichabod stared at him for a second as it dawned on him what Basil was saying.

"Please, sir! I feel fine. I know this man; I can possibly talk him down."

Ichabod weighed the words. Basil was a volatile bullet. "Don't make me regret this. Move it, people!"

•••

Aman

Pushing the mangled door out of the way, he ran to the small woman lying in a heap on the floor.

"Aynoor, Aynoor!"

She groaned like a wounded animal, head down, rocking on her knees. He grabbed her shoulders, "Aynoor! It's me!"

She lifted her head, eyes wild with shock.

She skittered back like a terrified spider when his tanned hand slipped the hood from his face. Deep brown eyes shone with pain. Words stuck in her throat when recognition suddenly dawned on her. "Aman? Aman!"

"Aynoor!"

"But why – how?" Instinctively, small hands clung to him. Searching eyes begged fervently for an explanation.

But he simply drew her into his arms and squeezed her. A sudden sob ripped through her.

• • •

Basil

Adrenaline shooting through him, Basil gunned down the gravel drive. "Alpha-23, about ten minutes away." He noted the time: 7:08 pm.

Moisture beaded his brow, and he shifted in his seat to dismiss the sinking feeling growing in his gut. He did not want to be right on this one.

"...possible acid attack..."

Acid.

Suddenly, he thought of Clarkson's wife. The acid attack victim.

Had Clarkson killed her? The image of the deformed face at the window struck him like a bolt of lightning. Had she been trying to get his attention? Questions swirled through him as his cruiser whipped down the street, his stomach twisting.

"...caller hung up..."

He punched the steering wheel. Idiot! The ride-alongs, the coffee, the committee – all staring in his face this entire time, and he had been too blind to see it. *Keep your friends close, your enemies closer.* He punched the wheel again.

"Alpha-19, I'll be there in a couple of minutes," said Sergeant Ichabod.

They hadn't told anyone about Laramie's body being cut into, and yet Clarkson knew. Of course, he did. "It's all there," he said aloud to no one. "The pieces all fit together!"

"...advise when you arrive and wait for backup..."

Bile rose in his throat as the enormity of it all hit him. He had saved the life of a serial killer. *You could have stopped him. You had his life in your hands*, an accusing voice whispered in his ear. *You let him go, and he continued on in his carnage, carving into women's bodies...*

"No!" he yelled suddenly, his fingers gripping the steering wheel.

"...use extreme caution..."

"...ten-four, Sarge!"

Tires squealed as he slid roughly against the curb, the car jolting to a halt. Cedar Drive. Soon, the place was crawling with cars and officers.

•••

Clarkson lay on his side, paramedics working on him. He moaned in pain and rage.

Basil saw Mrs. Clarkson on the floor as well, the arms of a tall, dark-skinned man wearing a white t-shirt, navy hoody, and dark denim jeans holding her tight and rocking her body. She clutched him firmly, her eyes wide and vacant. Her face was fully exposed, and he slowly took in the thickened scars that once formed a beautiful face. A long, nut-brown braid lay between her shoulder blades.

He crouched down beside the two. "Mrs. Clarkson, can I ask you a few questions?"

She didn't respond or look at him.

The man indicated Clarkson with a tip of his head and spouted angrily: "He's evil! I knew I had to come; I knew it!"

Basil looked at him in confusion, but before he could reply, Mrs. Clarkson spoke in flat tones of shock. "He killed them all. Everyone. He..." her mouth worked furiously, "... did this to me," her fingers sliding over the patchy skin of her face, "and I didn't know – didn't see any of it!"

He remembered then Clarkson in Arizona's home at the time of the burglary. How could he have been so blind?

"It's all my fault!" she cried.

"No!" the man took her shoulders and stared into her face. "This isn't your fault!"

Basil knew partly how she felt. Conned. Swindled. Physically and emotionally. The man she thought loved her – the man they all thought loved her – had mutilated her and rubbed her face in it. She had gone to bed at night with a serial killer; eaten her meals with a serial killer; given her all to a serial killer.

But he knew, too, the guilt – that irrational suffocating feeling that would not release its hold easily.

"You're safe now, Aynoor," the man murmured, his face pressed against her hair. "He cannot hurt you, or anyone else, anymore!"

"Amen," Basil echoed quietly.

The paramedics took Reg Clarkson away on a stretcher, Sergeant Ichabod following in his vehicle.

It turned out that the man who'd called 911 was Nora's brother, who'd arrived weeks earlier from Pakistan. Apparently, Rani had told only Aman about his sister's whereabouts. Worried about her never contacting her family, he felt he needed to go looking for her. As she left a forwarding address at the place she rented, it was not too difficult for him to find out where she'd moved to. When locals explained that she'd been disfigured in an acid attack on the part of her family, Aman had become suspicious of Aynoor's husband.

"He must have brainwashed her terribly," Aman shook his head. "We would never hurt her! It's more common where I'm from, this type of honor killing, but we're not all like that!"

Not trusting Reg Clarkson, he watched the family. "I didn't trust the man, the way he seemed to imprison my sister and played on her vulnerabilities."

Learning about Aynoor's fear of strangers, he chose to watch her movements for a while before disclosing his identity. "And I feared she wouldn't speak to me," he smiled wryly. "Father is not the easiest person on earth, but he would never hurt her, and neither would Amir! Had I known she was this fearful, and that she believed I was a murderer on the loose, I would have announced myself much sooner!" Tears filled his dark eyes. "He ruined her face, he crushed her spirit, and shut her away, all because she developed this emotional attachment to someone as a way of dealing with the grief of losing her son. My nephew!" His jaw worked furiously. "She suffered all alone!"

DAY 1

Arizona

Arizona pulled herself to a sitting position as her hospital bed was wheeled next to his. She stared speechless at the rail thin man carefully tucked under the pastel hospital sheets. She took in the downturned mouth, and memories tugged at her painfully. He moved his boyish face to her, his eyes still closed, and he muttered in his sleep.

Marc. Her darling Marc! Was it really possible?

Suddenly, his eyes opened slowly, searching around this way and that until they focused on her face. He stared at her then, blinked, and stared some more.

She pressed a white-knuckled fist to her mouth to stop the scream that was suddenly building in her throat.

His brown eyes continued to probe her face, his brows scrunching up in that familiar way.

And then it happened. The spark of recognition lit up his eyes – a thick fog that slowly cleared away. "Ari...Arizona!"

"Marc!" She couldn't speak more. Something clogged her throat. A shiver danced over her body. She blinked slowly, her heart beating so fiercely that she had difficulty breathing. Tears suddenly welled up in her eyes, and she twisted on her bed, reaching over to touch his arm. She needed to feel him, to make sure she was not dreaming; that he was not an apparition. Her tongue was frozen to the roof of her mouth, but she wanted to crush herself against him, to feel his heart beating against her chest. Fingernails dug into her leg, and the sharp pain was deep relief.

This was no dream.

Now, her tongue thawed. The words flowed from her mouth disjointed and confused as her brain refused to keep pace. "It's me – Arizona! You have a son!" A sudden shudder seized her body, and the dam burst. She stumbled out of her bed, fell to the floor, refused help, scrambled to her feet, and crept into his bed, her shaking body pressed against his as sobs tore through. "You're truly alive!" Was it possible! Had her prayers been answered?

Shaking with sobs, they clung to each other. Words weren't necessary. How long had they been separated? Cheers went up from the nurses; a woman had found her supposedly dead husband, and a man had found his identity again!

It was dark outside now. Marc sat up comfortably in his bed, Arizona seated on a chair beside him, clutching his hand and staring adoringly at him.

Slowly, haltingly, Marc related how he'd gone to The Silver Spoon, a former bed and breakfast, to find a set of precious gems the late widow had bequeathed to their town. Rumors suggested they existed, and upon visiting her lawyer in jail, his theory was validated. Eager to be able to pursue a story of such interest, and at the same time help his town, Marc jumped at the opportunity to investigate.

"Where are the gems?" Arizona asked, her interest piqued as well.

Marc shook his head sadly. "I never found them; I never got the chance. I was nabbed when I broke into the house. I had no idea it was being occupied!" He suddenly shuddered at the memory, his face paling. "What evil existed in that place! What a twisted sense of vengeance he has!"

Arizona squeezed his hand, "*Had*, Marc, *had*. He can't hurt us any longer!"

Tears filled Marc's eyes, and his head sank back into his pillow. "I'm so thankful God brought us together again, Arizona."

"I never really accepted it could be suicide, Marc, believe me!"

"Oh, Arizona. My faith was tried; it was *really* tried. But even at rock bottom, I never truly believed God would leave me – or us."

Suddenly, there were three more people in the room. Arizona's eyes opened wide. "Mom, Dad? Malcolm!"

Her father bent to hug her, his eyes shining with tears.

"Oh, Arizona," Estelle's voice wavered. She looked then at Marc and, without reservation, grasped his thin hand. "Marc…I…"

Marc covered her hand with his other. "It's alright, Mrs. Beckam. I understand. Let's leave the past where it belongs."

"Mother…" Her eyes welled. "Please…call me Mother. I would be truly honored."

Mother? Arizona felt as if her heart would explode. Malcolm ran to her bed then and squeezed her tight, not wanting to let go.

"Our little boy." Arizona turned smilingly to Marc, whose mouth dropped open.

"My son," he breathed in awe, his trembling hand reaching for his boy.

"Here," Clanton Beckam said, moving forward. He picked up Malcolm and brought him to Marc's bedside. Arizona watched nervously, wondering how Malcolm would receive Marc. He hesitated for a moment, and then a small chubby hand reached for Marc's ear lobe. Marc's own trembling hand reached out to carefully stroke the boy's hair.

"Be careful!" Arizona laughed at Marc. "He has a penchant for ear lobes."

They all laughed.

"Oh," Estelle broke in. "We bought Malcolm something. You know, grandparents and all. I hope we didn't overstep too much." She looked genuinely worried. "A kitten. His very own."

Arizona laughed then. "I *was* trying to have a cat flap put in."

Basil

A wonderful monument to the history of Twin Coulees stood divested of its flesh and sinews. The fire had fed upon the ornate woodwork, reducing everything to charred ash. Tendrils of smoke still wafted skyward like a pulse that beat faintly – a desolate echoing of all that it had been.

Sullivan sat reclined in his easy chair, casted leg on his leather ottoman. He'd broken his ankle clean through. "Bones not what they used to be," he chuckled. "Snapped like a dry twig." Basil had stopped by the clean white apartment complex to see how he was getting on.

Basil wrapped his long fingers around a steaming mug of coffee. "Fire destroyed everything, but there is still DNA evidence we can procure from the bones. Science these days. Fortunately, we saved two of the women. Not enough insulin to kill them; we suspect he woulda gone back to finish the job later. Apparently, insulin does not kill too easily; takes long. But he force-fed his victims alcohol to speed the process up. Kept them for as long as needed to kill them, and then harvested their kidneys." He took a long sip and set his cup down. "He had a fridge and freezer full of kidneys! Some were floating in formaldehyde and sealed with plastic wrap. Can you believe it?"

"Formaldehyde?" Sullivan questioned.

"Sure, you can get the stuff off eBay. Of course, these are not transplantable! Man, Sullivan, it all was staring us – me – right in the face! The tablets he threw in his mouth, the one found on Arizona Stuart's carpet. Forensics did a chemical analysis on that one – glucose tabs. The things he said and did. How could I have been so blind?"

Sullivan slowly shook his head. "You know what they say about hindsight."

"Yeah, I know, I know. But, man, it just picks at me."

"And let me guess, he's smug about it all?"

"After playing the innocent card. But get this, Sullivan: forensics found a broken bird figurine on the floor. There was a video camera hidden behind one of the bird's eyes. Apparently, Clarkson was recording pretty much his wife's every move."

Sullivan whistled between his teeth. He pulled a newspaper from the table beside him. The headline read: "Reporter Back from the Dead with Missing Gems!"

"Apparently, the amnesiac on the news was our missing reporter. Article calls him a hero."

Basil nodded. "When removing the remains of six women, forensics found a small, steel box deep in the rubble. Apparently, the town's missing gems. There was a copy of Emma Watson's will in there as well, perfectly preserved. She left the gems to the town." He thought of Arizona and Marc finally reunited and felt a sudden emptiness inside.

Sullivan struggled to stand up.

"Here, let me," Basil jumped up.

He waved him off. "No, I still live alone and have to do for myself. Keep the muscles going, the blood movin'."

Basil sank back down and took in a deep breath.

"And you?" Sullivan turned to him again, his eyes probing Basil's face.

"I don't understand."

"You saved a killer."

Basil felt the old knot of tension at the back of his neck. "I know," he responded quietly.

"But you're not at fault here. Don't allow this to grow into another monster," he wagged a gnarled finger at him. "You can feed evil, and you can also feed irrational guilt."

Basil nodded, knowing exactly what Sullivan meant. "I guess if I'd not saved Clarkson, we wouldn't have known about the bodies buried under the house."

"Exactly." Sullivan hobbled to the kitchenette. "Maybe this town can return to some measure of peace. I think its people have learned a painful lesson."

"Lesson?" Basil questioned.

"Well," Sullivan stopped. "It often takes a tragedy to bring hidden feelings to the light – one's flaws, one's vulnerabilities come glaringly to the surface. You can think you know someone, but you don't." He leaned forward, a serious look on his face. "None of us is inherently good, but we can all do good. No one is better than the next; one may live a more decent life than another, but evil lies dormant in us all. Not much is needed to awaken this deadly beast.

Basil nodded slowly. Mully's face swam into view, his bulging eyes full of terror, the reddening skin of his face.

Had he not almost killed a man? Shame flooded him. For mere seconds, the lid of his own heart had lifted then, and evil had seeped out.

"It's time to stop running, son. From everything, from everyone, but *especially* from God."

Once again, Sully hit the nail on the head. How often had he blamed God for leaving him, for what happened to Jules, for really everything that went wrong?

Sully returned with the pot of coffee and a small package wrapped in thin crepe paper. "Open it," he suddenly smiled.

Basil looked at him questioningly and ripped the paper off. An exquisitely carved burl canoe fell into his lap. "Sullivan!"

"It is yours. A constant reminder for you that," he coughed, his lungs wheezing like age-worn bellows, "that the trials of fire can produce a refinement of spirit. Just like this piece of burl."

•••

Basil sank into the seat of his car, staring at the cellphone in his hand. The sun was melting in a fiery blaze to be replaced by a full moon. It hung there, soft and pale as it had done for centuries.

Drawing in a deep breath, he pressed the digits to a familiar number. Each dial tone seemed to match the drumbeat of his heart.

"Hello?" The voice was tentative and light. Music to his ears.

"Myra?"

EPILOGUE

Nora

TWIN COULEES, ALBERTA, SPRING 2015

He waited for her by his car. She had to do this alone – *wanted* to do this alone. Freedom had an entirely different meaning for her. She carried the large canvas under her arm, her small mouth stitched in a line of determination. A colorful scarf concealed most of her face, but if a slight breeze played with its edges and revealed more than she preferred, it didn't bother her.

Timidly, she walked up to his door and knocked softly. Not so long ago, a bedraggled woman in fear for her life had pounded on his window. The memory caused an ache she quickly pushed away.

That had been her. Nora. The little bird with clipped wings.

The door opened on the second knock, and a smiling woman opened the door.

"Please, is your husband home, ma'am?"

"Come on in, please! You must be Nora." Her voice was soft and welcoming. She was petite, like Nora, her hair in a neat ponytail.

"It is Aynoor, actually." I have something for your husband," she stammered, slightly self-conscious.

The tall, red-headed police officer then materialized at her elbow, a small infant tightly swaddled in his arms. His eyes widened with surprise. This is a wonderful surprise!"

Aynoor smiled weakly. True bliss, not some carefully constructed artifice. She felt a sharp twinge under her rib cage, but then it was gone.

Forward.

For a moment, she turned around. Aman stood by the vehicle, his face confident, assured. His smile steadied her, inspired her, filled her with courage.

This is for you, Constable," Aynoor thrust the painting at him, her hands trembling slightly.

"For me?" He looked confused.

"You kept me going when all was dark."

Basil took the canvas carefully and studied it. Stark and bold with strong, confident strokes of oil paint, the piece was titled *Rebirth,* a powerful rendition of a river on its journey.

The scene started on the left with a clear brook of water that babbled like a child in wonder of the world, growing stronger and more independent. Slowly, it morphed into a bold river that picked up speed and strength, roaring and thundering over sharp rocks like a confident marathon runner, persevering when the boulders became tight and large, pushing through until it trickled into a calm, peaceful stream – so clear that only the kiss of sunlight indicated its presence – curving over rocks like silk falling into itself. In a powerful climax, it swelled at the top of a sharp cliff, and then without hesitation powered over, a conqueror at the end of her journey.

Basil cleared his throat and swallowed. "You can most certainly paint!" In its bold and confident strokes, in the bright hues of paint, he saw himself as much as she saw herself.

Rebirth.

There was something wonderfully cleansing and refreshing about it. God had turned discordant notes into a beautiful symphony.

"Thank you!" His smile wobbled. "Thank *you*!"

ACKNOWLEDGMENTS

Writing a book is a solitary task in many ways, but the journey itself is far from it.

My deepest gratitude goes to that of my dear husband, Jeff, and my four beautiful children for their encouragement and unfailing belief in me.

Heartfelt thanks also go to the rest of my family for not only patiently waiting for many years to see this book in print, but for many words of encouragement.

I cannot forget my past and present students who never stopped asking about my book, and for caring deeply. I am so grateful for all of them!

I want to sincerely thank my editor, Paul Butler, for helping me raise my manuscript from skeletal beginnings and tenderly nurture it to fruition. Your wisdom and insight are worth more than many writing courses combined!

I cannot express enough thanks to Shawn Walker of the RCMP for his invaluable insight into the workings of the RCMP. Although I tried to maintain correct police procedure throughout this book, any missteps are mine alone.

Finally, I want to extend my heartfelt thanks to Janee Van Harberden and Nicolette Verhey for being so willing to read my manuscript and provide feedback.